New York Times bestselling author **Christine Feehan** has over 30 novels published and has thrilled legions of fans with her seductive and sensual 'Dark' Carpathian tales. She has received numerous honours throughout her career including being a nominee for the Romance Writers of America RITA, and receiving a Career Achievement Award from Romantic Times, and has been published in multiple languages and in many formats, including audio book, e-book, and large print.

For more information about Christine Feehan visit her website: www.christinefeehan.com

***Praise for Christine Feehan*:**

'After Bram Stoker, Anne Rice and Joss Whedon, Feehan is the person most credited with popularizing the neck gripper' *Time* magazine

'The queen of paranormal romance' *USA Today*

'Feehan has a knack for bringing vampiric Carpathians to vivid, virile life in her Dark Carpathian novels' *Publishers Weekly*

Christine Feehan's
'Dark' Carpathian Series:

Dark Prince
Dark Desire
Dark Gold
Dark Magic
Dark Challenge
Dark Fire
Dark Legend
Dark Guardian
Dark Symphony
Dark Melody
Dark Destiny
Dark Secret
Dark Demon
Dark Celebration
Dark Possession
Dark Curse
Dark Slayer
Dark Peril
Dark Predator
Dark Storm
Dark Lycan
Dark Wolf
Dark Blood

Dark Nights
Darkest at Dawn (omnibus)

Also by Christine Feehan

Sea Haven Series:
Water Bound
Spirit Bound
Air Bound

GhostWalker Series:
Shadow Game
Mind Game
Night Game
Conspiracy Game
Deadly Game
Predatory Game
Murder Game
Street Game
Ruthless Game
Samurai Game

Drake Sisters Series:
Oceans of Fire
Dangerous Tides
Safe Harbour
Turbulent Sea
Hidden Currents
Magic Before Christmas

Leopard People Series:
Fever
Burning Wild
Wild Fire
Savage Nature
Leopard's Prey

The Scarletti Curse

Lair of the Lion

DARK
BLOOD

A CARPATHIAN NOVEL

CHRISTINE FEEHAN

piatkus

PIATKUS

First published in the US in 2014 by The Berkley Publishing Group
A division of the Penguin Group USA (Inc.),
First published in Great Britain in 2014 by Piatkus

A CIP catalogue record for this book
is available from the British Library.

Hardback ISBN: 978-0-349-40316-8
Trade paperback ISBN: 978-0-349-40183-6

Printed and bound in Great Britain by
Clays Ltd, St Ives plc

Papers used by Piatkus are from well-managed forests
and other responsible sources.

MIX
Paper from
responsible sources
FSC® C104740

Piatkus
An imprint of
Little, Brown Book Group
100 Victoria Embankment
London EC4Y 0DY

An Hachette UK Company
www.hachette.co.uk

www.piatkus.co.uk

For my sister of the heart, Anita. Thank you for being in my life. We may not have the same birth parents but that has never stopped us from our fierce love and loyalty to one another. We may have lost Mom and Dad, but we've got our family and we'll always be strong as long as we're holding on to one another.

FOR MY READERS

Be sure to go to christinefeehan.com/members/ to sign up for my *private* book announcement list and download the *free* ebook of *Dark Desserts*. Join my community and get firsthand news, enter the book discussions, ask your questions and chat with me. Please feel free to email me at Christine@christinefeehan.com. I would love to hear from you.

Acknowledgments

Many thanks to my sister Anita Toste, who always answers my call and has such fun with me writing mage spells.

I have to give a special shout-out to C. L. Wilson, Sheila English, Susan Edwards and Kathie Firzlaff, who are always gracious enough to include me in our power writing sessions. We rock it, don't we?

As always, thanks to Brian Feehan and Domini Stottsberry. They worked long hours to help me with everything from brainstorming ideas and doing research to edits. There are no words to describe my gratitude or love for them. Thank you all so very much!

Special thanks to Dr. Christopher Tong, who is amazing at everything he does, from songwriting to language building. More than those things, his spirit is that of an incredible being, one I wish I could capture for all to see in the pages of a book. We'd all benefit!

Last, but certainly not least, thank you to my editor, Cindy Hwang, for believing in me when I told her I had an idea for a difficult book and it ended up being three! She gives me the freedom to write the way I need to. And of course, the production department of Berkley, who have for the last three years believed in me enough to hang in there when they didn't get the books on time. I appreciate all of you more than I can possibly express.

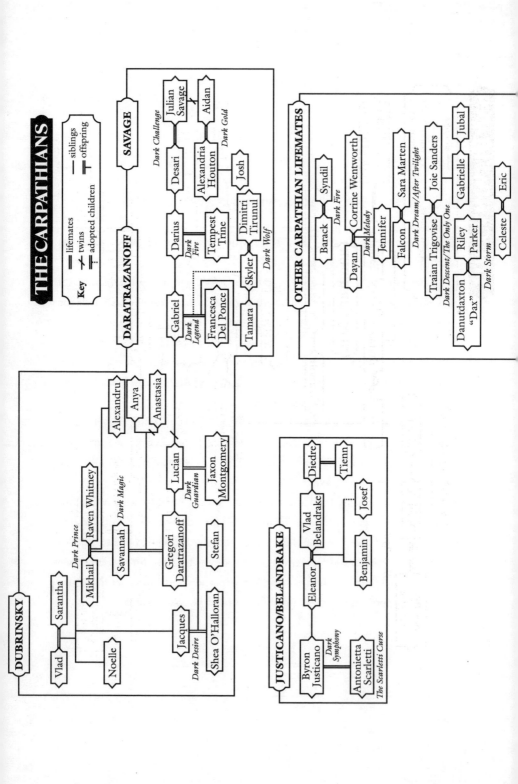

THE CARPATHIANS

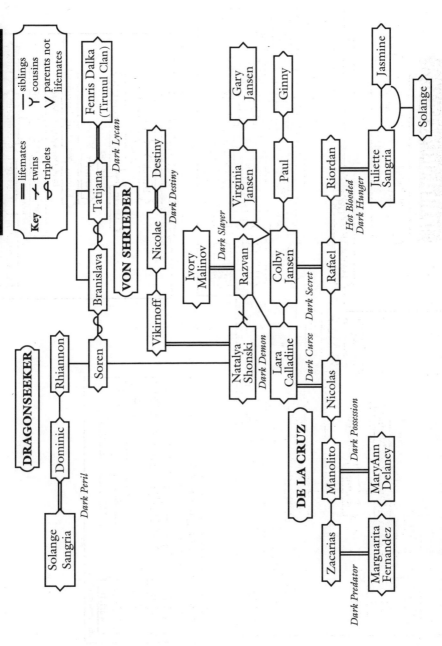

Key
= lifemates
≁ twins
triplets
— siblings
Y cousins
V parents not lifemates

DRAGONSEEKER

VON SHRIEDER

DE LA CRUZ

Solange Sangria
Dominic
Dark Peril

Rhiannon

Soren

Vikirnoff

Natalya Shonski
Dark Demon

Lara Calladine
Dark Curse

Nicolas

Manolito
Dark Possession

MaryAnn Delaney

Zacarias
Dark Predator

Marguarita Fernandez

Branislava

Tatijana

Fenris Dalka
(Tirunul Clan)
Dark Lycan

Nicolae

Destiny
Dark Destiny

Ivory Malinov
Dark Slayer

Razvan

Colby Jansen
Dark Secret

Rafael

Riordan

Juliette Sangria
Hot Blooded
Dark Hunger

Virginia Jansen

Paul

Gary Jansen

Ginny

Jasmine

Solange

DARK
BLOOD

I

Sound came to him first. A low, drumming beat growing louder. Zev Hunter felt the vibration of that rhythmic booming throughout his entire body. It hurt. Each separate beat seemed to echo through his flesh and bone, reverberating through his tissue and cells, jarring him until he thought he might shake apart.

He didn't move. It was too much of an effort even to open his eyes and figure out what that disturbing, insistent call was—or why it wouldn't go away. If he opened his eyes he would *have* to move, and that would hurt like hell. If he stayed very still, he could keep the pain at bay, even though he felt as if he were floating in a sea of agony.

He lay there for a long time, his mind wandering to a place of peace. He knew the way there now, a small oasis in a world of excruciating pain. He found the wide, cool pool of blue inviting water, the wind touching the surface so that ripples danced. The surrounding forest was lush and green, the trees tall, trunks wide. A small waterfall trickled down the rocks to the pool, the sound soothing.

Zev waited, holding his breath. She always came when he was there, moving slowly out of the trees into the clearing. She wore a long dress and a cape of blue velvet, the hood over her long hair so that he only caught glimpses of her face. The dress clung to her figure, her full breasts and small waist, the corset top emphasizing every curve. The skirt of the dress was full, falling over her hips to the ground.

She was the most beautiful woman he'd ever seen. Her body was grace-ful, fluid, an ethereal, elusive woman who always beckoned to him with a soft smile and a small hand gesture. He wanted to follow her into the cool forest—he was Lycan, the wolf that lived inside of him preferred the forest to the open—but he couldn't move, not even for her.

He stayed where he was and simply drank her in. He wasn't a man clever words came easily to, so he said nothing at all. She never approached him, never closed the distance between them, but somehow, it never mattered. She was there. He wasn't alone. He found that as long as she was close to him, the terrible pain eased.

For the first time though, something disturbed his peaceful place. The booming beat found him, so loud now that the ground lifted and fell with an ominous, troubling thump. The water rippled again, but this time he knew it wasn't the wind causing the water to ring from the middle of the pool outward. The drumbeat throbbed through the earth, jarring not only his body, but everything else.

The trees felt it. He heard the sap running deep in the trunks and branches. Leaves fluttered wildly as if answering the deep booming call. The sound of water grew louder, no longer a soft trickling over rocks, not a steady drip, but a rush that swelled with the same ebb and flow as the sap in the trees. Like veins and arteries flowing beneath the very earth surrounding him, making its way toward every living thing.

You hear it now.

She spoke for the first time. Her voice was soft and melodious, not car-ried on the wind, but rather on breath. One moment she was on the other side of that small pool of water, and the next she was sinking down into the tall grass, leaning over him, close to him, her lips nearly skimming his.

He could taste cinnamon. Spice. Honey. All of it on her breath. Or was it her skin? His Lycan senses, usually so good at scent, seemed confused. Her lashes were incredibly long and very dark, surrounding her emerald eyes. A true emerald. So green they were startling. He'd seen those eyes before. There was no mistaking them. Her bow of a mouth was a man's perfect fantasy, her lips full and naturally red.

The booming continued, a steady, insistent beat. He felt it through his back and legs, a jarring pulse that refused to leave him alone. Through his skin, he seemed to follow the path of water running beneath him, bringing life-giving nutrients.

You feel it, don't you? she insisted softly.

He couldn't look away. Her gaze held his captive. He wasn't the kind of man to allow anything or anyone to ensnare him. He forced his head to work—that first movement that he knew would cost him dearly. He nodded. He waited for the pain to rip him apart, but aside from a little burst through his neck and temples that quickly subsided, the expected agony never came.

What is it?

He frowned, concentrating. The sound continued without a break, so steady, so strong and rhythmic, he would have said it was a heart, but the sound was too deep and too loud. Still, it was a pulse that called to him just as it called to the trees and grass as if they were all tied together. The trees. The grass. The water. The woman. And him.

You know what it is.

Zev didn't want to tell her. If he said the words, he would have to face his life again. A cold, utterly lonely existence of blood and death. He was an elite hunter, a dealer of death to rogue packs—Lycans turned werewolves who preyed on mankind—and he was damned good at his job.

The booming grew louder, more insistent, a dark heralding of life. There was nowhere to hide from it. Nowhere to run even if he could run. He knew exactly what it was now. He knew where the sound originated as it spread out from a center deep beneath him.

Tell me, Hän ku pesäk kaikak, what is it you hear?

The melodic notes of her voice drifted through his pores and found their way into his body. He could feel the soft musical sound wrapping itself around his heart and sinking into his bones. Her breath teased his face, warm and soft and so fresh, like the gentlest of breezes fanning his warm skin. His lungs seemed to follow the rhythm of hers, almost as if she breathed for him, not just with him.

Hän ku pesäk kaikak. Where had he heard that before? She called him that as if she expected him to know what it meant, but it was in a language he was certain he didn't speak—and he knew he spoke many.

The drumbeat sounded louder, closer, as if he was surrounded on all sides by many drums keeping the exact beat, but he knew that wasn't so. The pounding pulse came from below him—and it was summoning him.

There was no way to ignore it, no matter how much he wanted to. He knew now that it wouldn't stop, not ever, not unless he answered the call.

It is the heartbeat of the earth itself.

She smiled and her emerald eyes seemed to take on the multifaceted cut of the gems he'd seen adorning women, although a thousand times more brilliant.

She nodded her head very slowly. *At long last you are truly back with us. Mother Earth has called to you. You are being summoned to the warrior's council. It is a great honor.*

Whispers drifted through his mind like fingers of fog. He couldn't seem to retain actual words, but male voices rose and fell all around him, as if he were surrounded. The sensation of heat hit him. Real heat. Choking. Burning. His lungs refused to work, to pull in much needed air. When he tried to open his eyes, nothing happened. He was locked in his mind far from whatever was happening to his body.

The woman leaned closer, her lips brushing against his. His heart stuttered. She barely touched him, featherlight, but it was the most intimate sensation he'd ever experienced. Her mouth was exquisite. Perfection. A fantasy. Her lips moved over his again, soft and warm, melting into him. She breathed into his mouth, a soft airy breath of clean, fresh air. Once again he tasted her. Cinnamon. Spice. Honey.

Breathe, Zev. You are both Lycan and Carpathian and you can breathe anywhere when you choose. Just breathe.

He was not *Sange rau.*

No, not Sange rau, you are Hän ku pesäk kaikak. You are a guardian.

The breath she had exchanged with him continued to move through his body. He could almost track its progress as if that precious air was a stream of white finding its way through a maze until it filled his lungs. He actually felt her breath enter his lungs, inflating them.

I'm not dreaming, am I?

She smiled at him. A man might kill for one of her smiles.

No, Zev, you're not dreaming. You are in the sacred cave of warriors. Mother Earth called the ancients to witness your rebirth.

He had no idea what she was talking about, but things were beginning to come back to him. *Sange rau* was a combination of rogue wolf and vampire blood mixed together. *Hän ku pesäk kaikak* was Lycan and Carpathian blood mixed. He wasn't certain what or where the sacred cave of warriors was, and he didn't like the word *rebirth*.

Why can't I move?

You are coming to life. You have been locked away from us for some time.

Not from you.

She had been with him while he was locked in that dark place of pain and madness. If there was one thing he knew for absolute certain, she had been there. He couldn't move on, because he hadn't been able to leave her.

He remembered that voice, soft and pleading. *Stay. Stay with me.* Her voice had locked them both in a sea of agony that seemed endless.

Not endless. You are awakening.

He might be waking, but the pain was still there. He took a moment to let himself absorb it. She was correct, the pain was subsiding to a tolerable level, but the heat surrounding him was burning his body. Without the air she'd given him, he would be choking, strangling, desperate.

Think what body temperature you wish. You are Carpathian. Embrace who you are.

Her voice never changed. She didn't seem impatient with his lack of knowledge. Before, when she was a distance from him, she hadn't been aloof, she simply waited. Now she felt different, as if she expected something from him.

What the hell? If she said to think about a different body temperature other than the one burning his flesh from his bones, he could give her that. He chose a normal temperature and held that in his mind. She spoke to him without words, telepathically, so she must be able to see he was doing as she asked.

At once, the burning sensation ceased to be. He took a gasping breath. Heat filled his lungs, but there was air as well. He knew her. Only one woman could speak to him as she did. Mind to mind. He knew her now. How could he have ever forgotten who she was?

Branislava.

How had she gotten trapped with him in such a terrible place? He sent up a small prayer of thanks that he hadn't left her there. *She* had been the one to whisper to him. *Stay. Stay with me.* He should have recognized her voice, a soft sweet melody that was forever stamped into his bones.

You recognize me. She smiled at him again and he felt her fingers brush along his jaw and then go up to his forehead, brushing back strands of hair falling into his face.

Her touch brought pleasure, not pain. A small electrical current ran from his forehead down to his belly, tightening his muscles. The current went lower, coiling heat in his groin. He could feel something besides pain, and wouldn't you know it would be desire?

It seemed absurd to him that he hadn't known all along whom she was. She was the *one* woman. The *only* woman. *The* woman. He'd known women, of course. He'd lived too long not to. He was a hunter, an elite hunter, and he was never in one place long. He didn't form attachments. Women didn't rob him of breath, or put him under spells. He didn't think about them night and day. Or fantasize. Or want one for his own.

Until her. Branislava. She wasn't Lycan. She didn't talk much. She looked like an angel and moved like a temptress. Her voice beckoned like a siren's call. She had looked at him with those unusual eyes and smiled with that perfect mouth, inciting all sorts of erotic fantasies. When they danced, just that one unforgettable time, her body had fit into his, melted into his, until she was imprinted there for all time, into his skin, into his bones.

Every single rule he'd ever made about women in the long years he had lived had been broken with her. She'd robbed him of breath. Put him under her spell. He thought of her day and night and fantasized far too much. He wanted her in every way possible. Her body. Her heart. Her mind. Her soul. He wanted her all for himself.

How did you get here? In this place?

It alarmed him that he might have somehow dragged her down into that sea of agony because he'd been so enamored with her. Could a man do that? Want a woman so much that when he died, he took her with him? The idea was appalling. He'd lived honorably, at least he'd tried to, and he'd never hurt a woman who hadn't been a murdering rogue. The idea that he might have taken *this* woman into hell with him was disturbing on every level.

I chose to come with you, she replied, as if it were the most normal thing in the world to do. *Our spirits are woven together. Our fate is entwined.*

I don't understand.

You were dying and there was no other way to save your life. You are precious to us all, a man of honor, of great skill.

Zev frowned. That made no sense. He had no family. He had his pack, but two of his pack members, friends for so many long years, had betrayed and tried to murder him. He was mixed blood now, and few of his kind would accept him.

Us all? he echoed. *Who would that be?*

Do you hear them calling to you?

Zev stayed very still, tuning his acute hearing to get past the heartbeat of the earth, the flow of water beneath him, reaching for the distant voices. Men's voices. They seemed to be all around him. Some chanted to him in an ancient language while others throat-chanted as the monks from long ago had done. Each separate word or note vibrated through him, just as the heartbeat of the earth had.

They summoned him just as the earth had. It was time. He couldn't find any more excuses and it seemed no one was going to let him remain right where he was. He forced himself to open his eyes.

He was underground in a cave. That much was evident immediately. There was heat and humidity surrounding him, although he didn't feel hot. It was more that he saw it, those bands of heat undulating throughout the immense chamber.

Great stalactites hung from the high ceiling. They were enormous formations, great long rows of teeth of various sizes. Stalagmites rose from the floor with wide bases. Colors wound around the columns from the flaring bases to the pointed tips. The floor was worn smooth with centuries of feet walking on it.

Zev recognized that he was deep beneath the earth. The chamber, although enormous, felt hallowed to him. He lay in the earth itself, his body covered by rich black loam. Minerals sparkled in the blanket of dirt over him. Hundreds of candles were lit, high up on the walls of the chamber, illuminating the cavern, casting flickering lights across the stalagmites, bringing the muted color to life.

His heart began to pound in alarm. He had no idea where he was or how he got there. He turned his head and instantly his body settled. She was there, sitting beside him. Branislava. She was truly as beautiful as he remembered her. Her skin was pale and flawless. Her lashes were just as long, her lips as perfect as in his dream. Only her clothes were different.

He was afraid if he spoke aloud she would disappear. She looked as ethereal as ever, a creature from long ago, not meant for the world he resided in. The chanting swelled in volume, and he reached for her hand, threading his fingers tightly through hers before he turned his head to try to find the source—or sources—of that summons.

There were several men in the room, all warriors with faces that had seen too many battles. He felt comfortable with them, a part of them, as if—in that sacred chamber—they were a brotherhood. He knew their faces, although most he'd never met, but he knew the caliber of men they were.

He recognized four men he knew well, although it felt as if a hundred years had passed since he'd seen them. Fenris Dalka was there. He should have known he would be. Fen was his friend, if someone like him could have friends. Beside him was Dimitri Tirunul, Fen's brother, and that too wasn't surprising. The brothers were close. Their last names were different only because Fen had taken the last name of a Lycan in order to better fit in during his years with them.

Two figures stood over another hole in the ground where a man lay looking around him just as Zev was. The man in what could have been an open grave looked pale and worn, as if he'd been through hell and had come out the other side. Zev wondered idly if he looked the same way. It took a few moments before he recognized Gary Jansen. Gary was human, and he'd waded through rogue wolves to get to Zev during a particularly fierce battle. Zev was very happy to see him alive.

He was familiar with Gregori Daratrazanoff. Usually Gregori wasn't far from his prince, but he hovered close to the man who struggled to sit up. Gregori immediately reached down and gently helped Gary into a sitting position. The man on the other side of the "grave" had the same look as Gregori. This had to be another Daratrazanoff.

On the other side of Gregori, a short distance from him, stood two of the De La Cruz brothers, Zacarias and Manolito, both of whom he knew and who had joined with him in a battle of some kind. The actual facts were still a little fuzzy. A third man stood between them.

In the center of the room were several smaller columns made of crystals forming a circle around a bloodred formation with what looked to be a razor-sharp tip. Standing beside it was Mikhail Dubrinsky, prince of the Carpathian people. He spoke very low, but his voice carried through the chamber with great authority.

Mikhail spoke in an ancient language, the ritual words to call to their long gone ancestors. *"Veri isäakank—veri ekäakank."*

To his absolute shock and astonishment, Zev understood the words. Blood of our fathers—blood of our brothers. He knew that was the literal translation, but the language was an ancient one, not of the Lycans. He had been born Lycan. He had heard the language spoken by Carpathians down through the centuries but he shouldn't have understood the words so clearly. *"Veri olen elid."*

Blood is life. Zev's breath caught in his throat. He *understood*. He spoke many languages, but this was so ancient he couldn't have ever learned it. Why was he understanding it now? Nothing made sense, although his mind wasn't quite as foggy as it had been.

Branislava tightened her fingers around his. He turned his head and looked at her. She was so beautiful she took his breath away. Her eyes were on his face and he felt her gaze penetrating deep. Too deep. She was already branded in his mind. She was coming far too close to his heart.

"Andak veri-elidet Karpatiiakank, és wäke-sarna ku meke arwa-arvo, irgalom, hän ku agba, és wäke kutni, ku manaak verival," Mikhail continued. The power of his voice rang through the chamber, raw and elemental, bringing Zev's attention back to him.

Zev understood the words. We offer that life to our people with a blood-sworn vow of honor, mercy, integrity and endurance.

What did that mean? This was a ritual—a ceremony that he felt part of—even though he didn't know what exactly was going on. The appearance of Fen and Dimitri was reassuring to him. The longer he was awake, the more his mind cleared. The two were of mixed blood, although both had been born Carpathian.

Mikhail dropped his palm over the very sharp tip of the dark red column. At once the crystals went from dark red to crimson, as if Mikhail's blood had brought them to life.

Verink sokta; verink kaŋa terád. Mikhail's voice swelled with power.

Zev saw sparks light up the room. He frowned over the words Mikhail had uttered. Our blood mingles and calls to you. He was mingling his blood with someone of power, that much was obvious from the way the columns throughout the room began to come alive. Several gave off glowing colors, although still very muted.

"Akasz énak ku kaŋa és juttasz kuntatak it."

Zev translated again as the columns began to hum. Heed our summons and join with us now. The columns throughout the room rocked, the multicolored crystals illuminating, throwing vivid, bright colors across the ceiling and over the walls of the chamber. The colors were so dazzling, Zev had to shade his sensitive eyes.

Crimson, emerald, a beautiful sapphire, the colors took on the strange phenomenon of the northern lights. The humming grew louder and he realized each took on a different note, a different pitch, the tone perfect to his ear. He hadn't noticed that the columns appeared to be totems with faces of warriors carved into the mineral, but now they came to life, the color adding expression and character.

Zev let out his breath slowly. These warriors were long dead. He was in a cave of the dead, and Mikhail had summoned the ancient warriors to him for some purpose. Zev had a very bad feeling that he was part of that purpose.

"Ete tekaik, sayeak ekäakanket. Čač3katlanak med, kutenken hank ekäakank tasa."

Zev swallowed hard when he translated. We have brought before you our brothers, not born to us, but brothers just the same.

Zev had been born Lycan and he'd served his people for many long years as an elite hunter who traveled the world seeking out and destroying rogue wolves who preyed on mankind. He was one of the few Lycans who could hunt alone and be comfortable and confident doing so. Still, he was Lycan and he would always have the need to be part of a pack.

His own kind despised those of mixed blood. It mattered little that he became mixed blood giving service to his people. He'd been wounded in hundreds of battles and had lost far too much blood. Carpathian warriors had more than once come to his aid as they had done this last time.

Zev looked up to find Fen on one side of him and Dimitri on the other. The two De La Cruz brothers stood with the stranger between them.

Gregori and his brother stood on either side of Gary, who now was getting to his feet with Gregori's help. Zev took a breath. He would not be the only man sitting on his ass while the others stood. He was getting up or would die trying.

Zev let go of his lifeline and the moment he did nearly panicked— another thing men like him didn't do. He didn't want her to disappear. His eyes met hers. *Don't you leave me.*

She gave him a smile that could allow a man to live for the rest of his existence on fantasies. *We are tied together, Zev. Where you go, I go. Only the ancients can undo a weave of the spirits.*

Is that what this is about? He wasn't certain he wanted to continue if it was.

Not even the prince can ask for such a release. Only me. Or you.

She gave him the information, but he had the feeling she was a little reluctant. That suited him just fine. He wasn't willing to relinquish his bond with her just yet.

Fen, I don't have a stitch on and I want to stand up. I'm not going to lie in this grave like a baby. For the first time he realized he was absolutely naked and Branislava had been beside him the entire time holding his hand—even when his body had stirred to life she hadn't run from him.

At once he was clean, and clothed in soft trousers and an immaculate white shirt. He struggled to get to his feet. Fen and Dimitri both reached for him at the same time, preventing him from falling on his face and making a fool of himself. His legs were rubber, refusing to work properly. For a Lycan, that was embarrassing, but for an elite hunter, it was absolutely humiliating.

Mikhail looked over at him and nodded his approval, or maybe it was relief at him being alive. Zev wasn't certain yet if he was relieved or not.

"Aka sarnamad, en Karpatiiakak. Saγeak kontaket ŋamaŋak tekaiked. Tajnak aka-arvonk és arwa-arvonk."

Hear me, great ones. We bring these men to you, warriors all, deserving of our respect and honor. Zev translated the words carefully twice, just to make certain he was correctly interpreting the prince's discourse with the ancient warriors.

Gary, standing between the two Daratrazanoff brothers, straightened his shoulders as if feeling eyes on him. Zev was fairly certain that somehow, those spirits of the dead were watching all of them, perhaps judging their worth. Colors swirled into various hues, and the notes blended together as if the ancient warriors questioned the prince.

"Gregori és Darius katak Daratrazanoffak. Kontak ŋamaŋak sarnanak hän agba nókunta ekäankal, Gary Jansen, hän ku olenot küm, kutenken olen it Karpatii. Hän pohoopa kuš Karpatiikuntanak, partiolenaka és kontaka. Saγeak hänet ete tekaik."

Gregori and Darius of the great house of Daratrazanoff claim kinship with our brother, Gary Jansen, once human, now one of us. He has served our people tirelessly both in research and in battle. We bring him before you.

Zev knew that aside from actually fighting alongside the Carpathians, Gary had done a tremendous amount of work for the Carpathians, and had lived among them for several years. It was obvious that every Carpathian in the chamber afforded him great respect, as did Zev. Gary had fought both valiantly and selflessly.

"Zacarias és Manolito katak De La Cruzak, käktä enä wäkeva kontak. Kontak ŋamaŋak sarnanak hän agba nókunta ekäankal, Luiz Silva, hän ku olenot jaquár, kutenken olen it Karpatii. Luiz mänet en elidaket, kor3nat elidaket avio päläfertiilakjakak. Saγeak hänet ete tekaik."

Zacarias and Manolito from the house of De La Cruz, two of our mightiest warriors, claim kinship with our brother, Luiz Silva, once Jaguar, now Carpathian. Luiz saved the lives of two of their lifemates. We bring him before you.

Zev knew nothing of Luiz, but he had to admire anyone who could stand with Zacarias De La Cruz claiming kinship. Zacarias was not known for his kindness. Luiz had to be a great warrior to run with that family of Carpathians.

"Fen és Dimitri arwa-arvodkatak Tirunulak sarnanak hän agba nókunta ekäankal, Zev Hunter, hän ku olenot Susiküm, kutenken olen it Karpatii. Torot päläpälä Karpatiikuntankal és piwtät és piwtä mekeni sarna kunta jotkan Susikümkunta és Karpatiikunta. Saγeak hänet ete tekaik."

Fen and Dimitri from the noble house of Tirunul claim kinship with our brother, Zev Hunter, once Lycan, now Carpathian. He has fought side by side with our people and has sought to bring an alliance between Lycan and Carpathian. He is of mixed blood like those who claim kinship. We bring him before you.

There was no mistaking the translation. Mikhail had definitely called his name and indicated that Fen and Dimitri claimed brotherhood with him. He certainly had enough of their blood in him to be a brother.

The humming grew in volume, and Mikhail nodded several times before turning to Gary. "Is it your wish to become fully a brother?"

Gary nodded his head without hesitation. Zev was fairly certain, that like him, Gary hadn't been prepped ahead of time. The answer had to come from within at the precise moment of the asking. There was no prepping. He didn't know what his own answer would be.

Gregori and Darius, with Gary between them approached the crystal column, now swirling a dull red. Gregori dropped his hand, palm down, over the tip of the formation, allowing his blood to flow over that of the prince.

"Place your hand over the sacred bloodstone and allow your blood to mingle with that of the ancients and that of your brothers," Mikhail instructed.

Gary moved forward slowly, his feet following the path so many warriors had walked before him. He placed his hand over the sharp tip and allowed his palm to drop. His blood ran down the crystal column, mixing with Gregori's.

Darius glided just behind him with the same silent, deadly way of his brother, and when Gary stepped back, Darius placed his palm over the tip of the bloodstone, allowing his blood to mingle with Mikhail's, Gregori's, Gary's and the ancient warriors who had gone before.

The hum grew louder, filling the chamber. Colors swirled, this time taking on hues of blue, green and purple.

Gary gave a little gasp and went silent, nodding his head as if he heard something Zev couldn't. Within minutes he stepped back and glanced over to the prince.

"It is done," Mikhail affirmed. "So be it."

The humming ceased, all those beautiful notes that created a melody of words only the prince could understand. The chamber went silent. Zev became aware of his heart beating too fast. He consciously took a breath and let it out. The tension and sense of anticipation grew.

"Is it your wish, Luiz, to become fully a brother?" Mikhail asked.

Zev took a long look at Zacarias and Manolito. The De La Cruz brothers were rather infamous. Taking on their family as kin would be daunting. Only a very confident and strong man would ever agree.

Luiz inclined his head and walked to the crystal bloodstone on his own, Zacarias and Manolito behind him. Clearly Luiz had not been wounded. He was physically fit and moved with the flow of a jungle cat.

Zacarias pierced his palm first, allowing his blood to flow down the stone, joining with the ancient warriors. At once the hum began, a low call of greeting, of recognition and honor. Colors swirled around the room as if the ancients knew Zacarias and his legendary reputation. They seemed to greet him as an old friend. There was no doubt in Zev's mind that the ancient warriors were paying tribute to Zacarias. Many probably had known him.

When the humming died down, Luiz stepped close to the stone and pierced his palm, his blood flowing into that of the eldest De La Cruz. Manolito came next and did the same so that the blood of all three mingled with that of the ancient warriors.

At once the humming of approval began again, and the great columns of both stalagmites and stalactites banded with colors of white and yellow and bright red.

Luiz stood silent, very still, much as Gary had before him, and just as Gary had, Luiz nodded his head several times as though listening. He looked up at Zacarias and Manolito and smiled for the first time.

"It is done," Mikhail murmured in a low, carrying tone of power that seemed to fill the chamber. "So be it."

Zev's mouth went dry. His heart began to pound. He felt tension gather low in his belly, great knots forming that he couldn't prevent. There was acceptance here—but there could also be rejection. He wasn't born Carpathian, but Fen and Dimitri were offering him so much more than that—they stood for him. Called him brother. If these ancient warriors accepted him, he would be truly both Carpathian and Lycan. He would have a pack of his own again. He would belong somewhere.

The feeling in the great chamber was very somber. The eloquence of the long dead slowly faded and he knew it was time. He had no idea what he would do when asked. None. He wasn't even certain his legs would carry him the distance, and he wasn't going to be carried to the bloodstone.

"Is it your wish, Zev, to become fully a brother?" Mikhail asked.

He felt the weight of every stare. Warriors all. Good men who knew battle. Men he respected. His feet wanted to move forward. He wanted to be a part of them. He was physically still very weak. What if he didn't measure up in their eyes?

You aren't weak, Zev. There is nothing weak about you.

Her voice moved through him like a breath of fresh air. He hadn't realized he was holding his breath until she spoke so intimately to him. He let it go, braced himself and made his first move. Fen and Dimitri stayed close, not just to walk him to the bloodstone, but to make absolutely certain he didn't fall on his face. Still, he was determined it wouldn't happen.

With every step he took on that worn, stone floor he seemed to absorb into him the ancients who had gone before. Their wisdom. Their technique in battle. Their great determination and sense of honor and duty. He felt information gathering in his mind, yet he couldn't quite process it. It was a great gift, but he couldn't access the data and that left him even more concerned that he might be rejected. Somewhere, sometime, long ago, he felt he'd been in this sacred chamber before. The longer he was in it, the more familiar to him it felt.

As he approached the crystal column, his heart accelerated even more. He felt sheer raw power emanating from the bloodstone. The formation pulsed with power, and each time it did, color banded, ropes of various shades of red, blood he knew was collected from all the great warriors who were long gone from the Carpathian world, yet, through the prince, could still aid their people. Mikhail understood their voices through those perfectly pitched notes.

Fen dropped his palm over the tip of the stalagmite. His blood ran down the sacred stone. The colors changed instantly, swirling with a deep purple through dark red. He stepped back to allow Zev to approach the column.

Zev wasn't going to draw it out. Either they accepted him or they didn't. In his life, he couldn't remember a single time when he cared what others thought of him, but here, in the sacred chamber of warriors, he found it mattered much more than he wanted to admit. He dropped his palm over the sharp tip so that it pierced his palm and blood flowed over Fen's, mingling with that of the one who would be his brother, and that of the great warriors of the past.

His soul stretched to meet those who had gone before. He was surrounded, filled with camaraderie, with acceptance, with belonging. His community dated back to ancient times, and those warriors of old called out to him in greeting. As they did, the flood of information through his brain, adhering to his memories, was both astonishing and overwhelming.

Zev was a man who observed every detail of his surroundings. It was one of the characteristics that had allowed him to become an elite hunter. Now, everything seemed even sharper and more vivid to him. Every warrior's heart in the chamber from ancient to modern times matched the drumming of the earth's heart. Blood ebbed and flowed in their veins, matching the flow of the ancients' blood within the crystal, but also the ebb and flow of water throughout their earth.

Dimitri dropped his palm over the crystal and at once, Zev felt the mingling of their blood, the kinship that ran deeper than friendship. His history and their history became one, stretching back to ancient times. Information was accumulative, amassing in his mind at a rapid rate. With it came the heavy responsibility of his kind.

The humming grew loud, and he recognized now what those notes meant—approval—acceptance without reserve. Colors swirled and banded throughout the room. Those ancient warriors recognized him, recognized his bloodline, not just the blood of Fen and Dimitri who claimed kinship, but his own, born of a union not all Lycan.

Bur tule ekämet kuntamak. The voices of the ancestors filled his mind with greetings. Well met, brother-kin. *Eläsz jeläbam ainaak.* Long may you live in the light.

Zev had no knowledge of his lineage being anything but pure Lycan. His mother had died long before he had memory of her. Why would these warriors claim kinship with him through his own bloodline and not Fen and Dimitri's? That made no sense to him.

Our lives are tied together by our blood. They spoke to him in their own ancient language and he had no trouble translating it, as if the language had always been a part of him and he had just needed the ancients to bridge some gap in his memory for it all to unfold.

I don't understand. That was an understatement. He was more confused than ever.

Everything including one's lifemate is determined by the blood flowing in our veins. Your blood is Dark Blood. You now are of mixed blood, but you are one of us. You are kont o sívanak.

Strong heart, heart of a warrior. It was a tribute, but it didn't tell him what he needed to know.

Who was my mother? That was the question he needed answered. If Carpathian blood already flowed in his veins, how was it he hadn't known?

Your mother's mother was fully Carpathian. Lycans killed her for being Sange rau. Her daughter, your mother, was raised wholly Lycan. She mated with a Lycan, and gave birth to you, a Dark Blood. You are kunta.

Family, he interpreted. From what bloodline? How? Zev knew he was taking far longer than either Gary or Luiz had, but he didn't want to leave this source of information. His father never once let on that there was any Carpathian blood in their family. Had he known? Had his mother even known? If his grandmother had been murdered by the Lycans for her mixed blood, no one would ever admit that his mother had been the child of a mixed blood. The family would have hidden her from the others. Most likely her father had left his pack and found another one to protect her.

The humming began to fade and Zev found himself reaching out, needing more.

Wait. Who was she?

It is there, in your memories, everything you need, everything you are. Blood calls to blood and you are whole again. The humming faded away.

"It is done," Mikhail said formally. "So be it."

2

F en clapped Zev on the shoulder hard enough to make him wince. "Looks like I'm your big brother. I knew eventually there would be an upside to meeting you. I've got another little brother to boss around."

Dimitri groaned. "Now we're in for it. He's going to strut around all puffed up. No one will be able to live with him."

Zev tried not to fall over. His stomach throbbed with pain. For the first time since he'd been so gravely injured protecting Arno, one of the Lycan council members, he looked down as if he might see the wound through the white shirt Fen had provided. His hand went up to cover the spot where it felt as if he had a huge hole torn through him. He half expected to feel the flesh gone right through the shirt.

The revelations from the ancient warriors were almost too much to process, just as all the information they had packed into his mind was. He swayed with weariness. He found he could barely think with his mind turning over and over trying to understand the things about him that had been revealed. Had he been in a dream state? Was it real? Right now, only the pain felt real. The rest of it felt surreal.

His fingers bunched the material of the shirt into a fist and he looked around slowly, carefully, wanting to see only one person. His breath caught in his throat. He felt his wolf leap forward as if to protect him. He was still disoriented, and it was impossible in his present state to process the wealth of information now imprinted on his brain. He found it difficult to stand, let alone think, and he needed her.

"Maybe you should sit down," Fen suggested, genuine concern in his voice. "I'm happy you're alive, Zev, but we may have called you back a little too soon." He glanced over Zev's shoulder to the man approaching him from behind.

Zev didn't think there was much question about it. He wasn't fully healed yet. He could barely control his body temperature. There was a note of guilt in Fen's voice that his mixed blood picked up when his mind seemed to be all over the place. "There must have been a reason to wake me."

He knew the prince had come up behind him. Mikhail made no sound, but the awareness of power couldn't be mistaken. He turned to greet the prince of the Carpathian people.

Mikhail clasped Zev's forearms in the welcoming of warriors. "You gave us all a scare, Zev. We weren't sure you would make it."

"Neither was I," Zev admitted. He looked around the chamber. He needed to see her. To touch her. Where *was* she?

"You need rest, Zev," Mikhail said.

As if he hadn't figured that out for himself. *Why did you wake me?* he asked Fen.

"Dimitri and Fen feel more comfortable in the forest and both have homes there. We can accommodate your preference, forest, mountain or even the village itself, but you'll still need care, at least until you're stronger," Mikhail continued.

He only wanted one person caring for him, and she was no longer in the chamber.

Where are you?

Was that him? He sounded possessive, even irritable that she dared leave without his knowledge. He didn't want her out of his sight.

"Thank you, I appreciate the offer of a house. I'm still a little shaky." He pinned Fen with his steel-colored eyes. He may have just come back from the dead, but he'd always gone his own way, fought his own battles and was a force to be reckoned with. There was another reason to awaken him before he was healed other than to present him for judgment before the ancient warriors.

Where are you, Branislava?

His snapped the question a second time, demanding an answer. He used his most commanding voice, one that brooked no refusal.

I need to reassure Tatijana that I live.

She had the same, perfect melodic voice, unaffected in the least by his domineering, *idiotic* short-tempered pack leader voice.

Wait for me.

He winced, hearing himself. He sounded like a dictator. He couldn't help how he sounded. It should have been a plea, not a command. She wasn't part of his pack, but he was used to obedience. Even the Lycan council took his word as law. More, he was annoyed that he didn't understand why it was so necessary to have her with him. It made no sense to him and until it did, until he could figure out why it was so important to keep her close, she wasn't going anywhere.

There was a small silence—a distancing—as if she'd been in his mind, but now had pulled away from him. His heart stuttered and he stretched, reached, unable to let go of her. He had been aware of the other men in the chamber talking around him, of the steady drip of water and the small hiss of flames, but now his complete concentration was on Branislava.

Zev willed her to return to him in spite of his overbearing, officious manner. He actually counted his heartbeats, waiting for her answer. Had he been strong enough, he would have gone after her. He knew he could follow her trail. Few eluded him once he was in pursuit.

He smelled her first, that blend of cinnamon, spice and honey. The moment she was close, he drew her scent into his lungs and was able to breathe fully again. He tasted the mixture that was unique to her, on his tongue, and instantly wanted—no needed—more.

He turned his head to gaze at her. The impact was the same as it always was when he looked at her. He hadn't been cured of whatever spell he was under. Looking at her almost hurt she was so beautiful.

Thank you. I don't know what's gotten into me.

Zev held out his hand to her, needing to touch her physically. It was strange to need anything at all, let alone physical contact. He ignored Fen and Dimitri's raised eyebrows when she didn't move. He continued to hold out his hand. Waiting. He said nothing at all, just let her make up her mind. *Willing* her to reach for him.

Branislava put her hand in his. His fingers closed around hers. Her hand felt small and fragile in his. At once everything in him settled and he felt whole. Complete. That was confusing as well. He'd always managed to be just fine on his own.

"I'd like you to meet Gary Jansen," Mikhail said.

"I remember him," Zev said. "Our last meeting was during the fight with the rogue pack attacking all the women and children. He fought like a banshee. Without him, I'm not certain I'd have made it through that battle."

As Gregori and Gary approached them, Mikhail added, "Gregori's like an old mother hen fussing over her chick. Now that he has Gary to drive insane, maybe I'll be lucky and he won't fuss over me so much."

"You're not ever going to get that lucky," Gregori shot back, in no way perturbed by Mikhail's needling. It was clear the two men were old friends.

Mikhail shrugged, a small grin lighting his piercing, dark eyes. "I thought that might be the case. One can only hope."

It was the first time Zev could ever recall seeing the prince, or Gregori, for that matter, relaxed.

He was aware of everything now as if his mixed blood had heightened every sense, as if both wolf and Carpathian were on the alert. The heat in the chamber. The water. The fact that Gary Jansen and Luiz Silva were both unattached males in very close proximity to Branislava. The breath hissed out of him in a long, slow growl under his breath.

He tugged on Branislava's hand, drawing her closer to him. *I don't want to fall on my face in front of the prince.* It was a lame explanation, but the only one he could think of for explaining why he needed her close to him.

"It's very good finally meeting you, Gary," Zev said aloud, offering his right hand to shake. Gary was very pale, but he looked incredibly fit for having suffered a mortal wound, essentially death and conversion.

"I'm glad you made it through," Gary said. "Gregori kept me up-to-date on everything that was happening." He bowed low toward Branislava, offering her a smile. "It's good to see you out and about. You look beautiful."

Right there in that sacred cave, surrounded by very perceptive warriors, Zev felt a kind of snarling rage burst through him like a live volcano. He actually saw red. Waves of crimson banded through the room, and in his mouth, he felt teeth lengthen. He fought back the change, refusing to allow the wolf side of him freedom.

He'd never experienced such an emotion or even one with such intensity. The Carpathian side of his nature seemed to be a little hard to control. He was going to have to get used to it—and so was his wolf. He doubted if the ancient warriors and the prince would be so welcoming to a snarling, raging wolf.

He glanced at Branislava to see how she took Gary's compliment. The man was being honest—there was nothing at all in his demeanor to suggest anything else—but still, Zev didn't think it was proper, when he was holding her hand, to have another man complimenting her. And bowing? Come on. He'd been human, not Carpathian. Showing off was ridiculous.

It is always acceptable and proper for a man to tell a woman she is beautiful. There was the merest hint of amusement in Branislava's voice. "Thank you, sir," she said more formally to Gary. *And bowing is very courtly and always welcomed.*

Fen raised an eyebrow at him. *Your wolf is showing.* Fen didn't even try to hide his taunting laughter. It was nothing at all like the gentle, kind, *soothing* hint of amusement Branislava had in her voice.

Zev sent him a quelling glare. He forced his attention back to Gary, determined to get his attention off of Branislava. "How did you manage to get in with this bunch?"

"I was their enemy," Gary admitted. "I saw an actual vampire attack and I joined a society that hunted vampires—except they weren't really targeting vampires. More often it was people they didn't like. I helped some people to escape, and Gregori was there to help them, too, although I didn't know that at the time. We met. That was quite a few years ago. My life was very different. I was skinny and tripped over my own feet when I walked. In my wildest dreams I never thought I could ever really fight a vampire and win, but over the years, I've had to learn."

"But you still were going to try back in those days," Gregori pointed out. "You never lacked for courage."

"I thought you were supposed to be a genius," Mikhail said. "Yet you chose to hang around Gregori." His grin widened. "And all the rest of us."

"Well, I can never say my life is dull," Gary said, with an answering smile that faded quickly. "You gave my life a sense of purpose."

Gary wasn't skinny now. He was fit and strong, with the look of a warrior who had seen many battles—and he probably had. He had been their go-to man during the day when the Carpathians were underground.

"I'm Darius." The man who looked much like Gregori introduced himself. "Gregori has told me so much about you. All good, which is rare for him."

Zev managed a smile. He scented a woman on Darius, and knew instinctively he had a lifemate. He breathed away the itch that seemed to come and go over his skin. "It's good to meet you, too." He'd definitely been awakened too early. His wound throbbed and pulsed with pain. No matter how hard he tried to push it away, the pain pushed back.

Zacarias De La Cruz, his brother Manolito and the newcomer Luiz joined them. Luiz was built like a Jaguar, compact with ropy muscles and a fluidity when he walked that couldn't be mistaken. Manolito was like Fen, Dimitri and Zev, a mixed blood.

Zacarias looked Zev over, bowed to Branislava without saying a word to her.

See, now that's courtly. Gary might be able to learn a few things from the man.

Branislava's soft laughter moved through his mind, but she didn't reply.

Zev, hurry through the introductions, you're looking like you might drop dead all over again, Fen warned.

Zev nodded at Luiz, gritting his teeth. He *felt* like he might drop dead as well, but that was impossible now. Two unattached males were very close to Branislava, and both were looking at her as if they might engage her in conversation at any moment. And just why the hell would that be so wrong? What had gotten into him? Joints and muscles ached. His skin itched. His jaw felt as if it might shatter, and he clenched his teeth trying to breathe away the need to change. His wolf prowled closer than ever to the surface.

"It's nice to finally meet you," Luiz said. "I've heard of you, of course."

Zev tried to reply, but Luiz's gaze kept straying to Branislava, and if he shook hands or attempted speech, all they would get was his wolf.

As if he knew there was a problem, Zacarias glided smoothly between Luiz and Zev. He didn't posture, but he was definitely a threat. Instead of backing down, the alpha wolf rose with a snarling challenge Zev could barely suppress.

Why is your wolf so close? Dimitri asked. *I can feel that you're fighting him.* He stepped closer to Zev, moving in on his other side protectively.

I don't know, but he wants out and he's looking for a fight.

Zev. Gregori reached for both Dimitri and Fen as well, as they were now tied to Zev. He knew all three could hear. *Your eyes have changed color and you're giving off a very dangerous scent. Should I remove the prince?*

Zev breathed hard to try to stay in control of the wolf raging to get out. He saw in images of heat, colors banding and shimmering. He pinpointed the hearts of every single person in the room. He heard them, loud and strong, calling to him.

Gregori, Zev is severely wounded, Fen reminded. *He can barely stand.*

He's dangerous, one of the most lethal men I've ever met, and there's no quit in him. He'll fight until he's dead. And he'll take as many with him as he can.

Zev wished he could reassure them all, but he wasn't certain anything more than a growl or snarl would come out of his mouth. He concentrated on trying to breathe, but it seemed as if every breath he drew contained fire so that his lungs burned, adding to the need to change. He kept his head down, knowing if Gregori and Zacarias could see the wolf rising, the other warriors in close proximity could as well.

Branislava moved closer to him, almost protectively, sliding under his shoulder. That small movement seemed to appease his wolf enough for him to breathe. Unfortunately, that small movement on her part instantly drew the attention of the men around them, including that of Luiz, who couldn't seem to stop staring at her. A low warning growl escaped before he could stop it.

Mikhail looked at him and then at Branislava speculatively.

Get me out of this situation now, Fen. I don't know what's wrong, but if that man keeps looking at her that way, I'm not going to be able to stop myself from attacking. Admitting to that weakness when he knew Branislava could hear was one of the most difficult things he'd ever done.

Fen didn't hesitate. "Zev needs to rest now. He's been awakened far too early out of necessity," he announced. "I hate to cut introductions short, but he needs to leave now." He indicated Zev's shirt.

Zev followed his gaze to the crimson stain spreading wider over the white material. He covered it with his hand. His palm came away coated with blood.

Mikhail nodded and stepped aside. Fen led the way to the outside of the chamber, with Dimitri close behind Zev and Branislava.

The moment they were out of sight of the others, Fen halted. "I'm going to take you out of here, Zev. You can't walk the distance and you can't shift right now." He indicated the blood. "That's genuine. I didn't put it there. Your wolf came too close to the surface and your body won't stand up to the change yet."

"Are you going to tell me what's going on? What's happening to me?" Zev demanded. He'd had enough of intrigue and his own strange behavior.

Let them get you home, Branislava said. *I can attend your wound.*

I need to know what's going on. He tried not to snarl the demand, but it came out that way despite his best effort.

I need to heal your wound. She didn't flinch in the face of the wolf. She used her soft, melodic voice that could bring any man to his knees. Even his wolf seemed to respond, subsiding enough that he could do as she asked.

He swore under his breath, but he nodded to Fen. Fen didn't wait to see if he'd change his mind. He caught up Zev and took him through the caves, going through the lower and upper chambers with astonishing speed. The caverns leading down to the sacred chamber were really miles of maze, a true labyrinth, but Zev knew instinctively that he could find his way back in spite of the rapid ascent.

The velocity wrenched at his body, but he didn't protest, wanting to get answers as soon as possible. They burst out of an opening between rocks that looked like no more than a mere crack when he looked back. Branislava, with Dimitri right behind her, emerged after them.

Which direction, Zev? Fen asked.

Take me to the house in the forest. He needed the familiarity of the trees and open air. He was Lycan and the forest would always be his first choice.

The terrible need to change, that snarling, raging wolf, had retreated, but the aftertaste was a blow to his pride. He'd nearly lost control in front of everyone—and he was a master of control. Not once in all his long years had he ever come that close. He knew he was a dangerous man. He was Lycan, born to a time when they still hunted prey. He had managed to overcome that hunger. He was able to fight without a pack. He negotiated peace among packs. To lose control was appalling, almost beyond his comprehension.

The forest felt cool and fresh when they entered it. The scent of ancient trees aided in calming his wolf. He breathed in the air, taking in familiar scents. He was aware of every living thing within a few miles. This was home.

The house was small, built of stone like so many in the area were. This one was deep in the forest, far from everyone else. Wolves inhabited this territory, and he immediately felt a kinship with them. It didn't surprise him to catch Dimitri's scent, very faint, mingling with that of Dimitri's lifemate, Skyler. They had been running with the wolves at some point earlier in the evening.

Fen didn't set him down until they were inside the stone house. He set him on the bed that had already been made up. The scents of Tatijana, Fen's lifemate, and Skyler were everywhere. Fen had called ahead and they had made the house welcoming for him. Still, it was significant that neither were present.

Branislava put a hand on his chest indicating for him to lie back. He put his hand over hers, just for a moment, as he eased down onto the bed. Her palm was right over his heart and her touch seemed to go right through him.

I know something is wrong with me, but I would never hurt you. That much he was certain of. It might be the only thing he knew for certain.

I never thought you would.

She pulled her hand out from under his to catch the edges of his shirt and rip it open. He winced when he saw the wound. It was an ugly mess, the hole far bigger than he anticipated. The edges were mending from the inside out, but it had a long way to go.

Branislava turned her head to glare at Fen and Dimitri. Zev realized she was angry—not at him—but at them. She turned back to him, her touch gentle as she placed both hands over the wound. He felt warmth in her touch, which seemed to grow hotter.

You need to go to ground, Zev. This wound needs to heal.

I need to know what's going on. Gregori said I was a dangerous man, and he spoke the truth. I can't lose control. I can't allow my wolf to take control from me in any situation.

Branislava sighed and sank onto the bed beside him. When she lifted her hands, they were free of his blood and he knew he was no longer bleeding. "We are lifemates," she announced. She didn't sound happy about it.

Zev frowned and slowly sat up. Puzzled, he looked to Fen for an explanation.

Fen shook his head, holding both hands up. "I don't know what happened, Zev. When you were so severely wounded, all of us fought for your life. No one wanted to let you go, but you were so far gone and there was very little time . . ." He broke off, shrugging again.

"I wove my spirit to yours," Branislava confessed. "It was the only thing I could think to do to keep you from dying. You wouldn't go if you would take me with you."

"You said either one of us could undo that weave," Zev remembered.

She nodded slowly. "That's true. But it will not release us altogether." She looked down at her hands. "I knew when I first saw you."

"That's impossible," Fen said. "He's Lycan first. How can a Lycan be lifemate to a Carpathian? A Dragonseeker?"

"I don't know the how of it, just that it is so," Branislava replied.

"Okay," Zev said softly, realizing she was distressed. He was beginning to be able to read her. "Now what happens?" Now, some of what the ancients had said to him about how everything was about blood was beginning to make sense. They called him "Dark Blood," not mixed blood. He was both.

Her heart was pounding too fast at the admission that she was his lifemate. He reached out and took her hand. "You have no reason to fear me.

Whatever this thing is between us, you tell me what you want to do. I would never force you into anything."

Fen ran both hands through his hair, and Dimitri turned away to stare out the window into the night.

Zev's frown deepened. "You're not telling me something I clearly need to know," Zev said. "Just say it."

"Until you claim her, until she is fully yours, you'll struggle with control. Your wolf is going to rise anytime a man is close to her. You think you're dangerous now, but wait until a little time has gone by and she's just out of your reach. Madness can set in. You're mixed blood, which means both your wolf and your Carpathian will drive you to keep her safe," Fen explained.

"Dimitri didn't claim Skyler for years," Branislava pointed out. "Tatijana told me all about it."

"It was a different situation," Fen said. He pinned Branislava with a stern gaze. "Much different, and you're well aware of that."

It was all Zev could do not to leap from where he was and attack Fen, just for the tone he used and the look he gave Branislava. He let his breath out slowly, forcing his years of discipline to come to his aid.

"Don't do that to her," he said, keeping his voice low. "None of this is her fault. How could any of us know what would happen?"

"We need you right now," Fen said. "You have to be 100 percent. Two more council members arrived this evening, and there are more Lycans in our village than we have Carpathians. Trying to kill every male in close proximity to Branislava doesn't make for good diplomacy."

Branislava flinched as if Fen had struck her. Every protective instinct of both species rose in Zev like an exploding rocket. His fingers bunched in the thick quilt on the bed, hiding the curved claws trying to burst from the ends.

"Fen, I think it best if you leave us for now." Zev managed to get the words out without growling. "We need to work things out between the two of us."

Fen sighed. "I apologize, Branislava. Zev is right, none of this is your fault. How could any of us know this was going to happen?"

"I knew," Branislava admitted in a low tone. "When I saw him there at the dance. When he took me into his arms. I knew then, just like I know we should complete the binding ritual."

Zev shook his head. "We'll talk it out and figure it out together. Fen is right, I am extremely lethal. I refuse to lie to you about that, but no one, least of all me, is going to tie you to a man you don't want."

"That's your Lycan talking," Dimitri said, "not your Carpathian."

Branislava attempted a small smile. "I already tied us together, remember? Our spirits remain woven together. Where you go, I go."

"But we can undo that," Zev reminded her. "You told me so yourself. You're not trapped, because that's how you're feeling, isn't it?"

Fen and Dimitri made a move as if to go but Branislava held up her hand. "I need to know why you insisted on waking him early. It's important to any decisions we make here."

"Zev is the one person the Lycan council still trusts. We have no idea who is friend or enemy. He knows Lycan politics and he's aware of personalities and every intrigue these people may try. The alliance is no longer as important as figuring out who our enemy truly is. Zev is the person who can do that."

"The council members are friends," Zev said. "I've spent my life protecting them and enforcing their laws. I can't just switch sides." He ran his hand through his hair. It was thick and long, untamed and hanging around his face, instead of being pulled back as he normally wore it.

"You would still be protecting them. You know assassins are trying to kill them. They're at risk just as the prince is. Hopefully you'll figure this out and keep them all alive," Fen pointed out.

Dimitri nodded his head. "You are truly our brother. Our blood runs in your veins. We all three are tied together in a blood bond. We would never have risked your healing unless the situation was dire."

Branislava's hand crept toward his, slowing smoothing the pads of her fingers over his knuckles where his fists were still bunched in the quilt.

Zev felt more of the tension drain away. At least he knew *why* he was all over the place. Finding how to control it might be difficult, but now that he knew the reason his wolf was bordering on being out of control, he was certain he had the discipline to overcome his knee-jerk reaction to other males near Branislava.

"I'll be honest with you both, I'm not certain I'm up for the challenge yet. I can barely stand, let alone protect the council members." He detested the admission, but he had to be straight with them. He could end up being a liability if they counted on him. "I could get you all killed if I can't hold my own in a fight. You can't be worried about whether or not I can protect myself."

Fen nodded. "We're aware of that. Mikhail said you'd say that. He wants you to consider allowing him, with Gregori, to heal you."

Branislava gasped. She whipped her head around to look at Fen. "That isn't done. You know that. Even I know that."

"Of course it's done," Fen said. "The prince is the most powerful man we have."

"Which is why it isn't done. Let us try again. Skyler is a powerful healer. We're Dragonseekers, Gregori on his own can aid us."

"You've all tried, Gregori included," Fen argued. "He's Lycan, they regenerate very fast. He's mixed blood and they regenerate even faster. He isn't healing, and you know it."

"The wound was too severe," Branislava admitted, her voice pleading.

Zev turned his hand over and took hers, placing her palm over his heart. "Don't be upset. I'll heal. I always do."

She shook her head and looked down at her lap.

Fen sighed again. "Actually, Zev, you're supposed to be dead. No one could have healed that wound. By weaving your spirits together, she cheated death, so to speak. She knew you wouldn't go into the other world and force her to go with you."

Zev shrugged. "I don't give a damn how it was done. As far as I'm concerned she was more than courageous, betting on me when all of you believed I would die—that I was supposed to die. I'm here. I'm alive."

He caught Branislava's chin in his hand and tipped her head up, forcing her to look into his eyes. "We'll do this together. We'll find out who is behind all this and then, I promise, we'll sort things out between us."

"You might have to do the sorting out between you *before* you find out who's behind this mess," Dimitri muttered under his breath.

Zev shot him a quelling glance. "Don't listen to him. What's between us is just that—between us and no one else. Understand?"

Branislava nodded, giving him another small smile that sent his heart into overdrive.

"Tell me about this healing process with the prince and why he so rarely does it." Zev tore his gaze from Branislava and looked directly at Fen, refusing to allow him to sidestep the question.

"One or the other can heal like anyone else. Gregori is known to be one of our greatest," Dimitri said, when his brother remained silent. "The combination of Mikhail and Gregori is more like a nuclear bomb going off. If they aren't precise, if they miss one small calculation, take the heat too high or . . ."

"I get it," Zev said. He sighed and tapped out a rhythm with Branislava's palm over his heart while he considered his various options.

It isn't done because it's considered too dangerous.

The hole in his gut hurt, a constant throbbing reminder of the huge wooden stake blown into him by a bomb as it tore apart a table. He really preferred not to remember how that enormous splinter nearly as big as his fist ripped through his body.

How much longer before I heal naturally in the earth?

There was a small silence. He turned his head to look at her, bringing the tips of her fingers to his mouth. He used the edge of his teeth to scrape along the pads of her fingers, waiting for her reply.

Wolves are very oral, aren't they?

It was the last thing he expected her to say. Laughter welled out of nowhere. He didn't laugh as a rule, and it hurt like hell to do it, but he couldn't help himself.

Yes, I suppose we are.

Amusement set her green eyes sparkling like emeralds. *I like that you have a sense of humor.*

"I've found, being around Fen and Dimitri, that I need a really good sense of humor," he replied aloud, raising his eyebrows at the two men claiming kinship with him.

"You're a riot a minute," Fen said. He crossed his arms over his chest and leaned one hip against the wall. "You tell me what you want to do in this situation. If you want to take the time to heal naturally in the earth you will heal—eventually. You're Carpathian and you're strong. It could take months, even a year, but you will heal."

Months? A year? Branislava had been in the ground with him. She knew whether or not that wound was healing fast or slow.

In my opinion you're healing very rapidly for such a mortal wound, but Fen's right, it could take several months, probably longer. You shouldn't have survived.

Zev sighed. "Did Mikhail ask you to waken me? Or was it your idea?"

Fen looked uncomfortable, but he didn't answer.

"Fen argued for days not to bring you out of the earth," Dimitri said. "Mikhail and Gregori insisted it was imperative. Both believe that without your knowledge of the Lycans and the council, we don't have a chance avoiding an all-out war, let alone securing an actual alliance."

Zev bit down gently on Branislava's fingertips as he considered the various possibilities. This woman sat in silence beside him, contemplating changing her entire life to become the lifemate of a virtual stranger in order to keep him from killing every single male who came near her. Duty. He sighed. He'd spent more than one lifetime doing his duty to his people. When did it end? He was damned exhausted.

You are not entirely a stranger.

There was that small note of humor in her voice. He realized she rarely spoke aloud, preferring to talk only to him. He'd noticed, the single time they'd danced together, that other Carpathians had flocked around her, but they had done most of the talking. She was very quiet, almost subdued, but her nature wasn't at all passive.

Beneath that cool, quiet surface was a fiery, passionate woman, as fierce as any warrior he'd fought with. He knew, because he'd seen her dragon. Bright, crimson-red scales tipped in gold, she'd been a sight in the sky. He was in her mind and saw that will of iron, honed in the ice caves where her father had kept her prisoner.

His heart thudded hard when he made that connection. Of course she would think being forced to become his lifemate would be a form of imprisonment. How could she not? She craved freedom, and yet, the moment she surfaced, almost the very day, she had met him and she had known they were lifemates.

"Tell Mikhail and Gregori, I'll do it," he said, making his decision.

Beside him she stiffened, but she said nothing.

You know there is no other choice for me. If there's a chance I can prevent bloodshed, I have to try.

Fen straightened, shaking his head. Clearly he wasn't any happier than

Branislava, but he'd done his duty, just like she would do, just as he chose to do.

Zev shrugged his shoulders. "We're warriors, Fen. It's what we do. Who we are."

Fen nodded. "They're taking a hell of a chance with your life, Zev."

"For Mikhail to consider doing such a thing, knowing Branislava tied herself to me, he has to have good reasons. He's our prince, I accepted that when I chose brotherhood. I'm sworn to protect the council and have a need to help those who are my people as well."

He wanted to lie in the cool earth and not think anymore. He'd made his decision. "I'll ask Mikhail to get the ancients to release our spirit weave," he added to Branislava. "Just in case something goes wrong."

3

Branislava abruptly pulled her hand from Zev's and got up, moving away from him and across the room to stare out the window. She radiated hurt. Her long, thick hair was banded with fiery red over the red-gold strands. He caught a glimpse of those green eyes, now changing color, deepening to an intense blue green like the deepest sea. Stormy. Turbulent.

He swore he could see sparks flickering in the air around her body as she stood with her back to him. Fen and Dimitri stepped back, and Fen lifted his hand.

That's our cue to exit. We'll tell Mikhail of your decision. If you make it out of this one alive, Fen added, *we'll come for you next rising and bring you to the cave of healing.*

Dimitri snickered. *You have a lot to learn about women, Zev. She's not the little submissive thing you thought, is she?*

He had never thought of Branislava as submissive—exactly. He'd seen that fiery dragon of hers and known she was a fierce warrior. But, okay, maybe he'd been a little arrogant thinking he could make decisions—all the decisions. He was particularly good at making decisions, giving orders and having everyone follow them.

"Fen, before you go, what's a 'Dark Blood'? What does that mean?" The moment Zev uttered the question aloud, the room went silent. Still. Even the insects ceased their constant droning. Fen and Dimitri slowly turned back from the doorway to stare at him. Branislava turned and leaned against the wall, her eyes wide.

"Where did you hear that term?" Fen asked, walking back into the middle of the room.

"In the chamber, when the ancients spoke to me. What does it mean?" He frowned at their reaction. "Is something wrong? Mikhail must have heard them."

Fen shook his head. "Mikhail summons them and he can understand them, but when they speak to the one who mingles blood with them, it is private, only between you and them. How did they come to use the term Dark Blood?"

Zev hesitated answering. He didn't need any more bad news. War was brewing and he was expected to stop it. His woman was upset with him, and he was facing possible death on the next evening. Worse than all of that was the pain that shook him each time he took a breath.

Branislava moved, drawing his attention. She was wearing modern but very feminine clothes. Everything about her was feminine. Just looking at her helped drain the tension from his body. She was the most beautiful woman he'd ever seen in his life. When she spoke, he heard music in her voice. When she moved, he heard the flow of water, that connection to the earth itself.

I didn't mean to hurt you, Branka. I'm tired. He was so damned tired he thought about just lying right there on the bed and letting himself escape the persistent pain. *But that's no excuse for not thinking before I spoke.*

We will talk about the weave of spirits when we're alone.

He marveled at her ability to sound so sweet when she was laying down the law. There was a note of absolute steel in her musical voice. The sound of it made him want to smile. He was alpha, he'd been recognized as alpha even as a child. Few in authority ever stood up to him, but here was a little slip of a woman, with porcelain skin and enormous green eyes, giving him the look from under feathery lashes that said she meant business.

"Zev. I need to know," Fen insisted. "What exactly did they say to you?"

"I thought you said the conversation with the ancients was meant to be private," Zev countered.

Do you know what Dark Blood means? he asked Branislava. He would much rather she deliver bad news to him than Fen, if it was bad. The ancients had welcomed him, not rejected him. If being a Dark Blood was bad, surely they wouldn't have called him family.

She gave the slightest shake of her head. *I heard Xavier speak of hunting a Dark Blood, but as far as I know, he never found one and I had no idea what it was.*

"Damn it, Zev, do you have to be so stubborn?" Fen demanded. "We're your brothers. We're mixed blood, the same as you are. We're under that same death sentence the Lycans dole out whenever they find one of us. Do you really think we'd suddenly go the other way and kill you over something you and the ancients talked about?"

"He's swearing at me," Zev pointed out to Dimitri with a little grin. He would have laughed but it would hurt more.

"Yeah, he does that sometimes. He thinks it's okay now because you're his little brother," Dimitri said, with an answering grin. He shrugged his shoulders. "It's best to ignore him. Swearing makes him believe he'll intimidate us into doing whatever he wants us to do."

Zev nodded. "I see. I suppose we have to let him think he's bossing us around."

"If we don't, he sulks," Dimitri said. "Just answer him so he doesn't go ballistic on us. I'm heading out in a few minutes to go hunting with Skyler. We've got our own wolves." He turned around and lifted his shirt to show the tattoo of two wolves staring back at Zev. "We're learning to hunt vampire with them. It's a lot more fun than listening to big brother give lectures."

"Nice," Zev said. "I agree. I'd rather be doing anything than getting a lecture from Fen."

"Keep it up you two clowns. Those wolves of yours can't protect you from me, Dimitri, and you're going to be healed sooner or later, Zev," Fen threatened.

"It's going to be sooner," Zev said. "I'll let Mikhail take his shot at this and see what he can do. I can't very well leave diplomacy to you." He counted his heartbeats. Five of them. "The ancients called me Dark Blood." He frowned. "It didn't make sense to me. They said I was of mixed blood now, but I was Dark Blood. I tried to find out what they meant, but they seemed to believe I would know."

Fen and Dimitri exchanged a long look. "I don't understand. Dark Blood is a bloodline. Like Dragonseeker. Like Dubrinsky. Names change but the bloodline remains the same. Dark Blood is the oldest lineage we have, and there are no more. Our last lifemated couple was lost to us centuries ago. They had a baby with them, and when the prince heard of their death, he sent out warriors to try to find the baby, a little girl, but they came to the conclusion she was killed by the vampire who slaughtered her parents," Fen explained.

"What else did they tell you?" Dimitri asked.

"That my grandmother became mixed blood and when her pack found out, they killed her. She had a daughter, a baby, at the time. My grandfather took the baby and disappeared, went to another pack, and that child, my mother, was raised Lycan. I know that she died in childbirth."

"The only way your grandmother could have been mixed blood would be if she was Carpathian and she mated with a Lycan. There would be no chance of her becoming *Sange rau*. Women don't become vampires," Fen said.

"So his grandmother could have been the child of the last of the Dark Bloods, thought to have been killed when her parents were," Dimitri said. "I remember that time. It was long ago, and we mourned the loss of that couple. They were—extraordinary."

"He was a warrior beyond what any of us had known," Fen added. "Everyone looked up to him. She was just as strong. They were often referred to as 'strong heart' or 'heart of a warrior.' When we studied battle techniques, it was always their techniques, their strategies."

"They became legend," Dimitri said. "No one could figure out how a vampire could have killed them."

"It must have been during the time the Lycans were being decimated by the *Sange rau*," Zev ventured. "It would have to be for the Lycans to murder my grandmother. How else would they have even known about mixed blood?"

"So if a Lycan family found a baby during that time . . ."

"Or *any*time," Zev clarified. "Lycans are good people. If they found a baby all alone, especially if they could see evidence that the parents were killed by the *Sange rau* they would have raised the child as their own. They could have even believed she was Lycan. She wouldn't know about life-mates, and if a Lycan claimed her and she fell in love with him . . ." He stopped. "Could that happen?"

Dimitri nodded. "Of course." He looked to his brother for confirmation. Fen nodded, and Dimitri continued. "It isn't the same, the all-consuming focus and love we have for our lifemates, but some women have found happiness with a man outside of our society."

"If Lycans had stumbled across this child, took her in and raised her as Lycan," Fen said, his voice gathering excitement, "then she wouldn't have ever known why she was different. She might not even notice the difference. When she wanted to be wolf, she could shift, and she might think that's what her family did."

Zev nodded. "It was centuries ago and they didn't discuss the how or why of things back then. They knew nothing of bloodlines or DNA. How she became a mixed blood is anyone's guess, but if her parents were so skilled in combat, she probably was, too. She most likely fought and hunted along-side her husband. When wounded, he gave her blood."

He, too, was beginning to believe in the possibility of solving the mys-tery. Some of the ancient warriors in the sacred chamber had been of the Dark Blood lineage and had recognized him. They knew the history of his grandmother, and that meant that somehow she'd made her way back to them.

"She gave birth to a daughter," Fen said. "And that daughter was your mother."

"Were there any other children? Did you have uncles? Aunts?" Dimitri asked, hope in his voice.

"My father never mentioned any other, but he was a secretive man. I doubt that he knew anything of my mother's family. I asked him and he just shrugged and said my mother didn't talk about them—ever." Zev shrugged. "I honestly thought maybe her family had gone rogue and my father and mother had been too ashamed to talk about them."

"If you really are a Dark Blood," Fen said, "Mikhail needs to know."

"It would explain why Branislava is his lifemate," Dimitri added. "His blood called to hers. Her soul is the other half of his."

At least, in the Carpathian world, he might be able to offer her something besides the detested mixed blood his people viewed him as.

I do not need you to be anything other than who you are. I see the heart of you. I see your character. It matters little to me what bloodline, if any, you are from. You do have the heart of a warrior and a great capacity for kindness. You are both fierce and compassionate. Both good qualities. There is no deception in you and I admire that tremendously.

His heart leapt at the compliment. No one had ever said anything like that to him, let alone the most beautiful woman in the world. She could make the blood sing in his veins with just a smile, let alone such a tribute. She definitely was the kind of woman that could bring him to his knees much easier than he would have wished.

Her soft laughter brushed against his mind. His stomach did a slow somersault. He loved the sound of her laughter.

I'm beginning to grow too fond of many of your traits, Branka. It would be difficult to go back to the emptiness of my life without your laughter and the sound of your voice.

It doesn't take much to make you happy.

He recognized teasing when he heard it. There was a secret brightness in her that pulled at him like a magnet. For an alpha like him, the idea that she didn't show herself to others was even more of a draw for him. Everything about her was feminine, yet he knew deep inside that she was a woman who would walk beside him, fight beside him and go through every hardship laughing with him, if he won her love.

I am your lifemate.

That doesn't mean you have to love me. I want your love, Branislava. Being my lifemate is wonderful, but that tie represents something else to you, and when we're together I don't want it to be out of duty.

There was a small silence. She walked back to the bed and sank down beside him. Or floated. He wasn't certain which because there was no hint of movement even on the mattress. She slipped her hand into his.

Don't ask Mikhail to have the ancients release you from our spirit weave. If I die . . .

I won't let that happen. We're tied together.

"Branislava." He said her name aloud.

For me, Zev. I'm asking this for me.

Branka, if things go wrong, I would take you with me to a place I have no knowledge of. I wouldn't know if I could protect you or not.

It was Branislava who brought his hand up to her cheek. She brushed her satin skin over his rough palm.

If things go wrong, I know I can pull you back. You're too strong to let anything take you as long as I'm tied to you. I absolutely know that about you. That's what the ancients meant when they called you "strong heart" and "heart of a warrior." You have a protective instinct in you I've never seen before. You won't stop. It's so strong, Zev, that you wouldn't die when most strong Carpathians would have succumbed. I know. I was there.

"This is amazing if it's true that you're a Dark Blood," Dimitri said. "Skyler can't wait to see you, Zev."

"Is she over our feud?" Zev asked.

Dimitri grinned at him. "One never knows with that woman. She's got wolves now and she's not afraid to use them."

Zev cupped Branislava's cheek with his palm and brushed the pad of his thumb along her jaw in a little caress. Her skin was softer than anything he'd ever experienced. "Skyler believes in retaliation if you are so foolish as to cross her sense of justice," he told her.

"I doubt that she holds a grudge," Branislava said. "She fought harder than any other to save you. Even when bullets flew, she didn't even duck. She was amazing." She flashed a small smile. "But then, she is Dragonseeker."

Fen laughed. "What she's saying is the Dragonseeker women are known for their retaliation if you get out of line with them. You might do well to remember that, Zev, old buddy."

Zev's eyebrow shot up. "Are you forgetting that your lady is a Dragonseeker? I've felt the singe of her fire when she got riled up." He swept his hand over the top of his hair. Tatijana, Branislava's sister, had broken up a Lycan attack with her dragon, raining fire on them to drive them away from the shelter where wounded Carpathians had gathered.

Fen looked a little hangdog. "Not really. She does have that same little character flaw."

Branislava's eyebrows rose sharply. She flicked her finger toward Fen, and water poured down over his head. "I beg your pardon?" she asked in her sweetest tone.

Fen yelped and jumped out from under the icy spray. The water mysteriously vanished as if it had never been. Fen stood there dripping wet, his clothes soaked and his hair hanging in long tails.

Dimitri snickered. "I can't imagine what you were thinking, bro." He bowed low and very respectfully to Branislava. "Allow me to apologize for my nitwit of a brother. There is no such thing as a character flaw in a Dragonseeker woman."

She inclined her head, princess to peasant, keeping a sharp eye on her brother-in-law.

Well done, Branka, well played. I do enjoy a wicked sense of humor, Zev commended her.

"That was mean, Bronnie," Fen accused, drying himself with a quick wave of his hand.

"What's mean, my brother-kin," she said smiling complacently, "is telling my sister what you said about her." She drummed her fingers on her thigh. "I might have to tell Skyler as well. After all, she is a Dragonseeker, and you were referencing her."

Fen held up both hands in surrender. "Tatijana told me you were the sweet one."

"Are you implying she was wrong?" Her eyebrows shot up again.

"Zev. Do something." Fen sounded a little desperate.

Zev shook his head. "You stepped into this one all by yourself." He wiped his forehead, and his hand came away with tiny smears of blood. He tried to imagine it away as Fen must have the water.

"Lie back," Branislava instructed. "Fen, will you and Dimitri give him more blood? I'd like to call Skyler and Tatijana in to aid me. We'll take him down to the sleeping quarters and heal him there."

Zev shook his head. "I want us to talk first. We need to settle things between us."

"Skyler is with Tempest, Darius's lifemate," Dimitri said. "She's playing with their son. He's a beautiful boy and very serious, quite like Darius and Gregori. I'll call her back."

"She loves children," Fen said.

"She's worried that because we have mixed blood she won't be able . . ." Dimitri trailed off, his gaze settling on Zev. "If your grandmother was Carpathian and became a mixed blood before she had her daughter, which she must have, that would mean . . ."

"It's possible to have children," Fen finished for him, his eyes lighting up.

"How do we find out if this is what really happened?" Dimitri asked. "I can't imagine Skyler never having a child. One way or another, I know we will, but, Zev, if we can validate that you're from the Dark Blood line, we'll know it's possible."

"How can we do that?"

Zev, you need to lie down now.

Zev tried not to smile at the bossy little note in her voice. He'd never been bossed around. His father had given up on telling him what to do by the time he was twelve. Already, he had become lead hunter of their pack. For her, to keep that worried look off her face, he complied, even though he knew movement was going to hurt like hell. Gritting his teeth, he eased back slowly. His face went white. He felt the color drain. Blood spread across his shirt again and a low hiss escaped between his teeth.

He swore to himself. He hadn't realized just how still he'd held his body. Movement was agony. She wiped the beads of blood from his face with a soft cloth, murmuring soothingly to him. He couldn't quite catch the words. His pulse thundered in his ears, drowning out everything around him. The edges of his vision faded.

I'm not certain what the advantage of being Lycan, Carpathian, Dark Blood or mixed blood is right at this moment. I thought I was supposed to heal fast, he said sarcastically to Fen and Dimitri.

You're supposed to use the gifts given you, Fen said, *and get the hell out of the way when bombs go off. Had you moved a little faster, you would have escaped, but no, you just had to play hero and get your ass handed to you by a table, no less.*

Zev tried not to laugh. When he did, fiery pain ripped through his gut. *I need to learn my woman's water trick.*

Branislava pushed back the hair tumbling into his eyes with gentle fingers. "My sister and Skyler are on their way."

His eyes met hers. He knew she looked at the wolf. *I said I wanted us to talk.* There was that voice again. Alpha. A command.

She couldn't have everything her way, especially not this. He wasn't going to go to ground without resolving a few of their issues. Not and go the next evening to try Mikhail and Gregori's combined radical treatment that could kill him. He wasn't stupid. If Fen was uncomfortable with the idea of it, then it was dangerous. Fen might kid around with him, but there was genuine affection and respect. Fen wasn't a man to proclaim his feelings, but he had accepted Zev as his brother and he definitely felt the need to protect him.

Branislava bit her lip. Her long hair banded with color, that deep swirling red that looked almost like glittering rubies falling over dark red wine. Her natural red gold nearly disappeared, although he could make it out through the changing color.

I would be very grateful to you and the others to take this pain away and see what you can do with the wound, he said, *but I'll wait to go into the ground until we're alone and we have a chance to talk. Can you live with that?*

Barely.

She gave him that look from under her lashes, the one that said she meant business, the one a secret part of him found amusing. God, she was beautiful. *How the hell did I get to be so lucky to have someone like you be my lifemate? I'm about as rough as a man can get and you—you take my breath away.*

She ran her fingers down the shadow along his jaw. *You are a very charming man, and I can see you'll find your way out of trouble very quickly.*

That was news to him. No one had ever said he was charming, but he'd take it if that meant she agreed with him. *So we'll wait to go to ground.*

The thought of that cool earth surrounding him was almost too much. The rich minerals and rejuvenating soil called to him. For a moment his lashes drifted down as he imagined sinking into the soil and allowing it to cover him. . . .

His eyes flew open, narrowed at her. *Rich minerals? Rejuvenating soil? Woman, what do you think you're doing? I'm Lycan, not Carpathian. I would never think in those terms.*

Her soft laughter brushed through his mind. *It was worth a try. And you are both.*

He wanted to kiss her. The thought came out of nowhere. He was staring up at her, at the laughter in her eyes and her full lips that were slightly parted, and all he could think about was tasting her. That wild honey and cinnamon mixture.

He had taken her with him when he'd left the Carpathian Mountains for the forests of Russia. She hadn't known it of course. That was his secret, that need to relive that moment he first saw her, when he'd first held her in his arms and replay it over and over in his mind. Her body had moved against his and he knew there would never be another woman in his life.

He had no idea of lifemates, but he did know the real thing when he felt it. He had been alive a long time and he had never wanted a woman for himself—until Branislava. There had been something so mysterious and elusive about her. She had intrigued him from the moment he saw her, and after the music stopped and he'd had to let her go, she was forever imprinted on his body.

I have often regretted that I did not kiss you that evening, Branislava admitted.

He could have groaned aloud. Of course she was reading his thoughts. *Branka, you're far too innocent for a man like me. You can't go around saying things like that to me when we have company. Wait until we're alone.*

Her fingers were back in his hair, her touch sending little darts of fire through his body—the body that shouldn't have been able to feel anything but pain.

I like that you call me Branka when everyone else calls me Bronnie.

He smiled at her. *You will always be Branka to me. Or mon chaton féroce.*

She raised her eyebrow at him. *I can be fierce, but a kitten? And French? That is French, isn't it? How many languages do you speak?*

He grinned at her, enjoying their moment together. *Claws. Spitting. Mine. And about ten very well and I can get by in five others. Well, now eleven if you count Carpathian.*

She rolled her eyes, but she didn't claw or spit at him, which he took as a victory.

"When you two are done flirting with each other, you might consider the answer to our question," Fen said.

"What question?" Zev asked.

"Yeah, that's pretty much what I thought. You're so wrapped up in your woman that your brain short-circuited."

Dimitri gave a little snort of derision. "Where can we find the all-important information on your grandmother and mother, that's the question. Whether Skyler, Tatijana and Bronnie can have children if they're mixed blood like we are."

"Why would they be mixed blood?"

Fen groaned. "You've really lost it, wolf man. Totally."

"Did you just call me 'wolf man'?" Zev demanded. "I'm going to get up and kick your ass."

"Fen." Tatijana slipped into the room. "What in the world are you doing provoking Zev at a time like this? Can't you see he's ill?"

Zev groaned dramatically and placed a hand over his stomach.

Tatijana shot Fen a glare and hurried over to him. She hugged her sister. "How is he?" *How are you? I've been so worried.*

"He needs to rest and go to ground again," Branislava answered aloud. *I know, Tatijana. I'm sorry I worried you. He was slipping away and I had to stay focused on him.*

Don't feel bad. If it was Fen I would have done the same. You told me he was your lifemate and I believed you, although I have no idea how.

Zev managed another very real-sounding moan, which earned Fen a dark glare from both women.

"Are you kidding me?" Fen said. "Can't you see he's faking it?"

Dimitri snickered at his brother. *Now you've done it. The man's a hero with blood dripping all over the floor, a hole the size of Texas in his gut and you're mocking his pain to women. You need lessons, bro.*

"Fen, if you can't have just a little compassion when a man's at death's door, I suggest you wait outside for me," Tatijana said. "I'm sorry, Zev. I have no idea what's gotten into him."

"Oh, for God's sake," Fen burst out. "Zev, you'd better hope you keel over tomorrow, because if you don't, you're going to be taken out behind the barn and learn what big brothers are all about."

You're just digging that hole for yourself deeper, Dimitri commented, his amusement growing.

Before Tatijana could singe Fen's hair, which she looked as if she might do at any moment, Skyler rushed in. She flung herself into Dimitri's arms and kissed him. "You're amazing. Amazing and incredible. I'm so lucky to have you."

Dimitri sent his older brother a quick triumphant glance. *Did you hear that? Amazing and incredible. She's lucky to have me. What was that Tatijana said about you?*

Zev could barely contain his laughter. "Why is Dimitri so amazing?"

"He told me it looked as if it might be possible that we could have children together." She bent over Zev to inspect the wound.

Zev thought it was significant that Tatijana and Branislava moved aside for her. Skyler was much younger than both women but she was the acknowledged healer.

"Why in the world did they allow you to wake?" Skyler spun around and glared at Fen. "I told you he would need at least another two or three months in the ground before we could even start to believe he was out of the woods."

Fen didn't defend himself. Instead he apologized. "I know, Skyler. I'm sorry. Is there anything you can do to help? He's in a lot of pain."

Zev could tell Fen's reaction was genuine. Fen had put all teasing aside and focused on the young woman.

"Fen, it isn't that bad," Zev said.

Fen shot him a warning glance. *She can help. And she can feel your pain, whether or not you downplay it. She saved your life.*

Of course Zev knew that. She might be the youngest of the Dragonseeker women, but she was talented, strong and determined. He didn't realize she could feel his pain. Instantly he did his best to push the pain away, so that if she touched him, she wouldn't hurt like he did.

Thank you, Dimitri said simply. *I know it isn't easy when you're weak to do that.*

Skyler ignored all of them. She sank down onto the floor, her spirit leaving her body as pure, white-hot healing energy to enter Zev's. He was shocked at the heat. He could feel her cauterizing and sealing off veins and tissue deep inside. The pain lessened almost the moment she entered him, and he could hear her soft voice somewhere in his mind.

That which is torn, raw and gives pain,
I draw upon fire to heal and reclaim.
Light that is life, fire that seals,
I cast forth your power to each vessel seal.

Fen tore at his wrist with his teeth and held the dripping blood over Zev's mouth. "I offer freely, my brother. Take what you need to survive."

Zev's body suddenly seemed starved. He hadn't even known it until that very moment. He knew that Fen and Dimitri had come regularly to his resting place to give him and Branislava blood to sustain them through the healing process. He shouldn't be starving but he could feel every cell in his body, every organ reaching for that infusion of life-giving ancient blood.

When he knew he'd taken enough he instinctively ran his tongue over the laceration and to his surprise, the bleeding on Fen's wrist stopped and the wound closed. That was a neat trick he could have used a few times in the past years.

"Thanks," he said. "I appreciate all you've done for me, Fen."

Tatijana reached out her hand to Fen. "I knew you weren't really being mean about Zev," she said softly.

Fen brought her hand to his mouth. *I don't like this, my lady. I should have found another way. If he dies tomorrow night . . .*

Don't. Don't think it. Don't say it. Don't put it out into the universe. We discussed this. You and Dimitri argued with Mikhail and the entire council of warriors. They believe we have no choice, and if we're going to save lives, maybe we don't. The prince would never take such a risk unless he believed there was no other choice.

There's always another choice, Fen said. *Unfortunately none of us could find it. Waking Zev was right there and once that was put out there as the solution, no one went on to try for another one.* He sounded bitter.

Fen. She whispered his name into his mind—surrounded him with warmth and love. *That's your love and fear for him talking. You know better. Mikhail had to have looked at this from every conceivable angle before he decided to wake Zev.*

I know. Fen scrubbed his hand over his face. *You're right. But look at him.*

Skyler's had to stop the bleeding every single time we brought him close enough to the surface to give him blood. And now he's bleeding all over the place.

She's here. And she's taking care of it, Tatijana assured.

But look at the toll it's taking on her. Fen shook his head.

"Fen." Zev said his name very softly, but his voice was commanding. "It's my choice." He felt Branislava's fingers tighten around his. "*Our* choice," he corrected. "You laid it all out for me, and we both feel strongly that we want to take the chance to try to help out."

"I don't have to like it," Fen snapped. He turned on his heel and was gone.

Dimitri dropped his hand on Zev's shoulder. "You know how he feels about you. And he's always been overprotective, much, I'm sure, as you've been all your life."

Zev grinned at him. "It's different from this side of the fence."

Dimitri shrugged. "I'm used to it, and I know he gets like that because I matter to him. So I just let him do his thing and then I go my own way."

Tatijana leaned over to kiss Branislava's cheek. "I'll see you next rising?"

Branislava nodded. "Take care of him."

"You know I will."

Skyler came back into her own body, pale and trembling after using up most of her energy to do the best she could to heal the gaping hole in Zev's stomach. Dimitri immediately enveloped her in his arms, sheltering her protectively while he gave her blood to recover.

"Are you all right on your own?" Dimitri asked Branislava.

She nodded. "If we need anything, I'll call. Thank you, Skyler. Go have fun with your wolves."

"Before you go," Zev said. "How do we find out if the things we suspect about my grandmother and mother are true?"

"Mikhail, of course. He can ask the ancients." Dimitri lifted his hand and, one arm around Skyler, left the room.

Zev made a move to sit up, but Branislava kept a hand on his chest. He capitulated, but he didn't like lying there, not if they were going to have a serious discussion about their relationship. He placed his hand over hers, holding her captive.

"I know it feels like you have to do your duty and keep me from acting like a wolf among sheep, but, Branka, I have great control and there is no need for you to feel trapped."

"Our souls belong together. When you say the words of the binding ritual to me, we will be tied together for all eternity and there will be no going back," she explained. "You have the power. I would not be able to leave you."

He rubbed her arm, from the back of her hand to her elbow, his touch soothing. "*Mon chaton féroce.* I do not believe in cages. No matter how much I want you with me, you have to want that same thing. You don't know me, Branka."

She nodded. "I thought that until I spent time inside your mind. You're a good man, but a little frightening. The idea of being with someone so dominant is daunting." She touched her breast beneath her clothing. "Carpathians do scar, no matter what is said, if the wound is bad enough and isn't healed in time."

Her lashes swept down and she looked away from him. His heart turned over. He continued to stroke her arm. He couldn't hold her. He couldn't kiss away her fears or take away the fact that they were lifemates and she knew she was tied to him no matter what reassurances he gave her. He couldn't imagine being in her shoes. Despite the comfort of his pack, he had always been fiercely independent, even as a boy. His dominant nature would never allow anyone else to have control over him, yet this woman who feared his power over her held his fate in her hands. It was a two-way street.

"Branka," he said gently. Intimately—even tenderly, when he wasn't aware he could feel such an emotion for anyone. "Look at me. Really look at me. I have been in many battles with rogue packs. Too many times I fought alone and I've been wounded time and again. My body is a road map. I'm not afraid of scars on your body or mine. Stop worrying about our future together. Let's take one day at a time."

She was silent a long moment and then she smiled at him. "Night. We'll take one night at a time."

4

Zev woke to the sound of the rain pouring down. A song of nature. He wondered how he could hear it when he was so deep beneath the ground, under the house that was intended for his home. He didn't want to move or open his eyes. He held Branislava in his arms and in the first instant of waking, with the music of the rain and the warmth of her soft body curled next to him, the moment was perfect.

He inhaled the scent of her hair, all that soft silk falling over him. He was naked, skin to skin with her, and he recognized her as he never had before. His body was spooned around hers, protectively, because, even in his deepest sleep, that was his strongest instinct. One thigh was over hers and in his palm he held her breast, a soft, sweet mound that rose and fell with every breath she took.

She was awake, he realized, and just like him, she didn't move. She didn't want to chance disturbing that perfect moment, either. He kept his eyes closed, savoring just holding her. He could feel the subtle beat of the earth's heart beneath him, reaching toward the water pouring down to feed the veins and arteries that ran throughout the land nourishing all life. They were part of the planet's cycle of life.

"I spent two years allowing the earth to comfort me," Branislava whispered. "I lay listening to her heart calling out to me. The warmth she provided made me feel whole. I was so cold in the ice cave. Tatijana could just absorb the cold, but I couldn't. Here, beneath the earth, I feel whole. I'm warm and safe. I didn't think anything else could make me feel that way." She moved, turning her head to look at him over her shoulder. "I was wrong."

He brushed his lips over the top of her head. "Safe isn't living, Branka."

She smiled and settled back, her head pillowed on his arm. "No, it isn't. I heard you, that night we first met. I knew my lifemate was close just by the drumming of the earth's heart. Mother Earth woke me, nudged me to embrace life. There was an insistence when I woke and I knew. I wasn't going to join the celebration even though I knew Tatijana wanted me there, but I could already feel you so close. My soul reached for yours."

She made her confession in her soft, musical voice, the rain her orchestra. He could listen to her for hours, that soft turn of her voice, those perfect notes that somehow reached inside of him and wrapped around his heart.

"But you came." He nuzzled the top of her head gently with his chin. Her soft hair got caught in the rough shadow along his jaw, weaving them together just as she had woven their spirits. "Knowing what you were facing, you still came, and you danced with me. That was brave of you."

"I wanted to see you, Zev. I wanted to touch you and to feel how I would respond."

"What did you learn?"

"That I could be safe with you."

He heard the smile in her voice, a small teasing note. He growled and moved his head to nuzzle against her neck, his mouth whispering over her soft skin. He felt her sudden stillness, the quick inhale. He bit down on the soft, sweet spot between her neck and shoulder, just hard enough to make her yelp, then laugh.

"You're not that safe, woman."

"Zev, I know you want to ask Mikhail to release our spirits before you allow him to try to heal you, but it's important to me that you don't. Tatijana and Skyler are Dragonseeker. My mother's brother, Dominic, is here with his lifemate. He's Dragonseeker. Our lineage is old and strong."

She sat up slowly, stretching, the beautiful lines of her body seen only through his night vision, there in the absolute dark of their resting place. She'd opened the earth before he'd awakened, but the house sitting above them protected them from the rain.

She didn't don her clothes right away but turned toward him, just enough to allow him to see the raised scar running from her left breast to her right. Both ends went up and over the soft curves. He reached out and gently traced the scar, from the tip of one breast down the slope to the valley and back up to the tip of the other.

"I will show you someday, just how beautiful your body is to me," he promised, regretting that he was so weak.

She took a breath as if he had exchanged air with her, and she was able to breathe again. She nodded—seemed to steady herself—and then she went back to business, braiding her long hair with a wave of her hand.

"If something happens there, the four of us can pull you back. Skyler came up with the idea and talked to Tatijana, asking if it was possible. Tatijana went to Dominic and he agreed that it was. We share the same bloodline and we can weave our spirits together."

He shook his head. "No. Absolutely not. I forbid that. *No*, Branka." Was she crazy? Were they all crazy? If he died, he would take not just Branislava with him, but her sister and Fen, Dimitri and Skyler, and her uncle and his lifemate. "No." He said it again so she knew he meant it. "There's no discussion on this."

"Zev, if you die, there is no life for me. I am unclaimed. If I choose to follow you, I'm lost on my own in a world I have no knowledge of. If I stay here, I will live a shadowed, half-life. It is the only way I know to be certain we don't lose you."

He took a deep breath and the pain that had been waiting for an opening slammed into him, robbing him of that first real rush of air. He absorbed the blow and waited for his mind to accept what he had no control over.

"I have the right to fight for my lifemate and if my family chooses to fight with me, that is for them to say," Branislava said softly, defiantly.

He sat up slowly and imagined that he was clean and fresh, just out of a shower, and fully clothed. It was easier than he thought it would be. "No." He had to move, had to float to the surface on his own. His body needed a fresh supply of blood, but Branislava had given him more blood just before he'd gone to sleep and she would need to feed this evening.

Branislava followed him up to the surface, fully clothed as well. He regretted that. He didn't want to end their perfect moment with an argument, but he wasn't going to take the chance of wiping out the entire Dragonseeker line. The generosity of her family, of Fen and Dimitri and her unknown uncle, a stranger to him, was shocking. His own people would have killed him, sentenced him to *Moarta de argint*—death by silver—or hunted him down and attempted to kill him, because he was mixed blood. He would defend himself and blood would run in rivers.

They moved through the house in silence. He was just a little ahead of her, keeping his teeth clenched and his body as flowing as possible so there would be no jarring as he moved. Lying in the rich minerals of the earth had helped him tremendously. Branislava stayed close to him, but she remained just as silent. He didn't trust her silence.

His Branka was home in silence. It wasn't surrender or submission, it was her place of power, not retreat. She had spent centuries as a prisoner, trapped in the ice caves in the form of a dragon, unable to escape the evil of her own father. She had lived there, with Tatijana, in that cocoon of silence, but her mind had absorbed everything around her. Each victim of her father's, no matter the species, she had sought to learn from. Language, culture, the passing of history, how to fight, how to survive. Her mind was always busy. Zev was very certain, there in the silence, her mind was very busy now.

Fen and Dimitri met them just outside the stone house. The forest was enveloped in the blue-black color of night. The fast-moving storm had left the trees shimmering with crystal drops and overhead, as the clouds swept past with the wind, stars began to sparkle.

"Everything all right?" Fen asked.

Branislava nodded.

Zev gave her his most fierce, intimidating scowl and shook his head. "Not by a long shot. She has a harebrained idea that her entire family is going to tie themselves to me in order to keep anything from going wrong. Dimitri, that includes your Skyler. In fact, she conceived the idea. I absolutely forbid it." He glared at Branislava again just for emphasis.

She reached out to take the wrist Dimitri offered, her gesture casual. Every muscle in Zev's body coiled for action, a red-hot rage sweeping through him. The reaction of his wolf was completely unexpected and he was unprepared for the wildness rising in him. He tasted the hot burst of blood in his mouth, took in the scent of his enemy, his vision banding with colors.

Stop it. Her voice was low, but carried a command. *I'm feeding from Dimitri. Your brother-kin. It is natural and right and you need to think with your brains not your . . . um . . . you know. You need to put Wolfie back in his cave.*

Her laughter bubbled up, infectious and beautiful, spreading through him like a tide of joy. Once again it was her humor that saved him. He found it impossible not to laugh with her. *Wolfie? Really? I probably am thinking with my . . . um.*

The wolf receded, and he felt stronger for keeping it at bay when he was so obviously vulnerable to the very ugly trait of jealousy. He had refused to even acknowledge that he could feel such a petty emotion, but there it was, intense and demanding. She was right, he definitely had been thinking with his . . . um. He laughed again, grateful she'd freed him from his own failings.

Not failings. We aren't tied together. Your reaction is primal. You're a predator, Zev, a very lethal one, and your instincts are what have always saved you. Your instinct is to protect me and to keep all other males away from me. That's natural.

Zev took Fen's offered wrist, savoring the life-giving substance flowing into his starved cells and injured organs. *Dimitri is insanely in love with his lifemate. I don't think he notices other women are alive. More, I'm in his head. He thinks of you as a sister. It isn't natural.*

Her laughter stroked over him like a caress. *Just know that until you claim me with the ritual words and tie our souls together, that will most likely be your reaction. Wolfie will come flying out all in a primitive caveman sort of rage, snarling at everyone, me included.*

Great. What if a member of the Lycan council stared at her with hungry eyes? He nearly groaned. That wouldn't work, either. *Woman, you're going to be the death of me.*

Or your savior, she murmured softly.

"Don't you dare go against my wishes," he snapped aloud, all humor vanishing abruptly, his wolf giving him that razor-sharp, low, fierce tone of the alpha.

She enveloped herself in silence. He realized Dimitri had made no comment about Skyler and her crazy scheme. It was impossible to tell from Dimitri's stone face whether or not he agreed with his lifemate's insanity. Dimitri was logical, and what the women had proposed was not the least bit logical.

"You ready for this?" Fen's tone was grim.

"As ready as I ever will be," Zev said, shooting Branislava another warning glance.

Branislava sent him an enigmatic smile and took to the air. He had to admire her smooth, easy takeoff. She leapt, a graceful dancer's leap, shifting as she did so into a small owl. Everything about her was fascinating. Everything. He loved the sound of her voice, the way she moved, her sense of humor and her vulnerability. He wasn't so enamored with her stubborn streak.

Fen caught him up in strong arms, making him feel weak. It was a little humiliating to be carted around as if his injuries were so severe that he couldn't take baby steps.

Your injuries are that severe, Branislava reminded.

What was he going to do about her? If he asked Mikhail to remove the weave of spirits between them, she would be hurt beyond anything he might be able to repair. He took a deep breath. He had to stay alive. There was no other choice. Whatever Mikhail and Gregori planned to do to heal his wound, he had to be strong enough to survive it—for Branislava. He was *not* going to take her chance at a life away from her.

She'd been locked up, a prisoner her entire life, and now that she was free, he was determined to see to it that her life was filled with happiness. She needed to live. Resolution settled deep in him. He wouldn't risk the others, no matter what, but Branislava was already tied to him. He still didn't know much about lifemates, but if he couldn't stand being away from her, then it stood to reason that she would have a difficult time without him.

Fen took him to another cave. This one was completely different than the chamber of warriors. Everything in the cave was soothing, from the colors of the formations inside to the deep pools of water. One was quite hot, the other cool and inviting. The cave was large, but not even close in size to the warrior's chamber.

The walls were ringed with Carpathians, some he recognized and others he didn't. Tatijana, Skyler and Dimitri stood close to the circle where Mikhail and Gregori waited for him. Beside them was a very tall man with wide-set shoulders and long dark hair. His eyes were striking, a strange, almost metallic green, piercing right through a man when he looked at you. He had scars from burns running up his neck to his face. This had to be Branislava's uncle. Beside him was a much shorter woman who looked as if she'd be more at home in the wildest jungle than a healing cave. He felt exactly the same way.

Mikhail stepped forward to greet him, clasping his forearms. "Well met, brother-kin," he said. "We owe you a great debt of gratitude. This can't have been an easy decision."

Zev felt power running through the prince like a strong current of electricity. "If it prevents a war, it is the only one." He gripped the prince's forearms with the same strength, trying to convey that he was ready for this.

Mikhail nodded in approval before stepping back to allow Gregori to greet him as well.

To his surprise, Gregori afforded him that same warrior's tribute, clasping his forearms. "I greet a friend and brother," he said formally.

Zev returned the strong grip. "Let's get this done."

Gregori nodded his head. "Fen tells me he believes you are the last remaining Dark Blood. If that is so, you are strong enough to endure anything, Zev. Your bloodline is revered by our people. It is legendary."

Zev understood that Gregori was giving him encouragement and he appreciated it. He had already made up his mind that he could withstand the power of the combination of the two men's healing abilities. He inclined his head and stepped back. He had one more thing to do. He wasn't going to die this night, but still . . .

He turned and found her beside her sister. Branislava. She stood straight, her chin up, but she was very pale. Her hand was in Tatijana's and he detected a slight tremor running through her body. He willed his body not to fail him. She was only about five feet from him, but the distance seemed to stretch ahead of him for miles. He would have forded a river if that's what it took to get to her.

He managed to walk straight, upright, not betraying that every jarring step sent waves of sickening pain crashing through his body. He concentrated on her. Only her. His woman. He stopped directly in front of her and took both of her hands in his.

We'll do this together, mon chaton féroce, and I won't fail you.

She swallowed hard and nodded, her gaze clinging to his. She nodded several times. He leaned over, ignoring the excruciating pain and the feel of blood running down his body again. He needed to kiss her. He caught her chin and gently brushed his lips across hers. Her lips trembled beneath his, soft and warm and inviting. That was all, the merest touch, but it was enough to convince him that his every reason to fight for his life was standing right in front of him.

He looked at her a long time, breathing in her scent, tasting that addictive flavor of cinnamon mixed with honey, willing her to believe he would get them through this. When she nodded, he smiled at her, turned and made his way back to Mikhail and Gregori. Blood soaked the shirt that had been pristine white. He ignored it, just as they did. It was simply more evidence that he was nowhere near ready to investigate who was behind attempting to start a war between Lycan and Carpathian.

Fen and Dimitri helped Zev up to the bed of stone, where he stretched out. He thought the surface would be hard and rough, but it wasn't, and he settled into it. He wasn't certain what to expect, but just the small amount of movement had exhausted him. He was so comfortable he was afraid he might fall asleep. He felt Fen's hands opening the buttons of his shirt, exposing his wound, but he didn't look at him.

Both Fen and Dimitri touched his shoulder in a kind of salute, but neither spoke. They didn't have to. He felt their affection, the brotherhood they'd offered. For just a moment, Tatijana touched his mind and then Skyler. He had forgotten what it was like to have family. It had been far too many years.

Feeling a burn behind his eyes, Zev closed them. He became aware of the scent of the aromatic candles. Hundreds of them burned in the cave with a combination of healing fragrances. Mikhail stepped up to the side of the raised bed with Gregori gliding into position beside him. He felt their close proximity without having to see either of them. The combination of the two men radiated an extraordinary power.

A hush settled in the chamber. He felt a searing heat drive right through his stomach and his eyes flew open. Gregori stood over him, hands raised, palms facing the wound in his gut, the white-hot energy unlike anything Zev had ever experienced. Gregori's hands were a good twelve inches from his body, but he could have been touching him with a red-hot poker.

The Carpathians present in the chamber began to chant, the language ancient, the words powerful. Others outside the healing cave, in the far distance, joined, their voices rising to aid in his healing. There was something comforting in the knowledge that an entire community could come together to try to save a single member from death.

The heat generated by Gregori alone was so scorching hot his mind shied away from the fact that Mikhail would amplify it. Once the two joined together he couldn't imagine the degree of heat.

Mikhail spoke in a low, carrying tone.

Kaŋam kudejek kuntanak en Karpatiinak és kuntanak en hän ku pesänak. I call upon generations of the line of the prince and the line of the protector.

The Carpathians in the cavern replied back to him.

It kule megem, oma kontak, kaŋak hän ku pusmak. Hear us now, warriors of old, healers we summon.

Mikhail inhaled deeply and trusted his judgment.

Kaŋam kudejek kuntanak Köd-verinak, kontak és hän ku pusmak päläpälä. I call upon generations of the line of Dark Blood, warriors and healers alike.

The surrounding Carpathians called back.

It kule megem, oma kontak, kaŋak hän ku pusmak. Hear us now, warriors of old, healers we summon.

Mikhail continued.

Juttanak kuntamet en Karpatiinak és kuntamet en hän ku pesänak és kuntamet Köd-verinak. Join the line of the prince with the line of the protector and the line of Dark Blood. *It kule megem, oma kontak, kaŋak hän ku pusmak.* Bring them together as one.

Those in the chamber intoned back.

It kule megem, oma kontak, kaŋak hän ku pusmak. Hear us now, warriors of old, healers we summon.

Mikhail placed his hands on either side of Gregori's body.

Päläpälä mekenak tuli ku pusm és katt3nak hän ainaba jamatan ekänkak.

Together we bring forth the fire of healing and send it into the body of our fallen brother.

The Carpathian people called back in response.

It kule megem, oma kontak, kaŋak hän ku pusmak. Hear us now, warriors of old, healers we summon.

Mikhail added one last plea to the spirits of their ancestors.

Andak jamatan ekänkhoz wäke bekit kutni ŋamaŋ takkapet. Give our fallen brother the strength to endure this trial. *Pusmak jakamaka és saYedak hängem wäkeva ainaval, kont o sívanak, és umuš käktäveritkuntaknak.* Heal his wounds and bring him forth with a strong body, strong heart and the wisdom of our combined bloodlines.

The Carpathians responded with one last invocation.

It kule megem, oma kontak, kaŋak hän ku pusmak. Hear us now, warriors of old, healers we summon.

Mikhail's entire body glowed white, his hands shimmering with fire. The fire leapt from him to Gregori. Gregori's body stiffened, and then jerked hard as if he'd absorbed a terrible blow. Flames ran down his arms and flickered over his fingers. He plunged his hand into the hole in Zev's gut.

Zev's entire body convulsed. He heard the wolf howl, a distant, painful cry as it retreated, desperate to escape the burn of pure fire. His Carpathian side leapt toward the cleansing fire while the wolf raced away. Sweat poured from his body, so that his entire body was dotted with tiny beads of blood.

Connected as he was to the two men through the blood of the ancient lines, Zev felt the force as a form of raw electrical charge. Gregori battled to stay in control of so much power. Mikhail fought to hold back the sheer energy radiating from him. All Carpathian people were connected through him and he drew their strength and energy like a magnet. It was as if a hundred suns had been lit and he carried them all.

"You're killing him," Fen hissed. He gripped Dimitri's shoulder, his knuckles turning white. "It's too much, back off."

Mikhail shot him a glance of pure reprimand. Fen started to turn away, but couldn't. Tatijana reached out to him, slipping her hand in his in an effort to comfort him.

Skyler leaned back against Dimitri, looking over her shoulder at him. He wrapped his arms around her, pulling her body into the shelter of his.

Light escaped from Gregori's hands, streaking through the chamber, so bright many of them had to turn away or close their eyes. Several rock formations exploded. He didn't look away from his task, the terrible gaping hole in Zev's abdomen, but broke out into a sweat. Tiny beads of blood ran down his face. His features were carved with concentration as he directed the light into Zev's body.

Zev's body turned bright red, as if his temperature soared and he could no longer control it. His hair grew damp and his body writhed and seized.

His mind retreated from the pain, an agony such as he'd never experienced, his insides forced into regeneration, an unnatural fiery death and rebirth.

"You're losing him," Mikhail hissed. "He's a Dark Blood. Call to that part of him, the warrior in him. Call to the blood line of Tirunul."

From far away Zev heard the prince speak, but his voice was lost among other voices calling to him from another realm.

He felt the fireball of pure white energy moving through him, burning him clean, cauterizing and cleansing, but that too was becoming distant.

Zev, you have to fight.

That was Fen, demanding. Coaxing.

Come on, bro, this is your time. Don't let go. You can beat this thing.

He recognized Dimitri's voice—or thought he did. The fire consumed him, left him with no lungs, no heart, no mind. He was incinerated. Burned alive.

I am with you, Branislava whispered. *Wherever you are, I am with you always.*

She was alone, her spirit weave still intact with his and no other. She was surrounded by her family, the people who would have aligned their fate with hers, but she had done as he asked, believed in his strength enough to risk her life once again with him.

He held tight to her, even as his mind wandered into another realm. He saw them, shadowy figures, tall warriors with slashing eyes and fierce expressions. Women, beautiful and courageous, whose faces were stamped with the same passionate resolution as their men. All had one thought, one mind.

They were joined together for one purpose only—to heal the horrendous wound in his gut.

He felt the first stirring in his mind of something unfamiliar—yet so familiar. His blood heated, boiled, flowed through his veins like hot, molten lava. Dark and strong, his blood refused to be taken by the fire. His blood was liquid already and the fire couldn't change that. The white-hot energy annihilated everything in its path, forcing his body to either die or rise like a phoenix from the ashes.

His blood moved valiantly through his body, determined to keep him alive, to keep one step ahead of the fireball crashing through him. It pushed into his heart and out again, ran through him like the underground rivers no one ever saw or was aware of, when his heart wanted to falter. His lungs refused to work, to find air, so burned and raw they couldn't work.

Dark Bloods do not ever give in. They do not give up. They fight with their last breath.

He had no breath. There was no air, only that all-consuming fire raging through his body. He was already in the other realm, surrounding by the ancestors. Here, he could find his grandmother and his mother. Here he could find his great-grandparents, the last of his legendary line.

You are the last of the line. You are kont o sívanak, strong heart. You have the heart of a warrior and you cannot choose to remain in this land of shadows. You are needed.

This time he wasn't certain who spoke to him. The prince? Gregori? They had faded so far away he had almost let go of them. The ancients then. He felt confused, but he was not a man to ever give up. He wanted life for Branislava and himself. His choice would always be life for her. He wanted that chance to make her happy and experience a lifetime with her.

More, he was a warrior and his people needed him. It really came down to that simplicity. He felt strength rising from somewhere deep inside of him. Determination and purpose. His people—both species—had need of him and he would not fail them. His woman had given him faith he hadn't yet earned and he would not fail her.

He called to his wolf, knowing as long as he was split, he couldn't find his way back. He could face the fire, embrace it even, if that's what it took to be healed and survive for those who needed him. The crisis brewing in him wasn't about his ability to withstand the power generated by the prince and the healer—his bloodline saw to that—it was the division of his mixed blood. The Carpathian in him rose to do battle with the healer and the prince to fight for his life, but the wolf had no knowledge of such healing and he retreated, snarling and fighting, determined to drag Zev with him to a safe place where the fire couldn't reach them.

Zev was alpha, his wolf dominant among his kind. It was strong and reactive, a force to be reckoned with, and it refused to give ground once it took a stand. The longer the prince and the healer had to remain locked together, the more intense the fire grew. Time was slipping away. The battle was his to win or lose.

There, in that other realm, surrounded by the dead, his body engulfed in flames, he reached for his Lycan side, embracing his wolf. There was no hesitation or trepidation on his part. His Dark Blood and the blood of his brothers called to the wolf. Lycan and Carpathian blood didn't blend together so much as there were two separate species in one body with the host able to draw on the strengths of both.

He commanded his wolf to join with him, to absorb the fire burning through him. The wolf snarled and raged at him, prowling close to the surface, threatening the change, to take over the host body, wanting to shift from his present form to half man, half wolf in order to fight those who sought to kill them through the burn of the white-hot fire.

Zev couldn't wait any longer, he was slipping further into that realm. The shadowy figures became more substantial. The chanting of the Carpathian people faded into the background. The heat in his body became even more intense, an excruciating pain he couldn't stop. His wolf insisted the answer was to go further into the other realm, far away from the two men wielding fire.

Stay with me, Lycan. Stay with your mate. I have great need of you. Branislava joined with him, her sweet voice calling through the other realm. She had no fear of fire. She embraced the flames, absorbed them, became them.

The wolf went still, listening for just a moment to the musical sound. Zev struck at him instantly. The Carpathian imposed his will, the strong heart of a warrior, forcing the wolf to heed his word. He drew the Lycan with him back toward the surface, back toward the hot, hot fire—and Branislava.

Flames seemed to burn from the inside out, stealing his breath, robbing him of reason and the ability to think. The wolf nearly escaped him, but at the last moment, Zev managed to stop his wandering mind and bring himself wholly back into the land of the living. He gasped, lungs burning for air. He swallowed a cry of pain, and then the fire was gone and he could breathe again.

Gregori stepped away from him, swaying with weariness. He tried to catch Mikhail as the prince sat abruptly on the floor of the cave beside the raised bed, but he collapsed as well.

"It is done," Mikhail said. "He survived. He'll need blood."

"As do you." Dominic of the Dragonseekers, uncle to Tatijana and Branislava, crouched beside the prince and extended his wrist. "I offer freely."

Zev felt Branislava take his hand in spite of the fact that his body was still fiery hot. The terrible intensity of the heat had diminished so that he could easily withstand the aftermath. His injured organs, cells, muscle and tissue had been forced to grow, regenerating in minutes when it should have taken months beneath the ground.

He threaded his fingers through Branislava's, content to lie still. *It feels like a nuclear bomb went off inside of me. I thought, if I opened my eyes and looked down at my stomach, I might see a mushroom cloud rising into the air.*

Her fingers brushed over his bare skin, right over the wound that had been a gaping hole in his body. He could feel her touch, so light and delicate gliding over his stomach.

Thank you, Branka, for believing in me enough to do as I asked.

It was difficult, she admitted. *I had faith in your strength, Zev, but I also knew your wolf was very suspicious and might become a problem.*

Zev frowned, his gaze jumping to her face. *Tell me.*

When you were first injured, there in the meeting hall when the bomb went off and you tried to protect Arno, the council member, with your body over his and the table stake went through your stomach, your wolf wasn't happy to have us invading you. Our healing sessions involve going into your body and healing from the inside out with energy. Lycans regenerate. Both work, but Carpathians and

Lycans have two very different ways of dealing with injuries and your wolf was very suspicious. I had to do a lot of soothing.

Around him, the cavern had become alive with activity. He could hear the low murmur of conversations. Darius gave blood to Gregori, and Fen offered him his wrist. He took it, suddenly craving the rich nutrients.

I didn't know, I was too far gone, I guess.

He didn't like the idea of loss of control and I think we would have lost you then, but Skyler is a woman and she is very close to the wolves. He accepted her. Tatijana had healed you before and of course he recognized her and accepted her. I am your lifemate, his mate, and he accepted me. Also, Arno was working with him, a member of the council and that gave him reassurance.

Zev sighed and swept his tongue across the twin holes in Fen's wrist to stop the blood flow. Wolves always rose to protect their other side. *I should have expected him to rise. He's strong and fast and he would fight to the death anyone he thought might harm me while I was unconscious. Thank heaven he's so enamored with you.*

She raised her eyebrow at him. *Him? Only the wolf?* She gave a little disbelieving sniff.

"Can you sit up?" Dimitri asked.

Zev had no idea, but he hid a smile from Branislava. He liked her little displays of temper. The burning through his body had subsided slowly. He actually hadn't noticed it ebbing away as he talked with his lifemate. "I'm willing to give it a try."

Dimitri got an arm around him. Fen hovered like a new father with his firstborn. Zev resisted a sarcastic remark. Branislava stepped back to give him room, and immediately a hush fell in the cavern and all eyes turned to him.

Mikhail had gotten to his feet. If it was possible for him to look anxious—he did. Gregori moved closer, stopping Zev from moving with a hand on his chest while he slowly inspected the wound site.

"Tell me how you're feeling."

Zev shrugged. "The fire faded and I can breathe normally. I haven't been able to do that since I got caught in the blast. I moved a few inches and didn't double up in pain, so that's a good sign, but I'll admit I feel weak."

Gregori nodded. "That's to be expected. You'll need blood several times over this night and rest as well as more recuperation in the ground during the day tomorrow. When you rise, we believe you will be at full strength, if your body has healed as we expected."

"Let's try it then," Zev said.

The room was too still and quiet. The anxious look on Fen's normally expressionless, stone face was too much for him. Zev shot him a glare. "Stop looking at me like I'm one of your chicks and you're the mother hen. I've got this."

"You always think you've got it," Fen snapped back. "I've never seen a man more prone to getting stabbed, shot, sliced or ripped open, unless, of course, it's Dimitri. It's a wonder I don't have gray hair."

"You do," Zev and Dimitri said simultaneously.

The tension in the cave immediately gave way to a wave of laughter.

Zev braced himself for pain as he gingerly sat up, Dimitri's arm a strong bar across his back to aid him if he needed it. To his utter astonishment, there was no agony, no hurt, not even an ache or slight stitch. If anything, his muscles seemed stronger than ever.

He grinned at Gregori. "I'd have to say it worked."

"I want to check before you get overconfident," Gregori said. "Just give me a minute."

"You're in worse shape than I am," Zev said.

"You're the first person to ever survive," Gregori said.

That wiped the smile off Zev's face.

Gregori and Mikhail looked at one another and burst into laughter.

"Very funny, you two," Zev said. "I'm taking my lady and going home." He wasn't altogether certain they weren't serious and just a little hysterical with relief.

Branislava brought her uncle close. "This is Dominic and his lifemate, Solange."

There was no mistaking Solange fought beside the Dragonseeker. She was a warrior through and through.

Zev inclined his head. "I'm grateful to both of you, for coming and for your generous offer of weaving your spirits to mine."

"Clearly it wasn't necessary. Mikhail tells me you are the last of the Dark Blood line. I knew your great-grandparents. There were few as skilled as they were," Dominic said.

He drew Branislava close to him. He was certain now, that the Carpathians were right and he was of the Dark Blood lineage, but at this moment, all he wanted to do was rest and spend a little time getting to know his woman.

"Take another look at him, Gregori," Fen said. "We need to get him home."

5

"L et's sit on the verandah, just for a little while," Zev suggested. They had just risen from their day's slumber and he wanted time to be with her. "We can visit out here." While there was no actual pain, he was surprised at how weak he still was.

The night was beautiful. Deep in the forest it was darker than outside of it, because the trees blocked a good part of the moon. He caught glimpses of the glow as well as a scattering of stars through the canopy and branches. Somewhere close by a wolf howled and another answered.

"Skyler and Dimitri have taken their wolves hunting," Branislava said. "They're hungry. I can tell by the sound of their calls. The alpha is on the trail of something big."

"Few can hear the difference in the notes," Zev said, a little shocked. "Yet you can tell what that call actually means?"

She nodded. "I can hear what they say by the pitch, the notes in their voices. I can identify each member of the wolf pack that inhabits this territory. I also have learned all four voices of Skyler and Dimitri's wolves as well."

"That's incredible. I'm a wolf and I can do that, but didn't think anyone else could."

She shrugged and put her feet up on the railing. "I love music, Zev. I love all the various instruments and the sounds they make. I love to hear voices singing in perfect pitch."

He smiled at her. "And you love to dance."

"I do. Tatijana does as well. It felt like freedom to me, floating around the dance floor in your arms. I felt as if we were soaring above earth in the clouds."

"I can see I'll have to study dancing. I wouldn't want to trip over my own feet." He lifted his face to the breeze. Across from the house, mice scurried in the brush drawing the attention of an owl sitting silently above them in a particularly old and wide tree. It was dense with branches and needles that appeared silver whenever the moon shone through.

"That's impossible and you know it," she said, laughing softly. "I've seen you in a fight with your sword and knives and you're like a beautiful dancer, flowing around your opponents in the most graceful, fluid way I've ever seen. Even Fen admires your abilities," she added.

"I was very lucky to meet that man," Zev said. "He was very adept at hiding that he was a mixed blood. He managed to live a good century or more among the Lycans."

"Tatijana told me."

Branislava lifted her hands to her hair, an idle move, but one that lifted her breasts beneath the material of her dress. Now that they were relaxing at home, she had donned a long gown, one from another era. The corset hugged her breasts and ribs and the material flared over her hips to fall to the ground. The top was white eyelet lace and a panel ran down the front of the dress surrounded by a rich crimson material.

She had been in the form of a fire dragon for centuries and he wasn't in the least surprised to find she was attracted to the color red. She seemed extraordinarily feminine to him, preferring dresses to trousers.

He enjoyed sitting across from her, there in the night, just looking at her. "You could take your hair down," he suggested.

Her hands settled in the thick mass of red-gold silk. "It will be all over the place. It's a little on the wild side," she confessed in a little rush. "It isn't straight, but wavy and curly and straight all at once. And it grows so thick there's very little I can do with it."

"I'm well aware of that," he admitted. "I love your hair." Especially when it was wild and messy. He thought of it as bedroom hair to go with her bedroom eyes. With it down, she looked sultry and inviting. Every time she had it up, or in a long braid, his fingers itched to pull the pins out and just let it fall in cascade, like a flowing waterfall down her back. She might not like all that wild hair, but he was particularly fond of it.

She pulled out pins and the mass of silk tumbled around her face and down her back in waves of red gold. She shook her head with a small smile as if she thought he was just a little bit crazy. "There it is. A big mess."

"You look amazing. You always look amazing. What makes you happiest?"

"Freedom." There was no hesitation. She jumped up, stretched her arms wide and spun in a circle. "I have space. Look at all this space. I can fly up to the clouds or run in the forest with the wolves. I can leave and go into a city." She gave a little shudder. "Not that I want to, but the point is, I *could*."

"I'd love to show you the forests of Russia. And the cities there are beautiful," Zev said. "Like you, I couldn't live in one, I need the forest, but some of them are really extraordinary. I chased three rogues through France and while I was in Paris, after my duty had been done, I visited the museums and the artwork was almost beyond my comprehension."

"I have seen some paintings in books as well as the memories of tourists and a few of the villagers," Branislava murmured. "But not in person."

"When this is all done," he said, "we'll travel a bit, if you feel up to it, and see some of the world."

"The first time I was ever away from Tatijana was when she went with Fen to get Dimitri," Branislava admitted. "I stayed behind because there were so many Lycans here and we feared there might be an all-out war."

He regarded her with a somber gaze. "You are a warrior."

She shrugged her shoulders. "I'm Dragonseeker. The one thing for certain Tatijana and I learned in the ice caves was how to fight in a battle. Xavier tortured many warriors of all species and all of them shared information with us in the hopes that we could find a way to escape. Sometimes that was all we had to hold on to, the two of us planning battles and talking mythical scenarios to keep our minds active. I don't yet know many things, but I know how to fight if it's needed."

She looked so beautiful to him, there in the scattered moonbeams. Her hair fell around her, looking like living silk, long waves that emphasized her small, tucked-in waist. She moved with grace and he could imagine her as a dancer, but the idea of her in combat, especially against a wolf in Lycan form, half-man, half-wolf, was a little terrifying to him. She was almost dainty with her small bone structure and soft curves, far too feminine for him to think of her wielding a sword or a knife.

"I have excellent skills with most weapons. The modern ones are a little more difficult, because Xavier rarely brought in humans. They didn't last long or amuse him much when he tortured them. Their blood didn't help his ultimate goal, which was to be immortal."

Branislava wrapped her arm around one of the stone columns at the edge of the verandah and stared out into the dark of the trees. Zev noticed her hand trembled as the memories of her childhood and life settled over her. He pushed himself out of the chair, testing his strength. It was definitely coming back to him. He was far more tired than feeling as if he had been wounded or was ill.

He moved behind her and instantly felt the heat he equated with her. She seemed so cool when one talked to her. Low key. Quiet. But he was beginning to know her. Merged as he was so often with her, their spirits tied together, it was impossible not to see glimpses of who she really was— that person she kept safe from those around her.

Her reasons were all tactical. The realization swept over him, stunning him. She truly was a warrior. That fiery, passionate woman who she kept hidden was ready for warfare, for combat, just as he was always prepared for it. In a secret part of his mind, he hoped, when she was prepared to come to him, that she'd always be just as ready for their lovemaking.

He wrapped his arms around her from behind, locking his hands at her waist and drawing her back against his body. "Have you ever felt safe?"

She didn't pull away, but rather relaxed into him, keeping her gaze on the night. "In the ground after we were rescued. I could feel Mother Earth surrounding me, holding me in her arms, all that wonderful heat after that icy cold. I felt safe there. I stayed much longer than I should have and it made me feel as if I were a coward."

She looked over her shoulder at him, her eyes meeting his. "I'm not."

"I can't imagine that you would be."

"I've never really interacted with people. We spoke to the prisoners in the ice caves telepathically. Sometimes we had to build a bridge for them, but we didn't really have conversations like this one. Both Tatijana and I have gaps in our knowledge. We try to learn as fast as possible, but reading information or taking it from memories is not always interpreted the way the event actually happened."

A wolf called, this time closer to the house. The night carried the mournful note. Zev frowned. "Did you hear that?"

Branislava nodded. "That wasn't one of Skyler and Dimitri's wolves. Or Ivory and Razvan's pack."

"It wasn't one of the local packs either," Zev said, putting her gently aside and slightly behind him. He stepped up to the very edge of the verandah. "But he's hunting and he's calling to his partner."

He reached for Dimitri. *Did you hear? That is no neighbor of ours.*

We heard. Dimitri's voice was grim.

"Fen, Dimitri and Skyler as well as I were put on a hit list by the Lycans. They have sent assassins to hunt us down and kill us." He turned to look at her over his shoulder.

Branislava was no longer in her elegant dress. She wore trousers and boots, and a soft shirt under a leather vest. Her belt was slung low on her hips, holstering an array of weapons. She was ready for war.

He had never hunted with her on the ground before, and he was a little reluctant when he didn't know her skills. In the air, with her dragon, she was precise and had mad skills, but hand-to-hand combat was altogether different.

She sent him a look from under her long lashes. "Try me."

It was the voice rather than her look that convinced him. Her tone vibrated with determination and even a hint of eagerness. She was a predator beneath all that cool beauty and her fiery nature demanded action.

"I'll follow your lead," she added.

"Let's do it then." He stepped off the porch. For the first time he used his Carpathian abilities to acquire his weapons. His long coat swirled around his ankles, the entire inside decorated with weapons, most of his own making. His belt held more weapons, as did his boots. A silver sword hung at his waist. He pulled on thin gloves to keep the silver from touching his skin. He was mixed blood, both Lycan and Carpathian, and silver burned when he touched it.

We're coming to you, Dimitri, from the south. That's where I pinpointed the wolf's position. We'll make a sweep and see what turns up. Let your wolves know we're hunting with them.

He isn't alone, Dimitri warned. *He was calling to a partner.*

Yeah. I got that. Is Skyler in your line of sight? He was mostly worried about Dimitri's young lifemate. She had amazing skills and the Lycans belonging to a mysterious group who wanted war between the species had particularly targeted her for death.

He tried to keep the note of worry from his voice. The Carpathians were fairly new in their dealings with the Lycans and they tended to underestimate them. Because of an order centuries earlier by their council, Lycans avoided Carpathians as much as possible and the two species hadn't interacted.

They'll be military trained with weapons, most likely guns, he warned, including Branislava in the circle of information. *Don't forget, they're fast and strong and they hunt in packs. This one could have more than one partner. The one you see is not the one to worry about.*

He gave the advice to Dimitri, but he was more concerned with imparting the information to the two women, although both had fought Lycans before. Still, he was worried. Dimitri had fought with packs and against them at various times throughout the centuries. Dimitri knew wolves and he would know how best to fight them. He was also a mixed blood, a *Hän ku pesäk kaikak,* guardian of all, which meant he could utilize both Lycan and Carpathian gifts. He was fast and intelligent and enormously strong.

Lycans can leap great distances, never assume you're safe if you take to the air, he added, unable to stop himself from reminding Branislava, although she'd done battle with the rogue packs before.

Branislava moved in silence, staying directly behind him. He realized she was following exactly in his footsteps, choosing the same path. There wasn't so much as a whisper of her clothing brushing against the leaves. Not a single twig or leaf snapped or crackled beneath the soles of her boots. She might as well have been a ghost floating through the night toward her destination.

Zev was Lycan raised and Lycan in his mind. He knew forests and how to travel through them in silence, but she astounded him.

You gave me the knowledge, she said. *I'm in your mind and your ways are ingrained in you. I simply have to absorb that vast collection and I'll be up to speed. I refuse to be a liability to you when we hunt.*

He felt pride in her. Her confidence level as a hunter was far stronger than when she was in a social setting. He understood why. As a prisoner, she had never really had a chance to learn the niceties that most learned as children growing up. She had learned battle tactics from prisoners, but not how to interact socially.

Her behavior made sense. She remained quiet, absorbing the knowledge of those around her, learning quickly. She appeared to be no threat whatsoever to anyone. All the while she was honing her skills for combat. In that time, she was also trying to learn how to behave in social situations.

Unfortunately, she had met—and recognized—her lifemate. He had been mortally wounded, and all her plans of slowly absorbing the culture and society of Carpathians and humans alike had gone out the window in her efforts to save him.

His every sense was on full alert. He could hear the slightest movement, the mice scurrying in the vegetation, the various creatures that made their home in the underbrush. The insects continued to drone but he expected that. Wolves didn't disturb the natural order of the night. Still, he was uneasy and certain they were closing in on their quarry. He slowed his pace even more, inching his way through the brush, his gaze continually sweeping his surroundings, examining above, below and to both sides of them as well as in front of them.

He took two more steps and a frond attached to a very large fern moved slightly, a small jiggle. The wind was above them in the canopy, not moving through the forest around the large trunks. There was no legitimate reason for the branch to move as it had.

He stopped abruptly, but she didn't run into him. When he glanced at her over his shoulder, her gaze was fixed on the same branch. Pride welled up. Branislava knew what she was doing. She knew what to look for.

Zev held up his fist without thinking, sinking low in the brush. She obeyed the silent signal to halt, crouching even lower almost simultaneously with him. There was no sound, no whisper of movement. She was very good and he found himself giving her the respect he would a fellow woodsman.

Lycans feel the energy of Carpathians when they use any of their gifts, he cautioned her.

He was mixed blood and could contain his energy. Skyler was the only full Carpathian he had seen able to do it. Lycans couldn't sense her presence, not even after her conversion, and she wasn't yet a mixed blood like Dimitri.

He studied the ground around the fern. The forest floor was uneven. Roots ran along the surface like veins. Downed tree trunks, rotted and hollow were scattered around as if flung by a capricious hand. Leaves and pine needles were inches deep, undisturbed for hundreds of years—until now.

Zev spotted the twisted, bruised shoots at the root of the fern. Four large bushes intersected with the ferns springing up everywhere around them, nearly choking them. He could barely make out the sole of a heel of a boot, peeking out of the undergrowth. He touched Branislava's shoulder and indicated the telltale sign. She nodded.

Stay here. I'm going to move in on him, but be alert to any sound, any sway of a branch or ripple in the earth. If they know we're hunting them, this could be a setup. I'm relying on you to watch my back.

He turned his head to look into her brilliant eyes. She didn't look afraid. In fact, she looked calmer than he'd ever seen her. She felt calmer. She was definitely confident in her abilities and that gave him confidence in her.

He was just a little shocked at his reluctance to leave her. Many of the Lycan women fought off the rogues if their villages or homes were attacked. Many served in their countries' military, no matter where their packs were located. In his own elite pack, Daciana hunted with him, and he'd never doubted her or felt hesitant to leave her alone.

He didn't like Branislava out of his sight. That was the truth of it. He loathed to leave her side when danger lurked so close. He was fairly certain his unwillingness was due to his being her lifemate and not at all that he was afraid she couldn't handle whatever happened there in the forest.

A wolf called and by the timbre of the voice, he knew it was an animal. He recognized the pitch of Shadow, Dimitri's alpha. Another answered. That was the little female, Moonglow. Shadow howled a second time and Sonnet answered.

What are they saying? Branislava asked. *One note doesn't mean anything.*

She had taken him at his word and her telepathy was on a very narrow path, each word spaced and thin so the energy was dispersed almost before he could catch the words pushed into his mind.

It's a count. They've spotted four assassins creeping around in our forest. They must be looking for someone, and I would have to guess it is Dimitri's Skyler.

They'll get a shock if they get anywhere close to her. Satisfaction edged her tone.

We've got one close to us, so my guess is, they're hunting in pairs. There has to be at least one more.

He dropped to his belly and crawled through the brush toward the Lycan positioned between three heavy berry bushes. Hundreds of ferns had pushed up all around the bushes so that the fronds intertwined with the leaves of the plants, forming a natural shelter. The Lycan—and Zev recognized him as Rollo—was in a pack subordinate to the council member Randall's main pack. Randall's main pack was one of the larger that Zev knew of. The larger pack commanded three other packs subordinate to it.

Zev had often spoken to Rollo. He knew the man had a mate but no children, which wasn't uncommon. Few Lycans were able to have children other than the alpha pair. This was another man he'd liked. He was a good hunter. He'd served in the United States Marine Corps. He often ran with another man by the name of Ivaylo. Zev would bet his life Ivaylo was somewhere close by protecting Rollo's back.

He smelled the Lycan assassin now, the aggression, the mixture of trepidation and excitement that often came with waiting for combat to actually start. Adrenaline always kicked in when lying in wait to ambush someone.

Zev could hear Rollo's heart pumping like mad, a pounding beat that beckoned to him. He heard the blood flowing like water through his veins. His Dark Blood lineage—and he recognized it for what it was—had been called to the forefront. Mixed with Lycan and Carpathian, his senses were so acute it was almost overwhelming. He lay still, inches from his prey, letting his senses fan outward, seeking Ivaylo, the Lycan he was certain was Rollo's partner.

He knew they had served in the military together. The two men were fond of saying they'd joined together, left together and married their wives on the same day in a double ceremony. He stayed very still, waiting for the sign he knew would come eventually, revealing the second Lycan's position. Hunting was all about patience, and he had it in abundance. He hoped Branislava did as well.

Tension coiled. A tiny shrew ran over his hand, stopped and started four times before disappearing into the small field of ferns. Rollo sighed, the sound muffled as if his mouth was covered by his arm.

An owl dropped down fast, talons extended, making for the tiny shrew. The shrew made a high-pitched sound of distress. As the claws raked over it, the shrew dove into the crack between two small rocks. The owl missed its prey and with a small cry of disappointment, lifted itself back into the air with straining wings. The bird made for the tree several meters across from the ferns, flew toward a high branch and veered off sharply.

Zev followed the owl's line of sight. Sure enough, just as he expected, Ivaylo was lying up in the tree, covering his buddy.

Do you see him?

I was aware of him the moment the owl chose not to land. She was silent a moment, gave a soft sigh and then admitted the truth. *I saw the owl dive for the shrew, but when it veered off, your conclusion was in your mind before I had the chance to actually get there myself. But I would have.*

If we're going to make our way to Dimitri and Skyler to help them out, we can't have these two alive and hunting behind us, you know that, don't you?

Hunting was not the same as killing. Branislava was no soldier.

A wolf poked his head through the brush just a few meters from Rollo. Branislava inhaled sharply. This wasn't one of Skyler and Dimitri's pack, she could tell by the markings, but there were wolves local to the area and this one was too curious.

Zev swore softly under his breath. He knew exactly what they were doing now. The Lycans were aware that Dimitri was fond of wolves. They knew his reputation. *These two are lying in wait for the others to drive the wolves this way. In doing so, they plan on drawing out Dimitri and Skyler.*

A shot rang out. The wolf yipped and leapt into the air. Panting, eyes rolling in pain, it hit the ground hard. Several times it tried to rise, only to fall back again. When the wolf realized it was unable to walk, it tried to pull its body along the ground to the relative safety of the heavier brush.

A cold anger formed into hard knots in his belly. *That's sacrilegious*, Zev hissed. *No Lycan deliberately wounds a wolf. They're our brethren.*

These two don't seem to mind in the least. Remember, they're hunting Dimitri and Skyler, probably you and Fen as well. I think I can make my way to the wolf and try to stop the bleeding.

Branislava sounded confident. He couldn't fault her courage. She waited for him to decide. If she went to help the wolf, and that in itself was dangerous as the wolf was wild and now injured, he would have to take out Ivaylo in the tree to protect her. That would leave Rollo only a few meters from her, armed and eager to kill.

I can do this, Zev. I want to do this, she insisted. *Your great-grandmother hunted beside her lifemate and I intend to do the same. I have to start somewhere.*

He nodded his head slowly and signaled her to go. She didn't make the mistake of using Carpathian skills to shift into something small in order to make her way across the ground to the brush where the wolf was hiding. She remembered the two Lycans would be able to feel that energy immediately. Instead, Branislava used her toes and elbows to push herself backward, deeper into cover, into a narrow rabbit's trail.

Not a single leaf, vine or branch moved as she made her way inch by inch through the tunnel toward the wolf. She was small, but he was shocked that she could use that passage without revealing herself to the enemy who was definitely poised and ready for anyone to show their face.

Zev didn't particularly give a damn whether or not Ivaylo saw him coming. The man had a rifle in his hands and Branislava was approaching a wounded wolf. She would come face-to-face with the animal any moment and all hell could break lose.

Zev used his mixed blood speed, a blurring, impossible-to-see quickness, as he raced to the bottom of the tree and leapt high, his claws slashing the rifle out of the Lycan's hands and tearing him out of the tree simultaneously.

As they both fell toward the ground, Zev twisted in midair, using Ivaylo's body as a shield to keep his buddy from shooting at him. He knew Rollo's attention would be on the desperate fight between Zev and Ivaylo and not Branislava and the wolf. They hit the ground together, Zev landing on his feet in a crouch and Ivaylo on his back in the dirt.

Zev used the enormous strength of his mixed blood to drive Ivaylo deep through several layers of vegetation and soil with one hand. The other held the silver dagger, a twister like a corkscrew in his fist. He slammed it deep through the chest, penetrating the heart and driving it all the way through, pinning Ivaylo to the ground itself. A shot rang out and then another. Rollo rapid fired, desperate to drive Zev away from his buddy. Bullets spit into the ground all around Zev. Bark splintered as the bullets tore into the tree trunk behind his head.

Zev rolled away from Ivaylo's body toward cover. He caught a glimpse of Branislava and his heart leapt into his throat. She rose up behind Rollo like a bird of legends—the fiery phoenix. Her hair, in that long braid, swept back from her face crackled with fiery sparks as bloodred as any sunset. Her eyes had gone from deep emerald to green with red-orange flames roaring in the very center.

Rollo stood, the rifle to his shoulder, finger on the trigger, firing round after round. Behind him, Branislava's diminutive figure took on a fiery glow, as if deep inside her was the fire dragon raging to emerge. She seemed to grow in stature, rising menacingly behind the Lycan. The moon caught the flash of silver in her hand.

She didn't plunge the stake into his body from the back as he expected her to do. She leapt into the air, right over the top of him, both legs kicking down hard on the gun, slamming it right out of his hands. As she dropped down, she plunged the dagger straight through his heart. Her feet hit the ground and he stood there a moment swaying, his eyes wide with shock, both hands coming up to cup the hilt of the stake, as if he might find the strength to pull it out.

Branislava stepped back. Rollo toppled over at her feet, hands still clutching the silver blade through his heart. She raised her hand in the air and Zev tossed her his sword. She caught it in midair and came down in a slashing motion, using Carpathian strength to sever the head, all in one movement. Without stopping her swing, she continued to raise the sword and threw it back to him. Zev removed Ivaylo's head as well.

"I think that was showing off, *mon chaton féroce*."

She gave him an enigmatic smile. "Perhaps, but I got the job done. Will you let Dimitri and Skyler know while I try to save the wolf? I had to choose between the two of you, wolf or crazy lifemate, and since Mikhail and Gregori think you're so important, I thought I'd better choose saving you."

He nodded, heat blossoming out of nowhere. With every step she took, even with her fluid glide over the vegetation, she crackled with fire. It was as if sparks leapt off her skin and hair into the air around her, although there was no real sound, only the illusion of flames burning from the inside out.

Dimitri, two down here. Can you make a move toward us?

We're pinned down. They aren't aware we're here, but there are four of them and we're caught in the middle. I can pick them off one by one, but I'm not certain I want to leave Skyler vulnerable.

Zev could understand Dimitri's dilemma. He didn't like leaving Branislava, and she had the knowledge of hundreds of warriors over centuries. Skyler was nineteen and had been converted only recently.

They're using the local wolf pack to try to draw you out. We've got a wounded wolf here. Branka is attempting to save it.

We're keeping our wolves with us. I warned the local wolf pack to stay away, but eventually they'll come back to investigate. This is their territory.

Zev understood that as well. The Lycans would be patient. They had all night to hunt Skyler and Dimitri and the local wolf pack. They'd seek cover and just wait. Eventually the wolf pack would return. The wolves would scent rivals in their territory and want to drive them out. The moment they showed themselves, the Lycans would wound them, hoping to draw out Dimitri or his lifemate.

I'm making my way to you. Don't shoot me by mistake. I've noticed you can be a little bloodthirsty.

I feel compelled to point out your humor is becoming less Lycan and more Carpathian by the moment.

Zev found himself laughing. Life was good when you had family. He had forgotten these moments, small stolen moments together where one could find humor even in the midst of being hunted. He hadn't had a family in a long time—unless one counted Daciana, Makoce and Lykaon, three members of his elite hunting pack. He had always counted on them to have his back—and they'd never failed him.

He made his way over to Branislava. She crouched in the brush, one hand in the soft fur, head down. He sighed and put his hand on her shoulder. "I'm sorry, *cheri*, there was really nothing to do." Sorrow welled up. Though an animal, the wolf was brethren, and a wild, majestic creature that didn't deserve to be caught up in the war taking place.

She looked over her shoulder at him, tears turning her eyes to emerald. "I understand how Ivory could be tempted to save them when we shouldn't."

"Turning a wolf to Carpathian could be creating a killing machine. Ivory had spent time with the pups prior to converting them," he cautioned. "But the practice is dangerous."

Branislava nodded and allowed him to help her to her feet. "I'm well aware of that. Still, it was a struggle not to try. I recognized that he was far too gone, but the temptation was there."

"Are you saying we'll probably end up with wolf tattoos?" he asked, slipping his arm around her and pulling her close to comfort her.

"Yours will say 'Wolfie.'" She leaned into him, allowing her body to shelter against his for just a moment while she steadied herself. "I'll have all the wolves riding on my skin."

"Wolf-master," he corrected solemnly. "I'll be the master of the wolves and the wolf keeper."

That bought him a faint smile and a quick eye roll.

She turned her attention to the two bodies. "We can't incinerate them without the other Lycans knowing we're in the forest as well."

"They aren't going anywhere," Zev decreed. "It isn't as if they're going to rise as zombies."

"It could happen," Branislava said. "Tatijana told me all about the zombie apocalypse."

He laughed softly. "She's been watching movies, hasn't she?"

Branislava had to admit the truth of that. Nodding, but she raised her eyebrow at him. "If Lycans and Carpathians are real, zombies could be as well."

He brushed a kiss along the top of her head. "Vampires make puppets. Fen refers to them as ghouls but we'll call them zombies just for you."

"Let's go hunt the assassins. They've got Dimitri and Skyler pinned down."

"Dimitri doesn't strike me as the type of man to ever be pinned down," Branislava replied with a little sniff of disdain. "By the time we get there, he'll have taken care of business."

They hurried through the forest toward the coordinates Dimitri sent them. As they approached the area, they slowed. Zev was pleased that Branislava did so entirely on her own, not waiting to take her cue from him. More and more, he found he was comfortable with her hunting with him.

He signaled her to go low. He went high, making his way into the canopy of the trees like a large lizard clinging to the bark. His body took on the coloration of everything around him so that he blended perfectly with his surroundings. Smelling blood, he wasn't at all surprised to find the first body lying at the base of a wide tree trunk. The head sat on the chest and a silver stake stuck straight up through the chest. The arm of the dead Lycan was turned up, exposing the small intricate circle on the inner wrist. This man had been a member of the Sacred Circle, a religious-like sect many of the Lycans believed in.

Nice work. Have you located his partner?

Not yet. I'm working on that.

I'll move clockwise. Branka's on the ground searching in the same direction, using a grid pattern.

Skyler will take the opposite way to Bronnie, Dimitri said, reluctance in his voice.

Zev!

Branislava broke in, her voice wavering with distress, but she kept their path shrouded from the Lycans and he couldn't help but be proud of her.

The wolf pack is returning. The alpha almost stepped on me. I tried to send him away, but he smelled blood.

Zev cursed under his breath. The last thing they needed was to mix in a healthy, territorial wolf pack that could be used against them.

Do your best to warn them of the danger. That was all they could do. If the wolf pack didn't listen, it was on their alpha, not Branislava, although he knew she would blame herself if something happened to the other wolves. He mentally braced himself for the event that she would want to save them and he would have to tell her to let them go.

Zev moved to the next tree via the long, sweeping branches touching the tree he was in. He took a careful look around. His breath caught in his throat. His heart gave a wild leap of fear. Skyler was a good distance away, lying prone in the vegetation, a few bushes covering her, but she was exposed and a good sniper could easily kill her.

Skyler, take cover, he warned abruptly, fear skittering down his spine, everything in him straining to protect her, but even his incredible speed, leaping from branch to branch was not going to get him there in time.

A shot rang out and her body jerked. A small red geyser went up in the middle of the back of her head.

6

Zev expected to feel her death, just as all Carpathians had the first time she had been killed by the Lycans, but there was nothing at all, only emptiness.

Another shot rang out and then a third, both bullets going into the body on the ground. Clearly she was already dead, but the sniper wanted to make certain. Even as Zev watched in a kind of horror, Skyler's body jerked, the arms stretching out stiffly, the feet drumming the ground. She rose with multiple twitches and lurches, coming upright eventually, her raised arms stiffly out in front of her.

Her body turned as if it were a compass pointing the way to her killer. She lurched forward. Blood ran down her face through the exit wound in her right cheek. More blood stained the front of her vest. Each step she took was laborious, her body shaking with spasms and twitches. Her eyes went wide and round.

Zev's churning gut settled and he passed a hand down his face, scrubbing away the fear of losing Skyler to replace that intense emotion with sheer laughter. *Skyler watched movies with Tatijana, didn't she?*

It was nearly impossible to tear his gaze away from the spectacle of horror as Skyler continued her arduous journey through the forest toward the tree where the sniper had lain in wait for her. Another bullet hit her in her left eye. Her head jerked backward and stayed in the position for a few seconds while her feet stumbled back rapidly in an effort to regain her balance.

The brush to Skyler's left parted, and Branislava emerged, her face slack, mouth drooping, arms raised in front of her. She had the same jerky steps as Skyler had, as she reeled forward. Part of her arm fell to the ground and some of the flesh on her face sloughed off. She didn't look right or left but wobbled in the direction Skyler had been pointing out.

Skyler righted herself, although her head tilted at an alarming angle as she began her slow, stumbling progress toward the Lycan's chosen tree. Zev could see him now, raising his head in alarm, putting his eye to his scope, only to raise his head again as if uncertain whether or not he should make a run for it.

The sniper settled behind his rifle and squeezed the trigger, this time aiming for Branislava. Looking at her as her flesh began dropping off, Zev couldn't blame the Lycan. The bullet hit her chest, slamming her backward as if she was a paper doll. She stumbled as black blood welled around the entry point right over her heart, but she recovered, swaying and twitching before beginning her forward progress once more.

As they began to converge onto the tree, another bush opened and out stumbled a third zombie. Tatijana looked worse than Branislava, with her hair falling out, leaving a trail of clumps of red behind her. One foot appeared gone so that she tottered unevenly but steadily toward the tree.

The Lycan chose to retreat, gathering up his weapon hastily. He stood, reluctant to take his gaze off the improbable but very real vision of three dead women coming for him. He turned to make his leap from the tree.

The real Branislava slammed the silver stake home, driving it hard through his chest with her Carpathian strength. Tatijana wielded the silver sword, slicing cleanly through the sniper's neck, severing his head so that it fell almost at the three zombies' feet. Immediately the apparitions were gone, mere illusions Skyler had created to keep the sniper's attention away from the two women who stalked him.

Zev shook his head. *Nice job, Skyler. A little theatrical, but it worked.*

My tribute to Josef and a little payback in his name to these murderers. There was no remorse in her voice. Josef was her best friend and the Lycans had shot him. Skyler was known to hold a grudge and take revenge. *Josef would like my style.* This time her tone was a little smug.

Dimitri, there's no keeping these Dragonseeker women under control, and yours could be the ringleader, Zev informed him.

Four dead assassins and at least two more to go. The one Branislava and Tatijana had killed hadn't been a partner to the Lycan Dimitri had killed. He hadn't been in a position to cover the Lycan in the tree. Dimitri was working his way toward that man's partner.

Zev needed to concentrate on the sniper high up in the trees, with his bird's-eye view. He was certain he knew where to look for the dead assassin's partner. There was usually a pattern to the way the Lycans hunted, even from the safety of distance.

Skyler is a little wild, Dimitri admitted, laughter in his voice. *Who knew?*

You knew, Skyler chimed in. *You're the only one. And now I've got my aunts and my wolves. Remember that, Zev, the next time you decide to cross me.*

Zev heard the faint laughter of the other two women as Skyler shared her empty threat with them. He was already moving, once again using the tree branches to backtrack and find the second sniper.

Branka, check his wrist or arm to see if he has one of those circle tattoos.

He does, I can see it from here. It's the same one the other two men had.

Could this be religious fervor? He doubted it. He'd been to a few of the meetings. While Arno, the council leader he'd protected at nearly the cost of his own life, was an amazing, passionate motivational speaker, he wasn't overzealous. He held rank in the hierarchy of the Sacred Circle, believing in their tenets, but tempering those beliefs with logical thinking.

Zev spotted the sniper in the crook of a fir tree, higher up in the branches than his partner had been. He had climbed to try to get a better look at what his buddy had been shooting at. More than likely, Skyler had created the illusion only for the man she was concentrating on. This Lycan had seen an empty forest floor. He couldn't tell what, if anything, his partner had shot at.

The lizard moved along the branch with slow, deliberate steps, careful not to draw the eye as he slowly made his way to the branch that bridged the gap between the tree he was in and the one the sniper was in. He recognized the scent and his heart sank.

Damon Declaw was Daciana's older brother. They had eaten together a thousand times over the last century. They'd laughed together. Hunted together, and had even given each other blood when battle wounds had forced them to do so.

Daciana loved this man with all her heart. She looked up to him. Admired him. She shared stories with him of her hunting expeditions against rogue packs. He'd always supported her. Hard-core members of the Sacred Circle didn't believe in women carrying weapons. Damon had never once acted anything but proud of his sister.

Zev shook his head. He had no idea what he was going to do. Damon was lying in wait for a member of the local wolf pack, and that went against everything they were as a species. They protected wildlife, not used it as bait. Would he murder Dimitri? Or Skyler? Perhaps Branislava?

Swearing savagely under his breath, Zev began to make his way up the tree trunk. He moved slowly, keeping to a deliberate pace that wouldn't draw attention to him. He blended in with the tree bark and as he moved out onto the branch to get into position behind Damon, he realized he needed proof that his friend, Daciana's brother, was that far gone.

Skyler, can you cast the illusion of a wolf curious enough to walk out of the brush investigating one of the bodies? Don't bring it in too close to the body. He didn't want Damon's reaction to be protective, keeping the wolf away from a fallen friend, but rather to know if Damon would actually shoot the wolf to draw Skyler and Dimitri out into the open.

No problem. She was all business now, all hint of laughter gone as if she sensed he was pulled in two directions and she felt sympathy for him.

Zev knew Skyler was an empath, whether she knew it or not, but in this instance, it was far more likely that his Branka remained merged with him and easily read his dilemma.

I am with you whatever the outcome, Branislava whispered in his mind. He was flooded with warmth, with the promise of a future. She might not be ready to commit that moment, but she knew she would eventually and she wanted him to know it as well.

This man is a friend. If I kill him, how will I ever face Daciana?

If he had family in the Lycan world, it was Makoce, Lykaon and Daciana. She would never forgive him if he killed her brother. Never. And he wouldn't blame her. Still, if Damon was willing to break the rules of their society, what choice did he have?

Perhaps you will not have to, Branislava said. *Perhaps he will give you a reason to keep him alive.*

She always managed to say the right thing. He positioned the lizard above Damon's head and waited. A few moments later, Damon slid his weapon slowly forward and leaned over to place his eye at the scope. Zev saw the wolf as it cautiously broke through the brush with its muzzle. The animal waited patiently for a length of time before moving into the open, nose to the air, seeking the scent of blood and death.

She was a beautiful female, strong and muscular with a tricolored fur coat. Shades of black, silver and charcoal shimmered as the moon hit her.

She's not mine, Skyler exclaimed. *She's real.*

Damon hesitated, clearly warring with himself. Zev willed him not to pull the trigger.

Another wolf stepped out, this one also a female. She bared her teeth at the first one. The silvery female whirled around to face the threat.

Coming your way, Dimitri warned. *Sniper on the move.*

Four more wolves stepped into the open, snarling at the females. Neither paid attention.

Don't get caught up in the drama, Zev warned Branislava. *The alpha female wants the younger female to leave the pack and she's pushing her to get out. We've still got two Lycans out there hunting Dimitri and Skyler. If you get in their way, they could try to kill you.*

The canopy above the wolves swayed gently as a breeze blew across the leaves. It didn't quite penetrate to the forest floor below. An owl settled in the branches above, mostly hidden by leaves as its wings settled closely to its body. He peered down at the spectacle below. Another five wolves joined the circle forming around the two females.

Damon sighed and lifted his head, shaking it. Clearly he didn't want to shoot any of the wolves. A shot rang out, and the young, silvery female shrieked and leapt into the air. The wolves melted into the foliage around them. Damon cursed and slid his rifle once more into place. He used the scope to look around, trying to find a target other than the wolves.

The female tried to drag herself to cover, yelping in pain each time she attempted to rise. Damon cursed louder. "Damn you, Vasya, you didn't have to do that," he said aloud.

Zev held his breath as the brush closest to the wounded female moved just a slight inch, but there was no breeze, nothing to make the leaves flutter. The wolves had retreated, well versed in what the sound of a gun meant. He knew, by the way Damon hunched his shoulders and then settled into his weapon, that the Lycan had seen that telling movement as well.

A feminine hand inched its way out of the brush, the arm following, as Skyler tried to reach the wolf to drag her to safety.

"Vasya, don't do it," Damon whispered aloud, making it a prayer. "It's a woman. Don't pull the trigger."

Zev eased down behind Damon, positioning his body directly behind him, ready to stop him should there be need. He couldn't do anything about Vasya. He glanced up at the owl. It was gone. The takeoff and subsequent flight had been silent. Feathers on the owl provided that silent flight, but Zev was certain Dimitri was close.

He knew he was correct when a man's high-pitched scream startled the insects into silence. Simultaneously the rifle went off, the sound every bit as loud. Damon swore and used his scope once more to try to see what happened to Vasya.

Zev had his gaze trained on Skyler. The second bullet hit the young wolf, and Dimitri's lifemate dragged the bloody animal into the brush. He caught a glimpse of Branislava, crouched close. Another wolf, a huge male, leapt from a distance away, as if he'd come from a tree branch rather than on the ground. He raced across the open forest floor, cutting unexpectedly from one side to the next in a zigzag pattern.

Zev recognized Dimitri's big alpha, Shadow. Whether he was protecting Skyler or the fallen female, he was uncertain, but it didn't matter. Damon didn't shoot him. Zev stuck the tip of a silver dagger hard into Damon's back. All he had to do was use his mixed blood strength to penetrate through muscle and bone to reach the heart.

"Shove the gun out of the tree," he advised. "You know me. You know I'll kill you in a heartbeat. Don't be stupid enough to make any mistakes."

Damon stiffened, recognizing his voice. He let the weapon fall to the ground below. "I thought you were dead."

Zev's heart plunged. Had Daciana told her brother? Was she somehow connected to this betrayal? She was family to him. "Now why would you think that?" He kept his voice even, not wanting to sound in the least as if with that one question, Damon had unknowingly called his sister's loyalty in question.

Damon shrugged. "The news came down the pipe that the Carpathians had pulled some trick and tried to off the council. You died protecting one of them and the Lycans fought them, trying to get the other council members out of their territory."

"Link your fingers behind your head and just stay exactly the way you are. I mean it, Damon. Did Daciana tell you all that?" He reached out and casually cut through the belt looping around Damon's hip, dropping the cache of weapons to the branch. With a flick of the tip of his knife, he sent the entire belt to the forest floor.

A low growl escaped Damon. "My sister? I was told they killed her."

"Did you try to call her?"

"Over and over. I got no response. I tried her partner, Makoce, but he didn't answer, either. No one did."

"She's alive and well, Damon. She's guarding the council members as we speak. A faction of Lycans, not Carpathians, attacked the Carpathian village simultaneously with an attempt on the lives of the prince and our council members." Zev reached around him to flip up his sleeve, revealing the tattoo of the Sacred Circle. "All of those who tried to assassinate the council have that same tattoo."

"That's bullshit, Zev. We believe in morals and ethics, not killing our own kind or murdering other species."

"Yet here you sit, lying in wait to murder a young woman who has done absolutely nothing to you. You were waiting to wound a wolf just to use the animal as bait, knowing she had enough compassion to come to try to save it."

The accusation was harsh, but he felt harsh. He felt like shaking Damon until his teeth rattled and then taking him out behind the proverbial barn to beat some sense into him. What was wrong with his people? Lycans were good people, not fanatics who killed without thought.

"I wasn't going to shoot a wolf," Damon mumbled.

"But someone gave you the orders to shoot them," Zev insisted. "That was part of your mission. Draw out the woman by using one of our wild brethren."

Damon sighed. "It didn't make any sense, but someone has to pay for killing Daciana."

"I told you, you idiot, she isn't dead. And really, Damon, killing Skyler wouldn't bring her back if she was. What possessed you to join with these people? You have a brain, why weren't you using it?"

Damon didn't answer.

Zev was fed up with the entire thing. "If you had lifted that rifle at either the wolf or Skyler, I would have staked you on the spot, and you would have deserved it."

Damon sank back on his heels. "I don't know why I joined them." He sounded confused. "You're right. This goes against everything I believe in. It isn't like me not to check facts. This goes against the code of the Sacred Circle as well. We don't condone violence. Self-defense, yes, but not murder. Not luring a girl out into the open and shooting her." He dropped his arms and turned toward Zev. "What the hell is going on with me?"

"What part of 'stay exactly the way you are' didn't you understand?" Zev asked quietly.

Damon placed his hands, palm down, on his thighs. "I'm not a threat. I want to see Daciana. Maybe she can figure out what's really going on."

His voice rang with truth. Zev didn't know what to believe. He never would have thought that Damon would join in a murder.

He's telling you the truth, Branislava said. *I hear it in his voice.*

I hear it, too, but that doesn't mean a damn thing, mon chaton féroce.

Branislava heard the hurt in his voice. This man had been his friend—a close friend. Zev felt betrayed by him. Not just him, but his entire species. He'd spent his life doing his duty, protecting his kind and first they had turned on him and then shamed him with their actions, and now there was betrayal.

Zev lived by a strict code of honor. He expected little in return for his service, but he did demand loyalty. The pack was always about loyalty and this man somehow was equated, in Zev's mind, with his pack.

Bring him before the council, let them decide what to do with him, she suggested. *If one of them is behind this, wouldn't they stick up for him?*

Not necessarily. He was very reluctant to present Damon to the council for judgment, not after what happened to Dimitri. The council members had sworn Dimitri was safe and well cared for, but in reality he'd been sentenced to the worst fate—the cruelest of all deaths any Lycan or enemy could suffer. Granted, Dimitri was mixed blood, considered the dreaded *Sange rau*, an abomination that had been outlawed centuries earlier. Even so, Zev trusted few people and, at the moment, even fewer Lycans.

Branislava sighed. Dimitri strode toward them, looking tall and authoritative. She exchanged a long, guilty glance with Skyler. They had saved the young female wolf, but at a great price. She would forever be a part of Skyler and Dimitri's pack.

"Shadow insisted," Skyler said, both hands buried in the fur of the female. "He says she's his chosen mate."

"And you didn't help that along?" Dimitri demanded, looking from one to the other.

"Is there a way to influence an alpha wolf?" Branislava asked.

"If there is, the two of you would figure out how," Dimitri said. He dropped into a crouch beside the female's body, running his hands over her. "She's changing inside."

"She's been convulsing," Skyler said. "I tried to help her, block the pain. She's silent and stoic, panting her way through."

Dimitri's hands were very gentle as he stroked them over the female wolf. "Our little misty girl is beautiful, I'll give you that much."

"That's a good name for her," Skyler said.

Shadow crowded closer, touching his nose to the female. Misty's gaze clung to his and then included Skyler and Dimitri as if she knew they were part of Shadow's pack.

"The Lycan bodies have to be incinerated. All five of them, or six if Zev disposes of the last one," Dimitri said. "Do you think the two of you can do that?"

"Skyler can stay here with you," Branislava said. "I know where each is located and I can get the job done. She should be with Misty."

"The silver weapons have to be collected," Dimitri cautioned. "And after the bodies are incinerated, it's best to bury the ashes deep so no one will find them."

Branislava nodded. "I understand. I'll do it. Zev knows the last Lycan and he's very upset. I don't know what he plans to do with him."

"If you need help, Bronnie," Skyler volunteered, "Dimitri can handle this."

"I don't. I've practiced calling down the lightning and I've gotten fairly good at it." She could use more practice if truth be told. She was determined to be an asset to Zev when he hunted rogue packs and vampires. She couldn't imagine that he would do anything else.

Fen and Dimitri had imparted the stories of the Dark Bloods to both Skyler and Tatijana. They were extraordinary warriors, both the males and females of that line. It seemed that every lifemate was as well, as if that fierce soul called to the soul of another fierce warrior.

She was Dragonseeker and proud of her lineage. Claimed by a Dark Blood, she refused to be less than all the women who had come before her. She would be at Zev's side for every battle and she would learn to do the things necessary to be safe, and to ensure that he was as well.

Mon chaton féroce, there is no other woman like you and no other that will ever do for me. That is not simply your Carpathian lifemate talking to you. That is Zev Hunter, mixed blood, Tirunul and Dark Blood. Lycan and Carpathian. I fell for you long before I knew what a lifemate was.

She couldn't help the little spurt of joy rushing through her veins. She wanted Zev to fall in love with her for who she was, not because he had no choice. She wanted to fall in love with him for himself. She couldn't go through her life without choices. She wanted to be the one to choose her own path. If she made mistakes they would be her mistakes.

Zev complicated things for her, but she couldn't find it in her heart to resent him. How could she not be proud of him? How could she not look at him and be attracted to him? She might not want to be, but each time his gaze rested on her, her heart fluttered wildly. Her breath caught in her lungs and the scorching heat in her body raged. She was a fire dragon, and heat and fire were her world, but when her veins filled with molten lava and pooled low and heavy, coiling tight, the flames threatened to engulf her. She was tempted to find out just what that fire was all about.

She floated the first body she came to over to the next closest one. This was one of her scariest moments. She didn't want to set the entire forest on fire. The few times she'd practiced calling lightning, she'd been in a clearing. Twice, she'd had to call down rain to stop the grass and flowers from burning.

Taking a breath, she turned her attention to the sky. Clouds shot up like a tower, climbing fast, roiling and churning as if angry. Lightning forked throughout the whirling clouds, lighting them up in various places as the bolts sought a target. She let out her breath and focused, straining for control. Lightning, raw and crackling with power, whipped through the sky. She fought the white-hot energy, corralling it and bringing it down to strike the two bodies dead center.

It was a huge accomplishment. She wanted to leap up and down with joy. The moment she forgot what she was doing, that whip snaked back up to the sky, lashing everything in its path. Several trees burst into flames.

She hissed an unladylike curse under her breath, one she'd heard Zev use, and lifted both hands to the sky to fill the towering cloud with water. She concentrated on dumping it directly over the trees crackling with flames. At once the fire copied her hiss of annoyance, flickering defiantly for just a moment and then giving up.

She fanned the flames incinerating the two snipers, bringing up the temperature until they burned clean. The ashes cooled quickly, leaving only the silver stakes behind. After retrieving the silver, she opened the earth beneath the Lycans and allowed the ashes to drop deep.

Nice, Branka, Zev praised her.

Fen, obviously monitoring the conversation, wasn't quite so kind. *I'm coming back with a camera to take a picture of the trees with all those scorched branches, though. Josef has an Internet page where he likes to put up botched spells and really bad mistakes. I hear he puts them up for a vote and whoever's entry wins gets money.*

You wouldn't dare, Branislava challenged in her most fierce tone.

Of course I would.

Tatijana, you traitor, Branislava hissed. *Keep that man of yours under control. I've got to do this two more times and he'd better not come here and take pictures and give them to Josef.*

How did I get into this? Tatijana asked innocently. *I was just making certain you were all right, keeping an eye on you like we do with each other and he was . . .*

Sneaking. That's what he was doing, Branislava accused, trying not to laugh as she made her way through the forest to find the next pair of bodies.

I find the most interesting things in my lifemate's mind, Fen ventured, unrepentant. *This one is worth bucks.*

Zev listened to the banter, letting the shared amusement warm him, easing the sting of betrayal just a little bit. He nudged Damon, indicating to him to get out of the tree. This would be the telling moment. If Damon made a break for it, or tried to kill him, he'd been lying the entire time. Zev hoped that wasn't the case, but he wouldn't hesitate to kill Damon, even if it meant Daciana would be his enemy for the rest of his life.

Damon rose slowly, lifting his hands toward the sky, indicating he wouldn't go for a weapon. He knew Zev, knew him for the relentless, implacable hunter that he was. He could be a killing machine when he had to be. He was fast and strong and there was no give in him. Damon wasn't about to make any mistakes.

He leapt to the ground, keeping his hands in the air, making certain to land away from his weapons. Zev hadn't so much as moved, but the stake in his hand was in a throwing position and Zev never missed—not anytime Damon had heard of. He landed in a crouch and slowly stood, his arms up, palms showing his hands were empty.

Zev dropped down beside him. "Do you have any other weapons on you?"

Damon even kept his nod slow. "In my boot. Taped to my back."

"Put your hands down, you look ridiculous," Zev snapped. He had no idea what he was going to do with Damon. He wasn't going to take him before the council members to judge for his actions, not until he had a chance to look into Damon's mind.

"I honestly don't know what the hell I'm doing here," Damon said. "I have no idea why it sounded so logical to me. Then, when I'm up in that tree and the wolf poked her head through the brush, everything in me just rebelled at the idea of wounding her."

"I could cut off your head and read your memories," Zev offered, half serious.

"You're pretty pissed with me, aren't you?" Damon said.

"You have no idea. I need people I can count on. We've got a war brewing and assassins running around. Lycans have always been the peacekeepers, the protectors, and this time, it looks as if they're the ones starting the war. I was counting on you and Daciana to have my back while I'm trying to straighten this out. The last thing I ever expected was to find you here with a gun in your hand about to murder Skyler or Dimitri."

The Lycan alpha male, pack leader mentality got the best of him and Zev cuffed the back of Damon's head hard enough to make him stagger forward.

Damon rubbed the back of his head with a wry grin. "I guess I had that coming. Where's the rest of my team?"

"They're dead, Damon. What did you expect? You go hunting Carpathians in the forest at night, they're going to come after you, especially if you're trying to kill their women. You're lucky I was the one who found you." Zev glared at him. "I'm still thinking about killing you on principle alone. Don't think you're out of the woods yet."

Damon turned to face him. "They're dead? All of them? Lycans don't get killed that easily."

"The wolves warned us that someone was hunting. Did you think the Carpathians were going to roll over and just let you kill their women?"

"Stop saying women. I wasn't going to kill a woman. She was targeted because she . . ." He trailed off, looking confused.

"She saved the man she loved from death by silver. He was tortured. I saw him. The council didn't pass sentence on him; in fact," Zev stated, "the order was to keep him safe while they tried to reach an agreement with the Carpathians on the *Sange rau.*"

Damon scowled. "That's right. The prisoner . . ."

"Dimitri," Zev corrected. "He's a good man, call him by his name."

"Dimitri is *Sange rau.* He's a bad blood, a mixed blood, fully capable of wiping out our entire species."

"He's not *Sange rau,* any more than I am. He's *Hän ku pesäk kaikak,* which, in case you're actually interested, is *guardian of all.* He protects all of us, Lycan, human and Carpathian alike. He saved Gunnolf and Convel, both of them, and to repay him they went against the council's orders and convinced everyone that he had been sentenced to death by silver. Had Skyler not come for him, he'd be dead and we'd be at war with the Carpathians. If anything, the Lycans owe that girl a debt of gratitude."

Zev couldn't quite keep the note of anger out of his voice. He was furious with Damon. Lycans didn't behave this way. They had a code of honor they lived by—*he* had lived by it. So had Damon.

"Tell me again who told you I was dead."

Damon rubbed his temples. "I don't know. I was at a meeting. A service. I was worried about Daciana. There had been trouble in the forest at the summer cabins. I couldn't get ahold of her and I thought I'd try to get some news. You know all that talk they do bores the hell out of me."

"They?" Zev prompted. Overhead the storm clouds sizzled with whips of lightning. Thunder boomed, shaking the ground. *Branka, that's too close, pull in your power a little bit*, he cautioned. She was going to light up the entire forest if she wasn't careful.

I've got this, Branislava said. *No worries.*

Zev sighed. When a woman said not to worry, that was clearly the best time to be worried.

Damon scowled again, trying to recall who the speaker was. "He's there at the meetings all the time with Arno and Lupo. They give motivational speeches all the time. He's in Lupo's pack. Why can't I remember his name?"

Lupo Wolfe was one of the oldest council members who had been locked away to protect the existing council should any of the traveling members be lost.

Zev noted that Damon pressed his fingers to his temples again. "What's wrong?"

"I don't know. My head feels like it's splitting in two."

"Don't think about this anymore," Zev suggested, suddenly suspicious. There was a hint of blood, just a small trickle near Damon's nose. "Let's go find your sister. She can fill you in on what's happening. It will be good to have you around while we try to sort things out. We need help protecting the council members from our own kind. We don't know who the enemy actually is."

Lightning zigzagged through the trees, a giant whip, lashing through the forest like a cat-o'-nine-tails. He caught Damon and threw him to the ground just as one of the switches snapped over their heads.

Soft laughter rippled through his mind, almost a giggle, a sound Zev had never heard Branislava make. *Whoops. Sorry. Lightning whips are difficult to wield, aren't they?*

That sound wrapped around his heart and squeezed tight. *Get that under control. Dial it down. You've got way too much power and you're going to hurt yourself.*

He didn't want to admit to her that he'd never actually tried controlling lightning. He'd seen both Fen and Dimitri call down the lightning, but he was Lycan. He didn't call it down. He could see how it would be useful, but not in the hands of an overly enthusiastic woman.

Damon slammed him down as another sizzling streak of white-hot fire snapped over their heads, coming a little too close for comfort. Every hair on his body stood up.

Zev burst out laughing. *Woman! What are you trying to do?*

"This is some crazy storm," Damon said.

"More like a crazy woman," Zev countered, and pushed himself up. "Get your weapons and let's get out of here." *If you're finished playing . . .*

She came out of the trees, walking toward him, her long hair swept back in a braid that trailed down her back. The silken mass was fiery red. Her eyes shone like emeralds and she had a huge smile on her face. In her hands she spun fire, the flames streaking through the air in loops around her as she danced.

She looked exotic, stealing his breath with her beauty. The double rings of fire looped around her body and then rose as she wielded the whips, spinning them around her and then back to either side. The whips were golden in color, the flames crossing her body, sweeping under her feet as she leapt gracefully into the air and then rose above her as she came back to earth.

Zev's breath caught in his throat. Beside him, Damon's jaw dropped. Branislava's soft laugh of pure joy was contagious and both of them smiled at her.

The flaming whips changed color, going fiery red and orange as she made intricate patterns in the night, all the while her body moving to some melody only she could hear.

Zev glanced at the rapt expression on Damon's face and growled low, his gut tightening into knots. "Pick up your jaw and stop staring at her like you're going to eat her up. She belongs to me."

"You're kidding," Damon answered before he could censor his shock. "Sorry, she's just so sexy."

Zev cuffed him again, this time hard enough to send him forward, sprawling on the forest floor. "You don't need to think she's sexy."

"I don't think it," Damon glared at him from the ground, unable to tear his eyes from the fire dance. "I *know* it. No wonder you kept coming back here."

Zev sighed. He couldn't very well fault Damon for having eyes, but his wolf was definitely reacting all over again. He had to find some kind of balance. It helped that, as Branislava spun and danced, she looked only at him—danced only for him.

He could see that she felt free and young and happy, something she'd never been able to do. Clearly dancing was going to be a passion of hers. Her skin glowed as if the fire inside her burned passionately. He didn't want the moment to end for her. She'd had so little happiness or fun in her life, and playing with lightning whips gave her such joy. Damon thought the whips were poi, two chains with the globes for fuel attached to either end.

Branislava danced toward him, whirling around. *Come dance with me.*

He wanted to—he wanted to be part of her fun. It was important to him that she have all the time she needed to get to know him and that they shared moments just like this one together, but he had the responsibility of Damon.

If he's really hiding the truth and I just don't see it because he's my friend, it could be dangerous.

We have lightning. She spun the whips furiously.

Zev laughed. He wasn't going to use lightning whips, but he could improvise. "Stay here a minute, Damon. Right there on the ground. And don't do anything stupid. She's pretty mean with those fire whips."

He danced his way to her, picking up her rhythm, his sword spinning in the air. He could hear the music playing in her head, the drumbeats her feet followed. As he neared her, flames leapt from her whips to his sword, igniting the tip and racing up the blade. He spun the sword in front of him as he approached her.

Her laughter added to the music playing through his head as he drew one of his many knives and set it on fire, tossing it in the air as he spun the sword. He enjoyed every movement, the pattern of their feet, the graceful, flowing ballet as they moved around one another, all the while lighting up the night sky with their fire dance.

Never once did he lose sight of Damon. As much as he enjoyed himself, he knew if Damon made one wrong move, that deadly knife, so beautiful flying through the air, would find its way directly into his friend's heart.

7

"What am I supposed to do with him, Daciana?" Zev asked, jerking his thumb toward Damon. "If I give him to the council . . ."

"You can't," Daciana interrupted, kicking her brother in the shins with the toe of her boot as she paced by his chair.

Branislava had hastily prepared their verandah for company. The chairs were comfortable and the lighting muted. Mist blanketed the forest, obscuring the trees, cutting them off from the rest of the world. She was inside, moving around, and he smelled the aroma of coffee. How she could manage making coffee he had no idea, but she was taking her time so he guessed the first couple of tries hadn't worked out so well.

"You know what they'll do to him. They'll think he's a traitor and part of the conspiracy to kill them." Daciana looked across the porch to Makoce. "What do you think?"

"Does anyone want to know what I think?" Damon asked.

Daciana bared her teeth at him. "No. Absolutely not. You just sit there quietly. Do you have any idea the trouble you've caused? We're sworn to uphold the law and you've broken it a million times over. You're lucky Zev didn't kill you right there in that tree when you aimed a weapon at a wolf and then at Skyler." She kicked him again just for good measure.

"I want to know who gave the order to come here and kill Skyler and Dimitri," Makoce said. "If we can get that information, maybe we can figure out what's really going on here."

Damon leaned toward him. "Most members of the Sacred Circle believe the *Sange rau* can't be tolerated. They're the devil. They destroy entire packs. You know that."

"How many have actually been in existence since the very first one our people encountered? And do you know who hunted it for several years, fought it and eventually killed it?" Zev asked. "Do the members of the Sacred Circle even have a clue who actually killed the *Sange rau* responsible for so much death and destruction?"

In the far corner of the verandah, Fen stirred uncomfortably. He'd stayed quiet. Now he wished Tatijana was with him instead of inside with her sister. Every now and then he felt her laughter brushing through the walls of his mind and knew the two Dragonseeker women were getting advice from Skyler on how to make coffee.

Dimitri and Skyler hadn't arrived yet, but each time he touched Tatijana's mind, she and Branislava were chattering with Skyler. The couple was on the way to join them, having put the newly converted female wolf in the ground to heal. She was safe beneath their home, resting in the bed they shared when sleeping the rejuvenating sleep of the Carpathians.

"I heard a Lycan by the name of Vakasin and his partner, Fenris Dalka, killed him," Damon said. "It's written in the sacred book."

"Did the sacred book also include the information that when Vakasin returned to his pack, they turned on him and murdered him?" Zev asked.

"That's impossible," Damon denied. "They wouldn't do that."

"Oh but they did," Zev said. "Vakasin spent a couple of years tracking the *Sange rau*, fighting with him and sustaining terrible wounds. He needed blood and his partner, Fenris Dalka, provided that blood. When Fen was wounded just as badly, Vakasin gave him the blood needed to sustain his life."

"That's a common practice in a partnership," Damon said, clearly puzzled. "But it doesn't explain why Vakasin's own pack would turn on him after he spent a good portion of his life tracking down the infamous and nearly invincible *Sange rau*."

"Not unless Vakasin was Lycan and Fenris was Carpathian," Zev said in a low, carrying tone.

"Fenris Dalka is Lycan. His name is Lycan. He's been around the packs for years. I've heard of him, although I've never met him," Damon said.

"I came across the torn and dying bodies of men, women and children," Fen said from the shadows of his corner. "At the time, I was Fen Tirunul, not Dalka. It was a sickening sight. I thought I hunted the vampire. I was certain he was vampire, but he killed too many, left behind such devastation. Each time I caught up with him, he nearly killed me, and I was experienced with much skill. He was fast and enormously strong."

Damon whirled around, peering into the corner, trying to make out the man speaking.

"I came across Vakasin's tracks many times and saw where he fought and was wounded over and over. He was tracking the undead as I was, only it was no mere vampire. We joined forces, hoping to have a better chance of killing it."

"You? You're Fenris Dalka?" Damon demanded. "*The* Fenris Dalka?"

"The vampire we were hunting had used Lycans for his blood so much that eventually he became what you refer to as *Sange rau*, or bad blood. It is bad blood, not because a Lycan mixed blood with a Carpathian, but because he mixed blood with a vampire. Vampires are wholly evil. There is a big difference between the undead and a Carpathian."

Damon opened his mouth to reply, but Branislava and Tatijana returned with cups of coffee for Damon, Daciana and Makoce. Damon's gaze immediately jumped to Branislava's face as she handed him the hot mug.

"I have no idea if it's any good," she admitted. "It's the first cup of coffee I've ever actually made."

Tatijana handed a cup to Daciana. "Not the first, this is about the fifteenth, but we think this could actually be drinkable. We want the truth because we have to be able to make this for our guests."

"I'm sure it will be fine," Damon said, staring into Branislava's emerald eyes.

As usual, Branislava wore a long dress, looking very feminine, the material clinging to her breasts and emphasizing her waist and flared hips. A ribbon was woven into her long braid, and she moved gracefully to Zev's side, perching on the arm of his chair, drawing her legs up under her.

Zev immediately wrapped his arm around her waist and pulled her closer to him. His wolf was close to the surface, much closer than he would have liked. Damon was just too attentive to her, his interest far too evident. His wolf prowled and snarled and raked, demanding the freedom to rid the world of a rival.

Branislava leaned into him, her lips brushing his ear. *Hello, my little Wolfie. I've missed you.* She breathed the words into his ear, yet no sound emerged. He heard her only in his mind.

Warm air sent fingers of arousal dancing through his body. The tension in his wolf eased instantly to be replaced by amusement—and satisfaction. His wolf no longer wanted anything to do with Damon, but Branislava was in danger of him eating her up.

Daciana and Mokoce drank their coffee gratefully. Damon took a sip of his and nearly choked. He turned away from Branislava, desperate to keep from spitting the brew out on the verandah.

Branislava's soft laughter sounded intimate in Zev's mind. *He really shouldn't have come here to hurt the wolves, kill Dimitri and Skyler and upset you.*

Evil woman. His laughter joined hers. *I should have expected that you would exact some sort of revenge.* His laughter faded and he whipped his head around to look into her eyes. *You didn't poison him, did you?*

The temptation was there, not to kill him, just make him a little sick, but I resisted. Branislava sounded just a little regretful. She even glanced at Damon speculatively under the sweep of her long lashes, as if at any moment she might change her mind and lace his drink with one of the millions of spells she knew.

Zev wanted to be alone with her. He needed to be. How was he going to talk to her, let her get to know him? Give her the chance to fall in love with him? He was falling hard for her. It seemed that every time they had a moment alone, something happened to steal it away from them.

You're getting to know me, Branislava said. Her arm tightened around his neck and she brushed her lips against his ear, sending that warm air rushing like liquid lava through his bloodstream. *You know more about me than anyone else other than Tatijana. I'm beginning to know you as well, especially your wolf. I rather like him. He thinks like me.*

He never ever wants you to refer to him as Wolfie out loud. In Fen's presence especially. Or Dimitri's. Or Tatijana's and Skyler's, because I will never hear the end of it.

He had no idea why he didn't just object strenuously to her use of that name, but somehow when she whispered *Wolfie* so intimately into his mind in her soft, sexy voice . . . He sighed. He might already have tumbled right into loving her.

"Did you understand what Fen just told you, Damon?" Daciana demanded, pinning her brother with angry eyes. They were nearly golden, a clear sign that she was furious with him. "Carpathians can turn vampire just as we can turn rogue. There's a difference just as with us."

Damon carefully set the cup of coffee on the wide railing and leaned one hip against the stone. "I'm aware there is a difference between a Carpathian and a vampire."

"So use your head," Zev snapped. "When the sacred code was written, the *Sange rau* had slaughtered our people, completely decimated our ranks. It made sense to keep the women at home and out of harm's way. No one knew much about the demon who preyed on our people, and it was nearly impossible to kill, so they created the sacred code and it made sense to them."

Damon rubbed at his temples again, a frown creeping across his face.

Branka, look at him. Every time I mention anything to do with why he's here or the Sacred Circle or code, he gets a violent headache. I saw a small trickle of blood come from his nose earlier when he was trying to tell me who sent him here. He couldn't remember and became very confused.

Branislava sat up a little straighter, her attention centering on Damon. The wolf in Zev didn't like it, but he understood and it was far easier for Zev to control that dangerous streak of jealousy knowing why she was so focused on the Lycan.

"Damon?" Daciana prompted. "If you understand the difference between a Carpathian and a vampire, it isn't that big of a leap to understand the difference between the *Sange rau* and the *Hän ku pesäk kaikak*. The *Hän ku pesäk kaikak* translates to 'guardian of all,' which is what Dimitri is."

"And me," Fen said. "I hunted the *Sange rau* with Vakasin, and we shared blood when wounded. Vakasin became Carpathian and Lycan and I became Lycan and Carpathian. Neither of us were vampire or rogue. We were stronger, yes, and faster, and in the end that is what enabled us to defeat the *Sange rau.*"

Damon nodded his head several times but he pressed his fingers to his eyes. A fine sheen of sweat broke out on his face.

Out of the mist, Dimitri and Skyler came, walking hand in hand up the stone steps to the verandah. Dimitri looked—lethal. Zev couldn't blame him. Skyler had been targeted more than once by members of the Sacred Circle and they were relentless in the pursuit to kill her. Dimitri still bore the scars of the silver chains they'd wrapped him in from his forehead to his ankles.

Clearly, Dimitri gave off an aura of danger. Both Makoce and Daciana moved closer to Damon as if they might protect him from the *Hän ku pesäk kaikak.*

Dimitri ignored them and went straight to Branislava to drop a kiss on the top of her head. "Little sister, you were wonderful tonight. Thank you."

She touched him with gentle fingers in reply. Skyler exchanged a kiss on the cheek with Branislava and then Tatijana.

"I'm sorry we're late," Dimitri said. "We were attending the wound on the wolf." Again he didn't look at Damon, but his low tone carried easily and deliberately.

Damon ducked his head, shame creeping into his expression. "I'm sorry. There's nothing else I can say, other than I really mean it—I don't know what's happening to me."

"You're shadowed," Branislava said, her voice so low it was merely a thread of sound. "Mage-shadowed."

Tatijana's gasp was loud. She reached out to Fen, who took her hand instantly.

"I don't know what that means," Damon said.

Daciana and Makoce moved even closer to Damon, closing ranks on either side of him. "Please explain, Branislava," Daciana said. "None of us understand."

"He's showing all the signs. Look at him, Tatijana. He's confused when asked direct questions about who sent him here. If he tries too hard to remember he gets a severe headache. You do, don't you, Damon?" she asked.

He nodded. "The headache is so bad I can barely breathe, let alone think."

"When he pushes past the pain in an attempt to get answers to why he would go against his beliefs to murder a young woman or shoot and wound a wolf to use as bait, his brain reacts with an actual bleed. If you keep questioning him, trying to force him to remember, you'll kill him," Branislava stated with absolute conviction. "He is definitely mage-shadowed."

Tatijana nodded. "We've seen it many, many times."

There was a small silence. Fen whistled. Dimitri sank onto the porch swing, pulling Skyler with him. Daciana gripped her brother's arm and just held on tight.

Damon shook his head. "I don't know what that is, but there's nothing wrong with me except a nasty headache." He looked around at the somber faces. "There can't be."

His gaze dropped to his sister's face. "There isn't."

Daciana slipped her arm around him as if she could brace him. "What is it, Bronnie?"

"How do you get rid of it?" Damon asked. "There must be a way. I want it out of my head." He shuddered.

"Only a highly skilled mage can shadow a person without his consent or knowledge," Branislava said. "By that I mean someone of Xavier's caliber."

"Xavier's dead," Tatijana declared quickly. "There's no way he survived."

Fen wrapped both arms around her and pulled her close. "Obviously this couldn't be Xavier, my lady," he assured softly. "Whoever has done this infiltrated the ranks of the Lycans long ago or Damon would have noticed a stranger immediately. Lycans don't bring outsiders into their meetings."

"You were there, you infiltrated," Damon accused, as if he suspected Fen of corrupting his mind.

"I am Lycan," Fen said calmly. "I have Lycan blood just as you do. I am loyal to our people just as I am loyal to Carpathians. You might say, Damon, I have dual citizenship."

Damon rubbed his face hard. "I don't understand any of this."

"What can we do about it?" Daciana asked. "Can you help him?"

"It can be undone," Branislava said slowly. "Although it is risky. This mage has actually placed the shadow on his brain like a deep wound that has scarred over. I don't know how to explain this. It isn't the same as placing a sliver of himself into the person to possess that person at will. That can also be referred to as shadowing, although that's not an accurate term."

"Is it possible the mage is doing this to others?" Zev asked.

"Of course," Branislava answered.

Zev didn't think she was even aware of the slight trembling of her body. On the outside, she presented a cool, confident demeanor, but inside, he felt her fear, just like the terror that gripped Tatijana. The idea that Xavier or a mage as powerful as he was could possibly be behind the attacks was frightening to them.

"Could a mage mass-produce shadows, say, at a Sacred Circle meeting?" Zev asked as he threaded his fingers through hers and pulled her hand to his chest, over his heart.

Branislava and Tatijana frowned as they looked at each other. Tatijana appeared more agitated than Zev had ever seen her. Fen cuddled her close, clearly reassuring her.

"It isn't Xavier, Tatijana," Branislava said aloud. "Fen's right. Whoever did this has been slowly trying to gain control of the Lycans, just as Xavier wanted control of the Carpathians. Mages are not immortal, but some of them want to be."

"Neither are Lycans," Zev said.

"Technically, neither are Carpathians," Dimitri said. "We can be killed."

"But both species have longevity," Branislava said. "Much longer than a mage. Xavier wanted that for himself. It was the entire reason he kidnapped our mother and had us. He wanted our blood."

"You don't know if it's Xavier," Tatijana said. She looked close to tears. "You don't know. Who else if not him?"

Branislava took a deep breath. "If Damon allows me, I can try to find the shadowing. I would recognize Xavier's work anywhere."

Tatijana shook her head adamantly.

"Sister," Branislava said gently. "You know it is the only way for us to know for certain."

"No. Not you. Zev, don't let her. Skyler, Dimitri, you can't let her," Tatijana pleaded.

Damon dropped his face into his hands and sank down onto the stone floor, moaning. "I want it out of my head. Get it out."

Daciana and Makoce immediately dropped down beside him to comfort him, although Zev noticed that both kept at least one hand close to their weapons—the silver ones. They believed that he could be dangerous to them all.

"You didn't answer my question," Zev persisted. "Could a mage mass-produce this effect without anyone knowing?"

Branislava let out her breath. "Only a couple might be able to. Two. Maybe three. We were prisoners for centuries, Zev, and Xavier only had a couple of students who might have been that good . . ." She trailed off, her gaze once more jumping to Tatijana's face.

What is it, Branka?

She pressed her lips together as if by not speaking whatever she had thought of wouldn't be the truth. Her fingers curled involuntarily into his shirt, nails raking through the material.

"Get it out of me. Get it out of me," Damon yelled, his wolf surging to the surface, eyes glowing as he glared at Branislava.

Zev could see both Daciana and Makoce brace themselves to protect his woman, and he was grateful. "Damon," he spoke in a low, commanding tone. "You are a wolf. A Lycan. You're strong and you will not embarrass our people by this display."

Damon sucked in his breath and began to pant. Clearly his wolf fought for supremacy but he was at least fighting to control the shift.

"Man up and control your fear. Your wolf senses it and is rising to protect you. Get control right now." Zev's voice took on even more authority.

Damon nodded his head several times, continuing to breathe deep. He looked ashamed and a little guilty, but mostly desperate to do as the alpha commanded.

Zev gentled his tone. "All of these people are committed to help you in spite of your intention to kill them. *I'm* committed to helping you. You know me. I've never let a member of my pack down, and you've always been that to me. Family."

Damon looked up quickly, and this time determination was in his eyes, the red glow receding a bit.

"Take a look at the two women you're demanding things of when you don't have an idea what it even entails. They're terrified. Either could leave, but they haven't. They're right here with you. Pull yourself together and we'll get through this. We just need a little time to sort things out."

How dangerous is it to you, Branka, and I expect the truth, to go in and take a look around at his brain to see if you can pinpoint where this shadow is and perhaps who actually made it.

Branislava hesitated. She leaned close to him and in front of the others rubbed her face along his cheek. She seemed close to tears, although not on the outside. She was stoic, presenting a calm appearance to the others. He knew most of her performance was for Tatijana's sake.

This mage is highly skilled. If he really has the power and expertize to place shadows in a roomful of unsuspecting people, he is extraordinarily dangerous. He will have safeguards.

Then we'll talk to Mikhail . . .

Branislava shook her head. *Not yet. We know all of Xavier's spells. Every last one of them, good and evil. We would have a better chance of removing the shadow than Gregori, who would most likely try.*

Gregori has removed shadows, Dimitri assured.

Branislava sighed. *He confronted and removed a sliver of a being, which is not the same. A shadow is a portal, not part of the mage. It is different, Dimitri, and rigged with traps.*

"I apologize once again," Damon said. "I don't know what came over me."

"Probably the thought of someone else having the ability to manipulate your movements and override the beliefs so ingrained in you," Daciana replied.

"I could still hurt someone, couldn't I?" Damon asked.

Zev shrugged, not wanting to lie, but Damon needed encouragement. "Whoever this mage is that planted that shadow in you, Damon, didn't count on your strength. You didn't follow his dictates. You're much stronger than you know."

Damon managed a brief half smile. "I didn't think of that."

"You're armed to the teeth right now," Zev pointed out. "Even through all the revelations, you didn't go for your weapons."

He not only wanted to encourage Damon, but also remind Daciana and Makoce that the Lycan was well armed. Zev was fairly certain the Carpathians were well aware of the weapons and by now knew exactly where, on Damon's body, each was located.

If I go in and just take a look around, without touching anything, or attempting to remove the shadow, Branislava ventured, *I think I'll be safe enough.*

Thinking isn't good enough for me, Zev declared. *I'm not willing to risk you.*

He'll die. Sooner or later the mage will return to his shadow and realize that Damon is not acting as he should—as one of his agents. He'll kill him, or force him to do his bidding. Either way, Damon will die.

Zev pressed her hand closer. *We'll find another way to save him.*

While I've sat here with you, you've gone over and over in your mind fifty ways to get to him and kill him if he makes one wrong move. I'm not even certain you know you're doing it, Branislava told him gently. *I feel your deep affection for Damon, Zev, and you'll never get over it if you or Daciana has to kill him. But you would kill him. I know you would.*

Zev sighed. Branislava was right. He didn't want Daciana to have to slay her own brother, not even in defense of all of them. She might hesitate, in which case, Damon, under the mage's direction, might very well kill his own sister. Zev, as pack leader, had that duty, not Daciana.

"Branislava wants to take a look at the shadow. She won't remove it, not yet. She is just going in to look, Damon. Without knowing what or who we're dealing with, she doesn't have a chance of removing it. Do you understand? You can't fight her. You can't move or endanger her in any way. If you do, I will put a stake through your heart. If you prefer, we will shelve this and seek guidance from the council."

Bronnie, what are you doing? Tatijana asked. *You know how dangerous a mage-shadow is. What are you thinking? A mage can use the shadow to spy. He can force the body he's in to do anything he wants. You can't reveal yourself to him.*

Do you really want to go the rest of our lives without knowing who has committed such an abomination? I know I don't. Even if Gregori tries to remove the shadow, he won't recognize the maker. Only you or I can do that.

Tatijana pressed her fingers to her eyes and then turned her face into Fen's chest. *You're going to do this, aren't you, Bronnie?*

You know I have to. I'm just as frightened as you that it's him. But we can't be running scared the rest of our lives. We have to know.

What if it's . . .

Don't think that. He's dead, too. All of them are. This has to be one of the students.

Zev took a deep breath and let it out. Branislava was terrified. Surrounded by Fen, Dimitri and him, she was still terrified. He didn't want her to take this chance. He wasn't certain what the danger actually was, or how he could help her.

"Fen, this is so far out of my territory," he said. "Tell me what to do to make certain she's safe." Because Branislava was going to go inside Damon's head and find the shadow on his brain. Zev felt her absolute determination. She needed to know who had put that mark on him. Truthfully, all of them needed to know, but he would much rather be the one to take the chance.

"Mine as well. I know very little about mage marking and shadows. Razvan would certainly know more, but Tatijana and Branislava were there with Xavier for centuries, seeing everything he did. We'll have to trust Bronnie that she knows what she's doing."

Damon pushed both hands through his hair. He lifted his head and looked straight into Branislava's eyes. "I want this thing out of my head more than anything, but not at the risk of your life. It sounds like just looking at it might be dangerous."

She shook her head. "If I don't draw the mage's attention by tripping his safeguard, I'll be perfectly safe. I intend to be very careful. I've seen this done several times. It's a matter of having patience. I learned that particular quality in the ice caves enduring my captivity."

"What do you need me to do?" Damon asked.

"Have patience, too. Just sit there and let me see if I can do this. It may take a couple of tries."

She looked at Zev, and his heart turned over. *I'm really scared, Zev. If I trip that safeguard, he'll know we're on to him. He can strike at all of us through Damon.*

I can take care of Damon. You just need to be safe.

Branislava threaded her fingers together at the nape of Zev's neck and stared into his eyes. He looked back just as steadily, willing her to know that he wouldn't let her down, that he would be with her every step of the way.

"You're a very strong man." She smiled at him. *Wolfie.*

He managed an answering grin. Branislava turned to face Damon, sinking gracefully onto the stone floor to one side of Zev's feet, giving him plenty of room to move if needed. There was no point in wasting any more time, but she needed a moment to steady herself.

She looked out into the forest. The mist covered the trees like a gray blanket. She felt the tiny droplets on her skin. The wind teased her hair and kissed her face. *This is freedom, Tatijana,* she whispered to her sister.

She closed her eyes and let go of her body, trusting Tatijana and Fen to watch over her as she made this journey. Zev had to watch Damon. Traveling as spirit only, she moved slowly into Damon's open mind. He was just as terrified as she was, but for different reasons. She couldn't blame him—realizing someone else had infiltrated his brain and directed his movements had to be abhorrent to him. Once inside his skull, she stayed very quiet, unmoving, keeping her light as dim as possible to keep from tripping any safeguard. Spirit traveled as light, moving easily where a body couldn't go, but the High Mage knew that and had always prepared for such an invasion when he placed his shadow in someone.

When she was absolutely certain her light was as dim as possible she began to move around Damon's brain to find the shadow.

"She's not breathing," Makoce said anxiously.

Zev felt his own heart accelerate. Panic began to rise in spite of his determination to allow Branislava to ferret out the name of their enemy. Her body had slumped to one side, and Makoce was correct. Zev couldn't detect a breathing pattern. He looked to Tatijana for reassurance.

Tatijana's face was stark white. Her eyes glittered like two huge gems, and color banded through her hair.

"Tatijana?" he said softly, insistently.

Tatijana's body jerked as if she suffered a blow. Her gaze jumped to Zev's face. She hunched her body, pressing closer to Fen. "She's alive," she said softly. "She's making certain she doesn't trip a safeguard."

Zev resisted the urge to merge with Branislava, knowing he couldn't distract her, but the need was strong in him, his every protective instinct rebelling.

Branislava drifted closer to the brain, studying it carefully. The brain was large, barely fitting inside the skull, with several folds. At first the surface appeared wrinkled with hills and valleys everywhere. The individual cells, neurons, were connected very closely, almost too closely for her microscopic study to actually see where the shadow might be located. The neurons were necessary for information to travel through, chemicals signals entering the cell and then traveling through the filament to carry out orders. The mage had to have burned his shadow into the millions of cells living outside the brain.

Her spirit continued to move carefully. Her light was indistinct, making it difficult to see the ridges and valleys. Up close, the brain appeared quite gray when she inspected the densely packed cells, but the filaments, so closely bundled together appeared white. Mapping out his brain took time. There were millions of cells and the mage-shadow could be on any of them.

She had no idea of time passing, only that using such a faint light made her work extremely difficult. Fear was ever present. Xavier had been invincible, a man who tortured and killed hundreds of people from every species. No one, in all those long centuries had come to rescue them. No one had ever managed to defeat him, and it was difficult to think that anyone ever could after so much time had passed.

Evil endured. She knew it did, and Xavier was wholly evil. If anyone could ever find a way to come back from the dead . . . She couldn't go there, couldn't think like that. In any case, Fen was right, he couldn't be in two places at one time. But that meant . . .

She found it. The shadow was wedged in a valley, the mark a vicious swipe of black that ran partially up a ridge. Everything in her stilled. She was disconnected from her body, but that didn't stop the sensation of shock and horror from rushing through her. She recognized the mark. She'd seen it a hundred times. She knew who made it.

Branislava found herself back in her own body swaying with weakness. She pushed herself up and rushed off the verandah into the cool forest, into the miracle of clean, purified air. She kept running, her footfalls silent on the thick carpet of vegetation. Time passed, and she realized she wasn't alone. Zev paced beside her, not speaking, not asking questions, just allowing her to run for her life. Run for her freedom. Just run.

She stopped abruptly and with a small sob, threw herself into his arms. There was safety there. Goodness. Zev might have to kill, but he regretted having to do so. She couldn't detect evil in any part of him.

Just the sight of that lesion in Damon's brain—that portal for evil with the distinctive signature—was terrifying to her. Pure evil had a way of insidiously trickling into lives and taking hold or wrenching the life away from a good individual and forcing obedience. Shadowing was such an abomination, removing free will.

She shuddered and Zev pulled her closer, held her tighter, pressing her face into his shoulder while tremors wracked her body. She inhaled the clean masculine scent of him and took solace in his integrity and compassion. Zev was an alpha male, at the very top of a predatory food chain and yet he didn't abuse his power. Never once had he tried to take away her freedom. He worried about her, but he didn't cage her.

Branislava brushed her mouth over his throat and burrowed even closer, grateful he didn't ask questions of her. She wasn't certain she could even speak. Her heart had accelerated to the point that she feared it would pound right through her chest. Her breath came in ragged, gasping staccato bursts, her lungs raw and aching.

Zev stroked caresses down the back of her head, soothing her in silence, breathing evenly, allowing her to follow his breath, his heart, at her own pace. She closed her eyes and let herself relax into him, allowed herself to be safe in his arms. The moment she did, her heart automatically began to adjust to the slower, steadier beat of his. Her breathing evened out, following that calm, composed rhythm of his.

Bronnie. Tatijana reached out to her. *Are you all right?*

Give me a minute. I need just a minute. Make my excuses for me.

She needed Zev. She needed the comfort of his arms and his unfailing cool, the composed commander she could count on. He could take charge and think through every battle, every crisis. And this was a crisis.

She lifted her head to look at him, to look into his eyes, searching, she knew, for reassurance. It was there, his wolf's eyes meeting hers steadily. He waited, not asking questions or forcing her to speak, just as she knew he would.

She locked both arms around his neck and went up on her toes as she pulled his head down to hers. He didn't hesitate or ask her what she was doing.

Zev's lips brushed across hers and a million butterflies took wing in her stomach. She hadn't expected that reaction, but it was a welcome distraction from the panic gripping her. She closed her eyes, her lashes fluttering for just a moment as his mouth coaxed hers, with little kisses, his tongue running along the seam.

His gentleness brought tears burning behind her eyes. In all those years, trapped in the body of a fire dragon, freezing in an ice-cold world, she had never once imagined having a man treat her with such respect or love. It was a gift. Wondrous. She opened her mouth, and the world stood still.

He kissed her with absolute confidence and command, sweeping her with him into another realm altogether, pushing away fear and replacing it with something else unexpected. Tenderness.

Fiery heat welled up from her center, surged through her body, and rushed through her veins. She had tamped down the fire in her for what seemed like ages, until the fire dance with Zev. He seemed to "get" her. To know who she was inside. He wanted her to be herself, and kissing him was like taking her first real breath. Knowing she was truly alive. His mouth was a haven to be lost in. Fire consumed her, reducing her to ashes, allowing her to rise like the phoenix reborn.

He tasted exotic and wild, a feral, untamed wolf, bent on devouring her. Bent on loving her. She felt surrounded by love when she'd never thought to know that emotion between a man and a woman.

There was desire. Lust even. Zev was a man of strong appetites, but the strongest emotion, the strongest connection was love. She tasted it in his kiss. Felt it in the way he held her. She let go of those last fears of imprisonment and gave herself up to him. She gave herself up to the fire roaring through her body, the flames dancing higher and higher, fanned by her lifemate.

When he lifted his head and rested his forehead against hers so they could both catch their breath, she stared into his nearly glowing, mercurial silver eyes. The eyes of the wolf.

"Claim me, Zev. Right here. Right now. Bind us together," she whispered, needing him desperately. She wanted him, yes, but right then, knowing what and who they faced, she wanted to be a part of him. She wanted their souls to be one. "Claim me."

8

Zev took a deep breath and tried to think past the sudden roaring in his head. She was offering him her life. Her loyalty. Pledging her love. She was everything he wanted and she was gifting herself to him.

He rubbed her arms soothingly, wanting to do the right thing by her. His every instinct was to claim her fast, to bind her soul to his so that there was no escaping and no way for any other to tear them apart, but that felt too much like imprisoning her. Without the ability to undo the bind, in the end, once she was no longer so terrified, would she still want him? Or would she become resentful?

"Branka, you're very afraid. Whatever you found put you in a panic. I want you more than anything. I want us to be lifemates, but more, because there is a huge part of me that will always be Lycan, I want you to love me and choose me for yourself. You haven't had time to even get to know me. We're in the middle of a war, and each time I think we have the time for you to be alone with me, so we can talk things out, we're interrupted."

"Silly wolf." Branislava stroked his face with her fingertips. "I don't need words to get to know you. I have your actions to tell me who you are. I would never make such a decision lightly. I will have to face my worst fears, the demon of nightmares, and when I do, I want to be connected to you, because of your strength and determination. You're a man who suffered a wound no other would have survived. Do you know why you survived? It wasn't all of us who worked to save you. It was your own determination because you were protecting me. That's the truth, Zev. You saved yourself against impossible odds."

"I want you to be very, very certain. The ancients flooded me with all kinds of information, history and culture. The truth is, in the back of my head, I probably knew it all, I just had to have them point the way to access those long-ago memories imprinted on me when I was born. I know once I bind you to me, there's no going back. No escape." He forced himself to use that word so she would hear it.

Branislava nodded. "I see what you fear, but I am Dragonseeker, above all else, I am of that bloodline. I know what I am doing and I assume responsibility for my decisions. We are intensely loyal, just as you are. My soul cries out to yours. My mind seeks yours. My body burns for yours. But Zev, if you believe nothing else, believe that my heart belongs to you alone. There is no going back for me. I made that choice when I wove our spirits together. I made that choice when I stayed with you in the ground and when I returned to you when you asked me in the cave of warriors. I made that choice when I fought beside you and I am making the choice now when I ask you to bind me to you. I love you and want to be with you."

Zev felt a curious melting sensation in the region of his heart. The tight knots he hadn't even known existed in his belly unraveled. Branislava was a grown woman and she spoke her mind. He couldn't find hesitation in her mind at all. There was only resolve—and love. He felt surrounded by it and the wolf in him sang with happiness. The Carpathian felt that age-old need, that bond of blood that connected his people for centuries from ancient to modern times. He needed to bind his lifemate to him.

The words came from his soul, not just his heart. "*Te avio päläfertiilam.*" He used the ancient words of his ancestors, the sacred language imprinted on him from birth, carried in the bloodline of both Dark Blood and the house of Tirunul. "You are my lifemate. *Éntölam kuulua, avio päläfertiilam.* I claim you as my lifemate."

Somehow in uttering the words, he actually felt as if thousands of strands of silk began to weave them together soul to soul. He wrapped his arms around her tightly, holding her to him, willing her to feel the same wonder and joy that filled him.

"*Ted kuuluak, kacad, kojed.* I belong to you."

She kissed his chin. "*Ted kuuluak, kacad, kojed.* I belong to you, Zev, now and for all eternity."

"*Élidamet andam.* I offer my life for you."

"I offer my life for you," she repeated, looking into his eyes.

His heart gave a small stutter. "*Pesämet andam.* I give you my protection. *Uskolfertiilamet andam.* I give you my allegiance. *Sívamet andam.* I give you my heart. *Sielamet andam.* I give you my soul. *Ainamet andam.* I give you my body. *Sívamet kuuluak kaik että a ted.* I take into my keeping the same that is yours."

Branislava pressed kisses along the underside of his jaw and down his throat, murmuring the ritual binding words back to him, her voice soft, but firm. Zev felt love bursting through him, an overwhelming, perfect emotion completely tied to her. He knew what it meant to belong, and he was grateful he belonged to her.

"*Ainaak olenszal sívambin.* Your life will be cherished by me for all my time." He knew what the word *cherish* meant. He'd never cherished anything in his long life until Branislava had come along. Whatever they faced, however bad, he wanted this time with her, and he vowed to make every minute count, to make her feel valued as the treasure she was.

"*Te élidet ainaak pide minan.* Your life will be placed above my own for all time." He found that as he uttered each declaration, he felt the bond between them growing stronger.

Zev closed his fist in her hair and pulled her head up to his. Her lips parted. Those perfect lips he'd spent a lifetime dreaming about. He lowered his head to hers, his mouth claiming her even as his soul claimed her.

Te avio päläfertiilam. You are my lifemate. He kissed her over and over, devouring her molten fire, feeling an answering firestorm building in his body.

His mouth drifted down her chin, lower, down her throat to the soft swell of her breasts beneath the thin material of her dress. His teeth scraped gently, persistently back and forth over that pulse calling to him.

Ainaak sívamet jutta oleny. You are bound to me for all eternity.

His teeth sank deep and she arched against him, crying out. She buried her hands in his hair, clasping his head as he drank from her very essence. There was that addictive taste. Her honeyed cinnamon bursting through him, yet this time, there was heat, as if deep inside that smoldering fire was building, waiting for him to ignite a firestorm of passion.

Ainaak terád vigyázak. You are always in my care.

Zev swept his tongue across that sweet swell of her breast and lifted his head. He knew his face and eyes bore the stamp of a predator, but he hoped she could see—and feel—the love in him. His body raged at him. He wanted her with every single cell. That was there for her to read as well. He didn't bother to attempt to hide the way he wanted her.

He was a rough man, demanding, and he wanted her in every way he could conceive, but he hoped she would always feel safe with him, that she would know he would put her pleasure above his own first.

Branislava smiled at him and slowly unbuttoned his shirt, running her hands over his bare chest. A tremor went through his body. She leaned forward and licked along his heavy muscle, swirling her tongue over his flat nipple before nipping at his skin with her teeth.

His cock jumped and thickened beyond anything he believed possible, stretching the material of his trousers. His hands dropped to the buttons to ease them open, desperate for relief. The material was far too painful. He figured the night air might help to ease the urgency of his need, but the moment he released that heavy erection, he felt as if he'd opened the cage of a raging monster.

The small droplets of mist touching his sensitive skin only added to the pleasure building in his body. Branislava dropped one hand down to stroke a caress over his shaft and then slide her thumb across the large head, before closing her fingers around him. At the same time, her teeth drove deep.

The sensation was almost too much. Pleasure ripped through him, bordering on pain it was so finite and exquisite. He felt the wolf rising, a howl of pure bliss as she took his blood into her. He needed to feel her skin beneath his hands, all that soft silky skin.

Get rid of your clothes, he whispered into her mind, half command, half entreaty.

Before the thought had completely pushed from his mind to hers, the long flowing dress was gone and she was naked against him. He found he liked the feel of her bare while he was nearly fully clothed. They were deep in the forest, the mist surrounding them, enclosing them in a blanket of privacy, and Branislava stood completely naked feeding from him, offering her body to him.

Zev ran his hands down the smooth line of her back to her buttocks. She felt firm and strong as he gripped tight, massaging her firm cheeks and the sensitive bundles of nerves hidden beneath that flesh, half lifting her against him. He didn't want to wait. He wanted her right there. Right then. He felt as if he'd waited centuries for his woman and he knew nothing he could imagine would match the red-hot fire in her body.

Branislava flicked her tongue across the small wound on Zev's chest. His body was hot, burning as if he had a fever. His hands on her buttocks were rough and demanding, sending a little thrill through her. She hadn't thought that such a dominating lover would appeal to her, but she found a secret excitement in the way he touched her.

She liked that he felt possessive of her. That he took their vows to heart. Her body did belong to him and she wanted to please him with it. She wanted him to enjoy her. It mattered to her that she brought him every kind of pleasure she could. In return, she trusted he would do the same for her.

His hand moved between her thighs, forcing her legs open. She looked down, and deep inside she gave a little gasp of shock. She hadn't considered that he would be so large, but he was a big man and a wolf—she should have known. More, his hands looked huge as he ran them up her leg, near her center.

Her heart gave a wild lurch and tiny flames of arousal danced up her thighs in his wake. She closed her eyes when his hand covered her mound. She could feel hot, damp liquid seeping onto his palm.

"Look at me." It was a command, nothing less.

She lifted her lashes, her gaze jumping to his. Again her heart gave the same stutter and more liquid fire leaked into his palm. Her pulse pounded and her breasts ached. Her stomach tightened with coiling tension.

He lifted his palm to his mouth and licked at the cinnamon honey. "You taste delicious. Just like I knew you would. I want to eat you up, *mon chaton féroce*. Every drop is mine and I want it all."

Her knees almost gave out. His face was stamped with a driving lust, a hard possession that only thrilled her more. He wrapped her in love, she felt that as well, but right now, this moment, she wanted the wolf, the wild, untamed wolf that looked at her just as Zev was doing. Glowing eyes, a fierce expression on his face. Domination in every line on his face and on his body.

There was something almost illicit about being naked there in the forest while he was clothed. She tried to keep her eyes on his, tried to keep her gaze from straying to his very hard erection, but it was difficult, a lesson in discipline.

"Do you understand what I want to do to you?" he asked, his voice low and so sexy she shivered with excitement. "What I'm going to do to you?"

"Yes," she admitted, her voice not her own. Truthfully, she wasn't all that certain of what he meant, but it didn't matter. She was willing. Her body burned for his. "But, Zev, I have to be honest with you. I tried to do a crash course in how to please a man once I met you, but the information I have might not be very reliable. I looked it up on the Internet and it was all a little confusing. Diagrams and anatomy, which I understood but wasn't certain how to implement."

His eyes glowed at her, darkened with desire, and his slow, sexy smile was definitely wolfish. "You don't need a crash course, Branka. I prefer to be your teacher. I want to teach you the things that will please me. I am looking forward to discovering the things you enjoy."

As he spoke his large hands cupped her breasts. "You have such beautiful breasts." His finger traced the ridged scar riding up one creamy slope. He bent his head to trail his tongue along that path. "Everything about you is beautiful, *mon chaton féroce*."

His unblinking gaze stayed on her face, watching her reaction as he captured her nipples between his fingers, rolling and tugging until she could barely catch her breath. Her nipples seemed directly connected to her most intimate core, electrical shocks streaking through to her very center. He leaned down, still watching her face and sucked her right breast into the heat of his mouth.

She heard herself moan. A flash-fire ignited in her breasts, fueled by his hands and mouth, flames leaping into her belly, burning hot and wild. Zev switched to her left breast, using the edge of his teeth. The small flash of pain added to her heightened pleasure, to the madness rolling through her body. She couldn't believe how much the scrape of his teeth and the stroke of his tongue combined with the heat of his mouth to drive her insane with need.

Her body definitely belonged to him. His hands moved possessively down her rib cage to her waist, his mouth following. Every muscle in her body melted under the blaze he created. She feared she wouldn't be able to stand when he dropped to his knees in front of her. She rested one hand on his shoulder, needing the support, her body shaking with need.

The mist around them began to glow a strange golden red. Her body was hot—everywhere. Her hair gave off sparks, crackling with fire, the red deep and true. Streaks of gold leapt like flames dancing out of control through the silken mass of her braid.

His hands felt rough on her skin, a contrast to her own smooth skin. His expression, when she looked down at him, had gone feral, his wolf's eyes hungry and focused, making her heart pump wildly and the tension in her feminine core coil tighter.

He swiped his tongue through her folds and she cried out, her hand going to his hair, fisting there as sensations poured through her body like fuel on a fire. She wasn't certain either of them would survive the conflagration building in her like a volcano.

He began to lap at her like the hungry wolf he was, stealing every bit of cinnamon honey he could pull from her body. His hands were hard, holding her thighs apart, holding her hips still as he indulged his whim of devouring her. Her cries rose to a crescendo, but he didn't stop. Her fist yanked at his hair, but his mouth was merciless. The fire built and built, raged and roared, but he refused to stop, taking her to the edge of some dark precipice, but never quite letting her fall over.

When she was certain she would go mad with need, when her pleas rang through the glowing mist, he took her to the soft grass, his clothes gone. He looked absolutely intimidating kneeling over her. She could barely breathe, barely think, her head tossing back and forth, her hips writhing and bucking.

He stroked her center with one long finger. Her body arched, her mouth opening in a silent scream. "I love how responsive you are, but hold still. I don't want to lose all control until I know you're ready for me."

She was ready? Was he crazy? How much readier could she get? If he didn't do something soon she was going to spontaneously combust.

This time he stroked a finger inside of her, sinking deep while her muscles clamped around him tightly. His breath hissed out. "So hot. That's right, *mon chaton féroce*. Burn for me."

How could she not? Only he could put out the fire he'd started and he wasn't cooperating. A small sobbing gasp escaped as a second finger sank with the first, stretching her. Again the bite of pain added to the electrical charges streaking through her bloodstream, finding every bundle of nerves in her body and igniting them.

She whimpered when he removed his fingers, but a heartbeat later, they were back . . . Not his fingers this time. Her heart pounded as he began to push inside of her. He held her legs straight up into the air, kneeling between her thighs so her legs were spread wide, to more easily accommodate his invasion. He was unyielding as he entered her, not slowing, but a patient steady pressure, forcing her body to accept his. Her muscles fought him, but gave way as he continued that ceaseless forward pressure until he lodged against a barrier.

Zev gasped. Swore. "You're so damned tight and hot." He managed to get the words out between clenched teeth. He had to fight to keep from losing control. He needed another minute and she *had* to stay still. Her sheath was heaven, fiery silk, alive and scorching hot, surrounding him, gripping him tightly and stealing all discipline. He didn't want to hurt her and ruin this moment for both of them.

Branislava was senseless, writhing under him, trying to force him into her, her body desperate for his. He brought his hand down hard on her buttocks. Her eyes flew open, her gaze widening. Around his cock, hot liquid spilled out, enfolding him. Her nerve endings were wired for pleasure and everything he did seemed to add to it.

"Hold still," he snarled, baring his teeth at her in warning.

She gasped and tried to obey. He didn't wait for her to lose control again, he surged forward, driving deep, claiming her body for himself. He was a large man and he knew it would take her body a little bit of time and effort to fully accommodate him. He lodged against her womb, watching her for signs of discomfort.

Branislava's eyes pleaded with him as her head tossed back and forth. Yanking her legs over his shoulders, spreading her even wider, he let his wolf loose. He began to surge into her, thrusting hard, over and over, setting a relentless, merciless rhythm. Each stroke sent flames burning hotter, her sheath winding tighter, or maybe his cock swelled even more, but the friction bordered on ecstasy.

He wanted more, always more, driving deeper, until at times he feared he might lodge in her stomach, but the pleasure engulfed him, wrapping him in her fire. He had known all along she would be like this, hot and wild, her passion a match for his. He was rough with her, and she answered with pleas for more, wanting, like him, to burn in that inferno.

Around them, spreading out from beneath her, the ground began to glow as if their wild joining drew the magma deep from beneath the earth itself. Tiny tongues of red and gold licked at the grass surrounding them, but he couldn't have stopped if his life depended on it. His breathing became harsh, and his lungs burned for air. The cooling mist settled over his body like a thousand tongues as around him the world seemed to erupt into flames.

He felt his body swell, lock into hers, holding her while she gripped him with scorching tight muscles. Somewhere in his toes, it started, that fireball of sheer bliss, rising like a firestorm, crashing through his body, overtaking him before he could catch his breath.

He let his head fall back as she milked him, drawing his seed out in long, rocketing spurts while her orgasm roared through her, tearing through her core in vicious waves that ripped through her stomach to her breasts.

He felt every strong convulsion of the rippling walls around his cock, the waves of fire engulfing her, consuming him, burning them both clean. She lay, panting, staring up at him with shocked, emerald eyes, the sparks in her hair subsiding. He watched her with those same hungry eyes, holding her body locked to his, refusing to let her go yet.

She made no move to try to roll away from him, but lay there, her legs over his shoulder, her breasts heaving, the combined scent of them permeating the air. She was the most beautiful thing he'd ever seen in his life. Her eyes were just a little dazed, her lips parted and her body flushed with a soft glow, much like the surrounding mist.

"Do you know what you are?" he asked.

She shook her head, still fighting for her breath.

He loved the way her breasts rose and fell with her struggle. "Perfect. You're perfect. There could be no other woman for me. Only you. I don't think you ever have to worry about satisfying my appetites."

She reached out to touch the small inch of his heated flesh where they joined, the only part of him that wasn't still inside of her. "I want to please you, Zev." Her fingers danced over his hard, velvety shaft, almost reverently.

Just her gentle touch set his cock jerking in anticipation. "Have no doubts that you do . . . and you will. I'm a man who will always let you know, firmly, what I want or need. I'll expect the same from you. If you're ever afraid of anything I ask you to do, just tell me and we'll work it out. Don't just say no and refuse me. That's important to me, Branka. I want you to trust me enough to talk to me about anything that frightens you."

"I didn't know fear could be so sexy," she whispered. "The not knowing added to the excitement."

"And you, woman, are as hot as hell. Or heaven. Is heaven hot?" He flashed her a grin. "Even the mist glowed for us."

Branislava looked around her as the colors in the mist began to fade. "That might be a cool effect, but honestly, do we want the neighbors knowing every time we make love?"

Zev laughed. "We nearly burned down the forest. We might be banned from the neighborhood."

Very gently, he rubbed her calf and then her thigh, his fingers moving up to massage her buttocks before he placed her foot back on the ground. He did the same with the other. His gaze moved over her body, and his smile faded to a frown. "Did I hurt you, Branka?"

"No, of course not. If you hurt me, you'd be fried in a few places that really matter to you. I'm a woman who believes in retaliation, remember?"

He leaned forward and another aftershock sent her tight muscles strangling his cock, so that his breath caught in his lungs. He placed both hands on her flat belly, fingers splayed wide to take in as much skin as he could.

"I love that little trait in you."

Her green eyes smoldered with her hidden fire. She still burned hot and it was difficult for her to conceal her true self behind her cool façade. He loved that quality in her as well, all that fire contained in her slender body just waiting for the right moment to ignite.

His body slowly began to relax and he allowed himself to slip from inside of her, that secret haven he would always be addicted to. Sitting back, he let his gaze drift possessively over her. Surrounded by the mist and trees, they remained quiet together, just the two of them, carving out a small moment for themselves there in the night.

Branislava was the first to move. She knew Zev would never hurry her, or push her to return to the others and face whatever horror she had discovered that had sent her running into the night. She used his shoulder to draw herself up beside him. Immediately he wrapped his arm around her hips, holding her to him.

Her heart gave a little lurch and began to beat faster. It surprised her that Zev could do that to her—that anyone could. The moment he touched her, her body reacted with need and hunger. She hadn't known just how intense physical attraction could be until he had come into her life. Her wolf. She looked down into his eyes and again her heart stuttered.

He focused wholly on her, a predator targeting his prey, looking as if he might devour her all over again.

"I've got to clean myself up," she said softly, regretfully. She enjoyed standing there, his seed running down her thighs while his hands massaged her buttocks.

"I like you just the way you are," he objected.

She laughed. "You would, but I think we should behave ourselves and go back to our guests. They are, after all, sitting on our verandah wondering what happened to us."

"We lit up for the forest. I doubt they can't figure it out."

Color and heat infused her body but she shrugged delicately. "Still, we have company."

"You're always going to insist I be civilized, aren't you?" His fingers stole up her thighs, taking her breath.

Branislava's fingers anchored in his thick hair. He leaned into her and bit her left buttock and then her outer thigh, making her yelp, flooding her body once more with hot, welcoming liquid. As his teeth teased her, his fingers moved inside of her, pressing deep, exploring her heat all over again.

She was already so sensitive just that intrusion sent her body reeling again. She gasped, air exploding out of her lungs, her mind melting as he found the small spot that made her crazy with need.

"What are you doing? We have a duty . . ."

"Your only duty is to please me," he murmured. "Straddle me."

She shook her head, but complied, placing one foot on either side of his legs. He caught her hips and urged her down right over the top of him, so that she was crouched just above his lap. Her eyes stared into his.

"That's my duty? To please you?" she echoed, amusement warring with her rising sensuality. She loved the feel of his hands, the look in his eyes. Already she could feel the heat of his thick erection pressing at her dripping entrance.

"Your *only* duty," he emphasized.

His hair was thick, a wolf's pelt, long and falling around him. His chest was heavy with defined muscle, his face carved and beautifully masculine. She loved the look of him, the strength of him and the stamp of absolute authority he wore so easily.

"Well then, if that's my *only* duty, I'd better be excellent at it," she replied, and sank down right over him, completely sheathing him, watching the way his hooded eyes went completely wolf.

He filled her, stretching her all over again, insisting her tight muscles give way for his intrusion. She seated herself on his lap, adjusting first one way and then the other, pleased to see the breath hiss out of him each time she made a small movement.

"I'm not certain how best to please you," she murmured, lifting her hips slowly and then riding him down even more slowly. "Like this? Does this do anything for your pleasure, sir?"

His fingers dug into her hips, but he let her take control. "I think you're on the right track."

Her eyebrow went up. "You think? Hmmm, perhaps you'd like this better?" She rose again, her hands on his shoulders to steady herself as she slowly made little circles with her hips, her muscles tightening, clamping down as she spiraled down, increasing the friction on his sensitive shaft.

He swallowed, the breath slamming out of his lungs in a long groan of sheer pleasure. "That's it, that's what I want, but a little faster." His hands guided her into a faster rhythm. His voice turned hoarse and raw. "A little harder."

Branislava laughed softly, throwing her head back, letting the fiery sensations take her. She rose again, riding him now, a harder, faster rhythm, just as he preferred.

"This is where you belong," he declared. "Me, inside of you. You surrounding me. Locked together just like this."

She felt like she belonged. She loved the way his body impaled hers, stretching her so deliciously, just skimming that edge of pain, but not quite, just sheer pleasure streaking through her body with every stroke.

He began to move her body with his enormous strength as his breath hissed out of his lungs, his hands urgent and hard, bringing her body up and down so that her ride was blissfully wild. Branislava closed her eyes, and let her head fall back, let his harsh pace consume her, take her to another realm, where there was only the two of them. Only *this*.

There was a sense of total belonging, not imprisonment. She craved him, desired him and even needed him, but there was such an awareness of freedom. He made her feel as if she could soar through the skies unfettered, at any time. He made her feel beautiful and sexy. He made her feel no other woman would ever do for him—only her.

His body moved in hers and a surge of electricity charged through her so that every nerve ending burst into life. Her world narrowed until there was only Zev and the way they fit together, the way he moved like a piston, the hard pace that sent streaks of fire rushing through her bloodstream and centering in her deepest core.

Zev urged her into a wilder, faster pace, his hands hard on her hips, as he thrust into her over and over. She rode him with abandon, floating in a dream world of pure feeling. Once again the ground beneath them heated as if the combination of the two of them drew magma up from the very depths. Her skin grew hot, as did his, and around them the mist glowed that strange red orange.

"How can you be so scorching hot?" he asked. "Silken fire gripping me in a tight fist."

She reveled in the wonder and raw desire in his voice. She loved that she made him feel this way, the same amazing way he made her feel. She rode him at a furious, fiery pace, and when he leaned forward to lick at her breast, the fire that had been building and building, crowned, exploding through her with tremendous force, taking him with her.

For a moment the edges around her vision went red with flames. She felt them licking over her skin like a thousand hot tongues. She circled his neck with her arms and leaned against his chest, resting her head on his shoulder. "I don't know how you do it, Zev, but when I'm with you like this, every bad thing in my life is gone. You wipe it away, so that for these precious moments, I'm a clean slate and the only thing written there is your name."

"That's an extraordinary thing to say to me," Zev said. "Thank you."

She turned her face into his neck. "I thought, once we were out of the ice caves, that we would never have to deal with anything as evil as Xavier ever again."

Zev's hand slid up her back, pressing her closer to him. There was intimacy in his touch, but in a comforting way. His fingers reached the nape of her neck and began a slow massage. He didn't say anything, and she was grateful. It was important to tell him the things she needed to while she had the chance.

"I'm not naïve. I know the problems facing our people, so I was prepared for hard times, although a war with the Lycans might have been more than I ever considered. Still, I know I could handle it."

Branislava rubbed her face back and forth in the warm space between his neck and shoulder. He smelled masculine and strong and right then, when her fears began to resurface, she needed him.

"Mage-shadowing is truly evil, Zev. The mage can access his victim at any time and force compliance. Often the victim is worn down over time, especially if their will is strong, as in the case of my nephew, Razvan, until they're weak and confused. The mage strikes them then and can force them to do things completely against everything they believe in."

"I don't understand the difference between a splinter and a shadow."

"Xavier used a splinter of himself in Razvan so that he was living inside of Razvan's body, but a shadow is an actual portal for the mage to travel through. The splinter can leave the body at any time and seek another host. Few leave a splinter of themselves behind for any length of time because there is a danger to the maker, should the splinter be found and destroyed. A shadow is a doorway to be accessed at any time. The risk of discovery is very small and one can build in all sorts of traps."

Branislava slowly sat up. A small shiver went through her body when the action caused friction against her most sensitive spot. "I'd much rather stay here for the rest of the night with you, locked together like this, but we have to go back."

He sighed and ran his hand down the back of her head, caressing the silky braid. "Fen is having trouble keeping Tatijana from looking for you," he admitted. "She wanted to follow you and make certain you were all right."

Branislava nodded her head several times, but made no move to get off his lap. If anything, she tightened the muscles surrounding him as if she could hold him to her forever. "I did leave rather abruptly. That poor man. Damon. I guess I shouldn't have ruined his coffee. I can't imagine what he thinks I found in him."

"What did you find?"

Her entire body shuddered. She pressed her lips together and looked around her as if she might spot an enemy spying on them. Very gently she used his shoulders to pull herself up, a little reluctantly, but she did it.

"I'll tell you when we're back at the house. Not out here. Not in the open."

Zev didn't press her. She looked scared. Whatever she had found in Damon's brain had been traumatizing enough to send her flying into the night. She needed to work it out herself and come to terms with it before she faced everyone.

"I suppose this means you're going to get dressed." He changed the subject, using a sulky tone, hoping to use amusement to distance her mind from the trauma.

"I think it best," she said, giving him a look from under her long lashes.

"I don't. Maybe you could just stand there for a few minutes and let me admire you." He was already clean and fully clothed, back in his normal everyday ready-for-combat clothes.

She smiled, shaking her head. "Your appetite is insatiable."

"I'm a wolf, what did you expect?" He bared his teeth at her, looking hungry all over again. "My appetite for you is insatiable. It's my sincere desire to ensure that every time we make love you are so enraptured and captivated by my expertise that you can't wait for the next time, because, believe me *mon chaton féroce*, there will be many, many next times."

Her laughter was genuine, and her bare breasts, rising and falling with her breath, drew his attention like a magnet. He reached out to cup her left breast and leaned forward to draw her exquisitely soft mound into the heat of his mouth. She laughed again and this time, tried to insert her hand between his mouth and her breast. He growled, refusing to relinquish his prize.

"You are a very bad wolf," she declared sternly. "Let go."

It's mine.

"I know, but you can't be so greedy. We have to go back and I need to get dressed."

I can give you another orgasm just like this. It will be good practice. His tongue flicked and danced. His teeth tugged and rolled. He suckled strongly. He could feel her instant heat, the flush in her body. Honey and cinnamon permeated the air.

"I'm sure you can," Branislava said firmly. "But don't. And you don't need any more practice. If you get any better at sex we'll both spontaneously combust. It will happen, Zev, and it will be all your fault. We're lucky we didn't burn down the forest."

He gave one last lick along her nipple, savoring the way her body shivered in reaction, before he straightened. "I plan on practicing quite often, Branka. Every rising. Two or three times a rising. Maybe more. Wolves need to be fed, and you can't let them get bored. Taking on a wolf is a full-time proposition."

"Tatijana never said she had this much trouble with Fen," Branislava declared, waving her hand to cover her body with her flowing dress.

Zev bared his teeth at her. "But then I'm the alpha elite, aren't I?"

9

Branislava curled her fingers tightly inside of Zev's hand. She was grateful to him for following her wishes to the letter. He didn't ask her questions, he simply did as she asked. The heat, so deep beneath the ground, wrapped her in a cocoon of safety. Ordinarily, a cave would have been her last choice for such a meeting, but the sacred cave of warriors was the only place she could think of that a mage could not possibly overhear.

She could taste fear in her mouth, a horrible, coppery tang she couldn't quite rid herself of. Tension knotted her belly and left her feeling shaky. She tried to follow the rhythm of Zev's steady lungs, breathing in and out and portraying confidence to those gathering at her request.

Somehow, Zev had gotten everyone to leave their home without her having to say more than she thought it was possible to help Damon the next rising, but they had to prepare. No one had questioned her too closely, although Tatijana had known the truth. Their eyes had met and she saw knowledge there, but like Branislava, Tatijana had remained steadfastly silent. Both refused to give name to evil where they resided.

"Bronnie," Mikhail said softly, "Gregori has completed all safeguards as you asked."

Gregori joined the tight circle, there in the cave of warriors, seating himself beside the prince. "Damon is safe as well. He can do no harm to us," he added.

"Daciana, Makoce and Lykaon are close and all three are acting as normal as possible under the circumstances," Fen told her. He kept his arm around Tatijana, keeping her close beneath the protection of his shoulder.

"Tell us what has disturbed you," Mikhail prompted. "Why you asked for these cautions to be taken."

Branislava touched her tongue to the roof of her mouth. Skyler and Dimitri sat directly across from her in their circle of power. Skyler had drawn a protection circle around them, just to be safe. The chamber had been cleansed as well, but still, her heart pounded and her mouth stayed dry.

"Tatijana and I were held captive our entire lives up until two years ago," Branislava said. "Most of that time, Xavier kept us inside the ice wall, in the form of dragons. We could see and hear everything that he did. It's impossible to tell you how difficult it was to see him bring in victim after victim and systematically destroy them. We could see every spell he cast. Essentially, we were his students, although he certainly never considered that we might be learning as we watched."

She glanced at her sister. Tatijana's eyes were downcast. The memories of those endless, horrific years lay heavy on both of them. The dark time was too close, and both wanted to push the shadows away.

Immediately the candles in the sconces blazed into life, illuminating the room. Zev's hand moved to her thigh in a gesture of comfort. His fingers splayed wide, wrapping halfway around her leg, as if gluing himself to her. His strength gave her added courage. She was grateful to him for providing added light. Evil sought darkness and shadow, slipping through those avenues to commit ugly deeds.

The sound of water seemed overly loud in the large chamber. The stalactites and stalagmites were ominously silent, so that the carved faces of the ancients appeared somber and staring. She shivered as her heart thundered in her ears.

"To think that one man could commit such evil over so many centuries is beyond comprehension," Branislava said, her voice dropping lower. "While Xavier was the face of the mages, the man befriending Carpathians and betraying them, he was not alone in his plans to become immortal."

Mikhail turned his head toward Gregori. They exchanged a long look, as if perhaps her revelation did not come as a huge surprise. Neither responded aloud, allowing her to give them information at her own pace.

Branislava wiped the back of her hand across her mouth. "Naming evil, uttering its name, can bring it to you. We learned that long ago." She looked at her sister and there was fear in her eyes. "There were three of us born to our mother. Soren, Tatijana and me."

Gregori's head went up, as if scenting danger, his silver eyes slashing through her growing terror.

"There were three of you," he hissed softly. "The bloodline of the High Mage."

Branislava nodded her head slowly.

I call to thee with in mind the three,
I feed your life blood, three must be.
Children of air, earth, fire and sea,
I call you into our world to be.

She whispered the words. "Xavier manipulated the birth of triplets, ensuring Rhiannon, my mother, would continue the bloodline of the High Mage. But we were not the first triplets born into the mage line."

"So Xavier is one of three," Mikhail said, letting out his breath. "Triplets."

Branislava nodded again. "That secret was kept beyond all others. They were identical in every way. They moved alike and talked in the same voice. They were rarely seen together and never where others might discover the secret. It allowed them to be in more than one place at a time, or provide an alibi should someone accuse Xavier of evildoing."

"Which is why no one discovered he was the one who had killed Rhiannon's lifemate," Fen said. "He was able to keep her prisoner for so long because so many Carpathians swore he was teaching them a class in safeguards when the murder and kidnapping took place."

Mikhail leaned toward Branislava, his dark eyes on her face. "Why did you not tell us of this threat immediately? The moment you were rescued?"

Branislava couldn't look away from those penetrating eyes. Her breath came out in a long rush. "Xavier killed them. Both of his brothers. He killed them like he killed Soren. He was obsessed with blood and the power of it."

She turned to look at Zev, her voice dropping another octave, as if whispering would prevent evil from hearing. "All three were on a quest for Dark Blood. At that time we didn't realize it was a bloodline. They believed that anyone possessing Dark Blood could build an army of soldiers that would be invincible. But they never found what they were looking for."

"Perhaps they did," Mikhail mused aloud. "Fen, you and Dimitri ran into more than one *Sange rau* you believed had been newly made. It is possible someone has or had access to Carpathian blood and is using it to create their own superior soldiers."

"So one targets the Carpathian species to bring them down while another goes after the Lycan species," Gregori said. "The third must have gone after the Jaguars."

Branislava nodded slowly. "We believed them to be dead," she reiterated. "We believed Xavier killed his brothers for his own purposes."

"Did you see them actually die?" Fen asked.

Branislava nodded. "Xavier cast a spell with one of them, his brother, Xaviero. They were working on a dark spell to enslave the living. They took blood from us to fill the ceremonial chalice."

She rubbed her arm where the faint slashes laced up and down her forearm and wrist as if the wounds were open and throbbing. Tatijana mirrored her actions.

Zev gently took her arm and rubbed his palm in long, caressing strokes over the faded marks in her soft skin.

Branislava touched her tongue to her dry lips. "They both drank from the chalice. Xaviero even saluted us with the jeweled cup." She swallowed hard, a small shudder running through her body. "He had this way of smirking at us that was terrible. We knew when he looked like that, he was going to do what he loved best . . ." She trailed off.

Zev immediately surrounded her with warmth and wrapped her up in love. Deliberately, she allowed herself to look up at him. He was strong and comforting. Good. A decent and honorable man. The memories of Xavier, Xaviero and their brother Xayvion left her sick inside. Sometimes she felt she might never get the memories of true evil out of her mind, but being with Zev certainly allowed her to distance them.

"What was that?" Gregori prompted. "What did he love best?"

"Hurting others. He was very depraved. Much worse than Xavier or Xayvion." Branislava pressed her lips together tightly. "He liked keeping his victims alive and toying with them for hours, even days. Man, woman or child, it didn't matter. And like Xavier, he loved an audience." She pressed her hand to her mouth, feeling sick. "I can't talk about him anymore. I can't think about this."

"I'm sorry," Gregori apologized immediately. "It isn't necessary. I think, judging from your reaction, we don't need or want the details."

Immediately there was a current of soothing warmth swirling through the chamber. She took a deep breath and nodded gratefully at the prince's protector.

"You said that Xavier and Xaviero drank your blood from a jeweled chalice," Mikhail prompted. "What happened next?"

"While Xaviero gave us his horrible smirk, Xavier stood beside him with the ceremonial knife in his hand. There was no warning at all, he just turned and plunged it into Xaviero's heart. We both saw him do it."

"What happened to Xaviero?" Dimitri prompted when she fell silent. "What did Xavier do with the body?"

She rubbed her eyes, trying to recall every detail. "There was vapor rising from the floor, like a dense cloud. I remember it because it was beautiful, about four feet off the pristine ice, curling up in these little, intricate, almost lacy patterns."

"Was that a natural phenomenon, or something they created during this ceremony?" Dimitri asked.

Tatijana and Branislava exchanged a frown. The incident had taken place centuries earlier. Both had tried to forget as much as possible. To deliberately recall memories of evil was daunting. Their minds retreated, trying to aid them.

"It was created," Branislava decided. "It had to be. To be that beautiful and intricate, it couldn't possibly be natural."

Tatijana nodded in agreement. "I could hardly look away from it. The lace would divide and multiply, each pattern, like a snowflake, different from the others."

"Go on," Mikhail urged. "What happened next?"

"Xaviero was staring right at us when Xavier thrust the knife into him. His body just kind of collapsed. He fell like a rag doll beneath the veil of vapor." Branislava related the details in a rush to get it over with.

"Did Xavier know you were watching?"

"We were always his audience, the only ones who ever saw him perform and lived through it. He wanted to show others what a genius he was, how clever and superior, but of course no one could know about his plans to become immortal and hold ultimate dominion over the world."

Tatijana nodded. "He played to us. He knew we were watching. The more complicated the spell, the more he wanted us to acknowledge his superiority. He loathed every Carpathian ever born and vowed to wipe them out."

"What of Lycans?" Zev asked.

"There were no species immune from his distain. Xavier couldn't understand why animals like the Jaguar or Lycan races had so many gifts. In his opinion, they were an utter waste of space on the planet, but he reserved his absolute hatred for the Carpathians."

Branislava allowed herself to lean against Zev. He was solid like a rock, and right then, she needed his strength. The cave was comforting, deep beneath the earth, in the heat where a mage would never survive. They were able to withstand the cold, even preferring the world of ice and snow, but they disliked the intolerable heat.

The temperature and humidity of the sacred cave of warriors would have left them gasping for air. Eyes and lungs would scorch. Skin would be burned, boiled in the 90 percent humidity. Eventually a mage would succumb, much like a human would to that world of heat. Branislava found solace in the thought.

"And Xavier's brothers?" Mikhail prompted gently. "Did they hold the same view of other species?"

Branislava frowned. "It was impossible to distinguish the three of them from one another unless they were casting—then each had a very distinctive signature. It was rare to see all three together, but the joint plan was to rid the world of Carpathians, Lycans and Jaguars."

"Not humans?" Skyler asked.

"They had to have someone to dominate," Branislava pointed out.

"What happened after Xavier stabbed Xaviero?" Zev asked. "We never actually established that."

"He dragged the body out of the laboratory." Branislava looked to her sister for confirmation. "He was dead, right? Xaviero was dead."

"We both saw his body fall," Tatijana confirmed. "Xavier picked up his feet as if he were trash and dragged him out of the lab."

There was a small silence. Fen looked across the circle to his brother. "We both studied a bit under Xavier. Did he ever once perform a menial chore manually? He had assistants who lived to serve him. If he looked at them they rushed to do his bidding."

Dimitri shook his head. "I'll admit, I can't recall a single moment when I saw him lift a finger. He instructed everyone else to do the work."

Fen arched his eyebrow at Branislava. "Was it his usual practice to drag dead bodies out of his lab? He tortured and killed on a regular basis. He must have had some kind of routine."

Branislava's heart jumped and then began to pound. Xavier had killed so many over the centuries, far too many for her to count. No species was left out of his circle of torture, he preyed on all of them. He worked out his dark spells alone . . . She bit her lip hard and once more raised her eyes to meet Tatijana's gaze. Her own horror was reflected there.

They had been young when all three brothers had been alive. It had been difficult to tell which one was performing an experiment, or which sliced their body with a knife and drank deeply. The three brothers looked and sounded alike. They all preferred to work their spells alone, but they didn't clean up after themselves. Not ever.

Why had Xavier dragged Xaviero's body out of the laboratory? Why hadn't he called one of his assistants?

"Would he have taken care of the body because he didn't want any of his assistants to see that there had been a look-alike?" Gregori asked.

Branislava wanted to answer in the affirmative, but she found herself shaking her head. Xavier had no compunction about using his assistants for a task he wanted kept confidential and as soon as it was completed, murdering them on the spot. Those disposing of the bodies would have no idea why Xavier had killed the mage interns, but they accepted it because dead bodies were common where they worked.

She began to rock back and forth. "Why would they stage Xaviero's death? Xavier didn't believe we could escape. None of them believed it. No, Xaviero's definitely dead." Even to her own ears, she sounded doubtful.

"What of the other brother?" Mikhail asked. "The one you called Xayvion? You said Xavier murdered both of his brothers. How did he die?"

Branislava wanted to crawl inside Zev's mind for protection. How could she have been so gullible? She had wanted to believe Xaviero was dead. All three brothers were cruel, true psychopaths without a hint of remorse or feeling for anyone. Xaviero just seemed to take his torture further than either of his brothers, as if he did it out of pure enjoyment rather than purely for experiment. She didn't doubt that Xavier and Xayvion were just as bad, but Xaviero always sent a horrifying chill through her when he looked at them encased behind the wall of ice. It was the one time Branislava was grateful for the protection of the ice.

"The same exact way. Time passed. I don't know how much, because time meant nothing. But it was a while. Xavier and Xayvion performed the same ceremony, and Xavier stabbed Xayvion and dragged him out of the lab by his feet. I never saw the actual body after it fell, only the feet and legs," she admitted. "But we never saw them again."

Mikhail rubbed his temples. Gregori flicked him a quick look. Branislava felt a surge of soothing heat circulating throughout the cavern. Mikhail sent Gregori a small smile as if thanking him.

"You said you couldn't tell them apart," the prince said. "Is it possible they were alive but because you believed them dead, you always thought it was Xavier performing experiments and spells? Could they still have been switching places?"

Again she wanted to say no. She would have recognized Xaviero's smirk. She was certain she would have. She'd been a terrified child, and he loved to torment her. He knew Tatijana was far more comfortable in the ice than her sister and he would deliberately make the ice colder and colder around

Branislava until it was impossible for her to control her body temperature to keep warm enough. She shivered and shook for days, sometimes weeks and months, her very insides so cold she thought she would freeze from the inside out.

"Bronnie?" Fen prompted.

She shook her head. "I don't believe Xaviero ever returned, not where I could see him. I don't think he could have resisted tormenting me."

"You asked us to meet you in this sacred place," Mikhail said, making it a statement, waiting for her to finish.

"No mage, not even a powerful one like Xavier or his brothers, could penetrate the safeguards of this chamber," Branislava said. "I'm Dragonseeker and I sensed that the moment I set foot on the ancient stone. I didn't want to chance being overheard, or speaking the name of evil aloud where it could find me. Xaviero is wholly evil, every bit as evil as Xavier. Although I would have sworn upon my very life that he was dead, I saw his very distinctive signature last night."

Mikhail let out his breath slowly and turned to look at Gregori. "I don't know why I'm not more surprised that this mess we're in began long ago with Xavier."

"Where did you see this mark?" Gregori asked.

"Damon, Daciana's brother, acted against his moral beliefs. Each time he was questioned, I could see that something kept him from remembering. His head hurt. His nose bled."

"Mage-shadowed," Gregori said. "You're describing someone mage-shadowed."

Branislava nodded slowly. "There's only a handful of mages who were good at it, but only three that I know of that might be able to mass-produce mage-shadows on unsuspecting victims. Damon recalled going to a meeting of the Sacred Circle, but he couldn't remember who was there encouraging him to join with the assassins targeting Skyler and Dimitri."

"His orders," Zev added, "were to wound wolves and leave them as bait in the forest. Dimitri has a certain reputation. His mission has always been to save the wolves in the wild."

"I thought Lycans had that same mission," Mikhail said.

"I thought they did as well," Zev said, a hard edge to his voice.

"Fortunately, Damon didn't take the shot he had and I didn't kill him. If I had, we never would have had a chance to discover that he'd been manipulated. I questioned him, and Branka spotted the signs."

Gregori's silver eyes bore into Branislava, making her want to squirm, but she stayed very still, determined to keep her composure.

"You knew he was mage-shadowed yet you checked for a signature without anyone to aid you if you got into trouble, didn't you?" His tone was low. Accusing.

She nodded, clutching Zev's hand in a death grip.

"You knew how dangerous it was, but you still did it—why?"

Gregori's voice lashed her like a whip. She even winced under the stroke. Beside her, Zev's head went up, his eyes going entirely wolf. Immediately a feral, wild scent enveloped her. She felt him coil.

"I would prefer, Gregori, that you watch how you talk to my woman," Zev said, his voice nearly hoarse with the effort it took to keep from growling. "Otherwise, you and I will be going outside to have a private discussion."

Shock showed on Gregori's face.

Mikhail coughed into his hand, clearly trying not to laugh. *Gregori, just in case you have never met yourself, that's you sitting over there.*

Gregori sent the prince a sour look. *Your amusement at my expense never fails to amaze me.*

The way you make friends everywhere you go never fails to amaze—or amuse me.

"*O jelä peje terád—sun scorch you, Mikhail,*" Gregori said irreverently to his father-in-law, the prince of the entire Carpathian race.

Mikhail's expression never changed, but his laughter was contagious. Gregori clearly tried to hide his own amusement, glaring at Mikhail, but in the end he knew Mikhail knew him far too well not to feel his laughter at his own expense.

"Please excuse me, Bronnie," he said aloud. "I know the dangers of trying to remove a mage-shadow and the thought of you attempting such a thing without protection was such a shock I spoke without thinking. I have removed splinters, but not a mage-shadow. I tried, but wasn't successful. It was . . . vile."

Branislava heard the sincerity in his voice and knew it had nothing to do with fearing Zev. Gregori didn't like bullying women.

"If it makes you feel any better, I would never have tried such a thing. That's why I asked you and Mikhail to meet us here, to decide what to do," she said. "I needed to know if my suspicions were true. Damon was adamant that the only place he'd gone was to a Sacred Circle meeting. There was someone there he couldn't name, a person he'd met many times, and yet each time he tried to recall him, he became quite ill."

Gregori nodded in understanding. "You suspect a mass shadowing?"

She pressed her lips together hard, her heart stuttering again, reliving that moment when she was quite certain who had placed the shadow in Damon's brain. She nodded slowly, frowning a little. "Who else, Gregori? Who could do such a thing? If not Xavier, then one or both brothers have to still be alive." Her voice quivered. She couldn't help it.

"And when you checked?" Gregori gentled his voice.

"It was as I feared. Xaviero."

Tatijana gasped and covered her mouth. She shook her head.

Branislava nodded. "It was, Tatijana. There is no mistaking his signature. He's alive, and he's infiltrated the ranks of the Lycans. Like Xavier, he is working to destroy anyone who might oppose his power."

Zev swore softly. "How could he manage it and none of us know?"

"I lived among the packs for centuries," Fen pointed out. "And I have mixed blood. I simply went to ground during the time of the full moon to avoid detection."

"He would be old and very respected," Branislava said. "He would demand devotion. Admiration. There is no way that he has stopped killing. He's addicted to it and enjoys it far too much, but he has discipline. He would torture and kill far from where he operates."

Zev shook his head. "There's no one like that."

"Yes there is," she insisted. "He's out in the open, living and moving among you. Don't look for a killer. He'll appear kind and benevolent. He'll blend in seamlessly with Lycans. He will have followers and they'll love him, almost to the point of worshipping him."

Zev frowned and rubbed his hand down his face as if wiping away the first image in order to try to replace it with the second. "You're describing half the leaders of the Sacred Circle as well as a few council members. It could be anyone, Branka."

"He'll need a laboratory for making his soldiers. And he has access to Carpathian blood." Branislava's breath caught in her throat and she closed her mouth abruptly before her next thought could spill out.

What is it? Tell me.

Zev's voice turned her heart over. So gentle and caring. She would break his heart if what she suspected was true. She shook her head.

Mon chaton féroce. If what you suspect is the truth, it will come out eventually. Better to get it over with now.

When Zev spoke in that French accent, his voice smooth, like velvet, she couldn't help but react to it.

Someone discovered your grandmother was mixed blood. They had to know she was Carpathian born. If Xaviero knew, he could have ordered her death. He would have access to her blood, the very blood all three brothers had searched for.

"Tell us," Mikhail said gently. "We need to know everything, including what you only suspect. Without all information, we can't make an intelligent decision."

Branislava's gaze clung to Zev's. Her logic was reasonable, though, and she knew it. Xaviero was alive. No one else would leave that same shadow behind. His signature had always been distinct. He had to have lived among the Lycans, infiltrating and becoming someone of importance. He would use his position to set up a network of spies. Those spies would keep him informed of every detail.

"Zev's grandmother was the child of the Dark Bloods. The last lifemated pair. They ran across the trail of the *Sange rau* destroying the Lycan packs systematically and of course they tried to help. When they were killed, Lycan survivors coming across their bodies and finding an infant believed she was Lycan. They took her with them to raise her."

"And Xaviero found out," Mikhail finished.

Branislava nodded. She held her hands out in front of her as if she could protect herself from the truth. "I believe that's what happened. It makes sense. Xavier wanted Dark Blood more than anything else, but he never found what he was looking for. Tatijana and I thought it was a type of blood that could harm others, not a lineage."

"Could Xaviero have had anything to do with the first *Sange rau*?" Zev asked. "The one responsible for killing so many?"

"I doubt it," Mikhail said. "But certainly Xaviero would have thought he'd stumbled across a gold mine. The very thing he needed to bring down Carpathians and Lycans alike. His problem was the sacred code was written by the council, and Lycans avoided Carpathians. He didn't have an opportunity to access Carpathian blood."

"Until my grandmother grew up and someone reported to him something they found suspicious about her," Zev ventured.

Branislava nodded. "They were so good at gathering information. They used animals, humans, every species available, and they got results. If she made a mistake, believe me when I say Xaviero would have been informed."

"She was raised Lycan," Gregori pointed out. "She probably didn't even know she was Carpathian. When others shifted, she did as well, not realizing she wasn't shifting the same way. She was a Dark Blood and she would have hunted and fought alongside her husband. She probably was given Lycan blood when she was wounded, and eventually she became a mixed blood."

"So he watched her." Mikhail pieced more of the puzzle together. "Xaviero watched her closely and he realized what she had to be. He wanted her blood and he couldn't chance that she was faster, stronger, and more intelligent and would defeat him. He whipped up a mob against her, probably to have her brought before the council, but they murdered her. He must have taken her blood to his lab and kept it to experiment with."

"Her husband took their child and ran," Zev said. "He would have gone far away and joined a different pack, probably in another country. He would have changed his name. That's what I would have done to protect my daughter."

"Did you meet your grandfather? Know him at all?" Mikhail asked.

Zev nodded. "He was very quiet and he spent most of his time hunting. I was pretty young. My mother died in childbirth, and my father said her father rarely came around after that. I saw him a couple of times and then one day he never came back."

"When you say 'hunting,'" Fen asked, "who or what was he hunting?"

Zev shrugged. "My father said he hunted down the men who killed his wife, one by one, at least that's what he thought my grandfather was doing." *I would understand if he did*, he added to Branislava.

Because it's something you would have done.

Branislava made certain she used the past tense. Zev was mixed blood, both Lycan and Carpathian. He might still think like a Lycan, but if his lifemate was to be killed, he would be a danger to everyone if he was caught in the deadly Carpathian madness—the thrall that took hold of males if they didn't immediately follow their lifemates.

His eyes met hers and her heart leapt. There was love there. Possession. Belonging. No matter what happened, she had this time, this unexpected passionate love that transcended her.

Once I knew my child was gone, I would have moved heaven and earth to find her mother's killers. Now, I go where you go. Always.

Branislava swallowed hard to clear the choking lump in her throat that had arisen from nowhere. *I think I'm quite mad about you, Wolfie.*

You're quite mad. And don't even whisper that name in these caves. We're surrounded by ancient warriors and Wolfie *just isn't manly enough.*

In spite of the fact that her worst fears had come true, Zev could make her laugh. Feeling her sister's gaze on her, she looked up, and Tatijana smiled at her. They were so close. This is what Tatijana had with Fen—this wonderful feeling of belonging, of being loved. She returned her sister's smile and found Skyler with her gaze.

Young Skyler, whose soul seemed older than all of them, wielded power so easily without even recognizing how extraordinary she was. Dimitri sat close to her, partially shielding her body from the others. It was clear she, too, was wrapped in love. They were lucky, the Dragonseeker women. All three had been very lucky.

"Would the bond between Zev's grandmother and Zev's grandfather be that strong? So strong that long after she was dead, he needed to find her killers?" Branislava asked. "She was Carpathian, and then mixed blood, but he was . . ." She trailed off. "Wouldn't he have been mixed blood as well? And the blood he had in his system would be Dark Blood."

"He couldn't have claimed her as a lifemate," Gregori said. "Not without the ancients bringing him fully into our world, but certainly their love could create a strong enough bond."

"Lycans love passionately, with everything in them, when they find their true mate," Zev said. He leaned forward, his gaze on the prince. "Would this mage keep a mixed blood alive in order to have a fresh blood supply? Because all along I've wondered how he would preserve my grandmother's blood. We have ways now, but centuries ago?"

Fen nodded. "Zev's got a point."

"Xaviero was used to living in an ice world. He could preserve the blood there," Tatijana pointed out.

"But he wouldn't share," Branislava said. "You know he wouldn't, Tatijana. They tried to outdo one another. That's why it was so easy to believe Xaviero and Xayvion were dead. That, and we wanted to believe it. If Xaviero had acquired the Dark Blood the three of them sought, he would have hidden it from the others and felt smug and superior."

Tatijana nodded her head. "Just talking about them makes me feel sick inside." She turned her face against Fen's shoulder. He immediately responded, rubbing his hands down her back and then up to the nape of her neck, fingers easing the tension from her stiff body.

"We must assume that both brothers still live and we face a very powerful enemy," Mikhail said. "This man Damon is a problem." His dark, penetrating gaze swung to Zev. "I presume he is a good man or you wouldn't have spared his life."

Zev nodded. "We've been friends a long time. Daciana and Damon are family to me."

Mikhail glanced at Gregori. "How do we help Damon without tipping off Xaviero that we know he's behind this mess? If you remove the shadow—" He broke off. "Is it even possible? You were upset at the thought that Branislava might have tried."

Gregori sighed. His silver eyes met Branislava's in understanding. "A mage this powerful would have equally powerful safeguards to protect his shadow. Tripping one would alert him, and he would immediately strike at us through his puppet. Failing that, to protect his identity, he would kill Damon."

Mikhail's gaze was steady on his son-in-law. "If we do nothing and allow this mage to have a window through Damon, what then?"

"His hold on Damon will strengthen with each use. Eventually, we won't be able to have the chance to save him. Anyone near the man is in danger at this point. Anything he sees or hears could get back to Xaviero."

Branislava nodded. "Gregori's right, Mikhail. That shadow can't be left inside of him. It should be removed as soon as possible."

"Can you do it, Gregori?" Mikhail asked. "And how high is the risk to you?"

Gregori closed his eyes briefly and shook his head without answering. Branislava's heartbeat accelerated. She clutched Zev's hand, every cell in her body rebelling. Every single fear she ever felt in those long years of captivity welled up to choke her—to choke back what had to be said.

Zev leaned down, his mouth brushing down her cheek, leaving a trail of fire in a chamber of pure, scorching heat. She was safe here. Xaviero couldn't find her there in the sacred cavern surrounded by the people she loved and who loved her.

"I've removed splinters in the past, Mikhail," Gregori said, "But never a shadow. Until I see what I'm facing, I can't say for certain. If Xaviero is capable of mass-producing shadows in groups of unsuspecting people as indicated, he's had centuries of practice and knows far more than I do on the subject."

"Gregori would have little chance to remove the shadow, not without knowing Xaviero's work," Branislava said. Once again her eyes met Tatijana's. Her sister shook her head, her fist jammed in her mouth to prevent a protest.

She took a breath and forced herself to say the one thing she feared above all others—the one thing she'd known when she saw the shadow and knew who had made it. "I'll have to do it."

10

Silence took hold in the sacred chamber of ancient warriors. Water trickled from the walls down to the pools, drops hissing as they hit the hot water. Steam rose as curling vapor and drifted around the stalagmites. The flickering light from all the candles cast expressions on the faces of the ancient warriors in the giant totems of minerals. It seemed as though the world held its breath.

Zev heard his own heart like thunder roaring overhead. His first reaction was visceral. *Absolutely not.* He wouldn't allow it. He didn't care what she said, or whether or not Damon would die, she wasn't going to put herself in that kind of danger. He hadn't known what looking at the shadow entailed or the jeopardy she had been in or he never would have allowed that. Gregori's reaction when she'd admitted she had done so was enough for him. She was *not* going to go near Damon ever again.

Branislava moved, a small flexing of her fingers, and he looked down to see his hand clamped around her thigh, his knuckles white. Immediately he relaxed his grip on her, certain she would have bruises, silently cursing himself for not being more careful. But damn it all . . .

"It's the only way," she said aloud, looking at him, looking straight into his eyes—into his soul.

She knew his primal reaction. She knew everything he was, Lycan and Carpathian, protested. She knew him, his instincts and his need to keep her safe. He could see her fear, so stark in her eyes, yet she was going to attempt to remove the shadow from Damon.

He couldn't contain the fury rising sharp and fast and terrible. His wolf leapt to protect her, to force obedience. Zev rose and stalked out of the chamber, leaving her there where she was safe from the madness gripping him. He wanted to shake her until she saw reason. He wanted to put her across his knee like she was an unruly child. He wanted to wrap her up in his love and keep her hidden away where nothing could ever touch her.

He kept moving, going from chamber to chamber, winding his way through the maze, uncaring if he was going up toward the ground level or farther down from the warrior cave. The *where* mattered little to him. Just the why.

Why wasn't her love for him strong enough to keep her from putting her life in danger? His fingers curled into two tight fists. Sharp claws cut into his palms. His skin itched and his eyes and jaw ached with the effort to hold back the wolf that would snatch her from the meeting and run off into the night with her.

"Zev."

Her voice was cool, like a gentle breeze. Rather than soothe him, it fanned the anger pouring through him. He swung around and caught her shoulders in a hard grip. "You shouldn't have followed me."

"Do you think I'm afraid of you?" she asked, her tone a low, musical melody his ear immediately tuned to.

"You damn well should be," he snarled. He kept himself rigidly under control, not shaking her when he needed to, but holding her so she couldn't move.

"Well, I'm not. I know you're upset with me . . ."

"Upset? Is this what you call *upset*? What an insipid word that is, and it in no way describes what I'm feeling. *Fury* might come closer. You have no right to make a decision to risk your life without even discussing it with me. Last night you didn't tell me what the real danger of looking into Damon's mind might be."

When she attempted to speak he held up his hand for silence. "You sugarcoated it for me. I've always done you the courtesy of telling you exactly what is going on. I've treated you with respect and I expected the same from you."

"That's not fair, Zev," she said, her tone low, her long lashes sweeping down to hide her expression.

He caught her chin in hard fingers and yanked her head up, forcing her to look into his eyes. "I don't particularly give a damn about fair right now. This isn't a good time for us to have this discussion."

He had to draw in deep breaths to keep his wolf at bay. Every few words a low, warning growl escaped. Heat imaging banded his vision in yellows and reds. He was alpha and no one, least of all his mate, disobeyed or defied an alpha in his pack, not without consequences. And they sure as hell didn't make independent decisions, not after the betrayal of Gunnolf and Convel.

For a moment her eyes glittered with pure fire. He saw flames burning behind the glittering gems. That she could be angry as well just took his temper up another notch. He caught the nape of her neck and drew her to him, his mouth coming down hard on hers. He kissed her, pouring his fury and terror at her courage into his domination.

She didn't fight him, which was a good thing. That would have only triggered more aggression, and they both knew it. He kissed her again and again, holding her still, his touch a little brutal, his kiss demanding and forceful. Her mouth submitted to his, but her tongue dueled and fought, her nails digging into his skin as she melted into him.

Her body was fiery hot, as if all the passion in the world was pent up in her soft form. He used his claws to rip through her clothing, tearing the material from her body in strips until she was entirely naked in his arms. He didn't know if she got rid of his clothing or he had, and it didn't matter. He walked her backward, kissing her over and over, the same forceful, dominant kiss he couldn't stop.

He kissed her as if there was no tomorrow, as if they had this one night together and he needed her to survive—and he knew he did. His kiss was overpowering, smoldering with such fire that tiny electrical shocks sizzled through her bloodstream and raced from her breasts to her melting core.

Her back hit the wall of the cavern and he trapped her there, using his larger body, bent on possessing her. He cupped her breasts while he kissed and bit his way down to her nipples. She cried out, arching into his mouth when he drew her left breast into the scalding heat. He showed no mercy, lavishing attention on her with hands, teeth and tongue until she was panting with need, her breath coming in heaving gasps of desire.

It's too much. I'm going to go insane. I can barely stand.

His wolf was almost impossible to control and each time she made a small movement, as if she might pull away, he became more aggressive, rougher in his handling of her.

Then get on your knees. He growled the command, his fist in her hair, half pulling her down in front of him.

She went to her knees obediently and he barely had enough sense left in him to cushion the ground for her. His hand circled the girth of his bursting cock. He pulled her head back, using the long rope of hair and pushed into her mouth without preamble. Immediately her lips closed around the sensitive head and he flung back his head and roared.

Fire consumed him, a tight fist surrounding him, drawing him deeper and deeper. Her tongue lashed at him with flames and the edges of his vision went red. He held her silken hair with both hands and pushed deeper into her mouth, taking complete control of the rhythm and speed. He tried to be careful, but the sight of her, so beautiful, her breasts flushed and bouncing with his every thrust, his shaft disappearing in her mouth was almost too much. She was beautiful beyond anything he'd ever known.

Branislava let her passion wholly consume her. She knew she had pushed Zev into his wild, uncontrolled state, giving his wolf nearly free reign, but she loved it. She loved how close to the edge he was, how rough he was. She loved knowing she could tame that feral creature and draw him back to her with her body. With her love.

His body was hers, wholly hers and she played him like an instrument. She hummed softly as she suckled him, the vibration traveling up his shaft to that oh-so-sensitive head. She increased the heat and friction as his thrusts grew more urgent. His taste was not only intoxicating but addicting. She couldn't get enough of him.

He thought he was in control, but she knew she was. This man belonged to her. His body belonged to her. She reveled in her ability to bring him so much pleasure. She wanted to give him more and more. Already she was dripping, filling the air around them with her call to her mate. Hot cinnamon-spiced honey trickled down her thigh and she couldn't wait for him to lap it up.

His hips bucked again and again, barely giving her a chance to breathe. It didn't matter, nothing mattered to her but pleasing him. Driving him wild. Giving him everything he needed to get past what she'd committed to doing. If this was his way, his show of domination, she would gladly accept it every time.

It didn't have to make sense to anyone but her. She loved stroking her tongue along his shaft. She loved the feel, shape and taste of him. She craved his taste. She could use her Carpathian senses to breathe, taking him deeper until she was constricting him, strangling him, and he was swearing, gasping and burning with her.

Her mouth was red-hot. Her skin the same. That wealth of fire in her rose to match the fury in her wolf. She hadn't been angry, but she had wanted him with every breath of air she drew into her lungs. She'd deliberately let him see that fire, knowing in his state he would mistake her passion for anger.

She had wanted him just like this—a firestorm burning out of control. She needed to feel his fury in the way he withdrew and then thrust deep again. Sometimes he just stopped, holding himself deep, his hands fisting in her hair while growls and soft cursing reverberated through her mind. That only added to her heightened pleasure. Her body responded with more liquid heat, the tension coiling in her so tight she feared she would have an orgasm without him inside of her.

His shaft swelled more and she felt as if she had swallowed a burning torch. Then he was gripping her even tighter while he roared again, his seed spurting hard over and over. He withdrew swiftly, before she could catch her breath, pushing her backward so that she tumbled to the ground, sprawling out in front of him. He was on her fast, revealing the wolf that he was, latching on to his prey with a growl.

He lowered his head to her burning center, and she screamed with sheer pleasure as he lapped up her thigh and straight into her core, plunging his tongue deep like a weapon. He took her over, giving her no time to breathe or assimilate his attack. He devoured her, eating her as though she really was his prey, drawing out the spiced honey he craved, using both teeth and tongue. Sometimes his fingers plunged into her and other times he held her open to him while he lapped at her ferociously.

It was a claiming. Nothing less. A declaration. She understood that. She understood his need to have her submit to him. She craved his wolf, the wild untamed creature that matched her own fiery nature. She could see the marks on her body from his hands, his mouth and teeth and she delighted in every one.

His mouth drove her insane with his tongue swirling through her heat, seeking more honey, pushing her higher and higher toward her elusive orgasm. His face, that beautiful, masculine face was stamped with lust, a pure dominant bent on teaching his woman a lesson. She reveled in the way he chose to teach her.

Her body shuddered again and again and she couldn't stop the little mewling noises escaping as his tongue slid through her hot, slick folds. His soft growls reverberated through her sheath, adding to the pleasure rocketing through her. He sounded like a hungry animal devouring his dinner as he drew more and more cinnamon honey into his mouth. His eyes glowed, the pupils almost completely dilated.

Her head thrashed and her hips bucked against his mouth, but he simply held her down with his superior weight, his hands hard, framing her entrance and the treasure he sought there. He focused wholly on his meal, on driving her up that cliff and holding her right there, perched on the precipice but unable to go over the edge.

Each time she was close and tried to force him to let her soar, he held back, blowing warm air over the fiery heat until she sobbed and begged him for release.

You don't deserve such a reward, mon chaton féroce.

She knew he would never leave her unsatisfied. Not ever. He was bursting with need himself, his shaft swollen and jerking. His hand already had begun to circle the girth casually as he glared at her. He sank back and turned his finger to indicate for her to get to her hands and knees and turn around.

Heart beating fast, she complied. She wanted him so badly. So much. She could barely think with the urgency of her need. He knelt behind her, taking his time while her body shivered and shook with such hunger she wasn't certain she'd ever be sated.

Without warning, he pushed her head down and caught her hips, pulling her back into him as he drove forward, entering her fast, almost brutally. Her body, already so sensitive and needy, caught fire, the flames streaking through her like a lightning storm, lashing her with a fury of pleasure so intense she wasn't certain she could survive the onslaught.

Don't stop. Never stop. She couldn't help herself. She could hear her gasping pleas and there was no way to stop her demanding cries. She needed the terrible gathering tension coiling tighter and tighter in her belly to dissolve, and only he could do that for her. Zev showed no signs of stopping, not even when she sobbed for release.

Zev controlled her hips, holding her absolutely still so she couldn't move, although she desperately wanted to. He thrust into her over and over like a piston, clenching his teeth against the fire streaking up his shaft and down to his balls. Even his thighs and belly were part of the rising inferno.

Each time he felt her close—too close—he backed off just enough to keep her from tipping over the edge. Her cries were music, his own personal symphony, adding to the firestorm building in his own body. He wanted her mindless with pleasure, stretched to the breaking point and maybe that little bit more so that each time they made love, he could take her to the next level. He wanted her to know who her lifemate was, the wolf, an animal capable of great love and loyalty, but also of intense passions and lust.

She chanted his name over and over, begging him to take out his fury on her body, wanting more, wanting to burn up in the flames, desperate to give herself to that ecstasy just out of her reach.

Tongues of fire raced up the walls of the caves. The ground grew hot, turning red beneath her. The droplets of moisture in the air glowed red orange, turning the small chamber into a furnace. Still he drove into her with wild abandonment, pushing her further.

Her body was hot to the touch, but nothing compared to the scorching heat surrounding his shaft. He felt the tension in her growing, coiling tighter and tighter. There was the beginning of desperation, a tiny shiver of fear that he might not stop before she went entirely insane. He stayed in her mind, careful not to push her too far.

She felt the terrible tension in her body rising without end, his relentless pounding pushing her higher and higher until she feared she would fly apart, without ever feeling the fiery explosion she so urgently desired. Her body had become a volcano of molten fire, an erotic fury, catching the night on fire, yet soaring was just out of reach.

She strained toward her goal, tossing her head, trying to guide him with her hips, but that didn't work—she couldn't move with his strength holding her still while he thrust into her again and again, a relentless, rough-driving invasion. The schism of fear snaking through her mind, threading through the frenzy of passion, that she might not survive this time, not with her mind intact, only enhanced the powerful sensations even more.

Zev. She whispered his name in her mind. Her talisman. Her anchor. The man who made her complete.

I'm here, mon chaton féroce. I'll catch you. Let yourself fall. He was there instantly, wrapping her up in love.

As if her body needed to hear his assurances, with that velvet over steel invader slamming deep, the volcano erupted, exploded, threatened to rip her apart as wave after fiery wave tore through her body from thighs to belly and up to her breasts. Flames licked over and through her, that beautiful fire she craved. She gave herself up to the fierce sensations, her sheath clamping down hard around his flesh, scorching hot, dragging him with her into the sky.

Once again she felt like a phoenix, the legendary bird, burning completely, cleansed in the fire and reborn. The scent of cinnamon filling the cavern added to her illusion. There was nothing left. She felt like a rag doll, worn out and unable to hold her own weight.

Zev kept her from collapsing forward, rolling her over into his arms, holding her close. She could feel his heart pounding, matching the rhythm of hers. Their breath came together in ragged gasps. He rocked her, brushing kisses over the top of her head, his arms strong around her, his chest a solid wall for her to lean into.

"I love you, Zev," she confessed. "Every part of you. Especially your wolf. The things you can do, the way you make me feel when we make love are absolutely amazing."

"I'm happy you're aware I'm making love to you. It's impossible to touch you and not have my wolf side go a little crazy." He smoothed his hand over her hair in a slow caress. "You make me a little crazy."

"Of course I know you're making love to me." She turned her head to look up at him over her shoulder. "Why would you think otherwise? You rocked the entire mountain."

He touched a thumbprint on her skin, a bite mark and two strawberries. "When my wolf is close, I get rough. I didn't try very hard to hold back this time."

She frowned at him. "I don't want you to hold back. I want all of you. You don't scare me." She paused, thinking it over. "Well, sometimes, for just a moment, not because I think you'll ever hurt me, but because the feeling is so amazing I'm afraid I can't stay sane through it. Never be afraid to love me how you need to. I can handle rough. I love rough."

He kissed his way down her neck. "Tell me whenever you're afraid, Branka. We can stop until you feel safe."

"That's part of the perfection for me," she admitted. "That delicious sense of being prey for your wolf. You have your wolf, and I have fire. So much, Zev. I burn so hot."

His chin nuzzled her shoulder. "I love your fire, Branka." There was a smile in his voice and his arms tightened around her.

"Sometimes I think from all those years locked in the ice, the fire just smoldered, sitting there, freezing, desperate to come out, and now, every time you touch me, it ignites the blaze." She sighed, snuggling closer into him. "There's so much heat in me, building and building and it starts spilling out and I can't contain it. Then you put your hands on me or your mouth and I just go up in flames."

He kissed the nape of her neck and bit down gently on her shoulder, sending chills through her body. She could stay there with him for all time, feeling safe and thoroughly loved.

Zev looked around the cave. It had been lit up with her fiery energy, but now it was dark and bleak again, no more red-orange glow, no red ground or flames crawling up the walls.

"I love you with all my heart and soul," he said. "I don't want to lose you."

"Zev." Branislava nuzzled his throat. "I'm sorry I hurt you. I can't imagine you asking me if it's okay for you to go hunting rogue packs."

"Don't try to compare the two," Zev warned, bristling all over again. "When I hunt rogue packs, you'll be right there with me. This is entirely different. I can't possibly protect you when you try to remove this shadow from Damon. Better that I just kill him and get it over with." He rose in one smooth, fluid motion, taking her with him, setting her on her feet. "Maybe that's what I'll do and the argument will be finished."

She lifted her hand to smooth the lines carved so deep in his face. "We're not arguing, Zev. I'm not arguing with you. I made a mistake. I should have talked it over with you before I opened my mouth. I'm afraid to face Xaviero. He always terrified me. The thought of him out there hurting other people is just as terrifying. Someone needs to stop him, and believe me, I wouldn't mind taking the easy out and backing off, letting someone else take the lead against him."

She waved her hands to clean and clothe herself. Zev tried not to smile. She was in a different outfit from the one he'd shredded. He followed her lead, refreshing his appearance.

"So you'll tell the others you won't be taking the shadow out of Damon."

"If that's what you want me to do," she said, her gaze on his expression-less face. It was impossible to read him. "Zev, I want you happy. I want to please you. I don't have any experience here, and you make it difficult some-times. Do you really think I want to get anywhere near Xaviero?"

"Come here," Zev pointed to the spot directly in front of him.

His voice turned her heart over. So much love turning his usual com-manding tone to a velvet caress. Branislava moved without hesitation, stop-ping exactly where he'd indicated. Zev tipped her face up, his hands sliding along the curve of her cheeks and along her jaw, to her neck, tilting her face to his. His mouth came down on hers, not with his fury, but with such tenderness she felt the burn of tears behind her eyes.

His kiss was gentle, almost reverent. She felt love pouring into her mouth, down her throat, spreading through her body so that there wasn't a single cell that wasn't saturated with the intensity of his emotion. When he lifted his head, she touched her lips with wonder.

"I can't believe you could do that," she whispered.

"I can't believe a woman like you even exists, let alone that I have the privilege of her belonging to me. I *am* a wolf, Branka. More, I've been an alpha almost from the day I was born. I've always been in the position of leadership. I expect that deference and when I don't get it, the alpha wolf reacts in the way it would to keep the pack together. I can't do anything about it. That's my makeup. That's who I am."

"I know Zev," she replied. "I accept that."

He stroked his fingers down her cheek, touching her with the same tenderness that had been so prevalent in his kiss. "I never thought there would be a woman for me. Not in all the long years. I've always known I had little tolerance for defiance from a pack member, so I knew I'd be worse with my mate."

"This woman definitely loves being yours. Just don't be worse with our children," she cautioned. "Dragons protect their young fiercely—especially fire dragons."

He laughed softly, for the first time the tension in him slipping a little. "I'll remember that. In the meantime, you remember that when a wolf hasn't had family, hasn't had a single person he loves, when he finds her, he holds on with everything he is. Maybe too tight."

Branislava wrapped her arms around his waist and hugged hard, pressing her face over his heart. "You don't have to worry, Zev. I hear your warnings. I understand what you mean. I'm not a woman who will be trampled on and I won't lose who I am because you're a strong man. I don't scare so easily, either. And I love every moment of our lovemaking."

He held her tightly. "You really are a miracle, Branka. My miracle."

She thought it was the other way around, but she didn't mind in the least being his miracle. "We're getting in the habit of leaving our guests. We'd better go back and tell the prince that Gregori will have to take the chance of removing the shadow from Damon, because I'm certainly not okay with you killing him. I'll have to try to explain to Gregori what to look for. If he trips a safeguard or can't unravel it, he'll die, and we'll lose Savannah and possibly their daughters."

"Damn it, Branka," he snarled her name, turning away from her with a quick, restless motion, pacing the length of the small cave as if he couldn't contain the energy inside of him. "You're manipulating me and I don't like it, not over this."

She shook her head. "I'm stating a truth. A fact. Gregori doesn't know the way Xaviero sets his patterns. I was there in the same room with him. I might have been locked behind ice, but I could see everything he did and I learned. I need to pass as much information as possible to Gregori so he has a chance of making it out alive."

He swore and drove his fist deep into the wall. She winced, knowing he felt helpless. She kept silent, waiting for him to come to the only real conclusion possible on his own. She didn't like it any more than he did, but in the end, the risk to Gregori was far worse than to her.

He turned around to face her, resting one hip against the entrance to the small chamber. "I'll go in with you. I can stay back out of your way, but if things get dicey, I might find a way to protect you."

She opened her mouth to protest.

Zev shook his head. "I'm not negotiating here. If you go after that shadow, I go with you to guard you. Take it or leave it."

Branislava nodded slowly. "We're better together than apart. You give me courage and strength, and he's my worst nightmare. Having you close might be just the thing that gives me the edge." Her nod grew firm. "I think that will work much better for both of us."

He held out his hand to her. "Let's get it done then. We'll let Mikhail know."

"We'll need to prepare," she murmured, talking to herself more than to him as they made their way back through several passageways toward the sacred cave of warriors. "Skyler and Tatijana can help me with a circle of protection. Both are very strong and I'll need them."

No one said anything as they entered the lit chamber, hand in hand. Zev sank down onto the smooth rock seat with Branislava beside him.

"I'll need a large open space," Branislava announced, "so if Xaviero becomes aware of my presence, he can't see anything or anyone that might betray our movements to him. He'll know when I remove the shadow that someone knows about him and he'll retaliate in some way. He'll strike at the Lycan council or at Mikhail. If anyone else is mage-shadowed, he can use them, and he will. I know him. He's going to be very angry that anyone would dare thwart his plan."

"Then we'll have to check each one of them," Gregori said. "Every single one, before you try to remove the shadow. We don't have to try to figure out who is doing it, you've already identified him. It's a matter of just looking and not touching."

"There are a lot of Lycans here," Fen pointed out.

"We can start with the key people, those in positions of power. The council members and then their guards," Gregori said.

"How long will it take to go through that many people?" Fen said.

"We've got a lot of help. Tatijana is capable," Gregori reminded him. "Skyler certainly is. Darius will help us. Certainly you and your brother can look into a skull and find a mark on a brain without disturbing anything. You're just looking, not touching anything, if you trip a safeguard, if anyone does that, the mage will know."

Mikhail nodded. "I can help as well and there are a few others we can ask."

"No," Gregori and Fen said firmly, simultaneously.

Dimitri added his opinion as well. "You can't, Mikhail. Xaviero is specifically targeting you. If he brings you down, he has a much better chance of defeating the entire Carpathian race, wiping out our species. Now, more than ever, you have to be safe."

Mikhail pushed both hands through his hair, the first real sign of agitation Zev had ever seen him make. Zev couldn't blame him. The man reeked of power. He couldn't open his mouth or take a step without anyone close feeling that power, yet at every turn, his own warriors stepped in front of him, blocking him from helping in times of need. Zev never wanted to be in that position.

He glanced at Branislava. Her eyes met his. He felt the impact like a punch to the gut, low and mean. *Am I doing that to you?*

She smiled at him. *Yes.* She was bluntly honest. *But like Mikhail, I allow it and I'm fully aware I allow it. He has choices, just as I do. Someday there may come a time when it's too important to him—or to me—and we'll both go against those trying to stop us. But right now, this all makes sense.*

Zev sent Mikhail a small, apologetic smile. "Your job isn't easy, Mikhail. No one believes it is and none of us wants to be in your shoes. We'll get this done as quickly and quietly as possible and report the numbers back to you."

"In the meantime," Mikhail said, "I can hide in my house while all of you take the risks."

Gregori's head snapped around, a frown crossing his face. *Mikhail, te ul3 sív és ul3 siel Karpatiikuntanak*—Mikhail, you are the very heart and soul of all Carpathians. *Te agba kont és te ekäm*—A true warrior and my brother. *Jŏremasz ainaakä han ku olenasz Karpatiikuntahoz*—Never forget who you are to all of us.

Mikhail nodded his head and sent a small smile Gregori's way, but it didn't reach his eyes. Zev could see the visual interchange, but he hadn't been privy to the private discourse between the two men, he only knew it had taken place. Gregori didn't look especially happy, and the prince didn't, either.

"Let's get this done," Fen said. "We don't have all night. We have to make certain Bronnie has enough time to remove the shadow from Damon."

"One last thing," Zev said. "What happens if there are a number of Lycans with these mage-shadows? Are you expecting Branka to get rid of them all?"

Gregori shrugged his shoulders. "Zev, we've learned to take one thing at a time. If we find more shadows, we'll discuss what to do before we take any other steps."

Mikhail shoved his hands through his hair once again. "I understand completely, Zev. If Raven or Savannah were pushed into putting their lives— or sanity—on the line, I would certainly object."

He sent Gregori a quelling glance when the healer made a move to speak. "We came of age in an era where our women were gone, and there was little possibility of ever finding a lifemate. We forget they are every bit as strong as we are. Our every instinct is to protect them from any possible harm. I make no apologies for that and neither does Gregori, nor should you."

There was greatness in Mikhail, Zev realized. He was quiet, much like Rolf, the real alpha on the council, but when he spoke his every thought carried weight. He was intelligent and compassionate. He didn't want others to serve him or fight his battles. His struggle, Zev decided, was fighting his own nature, the fierce predator that preferred action to waiting.

Branislava was Dragonseeker, a born warrior. Just as he was. She had a warrior's heart, and if he truly was the last descendent in the line of Dark Blood, those famous for their skills in battle, she was a true lifemate for one of that lineage.

I should have been more understanding. You were only answering your calling. There was regret in his voice.

Sadly, he knew himself. A man at the helm of an elite pack, the alpha who moved from pack to pack as an acknowledged leader dispensing justice and stopping problems before they got out of hand, had to have the fierce nature he had. There was no changing his wolf, nor did he want to.

I may have been answering my calling, she agreed, *but my first duty is to my lifemate. I made the choice to be bound to you. That was my choice and I stand by our vows. Your needs became mine. I trust that you feel the same toward me.*

The knots in his belly settled a bit. He wanted to scoop her up, drag her out of the cave like the men of old, declaring to the world she belonged to him.

Silly wolf. Of course I belong to you. And it just occurred to me. I don't know why I didn't think of it before. Our souls are tied together, but so are our spirits. I wove them together when you were so mortally wounded. They remain woven together.

How is that going to help this situation? He leaned toward her, recognizing her sudden excitement.

All you have to do is let go of your physical body. The moment you do, your spirit will travel with mine. If you allow me to lead, you will be right there with me, inside Damon, while I work on unraveling safeguards and removing the mage-shadow.

Clever girl. He let his admiration show.

And, Zev . . .

Her voice dropped low, a lyrical tone, one of sheer intimacy, one that penetrated deep into his every cell, wrapping itself around bundles of nerve endings and starting a smoldering fire deep in his belly. He gave her his full attention, focusing wholly on her.

I'm madly in love with your wolf. He can never be too wild for me. He makes me . . .

She broke off her words, but without warning he felt scorching hot silk wrap his cock in a tight, fiery fist, squeezing and gripping erotically. The sensation rushed over him, taking his breath away, leaving him gasping and hungry.

He sent her one warning look, his eyes taking on the glow of the wolf.

Her soft laughter teased at him. That was another huge trait he loved in her—the unexpected sense of fun she had. He hadn't really known laughter until she had come into his life.

You're such a gift, he said.

Around them, the others were standing. Stretching. Ready to leave to go check the Lycans. He couldn't move. Didn't dare move. She wasn't finished with him, not by a long shot.

She sat beside him, so close that he knew she wore clothing, but the illusion of skin to skin was perfect. She threaded her fingers through his and gave a little wave toward her sister and Skyler as they went out of the spacious chamber.

You have no idea what a gift I truly am, she said, her laughter mischievous.

Now he felt the hot, moist lap of her tongue on his shaft, the close of her mouth over him, the dance of her fingers on his heavy sac. She was killing him without actually touching him.

She started to rise to follow the others, but he caught her arm and jerked her back down beside him. At once he saw the flare of heat in her eyes.

"We're right behind you," he called to his brother, and waited until he knew all of them were gone. With one hand, he undid his trousers, with the other, he bunched her hair in his hand and forced her head down into his lap. Zev let his head fall back as she enveloped him in the warmth and love of her mouth.

She never failed to astonish him with teasing, with her heat and the way she was ready and willing to meet his every desire.

"Hello, my wolf," she murmured softly, licking at him like the fierce kitten he named her. "You do look good enough for a dragon to eat."

A blast of heat accompanied her soft declaration. He eyed her warily.

Her laughter vibrated through his shaft, and he forgot all about that little warning, giving himself up to her clever mouth and hands.

II

The three Dragonseeker women took their time building the circle of protection. Branislava and Gregori had consulted numerous times, choosing and then discarding several locations before settling on this one. The clearing was a good distance from the village and far from the home of the prince. There were no farms nearby and no real landmarks should Xaviero surface unexpectedly or detect her as she attempted to remove the mage-shadow.

Mikhail explained the theory to the Lycan council members and Rolf insisted all of them be inspected, although both Arno and Lyall, influential counsel members, protested adamantly, maintaining they didn't want a Carpathian invading their minds. An argument had ensued that had eaten into their time. In the end, Gregori had shrugged and given them an ultimatum. He wasn't going to risk the prince or any of their people. If they didn't want to be inspected, he told them to pack up and leave immediately.

It had taken a good half of the night, with ten Carpathians working to discover if any of the other Lycans were mage-shadowed. No council member was, but three more of the guards were. Daciana and Makoce were fine, as were the other two members of Zev's elite hunting pack, Lykaon and Arnau, Arnos's son.

The three guards, Borya, Pavlo and Igor, reacted as Damon had, horrified that someone else was inside their minds, possibly using them as puppets against their own council members, the members they'd sworn to protect. Zev realized it was possible that the guards who had attacked Rolf and Arno could have been mage-shadowed as well.

The three Dragonseeker women cleansed the meadow, using long wands of sage, cedar, sweet grass, lavender and copal, walking clockwise. White-hot light burst from their fingertips, creating a sacred space in the form of a sphere in the exact center of the meadow. It was important to separate their chosen circle of power from the rest of the space around it. Starting in the eastern corner, they walked counterclockwise, calling forth their four elements to guide and protect them. As they walked together they lifted their voices in unison.

We call to the powers of the East, Air.
We call to the powers of the West, Water.
We call to the powers of the North, Earth.
We call to the powers of the South, Fire.

Skyler took up her position in the northern corner first. She was of the Earth, close to the mother of all living things. She called on Mother Earth to protect and aid them with their task.

Hear our prayers, Great Mother,
We call upon you to protect us in our hour of need.
Thrice around this circle bound,
All evil sink into the ground.

Branislava took up her position in the southernmost corner. She was of the element of fire. She lived it. Breathed it. Understood it. She called upon her element to aid and protect them during their most difficult task.

I call upon that which is fire.
I bid you to build a wall a spire.

Breathe forth your breath,
Make it burn so that none may enter and away must turn.

Ivory took up her position in the eastern corner. She was a force to be reckoned with, a woman who lived her life on the outside of their society. She was lifemate to Razvan, Xavier's grandson and keeper of the wolves who hunted with her. The wind whispered to her at all times, sharing information and protecting her on every hunt. She called to her element of air to protect and aid them with their task.

Current of air that breathes,
Great goddess Hera, let your gales now blow.
Bring forth your winds, let them howl and sing,
Protecting your daughters and all within this ring.

Tatijana was last, gliding over to the western corner, taking up her position. She embodied the element of water. Cool, fluid, and at home in any form of water, she called out, asking for aid and protection for the coming task.

I call to water, blood of life,
Fix your gaze upon this sight.
Let water drop and lightning strike,
Keep evil out, protecting those inside.

Gregori stepped into the center of the sphere created by the women, looking more than impressive. Fen, Dimitri, Razvan, Zev and Darius formed a second circle of protection, ringing the first one of power. Inside that circle, the other three mage-shadowed Lycans lay sleeping.

"We're ready for Damon," Gregori announced.

Zev stepped inside the circle of protection the women had created, and the earth rippled beneath his feet. He sank down in the place he'd been assigned, knowing his spirit would follow Branislava's and leave his body unattended. He was still unused to the Carpathian way of shedding one's body and becoming pure spirit, and he wished he'd practiced some of their gifts more. He needed to be an expert in all things Carpathian as well as those Lycan.

"Zev, stay absolutely quiet and still," Gregori cautioned. "You have a strong personality and your instinct to protect Branislava is very fierce, but in this instance, you would do her more harm than good if you interfere. Have a word that you use between you. Something only you two would know. If she utters that word, she needs your aid. Feed her every bit of power you possess."

Zev nodded his understanding. Branislava was his—everything. He certainly would follow instructions to the letter in order to keep her safe. He was much happier knowing Gregori would be close as well. Gregori wanted to join them in order to learn Xaviero's signature shadow so that he could recognize it in the future. More importantly, he wanted to see the weave of safeguards, the hidden traps Branislava was certain she could uncover so he could aid her in ridding the other three guards of their shadows as well.

"I understand, Gregori. Consider it done."

"The three women present are a force of nature," Gregori continued. "They'll feed Bronnie their energy as she needs it, give her blood when needed. You have to remain absolutely still. You're her safeguard. Her guardian. Xaviero can't suspect she's removing the shadow, so her work will be slow and delicate. You're her last resort."

Zev nodded again. He had never been one to stay in the background in a fight, but in this case, it made sense to him. He might have been born with a small strain of Dark Blood, but he was wolf all the way, and he had no experience in this type of battle. Even his mixed blood didn't prepare him for a war of the mages.

"The men in the second circle will protect us from any outside harm," Gregori added. "Rely on them to have your back. They will stand in the face of any enemy. Your single job is to guard Bronnie and give her that power if she asks for it. No matter what happens around us, stay with Bronnie."

Gregori couldn't have gotten the point across any better. Without a doubt, what they were attempting was extremely dangerous.

Zev let out his breath as Daciana and Makoce led Damon to the sphere. He was blindfolded.

"Go to the edge of the trees and remain there," Gregori instructed the two elite hunters. "Do not set one foot on the meadow. It will be extremely dangerous to you."

Both were clearly already uneasy inside the circle of power. Daciana's hair had risen as an electrical charge had shot through her body. She nodded, squeezed her brother's arm and both Lycans trotted to the edge of the forest to join with Lykaon and Arnau.

Gregori waited until they were far enough away before turning to Damon. "This is your desire, to have the shadow removed from your brain?" Gregori asked.

Zev noticed the women remained absolutely silent. Should Xaviero pick this precise moment to enter his shadow puppet, there was no evidence to betray the identity of the women. Damon would hear only Gregori's voice. He couldn't see anything at all.

"Yes. Thank you. I'd very much appreciate you getting this thing the hell out of my head," Damon said, his voice coming in low growls.

His wolf was close, desperate to protect him. Branislava glanced fearfully at Zev. Should Damon's wolf take over, he would be extremely dangerous. They were threading the needle between the mage and the wolf.

"Damon," Zev said softly. "I am here, watching over you."

The tension seemed to ease in Damon at once. "If I go mad, Zev, I don't want to harm anyone, especially a woman." He inhaled, drawing the scent of each of the women into his lungs. One could blindfold a wolf, but you couldn't deaden his acute sense of smell very easily.

"I know, Damon," Zev assured.

"Promise me. You're my pack leader. It's your duty."

Technically, Zev wasn't really his pack leader. Damon wasn't a member of his elite hunters, but to Zev he was family, and that meant he was part of Zev's pack, elite or not. "You have my word. Just relax and let them do their work. Your wolf knows I'll keep everyone safe."

"We're going to put you to sleep, Damon," Gregori said. "It's much safer for all of us. Should the one who mage-shadowed you attempt to see through your eyes, he will find you in a deep sleep. It is night, he'll think nothing of your being asleep and leave again."

That was their hope. Whether or not their plan worked was something altogether different.

Damon nodded. "One way or another, just please get rid of it. If you can't, don't let me wake up. I'm not going to let him use me to assassinate a council member or kill a woman."

"Your heart is accelerating," Gregori said soothingly. "Remain calm. We're going to remove the mage-shadow."

Zev didn't want to think about what would happen if they couldn't. He wished Daciana was back with the council members, but they'd unwisely allowed her to stay near her brother.

Gregori held his arms up to the sky, palms facing the drifting clouds. Zev felt the swift buildup of energy inside the circle. The hairs on his body stood out as an electrical charge built up around them. Gregori chanted in a low carrying voice.

I command thee sky, darken Earth.

Clouds rushed overhead, boiling and churning, great dark cauldrons blotting out every star and bit of moon to be found.

Earth below now quake and tremble. Gregori's voice swelled with power.

The ground shifted, rising and falling around the outer circle, but didn't cross that line of protection. The clearing rippled with waves, as if the field was alive, a guardian keeping those within the circle protected.

Let flood waters take all who would enter.

Water bubbled from below, the hidden river rising at his command. Around the outer circle the ground sank, forming a deep trench. Water filled the ditch, developing a moat.

Gregori, arms raised to the boiling clouds, moved his hands in a graceful, but deadly pattern. The towering dark clouds lit from within, long forks of orange-red flames.

Mage fire, burn forth in rage, he commanded.

Thunder shook the forest, and lightning slammed from ground to sky and back again, five or six bolts sizzling through the sky to strike the meadow around the circle.

Entrapping shadow within your cage, he finished.

Gregori stepped up beside Damon and drew him into the middle of the circle. He started to wave his hand to send Damon into a sleep, but Branislava and Tatijana both shook their heads.

Xaviero will sense your presence. Your touch as a Carpathian is too strong, too individual, Branislava explained, using the common Carpathian path for communication so all of them could hear. *We need a mage spell that will feel like a real sleep.*

Wouldn't Xaviero spot a mage spell before a Carpathian one? Zev asked.

Carpathians were taught the spells from mages, Gregori said.

Branislava nodded. *True, and they were slightly different for Carpathians so a mage could always tell who had actually cast the spell or woven a safeguard.*

That still means Xaviero would recognize a mage spell, Zev insisted.

Branislava and Tatijana exchanged a small smile. Branislava shook her head. *Not if we changed the spell yet again. We had little to do behind those walls of ice but learn. We are every bit as adept as the three of them.*

Branka, I love your confidence. Zev had faith in her, but he knew how terrified she was of Xaviero. She hadn't wanted to face the mage and had only committed to erasing the shadow because she feared no one else could do it without harming themselves.

It's the simple truth, Zev, but we don't practice the dark arts like they do. We might know each spell—we felt it necessary to learn in order to reverse them—but we refused to use our gifts for anything other than good.

Or mischief, he teased, wanting to see her smile. Her complexion was stark white, her eyes enormous, looking like two emeralds pressed into her face.

She turned her head to look at him and gave him a smile that was worth more than all the gold in the world to him. His heart gave a little stutter and he placed his palm over his chest in a small tribute to her.

For a long moment, Branislava's gaze clung to Zev's. They stared into each another's eyes, hers questioning. He nodded slowly and then she answered his nod with one of her own, showing him they were in perfect accord.

Branislava closed her eyes and sent her own prayer to the universe, calling on all things good and right for aid.

Valerian, Lemon Balm, German Chamomile,
I call forth your essence to calm and wile.
Lavender, Catnip, heed my call,
Bring peaceful sleep so evil may not call.

Damon's eyes closed obediently under the blindfold, his face peaceful, not showing any of the stress that had been stamped there just minutes before.

Gregori unexpectedly reached out and took both of Branislava's hands. "You have great courage, Dragonseeker courage. This time you are not alone in your fight to save this man. We're with you and will aid you in every possible way. More, you are tied, spirit and soul to your lifemate. He is Dark Blood—from our strongest line of warriors. I have no doubt that you can do this and triumph."

In those strange liquid silver eyes that had always given her pause, as they were so much like those of the High Mage, Xavier, and that of his brothers, she saw the fire reflected there—*her* fire. She was the manipulator of fire.

She nodded her head again, and then glanced around the circle to each one of her sister-kin—the Dragonseeker women. Tatijana, so beloved, so close she would always be a part of Branislava. Young Skyler, so powerful and intelligent, a young sister full of life. Ivory, elusive and a skilled warrior, loyal and poetic. They surrounded her, ready to fight with her.

And Zev. Her wolf. Her everything. When had it gotten to be that way? She didn't even know, but he was her other half. She loved everything about him, and her faith in him would never waiver. He was her protector and he stood ready.

Branislava let go of her own body with confidence, becoming pure healing energy. It was always a bit of a wrench going from physical to astral, but once she shed her physical form, there was a sense of freedom unlike any she'd ever experienced.

She moved into Damon. He was calm, but she felt the watchful presence of his wolf. She sent the animal side of the Lycan both friendship and reassurance, grateful that Zev's aura was so strong. The wolf recognized him and settled without protest. She knew where the shadow had adhered to the brain, forming a lesion for Xaviero to use as an entry point. He could take control of Damon through the small stain and direct his activities. It was an abomination of life and free will and it wasn't tolerated by any society, yet Xaviero had managed to infect many of the Lycans without anyone's knowledge.

Branislava thought of this moment as her first real strike back at the High Mage. No one had ever managed to oppose him, not and lived to tell about it. She studied the area around the shadow. The ridges and valleys around the darker spot appeared to be untouched. She wasn't fooled. Xaviero's traps were clever and strong. He twisted light and bent it, weaving it into his spells so his most deadly traps always appeared to be the safest path to take.

Scattered throughout the grayish matter were those white cells—the filaments carrying commands. She saw the clever spots Xaviero had left around his shadow, those marks meant to trick an enemy into believing those were the places to avoid while the real danger was the very innocent-looking white filaments the mage used to send his commands throughout Damon's body.

She moved around the hot spots checking for the current of dark magic energy the mage couldn't help but leave behind. The moment she encountered it, she stayed perfectly still in her form as well as in her mind. Absolute calm was called for as she tested a strand of the weave like a delicate spider, her touch light, almost nonexistent. Had she still been inside her body her heart would have accelerated and her mouth would have gone dry. She felt the adrenaline and buildup of stress, with no real way to rid herself of it.

Your great advantage is that you have seen his work a million times, yet he has never once seen yours.

Zev. Her protector. He was to stay silent, waiting for his moment to feed her his strength, but there was so much more to their partnership. He had given her truth. He was so right. Xaviero had dismissed Tatijana and Branislava so easily, using them for his audience just as Xavier had done, but he had never credited them with brains or the ability to learn from him and his brothers.

You learned from all three. Doesn't that give you more knowledge?

Sadly, she'd learned all of it, both white and black magic.

Not sadly. You have knowledge that will help defeat a mage bent on destroying three species and ruling another. Don't you think there is a higher purpose for your skills? No one else can stop this mage.

Zev had a way of cutting through the emotion to get to the very heart of the truth. Again she examined those telling white filaments. Tiny microscopic hairs, so delicate she would have missed them had she not known what to look for. They were so thin, those weaves, one layer on top of the next so that a web of protection surrounded the shadow. Looking closer, she saw the weave formed a snare over the mark, but the hairs were darker, blending with the shadow.

I know this one. His classic blend of light and dark. He starts with white magic, using elements that are good, goes to those that are neutral and then calls upon darkness to hide within the weave he's made. He spins those strands over and over, a seven-point weave that is strong. But I can go backward and carefully remove the seven strands.

Branislava expanded her mind, calling on the power within, that smoldering fire always present in her deepest depth, running through her veins like molten lava.

Spirits I call you, twist and unbind,
That which was born of gray magic,
To entrap and entwine.
Dark is to light as light is to gray,
Each strand I unwrap,
To send darkness away.
Future to present, present to past,
Unwrap that which was woven,
So no more shall it cast.

One by one, those strands fell away, the tiny hairs pulling back to allow her to see the actual shadow she had to remove. Just to be certain she was safe, because she didn't trust Xaviero would not have a fail-safe, she took another careful look around the entire vicinity near the mage-shadow. There was no visual evidence of another trap, but she felt uneasy each time she got a little closer to the shadow and she kept her energy as low and as dim as possible, not wanting to accidentally spill across that shadow when she was certain there was another safeguard.

She studied the mark from every direction, first moving above it. She thought she caught a little glimmer, but it was gone before she could actually know for certain. She approached from the left side and saw nothing at all. From below, she caught the same flicker of movement, but it was gone as quickly as she noted it. From the right, a brief little shimmer told her for certain there was another weave.

She'd seen Xaviero use the technique many times. The safeguard continually moved position, several times in seconds so that it was nearly impossible to detect. Had she not known what she was looking for, she would have tripped his fail-safe.

Stopping this one was a little more difficult, but certainly not impossible. She had watched him, eye open and pressed to the wall of thick ice, so that the distortion, although present, hadn't prevented her from seeing the intricate motions he had performed, the dance of his hands, so graceful, almost beautiful when he was conjuring a deadly trap. She had been fascinated by the movement, almost mesmerized.

She followed that dance pattern so completely engraved in her mind with the flowing light of her spirit, although she started at the end of his pattern and traced her way to the beginning.

Seven points you have woven,
Seven points I unwind.
With each flash of light,
I unravel, I unbind.

The glimmer shone bright and then dissolved as if it had never been. Branislava took an imaginary breath. She had no idea of time passing, but she could tell what she was doing was draining. An out-of-body experience could drain one's energy on its own; working at mind games and unraveling deadly traps while fearing the High Mage would come calling left her a little tired.

Almost before she could acknowledge she was growing weary, she felt Tatijana pour strength into her. At once she was revitalized. Once again she moved toward the shadow. She had to do this in careful steps. She couldn't just take the mage-shadow away without alerting Xaviero. Should he suddenly check on Damon—and she was certain he would—he had to believe all was well and Damon merely slept the normal sleep of Lycans and humans. It was nighttime there and would be believable.

Why would he check on Damon? Zev asked.

He is High Mage, extraordinary and wholly sensitive to any disturbance in his web of evil. He won't know what is bothering him, but it will be there, like a nagging toothache. He'll need to check those puppets he sent to this area in order to see if something has happened. He'll want to rule out those closest to the Carpathians first.

How do you stop him from knowing you're working at removing his shadow?

By creating his safeguards over me.

She could tell by Zev's silence he didn't like the idea at all, but to his credit, he didn't say anything. She was the expert in this field, and he had no choice but to trust her judgment. This was her most telling moment. She had to move into place above the shadow, very close without touching it, and above and around her put both safeguards back.

Once Xaviero's safeguards are in place, no one else can give me energy but you, she said to Zev. *Only you can supply me through the spirit weave we have. That's our advantage because it is impossible for Xaviero to detect it. Any of my sister-kin can give you strength, but only you must feed me.*

It was almost as if fate or destiny had provided the necessary steps for them, creating a situation where she could fight Xaviero without all the advantages on his side. Keeping her spirit dim, she first wove the outer guard, wincing as she added the darker magic into the white and neutral elements.

She felt ill uttering the foul words, but she used her best version of Xaviero. Mimicking the three brothers had become a skill she and Tatijana had learned as children. Both practiced all the time as they grew up. She had never imagined their game of mocking the triplets would ever be a skill she needed, but she was grateful she was good enough at casting. She believed he wouldn't recognize her weave wasn't actually his.

When she was certain the top layer of his safeguard was in place and appeared just as she remembered it, she began to weave the glimmer directly overhead and so close there was barely room for even her spirit to maneuver. She knew she took too long. She had wanted to ensure she didn't make a mistake and she told herself not to hurry, but the longer her presence remained, along with the use of energy, she knew she would draw Xaviero like a magnet straight to her. He would come oozing out of his darkest hellhole, pouring himself into Damon, a giant venomous snake ready to strike.

She waited, lying low, staying huddled as small as possible, willing Zev to do the same. She should have warned him of the feeling one could get when confronted with pure evil. She didn't dare reach into his mind, not when she felt the first dark stirrings. How did one describe evil?

The feeling of dread came first, that tingle of awareness creeping with cold fingers down her spine. She felt the physical reaction as if her spirit was still inside her human form. The hair of her body reacted next, standing up. She had been encased in thick ice, entombed there for centuries, and always, she felt any of the three brothers long before they entered the room.

Next came the slimy sensation, as if green sticky oil spread over her skin, coating her, clogging pores and inhibiting her ability to breathe, so that she had to draw in air in short, shallow, ragged gasps, and only when it was absolutely necessary to do so or pass out.

Then the stenches came, a foul odor of complete corruption and decay that once in her lungs refused to leave for a long, long time. She woke in the middle of her slumber at times and still smelled him, so close, as if his bony fingers reached for her, to wrap around her throat, squeezing her last breath, laughing while he did so.

Her heart pounded. Her blood thundered in her ears. He was coming for her. It was really Xaviero. He was alive and he would find her. At once Zev was there, wrapping his spirit around hers, holding her close to him, sheltering her from the terror of such a nightmarish remembrance.

The moment she felt Zev's strength, the moment his love pushed against those terrifying memories, he drove away the evil smile and foul breath as Xaviero stuck his face so close against hers, watching her face go blue and her eyes go wide as she struggled to breathe. If she could have she would have touched her throat. She hadn't thought about those times in a long while. So close to him, knowing he was pouring himself into Damon's mage-shadow in order to see and hear what Damon could might have paralyzed her without Zev so close.

All at once, she felt him. His actual presence was far worse than the heralding of evil. Damon's mind filled with malevolent, revolting thoughts.

She knew instantly why Damon had panicked and wanted the mage-shadow gone. He was a moral man with high values and standards. Xaviero delighted in corrupting anyone good. He pushed immoral and malicious thoughts into Damon's mind, choosing the vilest, nasty and criminal acts he felt he could lead Damon to do.

She settled low, near the very base of the shadow-mark, praying he wouldn't find her. He studied his handiwork, his suspicion evident in his close perusal, although he obviously didn't really expect to find anything. She couldn't imagine he would ever believe—after having his way for so long—that an opponent would actually find him, let alone challenge him.

The only possible person would be his brother Xayvion, and she didn't even know if Xayvion was alive. Still, Xaviero had stayed alive and hidden because he was extremely careful. He took his time, looking over his handiwork before he decided he was safe to use his puppet.

She felt the swelling of his power and he commanded Damon to look around him. Damon didn't respond, but lay as still as death. She felt the swell of anger, bordering on rage. No one, least of all his puppets, could ever defy him. She felt the retaliation in the form of pain, as if a thousand needles pierced Damon's skull to stick into his brain.

Her spell held. She realized if Xaviero had tried to test the other five Lycans who had been sent to assassinate Skyler and Dimitri in the forest, he would have found nothing at all. He would have known they were dead. It might appear to him that Damon was unconscious, not sleeping. That suited her just fine. Xaviero would abandon Damon and go after one of the other remaining puppets. They had been given powerful sedatives to keep the High Mage from accessing their brains and memories while Branislava tried to remove the first mage-shadow.

Xaviero didn't give up easily. He wanted to know what had happened to his servants. He poked and prodded over and over, sending hot needles through the skull to try to wake Damon from whatever state he was in. When that failed he maliciously planted more disturbing thoughts, this time of wanting to kill his sister and Zev. He repeated the order over and over, driving it deep into Damon's subconscious through the portal he had made in Damon's brain.

She couldn't imagine how Damon would feel if he used any of the medieval ways of killing his sister Xaviero had ordered him to use and afterward returned to himself and had to live with his deed. She had no doubt now that Xaviero had been behind the sentence of death by silver passed on Dimitri, that horrible Machiavellian torture supposedly ordered by the council. She didn't doubt for one moment that he controlled at least one council member and perhaps more, and not necessarily through a mage-shadow.

Xaviero retreated. She didn't move or make a sound. Zev followed her lead. She was grateful he was so patient. As a hunter he had learned the value of patience and he didn't move or try to ask her why she waited. Time passed. It could have been ten minutes or an hour, she didn't know or care. Xaviero would return. He trusted nothing to chance and he'd been more than a little suspicious when he checked his handiwork.

Evil poured into Damon's mind like sludge. Thick and oily, the muck was foul. Xaviero rushed in fast, his murky light spinning one way and then the next, but no one had dared disturb his creation. He sent another spate of hot needles driving through Damon's skull, hoping to shock him awake. When it didn't happen, he left a second time, this time abruptly like a spoiled child angry with a broken toy.

The moment he was gone, Branislava moved out of hiding and began to unweave the two safeguards above her. She didn't want to remain trapped within that web of danger he had created should he return a third time. Again, she used patience, careful to make certain she didn't disturb one single fiber as she dismantled Xaviero's protections, piece by piece. She thought of him as a deadly, poisonous spider sitting in the middle of his giant web, just waiting for an unsuspecting victim to happen by. She refused to be his victim ever again.

The moment both defenses were down, she went to work, circling the darker shadow blending with the grayish matter in the ridges and valleys of Damon's brain. The portal wasn't raised at all; it just appeared as a smudge, nothing more, a small oval, elongated smear of charcoal that could easily be overlooked if one went searching. Right on the very tip of each side was a particular loop, a small flaw in the perfect oval—Xaviero's signature.

Xavier and Xayvion had argued endlessly with him, but Xaviero held firm. He thought each of them should have a distinctive signature no one else would recognize. Perhaps he had a precog episode where he "saw" Xavier killing him. But she doubted if that was real. After all, it was quite clear to her that they had faked the deaths, but to what purpose, she didn't know.

Had the triplets known that Tatijana and she would escape some day? That seemed very doubtful. They couldn't have known, and if they had, their solution wouldn't be to fake their deaths. It would be to murder her and her sister.

She sent up a silent prayer that when Xaviero replayed the entire event back in his head—and he would—he'd find she hadn't left behind a single telling signature. She was lucky in that while Xaviero knew his brothers' work and probably every one of the mages who had trained under Xavier, he had never actually seen her capabilities. Most likely none of the triplets believed that she or Tatijana might be able to cast. It hadn't occurred to the brothers that they had nothing to do to keep their minds active but learn— and that was such a distinct advantage.

She realized she was afraid of Xaviero, but was no longer completely and utterly terrified of him. Somehow, in confronting her worst nightmare, she had gained confidence in herself. She took a deep cleansing breath, or at least, thought that she did so. She pushed aside all doubt and concentrated on the fight to save Damon.

Hail grandmother, spirit of the North,
I call upon thee to defend me this night.
Hail grandmother, spirit of the South,
I call upon thee to attend this rite.

Without a body, she turned her own spirit both north and south in a salute of respect and gratitude, taking nothing at all for granted, but sending her plea out to universe.

Hail grandmother spirit of the East,
I call upon your forces to protect me with might.
Hail grandmother spirit of the West,
I seek your wisdom and guidance this night.

She turned her spirit both east and west, in a gesture of great reverence and admiration.

I call to thee Hecate, triple goddess above,
Maiden, mother, crone, see my plight.
Hecate, dark mother who heals the rights and wrongs,
I call forth your power so that I may remain strong.

She felt power running through her spirit. The white light began to glow a soft pink and then light red. Another breath and her spirit was dark red.

I seek the power to cast lightning's blast,
So that shadow may burn, undoing that which has been cast.
Twist and turn, heal but burn,
Peeling shadow away, let life now return.

From her spirit, lightning forked and then settled into one steady stream as if the fine tip was a laser. Slowly, with great care, making certain to remove the stain of Xaviero's shadow, she burned the layers away. It seemed to take forever, and all the while she feared he would suddenly realize and return. The moment the shadow was gone, she began the work of healing, sending rejuvenating cells to cover the damaged layer.

12

B ranislava had never been so exhausted in her life, but now wasn't the time to rest on her laurels. Xaviero had just lost his first battle and he wasn't going to be happy. When he was unhappy, others paid the price. He would go after the remaining three Lycans there in the Carpathian stronghold, and if he couldn't use them to strike at those he considered his enemies, he would send others very quickly.

She found herself back in her body, but she didn't have the strength to push herself off the ground. She sent up a silent prayer that she hadn't left any trace of herself Xaviero could find when he replayed the scene of his shadow over and over in his head, looking for the tiniest detail to ascertain his enemy.

She knew what his first thought would be, and that would buy them time. The three brothers had always enjoyed their ability to hide each other from the rest of the world. It gave them the freedom to do whatever they wanted in absolute secret, knowing they couldn't get caught. They always had a firm alibi. They felt superior to all others.

Branislava knew Xaviero would think one of his brothers had purposely opposed him. Who else could possibly manage to outmaneuver him? No one else was that brilliant. He would be raging, throwing one of his infamous fits. How many times had she seen him turn his anger on others?

"We don't have much time," she managed to gasp out. "Get the others into the circle. Gregori, did you see how to take down his safeguards? There's no need to rebuild them. Take them down and remove the shadow as fast as possible." Urgency was in her voice, desperation in her eyes. "We have only minutes to save them if we're going to."

Ivory crouched beside her, pressing her wrist to Branislava's mouth. Branislava couldn't help but almost gulp at the nutrients Ivory provided. Her body felt starved and thin. She was aware of Skyler providing blood for Zev. He held out his hand to her and she grasped it like a drowning woman would a life preserver.

Her heart pounded and her mouth was dry. He was coming for the others and he would be in a particularly ugly mood. She met Tatijana's gaze. She knew as well.

Gregori opened a pathway to the circle and this time it was Dimitri, Fen and Razvan who carried the sleeping Lycans into the protection of the sphere. They returned to the outside circle, ready to ward off any that might threaten those working to remove the shadows.

"Each of you choose one," Branislava said. "Remember, he'll come fast, pouring in like liquid, and he'll strike at both you and his victim."

She didn't bother to wait for an answer, but shed her body quickly and chose the one called Igor. She didn't know him, but Daciana had spoken highly of him. She knew where the shadow was and she didn't waste time looking around. If Xaviero had mass-shadowed these men without their knowledge, he couldn't take the time to vary each position. He would use that most advantageous to him, a region of the brain where he could command the thoughts and actions.

She found the shadow right where she knew it would be and began unraveling the safeguards, using the exact method she'd used on Damon. Layer upon layer of webbing disappeared and she reached the glimmer. Again, she took it down, going for speed rather than delicacy. Removing and repairing that mage-shadow required time whether she liked it or not, and she knew any of the three working on the Lycans could draw the attention of Xaviero.

She didn't want him going after Tatijana. In the ice caves, she had always stepped in front of her sister to redirect the attention of Xavier and his brothers away from her. Tatijana's health had always been just that little bit more fragile than hers and she never wanted any of the brothers to notice it. They were so wrapped up in their experiments and plans to become immortal and rule the world that they hadn't bothered with the sisters unless they needed blood.

As terrified as she was of Xaviero, perhaps she still deliberately drew his attention away from Tatijana. She knew her instinct for protecting her sister was extremely strong, but for whatever reasons, even as she worked feverishly to draw the lightning to the shadow, she had disturbed his traps enough to draw him to his victim.

She felt evil pouring into Igor's brain through the dark portal. Xaviero came fast, just as she had predicted he would. He'd already been seeking his three remaining Lycans, wanting news and to get as much damage as possible from his puppets before they, too, were cleansed or killed.

I know you're here.

His voice alone made her shiver, those cold fingers, like death, wrapping around her throat, ready to squeeze the life out of her while he smiled down into her eyes.

He doesn't know it is you, Zev whispered into her mind. *He's fishing. Don't take the bait. Keep working. You might trap some part of him here.*

Branislava pushed aside centuries of terror and called on the fire. She lived for that heat. The red-orange flames and white-hot energy. Always inside of her, she felt the magma smoldering, waiting for a chance to erupt in whatever form possible, whether intense passion, her mage spells or soaring through the sky, the fire was always close. She nearly forgot to control the energy leaping to her, ready to do her bidding.

She directed the fine point of a laser at the mark and began burning it away. She made certain she took the matter around the shadow as well, giving Xaviero no place to hide. It took time, time she didn't know if she had, but there was Zev and she had to trust him to watch out for her while she worked.

What are you doing, Xayvion? This was done for both of us. Your work with the Jaguars was beyond compare. Xaviero added the flattery in his most admiring tone. *We are so close to the completion of our plan. With Xavier gone, we have to be more innovative. Turn Lycan against Carpathian. I've waited for centuries for the perfect opportunity and I've found it.*

Branislava felt a small surge of triumph. Xaviero was so certain only his brother Xayvion could oppose him, he hadn't considered the lowly girls he'd tormented in the ice caves. They were beneath his notice other than for his amusement when he was bored.

She kept working, using the laser point of the lightning to move the burn along the outer edges of the portal, shrinking the area so that Xaviero could see that his choices were diminishing rapidly. If he wanted to escape, he would have to leave. Everything in him wanted a confrontation.

He struck hard and fast, the entire brain swelling, pressing into the outer edges of the skull so that the Lycan began to seize violently. Branislava had no choice but to stop her work and aid Igor or she would lose him. The moment she did, he would know his brother wasn't his opponent.

Keep working. Shrink his escape route, Zev advised. *If you begin to counter his every move, he will win this battle. Concentrate on removing that mark. I'll do what I can to protect Igor each time Xaviero throws something at him.*

Zev made sense. The longer the portal was open, the more damage Xaviero could do. But she didn't want Zev in harm's way. She kept working, forcing herself to be methodical and careful. Using the fine laser point of hot energy to burn away the shadow was difficult with Igor seizing.

Zev used his healing energy to move around the brain and take down the swelling, carefully avoiding moving fast, rather drifting through the fluid in an effort to keep from drawing the High Mage's attention. The seizures slowed and then stopped without Xaviero being any closer to knowing the identity of his enemy.

There was a small stillness that boded ill. Branislava continued to work, burning away the mage-shadow from the outside to the inside, narrowing the portal as quickly as possible without permanently harming Igor.

Without warning, worms erupted through the brain matter, tiny wiggling white worms with teeth. They appeared starving, biting viciously at the brain as if they would devour it. This time, Branislava knew she had no choice. She had to rid Igor of the malevolent creatures, or he would die in spite of all she had done. With trepidation, she opened her mind to counter his spell.

Zev blocked that opening solidly, refusing to give Xaviero a point of entry. *Use the laser to burn them away. Don't let him draw you into a match of spells, or give him any clue to your identity.*

Branislava did so immediately, skimming the laser over the brain much like a fire-breathing dragon. She had much skill in this kind of warfare and used her knowledge to rid the brain of the terrible worms feeding on it. They blackened and turned to ash even as she turned back and relentlessly continued closing the mage-shadow.

Xaviero shrieked his rage, erupting into a temper tantrum, something she remembered vividly from her centuries encased in ice. A thousand spears of ice pierced every conceivable spot of Igor's brain, striking everywhere, countering the lightning spear. There was no way to avoid the dangerous icicles stabbing from every direction.

Zev countered with heat, melting them, but not before both of their spirits were pierced with the mage's weapons.

How bad are you hurt? he asked anxiously. He was pierced through and through and felt as if his body was bleeding from dozens of wounds.

I can do this.

There was a hitch in her voice that caused him concern, but he had to trust her. *Keep working,* he advised. *I'll do my best to work on Igor's wounds.*

Some of them are deep. You have to repair them or we'll lose him anyway.

Branislava bit down hard on the need to hurry. She was so close and she didn't dare make a mistake, but her spirit felt ragged, torn, so thin, her strength waning. She couldn't get a boost from Zev, he was using everything he had in his attempt to save Igor and counter Xaviero's attacks.

She kept the laser in continuous motion, slowly squeezing the portal until it was almost nothing. She dared not feel triumphant yet. Now was the moment Xaviero had to make a decision. Did he try another attack and risk a part of him being trapped? A good mage could use that small part against him. Or did he flee without knowing the identity of his opponent?

Xaviero poured himself into the portal, but as he did so, he sent one last command to Igor. The Lycan's heart reacted as the stimuli raced through the pathways, laden with chemicals. Zev was fighting to repair the damage to the brain and Branislava was busy closing the portal to prevent Xaviero from returning. The heart seized.

The attack was massive. There was no way to stop the brain from shutting down. Branislava tried, refusing to give in, desperate to keep from losing the man she and Zev fought so hard for. No matter what they did, Igor didn't respond, Xaviero making certain he had thwarted them in the end.

Branislava's breath caught in her throat. *He'll go after the other two and do the same thing. Can you aid Gregori? Use a laser? With two of you it will be twice as fast.*

Zev followed her spirit from the dead body of the Lycan, just as determined as she was to save the lives of the other two. He didn't like the idea of splitting up, but he told himself they were tied together, spirit to spirit, and if needed, he could pull her out fast.

I'll do my best. He refused to flinch at the idea of using lightning. He had a healthy respect for nature, but the way the Carpathians regularly wielded it without harming themselves was amazing to him and something he was determined to learn—just not when trying to save a fellow Lycan.

Branislava's spirit entered Pavlo, the Lycan Tatijana was working on to remove the mage-shadow. Like all of them, Tatijana had never actually attempted to remove a shadow, certainly not one placed by a High Mage, and she worked slowly and methodically to make certain she didn't make a mistake.

The safeguards were down and she was removing the shadow from the left side, slowly burning away the mark using a sweeping motion from side to side.

He's coming Tatijana, Branislava warned, conveying her sense of urgency with her tone and the fact that she pulled lightning to her and began wielding the laser as fast as she safely could. *He killed Igor and he'll try for this one as well as the Lycan Gregori is working on. Pick up the pace. I'm going to try something new.*

Instead of going from the outside of the circle in, she began burning strips of the shadow from front to back, close together, so that if Xaviero tried entering, he couldn't do so easily. Tatijana quickly followed suit from the other side, racing to stop Xaviero's entrance. The moment they met in the middle, they began working backward, filling in the stripes so that every single tiny section of the portal was burned closed.

As Branislava began the final circle to ensure there was no hidden way in around the outer edges of the shadow where they couldn't see, she felt the sudden push against her as Xaviero tried to force his way through.

Tatijana gasped and cringed, her spirit moving back away from the shadow. *He's here.*

But he can't enter. Finish the outer edges of the circle and then begin the healing process on the burn. I'm going to help the others.

She didn't wait for her sister's reaction. She left Pavlo and just as quickly entered the last Lycan. Zev worked on one end of the shadow, slowly and meticulously. Gregori was at the other end.

He's coming and he's really angry. I'll help Zev close the portal, Gregori, but you have to keep him from Borya's heart. If he can't get to the heart, he'll go after another vital organ to kill him.

She knew Zev would want the job of protecting Borya. He felt passionate about protecting Lycans, but he wasn't as experienced in battling mages. Gregori was powerful in magic and he'd studied spells, both black and white, far more than most Carpathians ever had. She couldn't open her mind to Gregori's or that would give Xaviero access as well, but she trusted the healer to fight the mage off his patient.

Try not to let him see who you are. He suspects his brother is thwarting his efforts in a power play to take over the ruling of all species. If he continues to believe that, it could give us a small advantage. She was already wielding the lightning laser, using the same striping technique she'd used on Pavlo. Unfortunately, mages adapted fast and Xaviero would already expect his brother to close the portal in a similar fashion.

Good point, Gregori said, and built up his energy to block whatever the mage chose to throw at Borya.

Zev, start from the bottom and create strips as I'm doing, so we form a waffle pattern. Make your lines as close together as possible and we'll go back and fill them in when we're done with this.

She contemplated using a broader tip for the laser to take in more area, but the work was too delicate and the lightning difficult to control. She felt that wrenching sickness when Xaviero's foul stench poured into the skull.

Did you really think you could save these pitiful creatures from me? They are enslaved, mine to command. I refuse to allow you to use them for yourself, Xaviero exclaimed.

He's baiting again, Zev cautioned. *He wants you to taunt him with the fact that you saved one of them.*

It would have been easy enough to fall into that trap, but Branislava's confidence was growing with each encounter. She'd lost Igor, yes, but she had nearly trapped Xaviero in that shrinking shadow, and she and Tatijana had prevented his entrance into Pavlo, essentially saving his life. She didn't rise to the bait.

Once more, she felt black rage fill the skull, so powerful and strong it nearly pushed the skull bones apart. Gregori was there instantly, holding the skull in place. Xaviero shrieked, the sound reverberating through Borya's entire body. He sounded hideous, enraged, maddened with his inability to draw out his enemy. The sounds he made felt as if he was raking the inside of her head and ears apart, tearing off long strips of skin and turning her organs to jelly.

Your body is not here, Zev reminded her gently, calmly.

She was proud of him. He had not stopped working, even for a moment, while she had given a microsecond's pause. Xaviero would catch that mistake when he replayed the battle, but there was nothing she could do about it.

Will Borya's body turn to mush when it processes that sound? Branislava couldn't help but be anxious. She continued to work as quickly as possible and wanted to command Zev to pick up his pace.

In anticipation I had already plugged his ears, making him essentially deaf for the time being. There is a shield around his heart, Gregori assured her. *Xaviero will know it is Carpathian in structure, but certainly not who—although he might recognize my handiwork, you never know. Either way, it won't matter because he'll know there are at least two of us working against him.*

Branislava let out a brief sigh of relief, at least she felt as though she did. It was strange not to have a body, yet still feel the reactions of one.

Xaviero struck a second time, shooting electrical charges throughout the body, over and over, the neurons firing like crazy, the filaments nearly dancing at the surges racing through them to every nerve ending delivering the commands of the High Mage to his servant's body.

Gregori deflected each command, sometimes anticipating where Xaviero attacked next and other times rushing to get ahead of the electricity as it threatened to fry internal organs. The third attack was directed at the Lycan's lungs, so that every bit of fluid tore from the extremities to pool in a central location.

Terád keje—get scorched, you mage from hell, Gregori muttered under his breath, the curse finding its way into Branislava's head.

She knew what the healer was going to do, but there was no way to stop him, and in truth, it mattered little. Xaviero already was aware someone was in the Carpathian camp freeing or killing his puppets. It stood to reason that Gregori would be aiding Xaviero's enemy.

Thunder roar bring forth chains of light,
Cloud to ground let lightning strike.
Arch to channel magnetic field,
Current run so shadowed flesh does feel.

Xaviero shrieked and bolted. Branislava swore using very unladylike words to express her disappointment. She'd been so close to trapping him. A few more seconds and she and Zev would have closed the portal, shutting a part of Xaviero inside the burn. She could have killed it, diminishing the High Mage's power just a little.

She couldn't blame Gregori for retaliating, not when Xaviero was trying every way possible to kill the Lycan. She finished closing the portal, and both she and Zev sank down the moment they let loose of the lightning, their spirits in tatters. Both had been wounded by the ice spears and the teeth of the tiny white wormlike creatures Xaviero had sent to kill Damon.

I can finish up here, Gregori assured. *You both need to rest.*

Branislava knew it was the truth, but she wasn't certain she could comply with her mind racing and fear making her teeth chatter. Exhaustion had set in, far beyond anything she'd ever known. She did feel triumphant. In the end, Xaviero hadn't identified her. He had found Gregori. Who could possibly mistake the power of the Carpathian healer? But he hadn't identified Tatijana or Branislava, and that was a victory in itself.

Come on, mon chaton féroce, Zev said gently, his tone turning her inside out. *It's time to rest. You've done your part and there's nothing more to do but relax, take a little sustenance and lay in my arms.*

It sounded good to her. Branislava slipped from Borya's head and back into her own body. She slumped over, too tired to maneuver such an unwieldy heavy load with her spirit so tattered. Dimitri was there instantly, kneeling beside her, gathering her up and pressing his wrist to her mouth.

"Little sister, take what is freely offered," he said formally. "And be quick about it. You look so pale I think you're translucent."

"It's the red hair," Fen commented, helping Zev. "It makes her look like a ghost when she's not fed."

I'd retaliate with something brilliant but I'm just too tired, Branislava said truthfully.

She wanted to close her eyes and just go to sleep, maybe sink her body deep beneath the earth right where she was.

Tatijana emerged from the Lycan she just healed and smiled at her sister. "Fen is a terrible tease, isn't he? I'll kick him for you when I have the strength."

Thanks, Tatijana, Branislava said. *You're the best sister a girl could have.*

"I have strength," Skyler volunteered. "I'll do it for you." She suited action to words, landing a fairly easy kick on Fen's shin. "That's from Bronnie."

"Nice, Skyler." Fen scowled his most fierce scowl. "Dimitri, control your wild woman."

Dimitri shrugged. "You do find a way to rile them all up, don't you?"

Gregori emerged next and Ivory was immediately beside him, giving him necessary blood. They sat together in silence, the Lycans they'd saved still unaware and the one who lay dead a testament to Xaviero's cruelty.

Fen, Dimitri and Zev all swung around at the same time, facing outward, leaping to their feet. Zev could feel the disturbance coming at them. The energy was low, almost too low, but the intent was murderous.

"What it is?" Gregori asked. He closed the wound on Ivory's wrist at the last moment.

"Xaviero has found another way to attack us. He's sent another wave of his army racing toward us. This is a rogue pack and they'll kill and devour every species," Zev answered. "The Earth is telling me they're only a few kilometers away from this clearing. Those outside the circle of protection will be killed. We have to get to them. Leave those healing here."

Zev glanced at Fen and Dimitri. "I'll go at them from the front. They'll come at me hard. You close in from either side. Daciana and Makoce know what to do. They'll be in the thick of it. Gregori, can you mop up after the kill? It's a difficult job to continually sever heads, but it has to be done."

"Are you okay to do this, Zev?" Fen asked. "You're wounded, and so is Bronnie. Gregori's exhausted."

Zev shrugged. "It has to be done."

Gregori nodded. "No problem. If Zev can do this, so can I. I've fought them enough times now that I know how they work. No need to worry, I've made my own silver sword according to your blueprint of specs."

Zev turned his head to frown at him. "Mine?" His eyes met Tatijana's.

She grinned at him and shrugged. "I can't help it if you talk in your sleep. You passed out, remember?"

Branislava pushed herself up to her feet. Her head felt as if it might explode, a testimony to the ice spears Xaviero had sent. "Nice to know I can get all kinds of information out of you," she commented. It took a moment to get her legs back. She swayed a little, but then straightened her shoulders, shrugging off weakness.

"You and Tatijana take to the sky," Zev told her. "You'll serve us better up there. Both of you know the distances wolves can jump, so take that into consideration when you fly low."

Branislava nodded. She circled his neck with one arm and kissed him lightly. "We'll be careful. You come back to me."

He kissed her back, and then turned his attention to Skyler and Ivory. "You two both can use your connection with Mother Earth as well as your wolves. Pick off the strays and stragglers. Stay to the outside of the main pack coming at us. Remember to watch for traps. Your wolves will ferret them out better than you. Listen to the Earth, and don't get killed."

Skyler and Ivory both nodded.

"Gregori, open a path through the clearing. If we're lucky, we can run some of the rogues right into this trap," Zev said. "And if we're *very* lucky, they will not be led by a *Sange rau*. If you run into one, or even think there's one in the vicinity, call out to Fen, Dimitri or me. I'm not as adept at fighting them. I think Fen is the most advanced version of the *Hän ku pesäk kaikak*, so if it comes to that, we'll all follow his lead."

Fen nodded. "Let's get this done, before they find any of our people."

Gregori immediately lifted his hands, facing outside the protective, double-ringed sphere.

I call to thee Air which propels and blows,
I call to thee Fire which burns below.
I call to thee Water, send forth your gales,
I call to thee Earth that brings forth a mist that cloaks and veils.

Cleanse and clear,
Seal this pass.
Closing all,
After all here have passed.

Zev left the protection of the sphere first, with Fen and Dimitri fanning out on either side of him. Each of them tested the air and the ground beneath their feet. Gregori had opened a wide enough path that the chaos from the lightning forks didn't affect their ability to scan for information, but it did wreak havoc with the hair on their bodies. Dimitri sent Zev a small, quick grin and nodded toward Fen. He mouthed the word *skunk*.

"I can see you," Fen pointed out.

Dimitri raised an eyebrow, trying for innocence. "I have no idea what you're talking about, bro."

Behind them, Tatijana and Branislava followed closely. They needed to find a spot where they could shift and take to the air. Instead of looking for a large enough place to accommodate a dragon, they simply gave themselves running room and took to the sky as small birds, leaping high as they shifted.

Ivory and Skyler came next, moving fast, jogging toward the forest where they could better hunt prey with their wolves. Razvan angled to meet them, running fast through the trees to intercept them in the forest itself. Clearly, Ivory had shared every detail of the events and danger with him.

Gregori moved out of the circle last, walking with long, purposeful strides straight to the edge of the forest, where he turned, lifted his hands and sent his command once again to close the path behind him.

Lightning struck the ground and raced back into the sky. The ground shifted and water bubbled up. Inside the circle of protection, the three Lycans remained asleep, and the fourth, Igor, rested in peace.

Zev signaled to his elite hunters. They turned and melted into the forest, spreading out as they went. He could always count on them. Daciana with her steady hand and fast reactions. Makoce, handy with sword and short knife. Lykaon, who couldn't be matched with his ability to throw any object with deadly accuracy. Arnau, who seemed to have eyes in the back of his head and a steadfast nature, loyal to a fault. That was his pack and he believed in each of their abilities.

They knew one another very well, how they thought, where they would be in any given fight at any given time. They believed in one another and counted on each other. Now his pack was extended to Dimitri and Skyler and Fen and Tatijana. And his lifemate, Branislava. Somehow just knowing she was going to be in the sky in her fiery dragon form filled him with a kind of joy—or maybe the Lycan in him was so strong he just looked forward to battle.

Zev knew the way rogue packs operated. They should have gone for the outlying farms, killing livestock and overrunning the houses to kill as many people as they could. This pack was very focused, driving through the forest toward a single destination. The council members had been secreted to a protected cave while the Lycan guards they trusted were helping to guard the circle as Branislava and the others had attempted to remove the shadow.

No other Lycans had been told where the council members had been taken. The other Lycans had been deliberately kept away from the council. Since only three of those wearing the tattoo of the Sacred Circle were mage-shadowed, Zev was certain there were others opposing the current council members and their decisions. Xaviero had managed to turn many of those within the organization against the ruling body for the Lycans.

Still, if none of them had followed the Carpathians secreting the council members away, how could the rogue pack make a dead set right for their cave? He signaled Daciana, signing to her, making her aware of the rogue pack's target, knowing she would spread the word to the others in his pack.

He led Fen and Dimitri through the forest up into the higher mountains, outdistancing the elite Lycan hunters, knowing they had to get in place to protect the cave from the marauding wolves. They didn't hide the fact that they were *Hän ku pesäk kaikak.* There was no need anymore. If the council of Lycans didn't accept mixed bloods, there would be a rift between Carpathian and Lycan. If they did, Lycans would turn against Lycans, driven by someone in power within the Sacred Circle—someone who joined with a High Mage believing he would rule the Lycan world without interference from the council.

He sold his soul to the devil, he told Branislava.

Who is it? Who has betrayed the Lycans and aligned with Xaviero of his own free will? There were no more mage-shadows. If any council member was marked, we would have seen it. Branislava paused. *It is one of the council members, isn't it? It has to be.*

I believe it is. I think he has a way of communicating with Xaviero and he's given out their hidden location. Are you in the sky? Can you see the rogues?

Branislava was already in dragon form. The moment she had taken on the appearance of her fire dragon she felt confident and comfortable. She soared through the sky, the great wings flapping, lifting her up high into the dark, spinning clouds. Tatijana was at her side, a beautiful blue, her scales taking on a metallic shade each time lightning forked in the clouds, lighting the sky even a little bit.

They're directly below me, spread out in the way they hunt. I've counted twenty-seven of them. It's a fairly good-sized pack, although nowhere near the one that first came after Mikhail.

You're staying high?

I'm too far for them to notice. So is Tatijana, but if they get too close to the cave, we'll drive them back with dragon fire.

Of course she would. Fear or no fear, it didn't matter, Branislava and her sister would get the job done. He paused just long enough to place his hand on the ground. Ivory, Razvan and Skyler had come up behind the pack and were already at work, hunting strays. He felt their footsteps along with those of real wolves. Blood seeped into the ground from two different spots, so at least two of the rogues were down.

He was up and running in one smooth move, catching Fen and Dimitri.

We're ahead of them. Tatijana and Branislava are in the sky. My Lycan hunters are fanning out to come up on either side of the pack. Ivory, Razvan and Skyler are in the rear, separating and killing strays.

Bronnie, Tatijana, can either of you see anyone actually directing the pack? Fen asked.

I'll circle around and see if I can spot anyone, Branislava said.

Zev's heart jerked hard in his chest. Dread filled him. *No, no, don't do that,* he ordered sharply. *Which direction were you planning on turning?*

To my left.

She didn't argue with him and his heart returned to a normal beat. She trusted him, had complete faith in his leadership and that spared him a whole lot of heartache.

Fen, I think we've got a Sange rau hidden in the rocks close to the cave. The rogue pack is the distraction and the killer will use the fighting to enter the cave and kill the council members. He had committed the terrain to memory, just as he always did if the council were anywhere they might be in danger and the task to guard them was given to him.

When the rogue pack breaks into the clearing, I'll run with them. Branka and Tatijana can drive them back with dragon fire and I'll make for the cave entrance. I can protect the council members in that narrow opening. Dimitri and you have the most experience with a Sange rau and if you both go after him, you'll have a better chance of destroying him.

Fen gave him a small salute and the brothers veered off to circle around, shifting into vapor to streak through the air. Fen spotted the killer crouched in the rocks, blending into the formations, although not very well, indicating, as with the others he'd run into, that this one wasn't very old. Xaviero didn't seem to understand that it was a slow process, the mixed blood mutating them into stronger, more intelligent beings over years, not weeks. He signaled his brother to come up in front of the creature carefully. They both held their positions, waiting for rogues to make their appearance.

Zev waited for one of the rogues to rush past him, noting his colors and the way he looked. He immediately used his Carpathian gifts to give the illusion of looking the same as he fell into step. *I'm fond of my hair, Branka. Don't singe it just for fun.*

Be more worried about Tatijana.

In spite of the teasing note, he heard her worry and knew neither took the skirmish lightly. As the pack members burst from the forest and rushed the cave, he was swept along. At the last moment, as the dragons dove from the sky, he shifted, going invisible to leap out in front of the pack with his mixed blood speed. The moment he was inside the relative safety of the cave, the dragons let loose, breathing fire down like rain.

The flames poured down steady and strong, roaring over the half wolf, half human creatures bent on killing the council of Lycans, setting many of them on fire. The dragons used their wings to build a wind tunnel, fanning the flames so that they jumped from one rogue to the next. At least twelve went down in a fiery conflagration. The others halted abruptly, even retreating back into the forest. Two bolder ones swept through the clearing right through the flames, running for the cave.

In the forest, his elite hunters took on the remaining rogues. Skyler, Razvan and Ivory aided them, finding and destroying any who tried to get past them. Gregori used his silver sword, mopping up as fast as possible. Eventually, Zev's pack aided the Carpathian, making certain every rogue had been staked and their head severed.

Zev waited in silence as the two bold rogues entered the cave and began to make their way down the narrow passage, seeking targets. The first one ran right into him, never seeing the silver stake aimed directly at his heart. The wolf's eyes widened. His muzzle yawned wide, but no sound emerged. Behind him, the second wolf ran into him and cursed, shoving at his partner to move him along.

Zev stepped back, allowing the first wolf to fall to the ground, clutching at his chest and the protruding silver stake. The second rogue stared in disbelief, scowling, uncomprehending of what he was actually seeing. He actually bent down to look at his fallen companion. When he looked back up, Zev stepped into him, slamming the silver stake home.

The stake went through the first layer of skin and muscle and hit something hard, stopping abruptly, the silver snapping off in Zev's hand. Shocked, he leapt back just as a full set of teeth rushed toward his head.

13

Zev, some of the rogues have a protection against the silver stakes, Razvan cautioned, his voice grim. *We get them down, but the stakes shatter and don't go beyond about an inch and half into their bodies.*

It isn't all of them, Ivory continued. *Maybe a third of them, at least it's about one out of three that we've found when we kill them.*

Fen and Dimitri heard the warning as well. Razvan had used the more common Carpathian path of communication. They watched the *Sange rau* closely to see if he picked up the warning, but he remained quite still, hiding in the rocks, believing his camouflage would protect him from sight.

This one was not Carpathian first, Dimitri pointed out. *He was Lycan and created in a lab rather than naturally. Do you think he volunteered for the assignment, or Xaviero chose him, using a mage-shadow to force him into compliance?*

Fen shook his head, shrugging broad shoulders. *You can't ask yourself those questions, Dimitri. This man is dangerous to us and everyone else, no matter the start he had. He'll kill you the moment he sees you.*

He hasn't made a move toward the cave, Dimitri said, puzzled. *He should have rushed in there as soon as the first wave of rogues attacked.*

You've got a point, Fen said, and turned his attention from the *Sange rau* hidden so cleverly as a decoy. *Stay down, he must have a friend.*

Dimitri muttered a curse beneath his breath. *Like before, back in the village, Fen. They're hunting us in pairs now.*

Because they aren't ready to face us. Fen abandoned his more familiar path of communication with his brother and reached for the one forged with Zev. *There's a second Sange rau. He'll be coming for you. You're standing between him and his goal.*

Zev's heart dropped as he twisted to one side, only his speed saving him from the teeth rushing at him in the way a velociraptor might attack. The razor-sharp teeth skimmed along his arm, opening his skin, but it was the silver stake in his fist that did the most damage. Zev felt the burn as the *Sange rau* slammed it deep into his thigh.

"Hello, Zev," the *Sange rau* greeted as his hands settled around Zev's throat and he began to squeeze. "I've been waiting for a chance to meet you again."

Zev vaguely recalled the man. He'd been at the elite hunter's school and shown signs of murderous behavior. The school officials had called in Zev to work with him, wanting to make certain they were right in their assessment. Two council members had been on hand as well. It wasn't often an elite was turned down and not given a pack. Fredec was one of the few.

Zev didn't fight the stranglehold, but rather reached for the knife in his belt. He slashed up the right inner thigh of his opponent, continuing the flow of his strike to include the left inner thigh. He kept the movement continuous, slashing across the belly and moving his strike upward in a figure eight to hit as many arteries as possible.

Fredec let go of his throat and stumbled back away from him. Zev dragged air into his burning lungs, assessing just how bad the wounds on Fredec were. He hadn't been able to see where he was slashing, not with the hold the *Sange rau* had on his throat, but he'd managed to get two fairly deep wounds.

Fredec's lips peeled back in a snarl, his eyes going red. He leapt at Zev, tackling him, taking him to the ground. He was slippery with blood and Zev couldn't get a decent grip on him. The stake in his thigh hit Fredec's leg, shooting pain right through his body, the intensity shocking.

Zev fought past the nausea and sudden weakness, locking down on the grip of his knife. He kept the blade up so that when Fredec landed on him, his own knife in his hand, Zev could shove the blade deep into Fredec's chest. Once again, he hit some type of armor. The blade actually snapped off.

Cursing, Zev rolled, throwing Fredec off him, preventing himself from getting disemboweled but driving the stake in his thigh deeper. He yanked it out and slapped a large patch over the wound almost in one motion, sending up a silent prayer of thanks to Gary for the invention. The patch adhered instantly, rushing the mixture of compounds to his skin and deeper, to stop the bleeding and begin the healing process.

Fredec laughed as he regained his feet. He wiped his muzzle with the back of his hand, his claws growing, the nails curved and sharp. "You shouldn't have told them I wasn't elite. I'm superior to you. I always have been."

He wanted acknowledgment. He wanted to brag. Zev circled with him, wanting to give him the opportunity. "Someone must have seen something in you I didn't. One of the council members? They argued that day, and one of them advocated for you."

Fredec inclined his head. "You and the school board threw me out, but I got revenge. I killed every single member of that board. Now I'm going to kill you and then I'll have the pleasure of showing Randall that he should have listened to Lyall."

Zev's heart sank. Lyall was a trusted member of the council. He was there with them all in the chamber, secreted away from the guards in case any were members of the Secret Circle army.

The traitor in the council is Lyall. There was no keeping that information to himself, not when he was in a fight to the death with a *Sange rau.* The red eyes focused on him, gleaming with hatred and murderous intent.

Fredec was fast and intelligent, and if Lyall had recruited him as far back as when Fredec had entered the elite hunter school, that was half a century earlier. Fredec should have been much further along in the mutation of the *Sange rau.*

Someone needs to get to them. I am fighting the Sange rau. He didn't trust that Lyall wasn't murdering the entire council right at that moment.

Fredec feinted an attack, going for Zev's left side, his wounded side, but at the last second whirling around, slashing with the blade of his knife toward Zev's belly. Zev leapt back just barely out of reach, slamming his fist down on the wrist coming at him and then turning his fist so that his own blade made a clean, deep slice down Fredec's arm. It was an old trick learned many years earlier and Zev was grateful he had it in his arsenal.

Somehow he had to find a way to kill Fredec and help the council members. It was ingrained in him to protect them. Fen and Dimitri were occupied with the other *Sange rau*. Those fighting the rogues had run into the same thing he had, a thin plate of armor that seemed to be under the skin.

I'm making my way through the cave.

His heart nearly stopped. Of course Branislava would sense his anxiety. She would come. She was his lifemate, a true warrior who believed her place was fighting beside him.

He couldn't detect her presence. He was very sensitive to energy and if he couldn't feel her close to them, perhaps Fredec couldn't as well.

He's dangerous, he warned, suddenly shifting onto the balls of his feet and moving toward Fredec in a kind of dance, one moment here, the next over there, making it impossible for Fredec to touch him, yet constantly keeping the *Sange rau* on the defensive.

So am I, Branislava answered. *Keep him moving toward the entrance.*

She was made of fire. Flames burned through her veins and he heard her quiet determination. He didn't know what she planned, but he believed in her. He ducked Fredec's knife and avoided the raking claw hissing across his belly while he continued the offensive, pushing the *Sange rau* back toward the entrance.

Keep your grip on your knife high and be ready to plunge it into his heart. I'll do the same from the back.

Again he didn't question her, but kept up his flowing dance, flicking the knife at the *Sange rau*, small little hits, and then once more dancing out of reach. Fredec was a strong brute and was used to using his size and strength to his advantage. Fighting someone like Zev who had been in hundreds of battles and was very experienced with a knife, smooth, fast and deadly, had thrown Fredec off his game.

Each time Zev danced closer and flicked his knife at Fredec, he left behind evidence of his superior ability. There were dozens of small cuts all over Fredec's arms. Zev hadn't gone for the kill, but rather was wearing his opponent down with smaller slices that kept the *Sange rau* continually bleeding.

The blade of his knife began to glow, first a soft yellow orange and then a darker red. Heat traveled up the grip. He didn't let the change distract him, but kept moving, his feet following that pattern so familiar to him. He flicked Fredec's rib cage and heard his opponent gasp with shock. It was a shallow cut, but the blade of his knife was now glowing bright red, and from the amount of heat pouring into the grip, he knew that burn had gone far deeper than the actual cut.

Now, Branislava ordered.

Without hesitation, Zev moved inside those hamlike fists, and sank his knife deep into Fredec's chest. The hot blade seemed to stop for one moment, but then it drove through the thin plate of armor, melting it like butter. Behind Fredec, Branislava had done the same, plunging her knife deep into Fredec's back, her blade just as hot, melting everything in its way to the heart.

Fredec went down hard, his eyes wide with shock. Branislava stepped back. There wasn't much room in the narrow hallway leading to the chamber much deeper in the cavern for Zev to wield his sword, separating the head from the body, but he managed. She stepped over the downed *Sange rau* and they both ran for the chamber holding the council members.

Use extreme heat to get through the armor, Zev advised as he ran, sending out the advice on the common Carpathian path.

That red-headed woman of yours comes up with some good ideas, Fen stated, laughter in his voice. *That wasn't your idea.*

Fen signaled to Dimitri and his younger brother crept closer to the *Sange rau* hiding in the rocks. The "bait" hadn't moved an inch, remaining absolutely still. *Too still.* The wolves on Dimitri's body shifted, lifted their heads sensing an enemy, and were ready to leap off to defend him.

No, stay, Dimitri commanded and swung around, just barely avoiding a stake through his heart. The dagger went deep through the right side of his chest, the terrible burn of silver more of a shock than the actual hole in his chest. He went down hard, his legs going out from under him, blood pouring down his chest.

The *Sange rau* stepped close, maneuvering his footwork on the uneven rocks. Dimitri didn't try to move out of his way, but he used his knife, slashing open both of his opponent's thighs, going for arteries to slow him down.

The man roared with anger and pain. The silver had burned him just as badly as it had Dimitri and blood spewed from both legs.

Fen leapt from a rock above them, landing on the *Sange rau*'s back, driving him to the ground and away from Dimitri. They rolled in a tangle of arms and legs, grunting as their backs hit the hard and sometimes jagged rocks.

Dimitri remembered the patch included in their arsenal of weapons—the one Gary had insisted each of them take with them into battle. He pulled it out of the leather bag hanging at his belt and slapped it over the wound in his chest. Instantly he felt the heat, a burn that seemed to cauterize and then begin the healing process. He sent up a silent prayer to remember to thank the man for his continual efforts to provide the Carpathian species with aid. The patch amazed him, giving him a boost of energy he needed after such a blood loss.

Pushing himself to his feet, he staggered after the two combatants rolling around in a tangle of arms and legs, the occasional knife flashing for a moment. Grunts, snarls and curses added to the chaos of dust rising. The *Sange rau* left a trail of blood behind him, testifying to the knife wounds Dimitri had managed to inflict as he went down.

His wolves again tried to defend him, squirming in eagerness to be released. Dimitri had to warn them again to stay put. He didn't want the animals anywhere near the mixed blood with his incredible speed.

Fen grappled with the assassin, holding firmly to his wrists to prevent those talons from ripping open his belly or slashing across his eyes to blind him. Dimitri called on the heat of the fiery volcano, bringing it down the blade of his knife. He thrust it into the *Sange rau*'s back, feeling the tip strike a barrier and then begin to slide through muscle.

The *Sange rau* roared with rage, whipping around, claws extended, seeking Dimitri's belly. Dimitri used his mixed blood speed to leap backward as the wolf/vampire leapt forward, the maneuver astonishing. He went from a prone position to midair in one move, rushing toward Dimitri so fast he appeared blurred.

Fen mirrored his opponent's action, coming up behind him, using his legs as a springboard to leap after the *Sange rau*. Before those claws could reach Dimitri, Fen slammed his fist hard into the hilt of Dimitri's knife with his enormous strength, driving it deep through the assassin's back to pierce the heart.

The *Sange rau* shrieked and thrashed, lunging forward toward Dimitri, slamming both claws into his chest, digging through flesh to try to get at the heart. The long muzzle gaped open and clamped teeth around Dimitri's shoulder and arm.

Dimitri, as he had when he made the first leap away from the *Sange rau*, had drawn his sword. He swung low, cutting through both legs even as he threw himself back and away from the pain-maddened creature. As he did so, he tossed the sword to his brother. Fen swung the silver sword in a glittering arc, severing the head of the *Sange rau* from the neck.

"How bad are you hurt?" Fen asked grimly as he threw his brother the patch he carried and then sank a silver stake through the assassin's heart.

"What does it look like?" Dimitri demanded a little sarcastically.

Fen glanced over his shoulder at the woman striding toward them. Wolves surrounded her. "She looks royally pissed, Dimitri, and I can't say that I blame her. You set yourself up for this piece of garbage to use as a pincushion to give me a shot at killing him."

"We had to take him down fast and that seemed the quickest solution. You were a little slower than I'd hoped."

"I'm resisting the urge to kick your ass," Fen said, "but only because your woman has a thirst for revenge."

"Get out of here, go help Zev," Dimitri ordered his brother. "I'll be fine."

"If you don't bleed to death," Fen snapped, and stepped up to Dimitri, his teeth tearing at his own wrist. "Just hurry."

Dimitri had no real choice but to accept what his brother offered. Not offered. More like forced. There was no way to ever stop Fen from taking the role of the eldest brother, no matter how savvy or experienced Dimitri was in battle.

Skyler rushed up to her lifemate, her eyes dark with concern. The wolves pushed close to him as she inspected the damage. "Ivory and Razvan are working with Daciana and the others to hunt down the remaining rogues. There're only a couple of them left alive. Once we knew how to kill them, they weren't nearly as tough as we thought they'd be."

Dimitri closed the wound on his brother's wrist. "They weren't hunting in pack formation as they should have been," he explained to her. "The orders must have been to rush the cave. They were pawns to be sacrificed."

Skyler ran her fingers through his hair, pushing the damp strands from his forehead. "Don't sound so sad, Dimitri. These were rogues, Lycans who deliberately turned to killing for the pleasure of it."

She crouched down beside him, peeling back the patch Gary had given to all of them, her palms resting over the wound in his chest. He felt the heat of her touch burning through his body, but it was soothing, rather than painful. She mixed rich soil and healing saliva and pressed it into the stab wound before moving to the wound on his thigh.

"You're a mess, you know that?" she asked.

"Yes. You didn't tell me how the wolves did." He meant how she did. Practicing combat was entirely different than actually having to kill another living creature.

Skyler pressed her lips together and shook her head. He didn't ask again, but ran his hand up her leg to her thigh, keeping the contact while she worked on him.

"Is he going to live?" Fen asked.

"Yes," she said. "Don't worry, I've got this."

Fen nodded and left them, moving fast, rushing for the entrance to the cave. Behind him, he could smell fire, as the bodies of the rogues were gathered and burned. Just down from the entrance lay a dead *Sange rau*, his head macabrely lying against the wall, eyes wide and staring. Fen ignored him, leapt over the body and rushed toward the cavern where the Lycan council members had been secreted.

He entered quickly and ran into Zev, just stopping his forward momentum before they collided hard. As it was, he bumped him enough to drive him forward a couple of steps. Lyall sat on the floor of the cavern, his fingers locked behind the nape of his neck. He looked furious.

Randall glared at Lyall, his eyes red, his body more wolf than man. He looked frightening, a great bear of a wolf ready to slash and kill. Rolf looked saddened, shaking his head, one hand pressed to his eyes. Arno was the only council member not seated. He paced back and forth as if all the restless energy he had would erupt any moment into violence.

Mikhail was a good distance from any of the Lycans. Tomas, Lojos,

Mataias and Andre formed a barrier between Mikhail and the others in the room. Clearly Andre had been in a skirmish. As always, his eyes were flat and cold. No one moved. No one spoke.

Fen nudged Zev. *Did I interrupt something? I came a little late to the party.*

Lyall tried to kill Mikhail and the other council members. He rigged an explosive device, but your man Andre there caught him. Then Lyall apparently tried to turn a gun on the prince.

Shocking that he's still alive. Gregori will have a few things to say to Andre about that, Fen said, meaning it. *He believes if anyone tries to harm the prince, death is the only answer and I have to agree with him.*

Apparently Mikhail and the council members asked Andre not to kill him. He wants answers. Zev looked down at the floor. This was the part he detested the most about his job. A clean kill was one thing, extracting information was something altogether different.

If he wasn't Lycan, Fen said regretfully, *we could just go in and get the information, but Lycans have a natural barrier against mind probes—unless you cut off their head. We could talk to Gregori and maybe he could persuade the prince.*

Zev could tell he was half serious, and he was touched that Fen would try to think of ways to keep him from having to interrogate Lyall. *Thanks, but it's my job. The council will expect me to question him and get results.*

Branislava slipped her hand in the crook of Zev's arm. *Why don't you let me do it? I can ask him questions and I'm fairly certain he'll answer.*

Zev frowned down at her. Her green eyes had gone multifaceted, much like a dragon's, but then changed color. Her hair banded with a deeper, almost wine red running through the lighter red gold. Her smile took his breath away.

My father was the High Mage and he frequently interrogated people without ever laying a finger on them. It mattered little which species, not when he used a truth spell. It isn't that difficult and no one has to hurt anyone. Branislava leaned into him. *I can really be quite useful.*

Zev found himself smiling. His eyes met Mikhail's. "The council has asked me to interrogate Lyall to find out why he's committed such a betrayal of not only his lifelong friends, but all Lycans as well."

Mikhail inclined his head slowly. "I am not a man who believes in torture."

Lyall smirked. Randall snarled, a low, warning note that raised the hair on the back of Zev's neck and had Mikhail's guards whipping around to face the threat. Arno stopped pacing, his body rippling with the effort not to shift into the half man, half wolf that would signal even more danger.

Rolf held up his hand to stop his fellow council members from further action. "No one likes the torture of any being, not even a traitor such as Lyall, but to prevent war, sometimes things none of us like must be done."

Mikhail shook his head. "It isn't our way, Rolf, nor will it ever be."

Randall leapt to his feet as if he would extract the answers needed from Lyall himself.

"I believe we have a satisfactory solution for both parties," Zev said. "Branislava has offered to interrogate Lyall. She'll get the necessary information without harming a hair on his head."

Lyall's gaze jumped to her face. He glared at her, but then looked rather amused. "A Carpathian can't invade my mind no matter how hard they try. Do you think I'm afraid of her? Or that I'll answer her questions because she's beautiful? She might enslave Zev, but I'm stronger than that."

Branislava smiled at him. Her green eyes glowed with the fire of the dragon burning so bright in her. She glided closer to Lyall. Her long, thick hair crackled with energy. Power radiated from her. Her skin had a radiance Zev had never noticed before. She was truly beautiful, and Zev couldn't imagine any man resisting her, let alone the older Lycan who had spent a lifetime chasing women.

"Did you think I might sleep with you to get the information from you?" Amusement dripped from her voice like warm honey. "Aw, I see that you did. I have to disappoint you, sir, I only sleep with one man, and that wouldn't be you."

The chamber had gone utterly silent. Even Randall had ceased snarling and once more shifted back to his human form. Arno settled into his chair. All eyes were riveted on Branislava. Zev folded his arms across his chest, simply waiting. He had seen the power in his woman on more than one occasion. Lyall didn't stand much of a chance against her.

"What then?" Suspicion settled on Lyall's face. He scowled at her. "Do you think I'll be so intimidated because you come close to me? That perhaps

Zev can move fast enough to protect you if I choose to kill you instead of talk to you?" He held his hands straight in the air to show he was not bound.

"Have no worries," Zev said. "I am *Hän ku pesäk kaikak*—guardian of all, and I have been for some time, Lyall. Each of the *Sange rau* you have sent to kill me or one of the others has failed. You're a hypocrite to secretly use the very creature you publicly condemn against our people. None of them were faster. Are you mixed blood? I have seen you walk in the sun. If you were, you would be unable to do so. You cannot possibly be faster than me, should I choose to strike you down."

Lyall sneered at him. "Why would you ever say such a thing to me? You walk in the sun as well. How is it you can when no other *Sange rau* can? Do you think to lie to me? That I would believe such nonsense? You are so arrogant, puffed up with your own importance."

Zev had never asked himself that question. He hadn't realized he had mixed blood for a very long time and when he had become suspicious, he'd dismissed the idea because he could carry out his duties in midday. He shrugged his shoulders. "You don't have to believe me, but if you're considering suicide by elite hunter, I would not kill you, not before Branka has had the chance to question you."

"He is Dark Blood," Mikhail said. "The ultimate warrior. He is of Carpathian descent and the last of his line. Few could ever defeat a Dark Blood in battle, and the women who were their lifemates were every bit as fierce and as gifted. He can walk in the sun because he is Dark Blood."

Zev felt Branislava gasp, but she didn't change expressions or even glance at him. Still, he felt her touch, that hot slide of her palm against his chest— such a casual gesture but so intimate when his lifemate initiated the caress mind to mind.

Branislava smiled at Lyall, her soft, gentle, perfect smile, the one that lit up Zev's world. It seemed to have an effect on the Lycan as well. He lowered his hands, twisting his fingers together, and stared at her with a look of admiration and puzzlement.

"Before you make your try to interrogate me, I wish to answer the charge Zev has laid against me. I have no idea what he's talking about when he says I used the *Sange rau* against our people. I am not one of those abominations nor would I ever seek to align myself with one. Had I known Zev is what he claims, I would have issued the death sentence against him, commanding those loyal to our ways to have him killed immediately."

"You sound so righteous," Rolf said quietly, "yet you tried to assassinate the prince of the Carpathian people and kill all of us."

"I follow the doctrines and principles of the Lycan race." Lyall glared at Rolf. "To come here was wrong. We were warned never to mix with Carpathians. It is written in the sacred code and yet you, head of our council, agreed to such a meeting. You betrayed our kind, not me."

Arno made a soft sound, a mixture of despair and anger. "You've been my best friend since we were boys together, Lyall, yet you were willing to murder me. You stood for me at my joining ceremony. I don't understand how you could do such a thing."

Lyall had the grace to look slightly ashamed. His gaze avoided Arno's. "I tried talking to you numerous times over the last few years. You kept sitting on the fence." His tone grew accusing. "You wouldn't commit to doing what was right, even though you knew what you should do and how you should vote. The women's issue was the clincher for me. And coming here, to this place, to these people." His voice swelled with disgust. "You followed like a little lamb being led to the slaughter."

"Do you think we don't know about Xaviero?" Zev asked.

Lyall frowned. "I have no idea who or what you're talking about."

Branislava shook her head. "No, of course you wouldn't. He would never go by that name. He would be an older man, but not too old because he would want the admiration of the women and girls around him. He would be very good-looking, and soft-spoken, but his word would carry great weight. He would be a man you admire greatly, perhaps the only man you look up to. He would not be able to hide his very distinctive eyes. They glow like silver."

Lyall looked a little alarmed. The council members exchanged long looks of equal alarm.

"You mean like Zev's eyes?" Lyall injected sarcasm into his voice.

She shook her head slowly, and this time she addressed the council. "Real silver, glittering and changing from molten to hard. Lyall would have been a very close friend to him."

"You are describing Rannalufr. He has been around for centuries, nearly as long as me," Rolf said. "He has been a trusted advisor to our council for many, many years." He shook his head. "I cannot believe he would betray us."

Rannalufr means plundering wolf *in Old Norse,* Zev informed her. *Would Xaviero be so bold as to give himself such a name?*

That's exactly the kind of thing he would do, Branislava said. Aloud, she addressed the council members. "If this is the man I've described, he is not Lycan, but mage, and he's infiltrated your council for his own agenda—destroying the Lycan race. One of his brothers has destroyed the Jaguar species and the other nearly managed to eliminate the Carpathians. He is Xaviero, brother to Xavier. You are old enough to know of him," Branislava assured.

"I know of Xavier, but I have never heard of Xaviero," Rolf denied. "Not a whisper about a brother or brothers."

"They were interchangeable, identical and they kept the fact that they could be in three places at one time from the world because it suited them to do so," Branislava explained. "Xaviero is hard at work destroying your species. He's actually creating the *Sange rau.* No doubt, Rannalufr is a great chemist and such a boon to your people. You are indebted to him for his many kindnesses and his aid in discovering various remedies that help with strange illnesses that suddenly beset your people as well as other things. Am I correct?"

The council members looked at one another, their alarm growing. Lyall continually shook his head in denial.

"How is this possible?" Rolf asked. "I don't understand this. It *can't* be possible. Rannalufr has been to my home on many occasions, sat at my table and played with my children."

"And Lyall?" Mikhail asked quietly. "Has he not been to your home, sat at your table and played with your children?"

Rolf's gaze jumped to his old friend's face. "Yes," he said, sounding tired, answering for Lyall. "Yes he has, many times. I have loved him as a brother."

"As did I," Arno said sadly.

Again, Lyall looked a little ashamed, but he shook it off, shaking his head. "You betrayed our people, Rolf, Arno. All of you did. I merely am an instrument of justice."

"With your own army?" Zev leveled the accusation. "You just managed to recruit an entire army without anyone's knowledge in a matter of days or weeks because the council suddenly made a decision to come here? I don't believe you, Lyall. You use both *Sange rau* as well as rogue packs to do your dirty work."

"I am a chosen one, a martyr for our people with a higher purpose you cannot possibly understand," Lyall shot back at Zev, his tone self-righteous and firm.

"*That* is the mage talking. He 'joined' your little cause and he kept you fired up," Branislava said. "He offered you something to betray your friends, Lyall, what is it you covet most? Power?"

"He had power on the council," Rolf said. "He covets women."

Branislava's heart stuttered. She knew the cruelty Xaviero was capable of, especially with women. He enjoyed hurting his lovers and finding inventive ways of disposing of them. So many young mage women, so many human women. She didn't want to see those memories in Lyall's mind.

You do not have to do this, mon chaton féroce, Zev said. *There are other ways. I can get the information from him that we need.*

He always gave her an out, and Branislava was grateful to him for it. That generous offer allowed her to square her shoulders and send Zev a smile. She could do this because she wasn't alone. His soul and his spirit were woven to hers.

Branislava let out her breath slowly. "Lyall, I think the time has come to get a few answers from you."

"Ask me anything," Lyall said, crossing his arms over his chest. "You will get nothing at all from me."

Branislava didn't bother to argue. She raised her arms and wove a pattern in the air around her, as if she was creating a space, clean and pure and free of harm.

Cells to neurons interact and flow,
Carrying messages that I must know.
I see your stimuli, I know your game,
Reveal to me what is hidden so there will be no pain.

Around her, the air changed color, glowing with soft golden light. Her hair crackled and tiny flames seemed to lick up her arms. Lyall went pale and covered his face as if by not looking at her, she couldn't get into his head.

Current to neuron cells to grow,
Provide me with knowledge so I may know,
I take what is hidden and make it mine.

Lyall began to rock back and forth, making noises like a child in distress. He clearly was in no pain, but he must have felt Branislava in his mind, close to taking control.

Let there be no barriers,
Let there be no lies,
As I came, so now I must return,
Taking these memories so no other may learn.

Lyall screamed and rocked, shaking his head, tears rolling down his face. He pressed his hands over his ears as if he could drown her out—or keep her out of his head. Branislava entered his mind with trepidation, afraid of what she might find.

She felt Zev take her hand. She knew he hadn't done so physically; he was too busy watching Lyall to ensure the Lycan didn't try to harm her, but still, it felt as if he'd threaded his fingers through hers and entered that warped mind with her.

There was greed, certainly. Lyall wanted more than the power Rolf claimed he already had as a council member. He wanted to be the one everyone looked up to and followed, just like Rolf. She saw Xaviero and caught glimpses, small little vignettes of the encounters over so many years. Xaviero had been patient in stalking Lyall and learning about him. He had wanted a man in a position of power, one he could persuade easily and yet would believe that all ideas were his own. Lyall, over time, had become that man.

Xaviero had discovered his weakness for women. At first he had used flattery to ensnare Lyall, and then he began to mention his night with a particular woman and the things he had gotten her to do for him. Lyall's breathing changed, his mouth went slack and he practically drooled. The baser the stories, the more rapt Lyall's attention became. Xaviero led him down that path slowly as well, talking about how they were so superior to women and how women provoked them with the way they moved and dressed and smiled. How those women were meant to serve men such as they were. Powerful men who needed the relaxation such women provided.

Lyall wanted to hear those things and he accepted more and more of Xaviero's depravities as normal. He began to believe he was entitled to any woman he wanted, and his good friend agreed with him. By the time Xaviero had begun to share sadistic stories, Lyall was more than ready for them and eager to try them out.

It didn't take long for Xaviero to begin introducing the subject of the sacred code and how the council wasn't upholding the ideologies. At first the conversations were merely philosophical, but then they turned to how they could begin to right the wrongs. Always, Xaviero was careful, allowing Lyall to believe all ideas came from him. The mage was clever, admiring everything Lyall said, hanging on his word as if it were gospel. Lyall believed his good friend Rannalufr was his most ardent follower.

He had no memories of the *Sange rau*, but he had carefully begun to enlist followers for his army, recruiting those who were fanatical about keeping to the old ways. Over time he had a tremendous amount of followers. Unfortunately, Arno had helped, without realizing it, adding his voice to the ones preaching in the Sacred Circle meetings.

14

Branislava left Lyall's depraved and twisted mind abruptly. "He's fanatical and likes to hurt women, but he doesn't know about the *Sange rau* assassins Xaviero had made. He built an army with the idea that he would get rid of the council and the Sacred Circle would rule in its place. He, of course, would be the head of the Sacred Circle. He planned on having many young women attending him." She said the last with disgust.

She wanted to leave. To go back home and sit on her porch in the middle of the forest, listening to the wolves and the night creatures. She needed to be cleansed after being inside such a vile mind. "Lyall has no real sense of morality anymore, nor does he remember loyalty. He's addicted to the sadistic things he does to the women he sleeps with. If they protest, or if he grows tired of them, his good friend Rannalufr takes them off his hands. He's never thought to ask what Rannalufr does with them at his laboratory, nor does he care."

She rubbed her temples, realizing she had a headache. The man sickened her, and he'd been far too close to Xaviero for her comfort. Xaviero had found an apt pupil and disciple, although Lyall had believed it was the other way around.

"Rannalufr is definitely Xaviero and he found a corrupt, greedy man with a weakness for women and exploited it. Lyall went willingly down that path of destruction." She couldn't keep the distaste from her voice. "He knows nothing of Xaviero's plans, or of the *Sange rau*, although there is a laboratory where his lovely friend, Rannalufr, takes the women Lyall discards after hurting them. My guess is they endure torture and are eventually killed. After a few hours in Xaviero's company, the women probably welcome death." She'd seen it more times than she cared to remember.

Mikhail waved his hand toward her and she felt a little less covered in the stench of evil. "All three of the High Mages were very adept at choosing the right target for their enlistment. They had patience and they waited to discover the weakness of their victim. Lyall liked women and had he never met Xaviero, he might never have given in to his baser impulses, but the moment he was targeted by the mage, he didn't stand a chance."

"Are you expecting us to feel sympathy for the man who tried to kill us?" Randall demanded.

Branislava shook her head. "No, of course not. I want you to understand your enemy, and I don't mean Lyall. Xaviero spent years breaking him down, conditioning him to accept more and more violence toward women. That wasn't quite as hard as turning him against friends, but their political talks eventually had Lyall believing he was superior to all of you and could lead the Lycans back into the 'right' way of living."

Rolf sighed and sat back, hanging his head. "If you look too long at something evil, eventually you become evil. Minds are funny things. Lyall was a man of strong faith. He believed in the sacred code and the old ways, but he always kept an open mind. Becoming friends with Rannalufr and listening to him clearly allowed the mage to slowly corrupt Lyall's own values and morals." He shook his head sadly.

Branislava noticed Rolf used the past tense as if Lyall was already dead. He didn't look at him, as if that man sitting there on the floor rocking back and forth, hands over his eyes, was not the same man he'd known all those years—and in truth he wasn't.

Lyall couldn't bear to see his own crimes and depravities so exposed; on some level, whether he had convinced himself he was right or not, he knew the things he'd done were wrong.

"Bronnie." Mikhail's voice was gentle. His tone was like pure water, clean and fresh like a mountain stream, running over her and cleansing away some of the grime of evil. "Who directs his army? Who is in charge of these attacks against us? Is it Xaviero?"

"He is the puppet master. He would not issue orders himself. He will always appear innocent of any crime, so if caught, those around him will fight for him, truly believing his actions were never anything but kind."

Her legs trembled and she made an effort to steady herself. She was tired. Not from the battle or from using her spirit to fight off the mage-shadows, but from this—the ugliness of Lyall's mind. Of touching far too close to Xaviero and feeling the depth of true evil once again.

"There is a man, a wolf, tall, broad shoulders, a great bear of a man, much like Randall. He moves fast and has been active in the Russian military. He's highly decorated. His eyes are a deep blue and his hair is closer cropped than that of most Lycans. He commands Lyall's army."

Randall closed his eyes briefly, refusing to look at his fellow council members. "Is there a tie to Xaviero?"

Branislava nodded her head. "Yes. All three men have met on many occasions, and it was clear that Xaviero and this other man are friends away from Lyall. The looks between them, the way they smirked—they were planning to get rid of Lyall once his usefulness ran out. Of course, that's my guess from replaying Lyall's memories, so maybe not, but it is something Xaviero would do. Do you know this man I've described?"

"He's my nephew, Sandulf," Randall admitted quietly. "He was elite and then joined the military. He loves the battle and power. I wish I could say I'm surprised because he's always been a moral man with strong beliefs of right and wrong, but he craves action and above all else, attention and power. No matter how often I counseled him, he ruled his family with an iron fist and any in his pack had to be cautious."

"He seemed to have no problems with the idea of killing everyone here, the council, Mikhail and all of us." She swept her hand toward Zev and the other Carpathians in the chamber.

"Is he mixed blood? *Sange rau*?" Mikhail clarified.

"I have no way of knowing, you'll have to ask the council." Branislava swept a hand through her hair in a gesture of weariness.

I'm going to get you home, Zev said, tenderness nearly bringing tears to her eyes. *There isn't much more you can tell them.*

"Was he stronger, faster and a little more intelligent than most Lycans?" Mikhail asked.

Randall nodded. "That's why he excelled in his military career."

"He must have been made many years ago," Mikhail noted, with a warning glance at Zev. *Xaviero had the blood he had sought—your grandmother's blood. This Sandulf is more likely full Sange rau and participating more closely with Xaviero in building his army of mixed bloods, although where the mage is getting Carpathian blood now, I don't know.*

She was too close to the truth tonight, Branislava decided. Too close to the answer to the question Mikhail had just posed. Bile rose and she turned to Zev, uncaring if they needed to stay to protect anyone else. She wanted to go home. She needed to be outside and away from these men and the vivid memories pressing too close. She felt as if she had given everything she had to give.

Zev's arm circled her waist and he brought her under the protection of his shoulder. "We're a little beat up, Rolf. Daciana and Makoce as well as the others are close. They're burning the rogue bodies as we speak." He nodded toward the prince. "Mikhail, if you don't mind, we'll let Fen and Gregori take over here. I'm going to get Branka home."

Mikhail's dark eyes slid over her. He gave them a slow nod. "Thank you for your help, Bronnie. I know it couldn't have been easy for you."

She forced a small smile and let Zev take over, allowed him to say their good-byes to the council. She turned away from the broken man on the floor. Confronted with his crimes, knowing someone else had seen into his rotting, depraved brain and had seen the secret things he'd done to so many young women, he couldn't bear to look at anyone.

Zev suddenly shoved her aside—pushed her hard so that she staggered away from him and fell against a sharp boulder jutting from the side of the cave. When she managed to turn her head, she saw her lifemate grappling with Lyall, his fists clamped around both wrists, knee rising hard into the man's groin and then his foot driving into the inside of Lyall's knee. The council member collapsed, Zev going down to the floor of the chamber with him, transferring his grip from wrists to head.

The crack was audible as Lyall's neck broke. Zev's hand flashed with silver and the stake was driven through the council member's heart. Zev stepped back and drew his sword. Without a word he severed the head, wiped his blade clean and shoved it back into the sheath.

His gaze jumped to Branislava. *Are you hurt, Branka?*

She shook her head. Her hands smarted a little, along with one hip and part of her shoulder, but all she cared about was getting away from blood and death and the stench of evil. She hadn't even felt the attack as Lyall had come at her, his energy masked as Lycans could so easily do.

Zev didn't look at anyone else as he took her hand and walked out of the chamber. Behind them, she heard Rolf comment.

"That takes care of what to do with Lyall, doesn't it?"

Sadness overwhelmed her. *Once, Zev, very long ago, Lyall was actually a good man. He had a weakness for chasing women and he knew it and tried hard to curb it. He believed in the sacred code strongly, because, like so many other of the old ones, he nearly lost everyone dear to him when the first known Sange rau destroyed so many of the packs.*

Zev pulled her closer to him. They stepped out of the cave into the night. At once the fresh breeze touched her face and made her feel as if she could breathe again.

"I'm sorry for him, Branka," Zev said gently, "but the man you describe has been dead for a long time. There was no redeeming him or the things he's done."

She shuddered. She knew better than anyone—no, that wasn't true. She looked up at his face, her hand smoothing those lines etched deep into a face of masculine beauty. Zev had been with her. He had seen the fall into depravity just as she had. She didn't have to carry that burden alone.

"I'm very much in love with you, Zev Hunter," she whispered, and circled his neck with her arms, leaning into his strength.

She laid her head on his chest, her ear over the steady beat of his heart. He felt solid and strong, like a great oak tree with roots that went deep. He was a steady man, one she could always rely on. *I appreciate you so much. I really am lucky to have you.*

"You're very tired, *mon chaton féroce*," he replied, his voice even more gentle than it had been. "Perhaps it is time to go to ground."

She shook her head. "Not yet. The night is nearly over, Zev, but I need to be out in it. Somewhere beautiful and clean, somewhere I can breathe." Without lifting her head, she looked up at him.

He smiled down at her and her heart turned over. "I think I know just the place. It's a distance, but well worth the travel."

She wasn't going to warn him that they only had a couple hours left before the sun began to climb into the sky. She wanted to go with him, somewhere new and exciting, somewhere fresh and clean where she could breathe properly. Somewhere . . . *away.*

Zev stepped away from her and shifted, so smooth, so easily. She admired that fluid way of his. He learned fast and never hesitated once he made up his mind. Branislava followed his lead and shifted into the form of a night owl. She followed him into the sky, her wings spread wide, the air rushing around her and ruffling her feathers so that she felt free and a little wild.

Below her, everything on the ground dropped away. She left behind the carnage of battle. The smoke rising in the air couldn't find her as she hurried after Zev. He led her over the forest and up over the first mountain ridge. Below them the glacier-fed lake appeared deep and ice-blue. Small farms dotted the countryside and she spotted the animals, cattle sleeping, horses moving slowly, chickens roosting.

Life was normal around them. She needed to see that. In those houses, children slept with their parents watching over them. Zev kept going, along another mountain ridge where the trees were so close together that it was impossible, even with the eyes of an owl, to penetrate to the floor below.

A waterfall burst from the side of a mountain, crystalline and shiny, tumbling to the wide pool beneath it where giant ferns ringed the water and shrubs and plants congregated close. Water formed bright ribbons dissecting the ground below them as they continued to fly over the next mountain ridge. She followed him, caught up in the rapture of soaring through the sky, the wind on her body and the ever-changing scenery below her breathtaking.

The caps of the mountains ahead were snowy white, a pristine world of icy beauty. The part of the mountain Zev sought had long ago been a volcano. The glacier followed the deadly eruption, creeping over the fire-lit mountain, turning the red rock to an icy blue. The effect where the ice thinned was stunning.

He dropped down into the crater. She could see the surrounding mountain was all snow and ice, but in the cradle, trees and plants and even flowers grew, birthed by the years of wind bringing seeds to the rich soil inside the shallow crater. A fine green grass lined the floor, tiny little shamrocks of ground cover. A few trees grew, their limbs healthy and strong, reaching for the sky in their warmer nest, unseen and untouched by anyone. Protected by the ice and snow, the little oasis had gone unnoticed.

Zev settled on the floor itself, waving his hand to cushion the ground with a bed of petals. Branislava shifted, taking her human form, turning in a slow circle to inspect their surroundings. When she had first seen the snowy mountains, her heart had given a little jerk of apprehension, but she should have had more faith.

"It's beautiful here, Zev. How did you find it?"

"Patrolling. Looking for rogues. A couple of times, before you woke, I went out looking out of habit." He grinned at her. "And I like to fly."

She had to smile back. He looked relaxed and happy, a far cry from the grim man who had to fight too many battles. "It's time someone saw to your wounds." She pointed to the bed of petals.

"That's for you. And this patch of Gary's worked very well. Lycans rejuvenate fairly quickly. Remember, I'm also mixed blood and that gives me a boost as well."

She fixed him with a stern eye, even as she lifted her hand to her hair and pulled out the tie binding her braid. With a wave of her hand she freed the long thick mass from its weave, shaking her head so that the silken strands fell around her like a cape of red gold. "I would very much like you to lie down so I can see to your wounds, Zev," she told him.

"Dragon flames are beginning to glow in your eyes," Zev informed her. When she was like this, demanding, sexy, every move sensual, there was no way to resist her. He could see that fire always smoldering just beneath the surface rising, growing hotter.

His body reacted to that note in her voice, the stroking of his skin with her tone, the heat in her eyes as she looked him over. Her tongue darted out and moistened her lips.

She tapped her foot. "I'm waiting."

"So am I," he said softly, trying not to use his alpha voice, but it was there, that growling command he had been born with.

She tipped her head to one side, her eyes slumberous and sexy, long lashes sweeping down almost demurely, but when they came back up, her eyes held flames dancing through a background of emerald green.

She waved her hand down her body, and her clothes disappeared. His breath caught in his lungs and stayed trapped there. Her form was exquisite to him, all those soft, full curves and the tucked-in waist. Her hair fell around her, framing her high breasts and the nipples peaking hard already. He knew if he pushed his hand between her legs she would be hot and wet for him.

"You are so beautiful, Branka. For me, to me, there is no other who can compare."

She placed one hand on her hip and continued tapping her small, bare foot. He wanted to drop to his knees and yank her close, and taste the cinnamon honey he scented drifting toward him. Instead, he let her have her way, shedding his clothes, watching her eyes as her gaze dropped to his heavy erection. His hand went to his thick cock, circling it, feeling the sensual burn already. He took his time walking over to the bed of petals. It wasn't easy with his groin full and hard and so ready for her body, but for her, he would do anything.

The moment he lay on his back, she was straddling his calves, removing the patch and leaning over him, her soft breasts brushing across his skin. Her tongue lapped at his wound with healing saliva. She whispered softly, a small healing litany he heard in his mind rather than aloud.

Zev's pulse thundered in his ears. While she lapped at his wound, her hands were busy on his shaft, his balls, fingers sliding over him in a delicate dance and then suddenly switching from a soft caressing brush, to a fist pumping him, her thumb sliding over the large, sensitive head to smear the leaking pearls around.

Her hair fell in a pool of red into his lap, teasing his cock, adding to the chaos growing in his mind. The sensation of living silk sliding around and over him, her tongue and hands was almost too much to take. He kept his hips from bucking and his hands from fisting in her hair and dragging her mouth to his cock using his years of discipline—but it wasn't easy.

She lifted her head to look at him. His heart nearly stopped. The stark intensity of her fiery passion shone in her eyes. Already her skin took on a glow, the color changing from pale porcelain to a flushed deep pink. With each move she made, her hair crackled, alive with energy. Very slowly she moved her body up his, the hot vee between her legs leaving behind evidence of her arousal on his calf. She moved over his thighs and straddled his groin, refusing to give him the satisfaction of sheathing his rock-hard weapon.

Once again she removed the patch and flung it away from her, licking up his belly and over his ribs, over every scratch and bruise until she reached the stab wound in his chest. He heard that soft healing litany echoing through his mind, a melody of love that surrounded him, enfolded him with fire. Branislava. His lifemate. She was fire and passion. She was love to him. Everything good in the world. When she healed him, she didn't just heal with her love and her gifts, or even the miraculous saliva of her species. She also healed with her fiery passion, and the urgent need she had for his body.

When her mouth moved over his wounds, when her tongue lapped at his lacerations and bruises, there was blatant seduction along with her healing balm. His body reacted, every nerve ending springing to life, alert and pouring heat through his bloodstream. He brought his hands up to her breasts, massaging and kneading, his fingers settling on her nipples to tug and roll.

The pretty pink flush on her body deepened. Her skin, soft and supple, burned hotter. Over the base of his cock, where her body met his, a fire seemed to ignite. He was fast losing his ability to accommodate her. He issued a warning growl, letting her know he was about at his limit.

"I'm working here," she murmured, flashing a reprimand at him from under her lashes.

He caught her arms and rolled her under him, his knee inside her thigh, pushing her legs apart. "So am I." His voice was harsh with need. "I'm starving and I want to eat you up."

He did just that, lifting her hips and dragging her to him, lowering his head so he could devour her. She screamed, a loud cry of bliss as his tongue plunged deep and drew the cinnamon honey he craved from her body. It was warm and thick, like molasses and he found himself growling like the wolf he was, ravenous for her. He held her firmly as her body tried to roll and buck.

"Be still," he ordered harshly, when he could find a moment to speak. When she didn't comply with his order, he smacked her bottom to get her attention. Her nerve endings fired with passion, more delicious honey spilling into his mouth. He couldn't resist trying it again and again, and each time he got the same results, more of what he needed. Each time the honey was hotter and spicier, the taste more delicious than ever. He licked at her scorching sheath, and then nuzzled her, inhaling her perfect scent. He couldn't resist taking little nips up her inner thigh, tiny teasing bites that had flames of desire licking up her legs.

He moved over top of her, catching her wrists, pinning them over her head so he could look down at her body, sprawled beneath his larger one. Her breath came in ragged gasps so that her breasts heaved and moved invitingly—temptingly. He leaned down and captured the left one, drawing the soft mound into the heat of his mouth.

She moaned softly, her body rippling as his tongue stroked her nipple, and then he suckled strongly. Her head thrashed. Her hips rose beneath him. It was all music, part of the night. He loved the sounds she made and the way her body was so ultra-responsive to everything he did to her.

He kissed his way over the creamy curve of her breast to find her pulse beating so wildly—so temptingly. He heard the answering beat deep in his own veins and without warning, without preamble, he sank his teeth deep. She cried out, sobbed, lifted her hips and writhed. She tried to lift her arms to circle his head and hold him to her, but he held her helpless, enjoying bringing her so much pleasure. He felt it in her mind, her need rising like a volcano.

He drank her essence, taking her into his body, that same spicy taste just as addictive. He wanted to be the wolf and eat her up. There was something so beautiful in her face, in her glowing body as she lay beneath him, her pleas growing more desperate as her need intensified.

When he had taken his fill, he gripped her wrists hard and looked into her eyes. "Stay still, just like this." He leaned down and kissed her mouth, that beautiful mouth he wanted to spend a lifetime playing in and kissing and loving.

"I don't think I can," she admitted a little desperately.

He licked down her ear and nipped at her chin. "Then I'll help you. Because this is for me. I want to drive you insane and watch you catch fire. We're safe here. There's no forest to burn down. I can light a match and watch you burn."

As she lay there, vines rushed from the ground and circled her arms, forming two long sleeves that went from wrist to bicep.

"There you go, *mon chaton féroce.* There is no moving when I want you still." He sat up and ran his hand possessively down her body from breast to belly, splaying his fingers wide to take in as much of her skin as possible. "I can take my time with you. You can scream to your heart's content and your body can go up in flames over and over and no one will interrupt us."

He smiled down at her shocked expression, watching the flames in her eyes grow even brighter. More cinnamon honey spilled from her body. More than anything, the faith in her for him, the trust she had, excited him. She gave herself into his keeping, knowing he would bring her only pleasure— and he intended to do just that.

"I'm wolf, Branka. Wolves are often rough, bordering on brutal. But I touch you with love. And I'd never want to harm you. Tell me to stop if you don't like something."

"Fortunately for you, I like the way you love me. I like rough, bordering on brutal. If I don't like something, you'll hear about it fast," she assured. "And, Zev, I know you would never harm me."

She killed him with her soft seductive voice, with the thrash of her body and the bucking of her hips as if she couldn't wait for him. Deliberately she spread her thighs for him. Opening herself for him. Silently begging him for more. For anything.

He laughed softly. "You're so eager, my love. Let's just see what fun I can have with you." He rose over top of her, on his hands and knees, moving up until he was nearly on her head. His cock felt heavy with need, his sac sliding sensuously over her breast and bumping her chin. Using one hand, he wrapped his fist around his shaft and brought the head to her lips.

"I dream of you sucking me dry. That beautiful mouth of yours wrapped tightly around me, so tight like a hot fist. I had that dream from the moment I laid eyes on you, your mouth so beautiful and tempting. I love you lying here beneath me, helpless, an offering. *Mine.*" He smeared droplets along the seam of her mouth. "Mine to play with, mine to love."

Her tongue darted out and caught his offering. She licked at every last drop and then strained toward his cock. "Please," she finally said, her eyes growing even brighter when he held himself just out of reach. Her body glowed even hotter.

He pushed into her mouth, sliding deep, groaning with bliss. He shared the feeling with her, mind to mind. She rewarded him with stroking his shaft with her tongue and then teasing at the sensitive spot beneath the flared head. He closed his eyes briefly, unable to believe that she was his. Everything in her reached for him. She gave herself wholly over to his care.

Love welled up, sharp and terrible and all encompassing. More, Branislava didn't think about herself or her own needs when she attended to him. She focused solely on his pleasure. Her every move was filled with love and he couldn't help but feel it in the eagerness she had each time they came together like this.

She gave a little cry of protest when he pulled out of her mouth and slid down her chest, between her breasts, his mouth nibbling at her chin as he slid farther down to her belly. He kissed and bit lightly, stimulating her body more, watching the fire growing hotter in her until the little sparks began to snap around them like fireflies in the night.

He loved that. Her passion. Her fire. He wanted her to have the chance to set the night on fire where nothing could get harmed. High up the snow-covered glacier, they were safe. Even if a tree caught fire, there was nothing else to burn, and he'd already made certain the foliage around them was safe.

Zev kissed his way across her quivering, flat belly to her mound and then swiped his tongue through her soft folds again, watching the delicious shiver go through her body with satisfaction. Her fingers dug into the rich loam. He noticed the soil under her begin to glow with a soft red light and where her fingers sank into the dirt, the red appeared crimson. Joy burst through him. Loving her was an adventure, a beautiful, incredible journey of love.

He spread her legs farther apart, pulling them over his shoulders as he knelt up against her, easily lifting her bottom from the bed of petals. Her eyes were huge, the green nearly gone to be replaced by those hot, flicking flames. Her skin was hot to the touch. His cock jerked in anticipation of her scorching sheath wrapped tightly around it.

"Hurry," she panted, trying to move her body in a kind of desperation to find his cock. She never tried to hide her eagerness from him. She always hungered for his body, just as he hungered for hers.

He laughed softly, his happiness spilling over. He had no idea why he'd been given such a miracle, but he knew he would always treasure her. She was a gift beyond anything else in the world. He took one more moment to just look at her, lying there, breathing raggedly, her eyes flickering with flames, yet pleading. Her body was flushed and hot with sparks leaping around her and the ground beneath her rising in temperature directly in proportion to hers. Her hair was everywhere, that mass of red silk, a fiery fall he was madly in love with.

He entered her in one, swift, brutal thrust. She screamed. Her voice rose to the misty clouds, such perfect music of pure pleasure. His voice blended with hers, a husky long wolfish howl of pure ecstasy as her muscles gripped him with scorching-hot silk. She was so tight he had to drive through her sheath like a piston, forcing his way through the tight-wrapped silk to lodge deep.

He used his mind to free her arms, not wanting her to feel discomfort. In any case, he loved the way she clutched him, driving her nails into his skin and holding on to him as if he was her only anchor. Immediately she slid her hand down his belly to the junction between his legs, where their bodies joined, her fingers stroking back and forth over the base of his cock.

"You're so beautiful, Zev," she whispered, her breath coming in ragged gasps.

She was the beautiful one. Around them, the ground took on a red glow as he began to move, long, excruciatingly slow strokes, dragging over her sensitive bud, burying himself deep, all the while watching her face. Her head tossed and her lips parted. Her skin grew hotter. The fierce heat spread like wildfire while the storm built inside of her.

"More," she pleaded. "Give me more."

He laughed softly. "You're an insatiable little thing, aren't you? A very demanding woman." He loved her that way.

He took his time, holding her hips in place, refusing to give in to her demands, setting a leisurely pace that drove her wild. She squirmed and writhed, trying to force him into a more forceful speed, but he refused to cooperate, watching her skin flush even more red, watching the sparks leaping around her body and the glow spread across the ground as she tossed her head and pleaded with him for release.

He kept her on that edge, building the tension, feeling her coil tighter and tighter. She screamed again when he suddenly shifted gears, riding her hard, setting a brutal pace, wanting to drive her up as high as possible, to stay inside of her for as long as possible. She began her song, that soft melodic chanting of his name, tears swimming in her eyes, fingers digging deeper into his biceps.

He let himself lose all control, reveling in his ability to do so. Branislava not only could handle it, but she welcomed the madness that took him. Her body was made for his, for the pounding pleasure and the incredible, impossible heat. The firestorm leapt from her to him, burning through his every vein, pooling in his groin like the molten lava rising in her.

They burned together, the scorching heat growing hotter by the moment until a fine sheen of sweat spread over his body. Still, he didn't stop, couldn't stop. He lost himself in her, all that fire, burning with her, getting closer and closer to the very heart of the volcano. He felt the first wicked ripple, her sheath clamping down hard around him, fisting him in living silken flames. The volcano erupted, shaking them both, a fireball bursting through her, through him, her body milking and squeezing every last drop from him as they burned together.

The orgasm tore through her, her panting cries filling his mind with pure joy. His body sang along with his heart. He savored every second of her orgasm and his, the heat and fire, the ecstasy unmatched by anything else he'd ever known.

Very slowly he lowered her legs to the ground, slipped from her body and collapsed beside her. She turned into his arms immediately, snuggling close to him, her body still shuddering with aftershocks. She was burning hot against him, her skin like the smooth silken fire that had wrapped around his cock so lovingly. Her hair tumbled over his chest, adding to the sensation of being covered in silk.

"The night air feels good, doesn't it?" she said, when she could catch her breath.

She was right. The cool of the snowcapped mountains felt amazing against the heat of his skin. The ground was a hot bed of petals, but it was cooling rapidly. "The night's fading, Branka. Let's just stay right here. We can open the ground and rest here."

She pressed kisses along his neck. "I like the idea. It's so beautiful up here." She glanced toward the tree. "And look at that, we didn't even burn down the tree."

He brushed a kiss on top of her head. "It does look a little scorched. Look at the base and the leaves."

She laughed softly. "I don't think so. You're making that up."

"Maybe." He wasn't so sure. The ground had definitely heated up around the base of the tree, probably affecting the roots underground.

"You make life fun when everything around us is a little crazy, Zev," she confided. "Thank you. This is the perfect place, far from everything and everyone."

"It's the two of us, Branka," he pointed out. "We're good together. We belong."

She nuzzled him again, inhaling his scent. "You always seem to know what I need."

He laughed softly. "Of course I know what you need. I take my vows to you seriously. You'll always be first."

There was a stirring in Zev's mind. Faint laughter. *Do you want to tell me why the lake has risen three inches? I think half the glacier melted. Down here, everyone thinks there's a possibility that the volcano is becoming active. I told them you two were setting the night on fire,* Fen taunted him.

I don't believe you.

How did I know you two were up there? The entire top of the mountain glowed right through the mist. You can bet it caused quite a stir down below with farmers rushing out to make certain the volcano wasn't about to blow and kill them all.

Ha. Ha. You're so funny. Zev was beginning to grow just a little uneasy. Fen sounded amused, but not necessarily as if he was making it up.

Not three inches. We didn't melt the entire glacier. Although they could have. Branislava had burned hot enough to melt the ice cap.

Don't bet on it, bro. And go to ground. Both of you are exhausted.

Zev gave him the mental equivalent of rolling his eyes. Dimitri had warned him about Fen's penchant for being the older brother and how he'd forget that Zev and Dimitri were not only entirely grown-up but had been around for centuries.

Zev wrapped his arms around Branislava, holding her close. "I thought we'd be safe up here, *mon chaton féroce*, but already, Fen is asking why the lake below has risen three inches. He claims we melted the glacier."

"He's such an exaggerator," Branislava countered, content to bury her face in his neck. She lay quietly for a moment. "He is joking, right? We didn't really melt the glacier, did we?"

"Hell if I know," Zev said, too content to move and go check. "We could have."

"What else did he say?"

"The mountain glowed red through the mist, and the farmers all thought the volcano was active again. But you know he likes to tease."

She started laughing. "You have to admit it would be kind of funny if it was the truth. Can you imagine the prince asking everyone for reports? Worse, what if he told Gregori to do a flyby to make certain the mountain was safe?"

"He'd get an eyeful with the two of us lying here naked," Zev said. He glanced up to the sky. Dawn was breaking, light penetrating through the clouds of mist. "We do need to go to ground and heal a bit, Branka. Your spirit and my body. We're both a bit battered."

"I suppose so. This feels like such freedom to me, Zev. Thank you again for finding this place for us. I really love it."

He tipped her chin up with his thumb and kissed her thoroughly. "Open the ground, *mon chaton féroce*, and let's get some sleep."

Branislava waved her hand and opened the ground close to them. "If we did melt part of the glacier, you know we'll never hear the end of it. My sister and Fen and Skyler and Dimitri will never stop giving us a bad time."

He floated them into the deep hole. "Let me just say, Branislava, if we did melt the glacier and the lake has risen three inches and we're teased for the next ten centuries, it was *so* worth it."

Her soft laughter told him she agreed with him.

15

Branislava stared down at the deep blue lake shimmering below her. She studied the water lapping at the shore very closely. *I don't think there's more water in it than there was last night,* she told Zev, but her voice indicated she wasn't certain.

Zev moved up beside her. They hovered together over the body of water, two trails of vapor, looking a little like comets in the night sky. Laughter welled up. *Take a look at the reeds and the trees. They're in the water, Branka, and they weren't like that last night.*

You can't possibly know that, she protested, but again she didn't sound sure.

Of course I can, he said, keeping as sober as possible. *Elite hunters have to notice every detail around them. I registered the lake last night . . .*

She stirred in his mind, giving him the impression of a raised eyebrow. *I thought you were entirely focused on me.*

Exactly, he replied smoothly. *With the small exception of noting the water and shoreline as we passed by.*

Her laughter teased at his mind like the brush of butterfly wings. *I will concede the reeds seem to be a bit more under water than I remember them. And maybe the two trees on the southern end look as though the waterline moved up, but that's all. I checked the snow pack and there's absolutely no problem with it, and the glacier is totally intact.*

I'm certain the prince will be happy to hear that. And we can reassure him that the volcano remains dormant. Zev's voice was droll.

She laughed again, sounding carefree, a sound which he hadn't heard from her ever. He loved that he'd found a way to get her to relax, to forget about what she'd seen and heard in Lyall's mind. Lycans and Carpathians would have to find a way to ferret Xaviero out and rid the world of him, but Zev wanted to keep Branislava as far from the mage as possible.

They took their time, hunting leisurely for sustenance, dropping down near a farm to talk casually with the farmer and his wife. They laughed together at the antics of horses, and Zev helped the farmer put a tire back on his broken cart. When they had fed, they left the couple sitting on their front porch, smiling happily, remembering the nice couple who had stopped by to inquire about the beautiful handmade quilts the wife had hanging up to sell for extra money. Her pocket was fat with cash and one of the quilts was missing.

"That was fun," Branislava said, hugging the quilt to her. "They're nice people."

Zev took the quilt from her and threaded his fingers through hers. "I agree. We'll have to check on them once in a while. It's always a good thing to make friends with neighbors and locals. Mikhail is quite charismatic and he takes the time to fit in. Those living in the village are very loyal to him."

"Are we going to make our home here?" Branislava asked.

He caught the little note of apprehension in her voice. He brought her hand to the warmth of his mouth, his teeth nibbling at her knuckles. "I told you we would always stay close to Tatijana. I like it here, and if we use these mountains as our base, with our ability to fly, we can get to places very fast if need be."

He stopped walking, turning to plant himself directly in front of her. "When I said I would cherish you for all time, Branka, that I would put your happiness above my own, I meant it. You never have to do anything you don't want to do." He slung the quilt over one shoulder and tipped her chin up with his fingers. "I treasure each moment we have together, I do, but if I have to go off hunting rogues, or tracking vampires or the *Sange rau,* it will always be your choice whether or not you leave our home and accompany me."

Tears swam for a moment in her vivid green eyes but she blinked them away rapidly and managed a mock scowl. "If you think I'm going to let you go off somewhere hunting rogues, vampires or *Sange rau* without me, you've got another thing coming. Someone has to look after you." She reached up to circle his neck with her arm and pulled his head down to hers. "You take too many chances, Zev, and I'm not willing to let you go. So stop." She punctuated each word with a fierce kiss.

His heart turned over and heat rushed through his veins, not just the heat of desire, but the heat of love. He had no other way to describe it. She ran through his veins like life's blood, an addiction and obsession, that scorching hot love she poured into him every time she entered his mind, or kissed him as she was doing. Every time she touched him, sparks leapt between them, igniting an overwhelming rush of pure love he felt for her.

He wasn't a man with fancy words. He never would be. He was a predator, a wolf, an elite hunter and rough as hell. But he knew without a doubt that he loved her fiercely, with every cell in his body, with every beat of his heart. Had he been a poet he would have written her something beautiful, but he only had his body to show her how he felt.

He kissed her, pouring that hot, ferocious love he had for her into her mouth. He was demanding and rough and insistent, sweeping her up into a vortex of fire, as alpha as it got, forcing her response, yet knowing she gave it to him freely.

Branislava clung to him for a moment when he lifted his head. She kept her body tight against his, as if he was her sanctuary. He wanted to be that haven for her, a shelter she could always count on. He closed his arms around her and held her to him, counting her heartbeats, listening to the rhythm of her breathing until his body followed the tempo of hers.

"Are you all right, *mon chaton féroce*?" he asked, brushing a kiss along the top of her head. "You don't have to come with me for this meeting. I know anything to do with Xaviero distresses you."

"I'm just holding you, Zev. Keeping you close, gathering strength from you. You never seem to get upset, not even in the worst crisis. You just feel calm inside. I want to be like that."

He laughed softly. "Branka, do you know what *mon chaton féroce* means?"
She nodded, puzzled. "My fierce kitten."

"*Exactly.* You are fierce and passionate and fiery and I love all those things
about you. In a fight, I can count on you to keep your head and get the job
done, even if you're afraid. There's no need to be anything other than who
you are, who you're meant to be."

Branislava gave him her radiant smile. "You always know the right thing
to say." She took a deep breath. "I'm ready to help you figure all this out. I hope
we aren't the ones who have to try to hunt Xaviero down. I know that's what's
coming next and believe me, Zev, when I tell you he is extremely dangerous."

"I am well aware of that, Branka," he reassured her.

"Have you ever met him? The one they call Rannalufr?"

He nodded his head. "I work for the council. I protect them, and when
they issue orders to settle disputes among packs or within packs that aren't
being resolved by the alpha, I go. Council members are guarded at all times.
I have to know where they are and who they're with. The short answer is
yes, I've met Rannalufr. He seemed a kind older man to me, one who speaks
in a low, gentle voice and seemed always to give thought before he answered.
I liked him. I think most people who meet him like him."

"Does he belong to the Sacred Circle? Is he one of the leaders?" Branislava asked.

Zev slipped his arm around her waist and once again began walking
toward Mikhail's home. It was up the mountain and just on the edge of the
forest. "Yes. Many Lycans belong. Those belonging revere the old ways and
hold the lost elders up as examples of how Lycans should be."

"Did you ever belong?" she asked curiously.

"I've gone to the meetings, of course. The speakers are usually amazing,
Arno in particular, and yes, before you ask, Rannalufr as well. Both are
charismatic, but I tend to have problems with anything that narrows my
thinking or borders on fanaticism. Things have to be logical to me and living by old rules that no longer make sense is not in the least logical." He
sighed. "I don't get the progression."

"I don't know what that means," she said.

They followed a narrow deer path that wound through the trees, moving
deeper into the forest as they climbed uphill.

"Modern times are moving fast. Technology has changed everything, and it keeps changing at an alarming rate. If the Sacred Circle merely preached morals and how to treat one another with kindness, I might go for it, but they don't stop there. They have a political agenda and that agenda doesn't follow the dictates of the countries Lycans live in."

Branislava leaned down to smell a night flower. Walking beside him always gave her a secret thrill. He was tall and strong and he made her feel feminine—which she was—and delicate—which she wasn't. The sound of his voice mesmerized her. Zev never spoke in a booming or loud voice. He was soft-spoken, and yet his tone rang with authority. Everything about him spoke of absolute confidence, and she loved that in him.

"I still don't understand."

"We have integrated into modern society," Zev explained. "Each pack, no matter the country, serves in the military for that country and hold jobs just as humans do. We live side by side with them. It isn't logical to think we can go back to a code that was written long before technology came into being. Our women were once fierce warriors. Look at Daciana. She's every bit as good as—or better than—the male elite hunters and yet, because many centuries ago the first *Sange rau* nearly wiped us out by decimating our ranks, the sacred code decreed that all women stay home."

"But the council overturned that," Branislava pointed out.

"Against much opposition. The leaders of the Sacred Circle were furious and some even talked of forming their own council." His voice had dropped another octave and he shook his head.

The moon had risen, beginning to look quite full, although not yet at its peak. A yellow halo surrounded it. Branislava made out his face by the light of the moon shining through the branches overhead. Lines were etched there. Scars. Yet he looked a true example of masculine beauty to her.

"And you were sent to put them back in line." It wasn't a guess on her part, she knew she was right. She was becoming much more adept at reading him.

He nodded. "I had a talk with them, yes. I can be persuasive when necessary. There cannot be dissention, not when Lycans are so dangerous. We did lose a few packs. They went rogue, which I pointed out to the leaders of the Circle, and they stopped their preaching. It's okay with the council to discuss each issue and the members are always willing to hear any Lycan out before making a decision, but ultimately, all of us abide by their rulings."

They came to a small clearing. A large tree had fallen, the trunk lying across their path. The opening had provided room on the forest floor for shrubs, ferns and flowers to grow in abundance. Branislava flung out her arms and turned in a slow circle. The moon fell across her wealth of red hair, the light setting it on fire.

"What are you doing?" Zev asked.

"Living," she replied, still spinning around like a ballerina. "I'm living right here in this perfect minute. I have you, this beautiful spot, the moon and the night air." She inhaled deeply, drawing the scent of the forest and her wolf deep into her lungs. "What could be more perfect than this one moment?"

He stepped close, his arm circling her waist, yanking her to him hard, his feet already picking up the rhythm of a dance, moving to music the night provided. "Making love to you is always perfect. Kissing you is definitely perfect. *Dancing* with you is sheer perfection."

He held her close, listening to the moaning wind playing them a melody of string instruments. The heartbeat of the Earth became their drum, providing a steady beat. He moved her around the clearing, their bodies in perfect synchronization, flowing like water over rocks, gliding first one way and then the other.

Branislava felt his body move against hers, that rippling of sheer power as his roped muscles played beneath his warm skin. She laid her head on his shoulder, feeling as if she were floating in the clouds. There were moments of perfection and she wanted to recognize and capture each one and hold it close to her heart. She knew, better than most, that there was evil alive and well in the world and it would raise its ugly head soon. She needed this foundation with Zev, these perfect moments to add to their arsenal of weapons. She had to become a weapon just as Zev was already. They needed to be unstoppable.

"Can anyone join in?" Dimitri whirled Skyler right into the clearing, and then pulled her tightly against him, his smooth footwork guiding her over the twigs and leaves. "We heard your music calling to us and couldn't resist."

Branislava smiled contentedly. Dimitri still carried the scars of his brush with *moarta de argint*—death by silver. Somehow, Skyler had managed to force the terrible burns to fade almost to invisibility. Still, Dimitri was quite handsome, and he held Skyler in such a loving, intimate, protective hold that they looked as if they were one as they danced around the clearing. Branislava felt their love pouring from them both, as if it were so great neither could contain the emotion.

Fen and Tatijana dropped down unexpectedly from above. Zev didn't so much as flinch, so Branislava knew he had been aware of them close by. Fen waved his hand and more instruments joined in, adding to the music of the night. He pulled Tatijana into his arms. She fit perfectly beneath his shoulder and they began to dance.

The rhythm at first was soft and dreamy so that the men could hold their women close as they moved around the small clearing as easily as if it were a ballroom.

Before long, another couple showed up. Darius Daratrazanoff strode up, his lifemate, Tempest, beside him. He carried a child that could be no more than two. They moved together without a word, their son between them, as Darius whirled Tempest around beneath the moon. The child's soft laughter only added to the beauty of the moment to Branislava.

"Are we having a party?"

The question came from a group of Carpathians. Branislava vaguely recognized them. They made up a traveling band called the Dark Troubadours.

"Hey, Andor," Julian called to Darius and Tempest's boy. "Can we come and dance with you?"

Andor waved happily at him, breaking out into a huge smile that lit his dark eyes—Daratrazanoff eyes.

"Do you mind?" Desari asked Zev and Branislava. "This looks such fun."

Julian Savage and his lifemate, Desari, moved gracefully together. She was sister to the Daratrazanoff men. Beside them, Barack and Syndil danced close. Emerging from the trees already moving to the beat, Corrine and her lifemate, Dayan, arrived with their daughter, Jennifer. Clearly she was a child of music. She began whirling and twirling and shaking her bottom to the rhythm.

"No party," Zev said, "just holding my woman and doing a little dancing, but you're all welcome."

After a few minutes of dancing with Corrine, Dayan sank down onto the large tree trunk and drew his guitar to him. His fingers danced over the strings and music poured into the night. Barack immediately joined him, playing bass. Syndil listened to the heartbeat of the earth and then called drums to her, joining with the earth to add in her rhythm. Corrine and Jennifer danced together, whirling around the small clearing, the sound of Jennifer's laughter joining with Andor's.

Razvan danced Ivory right out of the forest, his eyes filled with laughter—something one rarely saw in him, unless they stumbled upon a private moment between Ivory and him. She clung to him, laughing with him, her gaze only for him.

Desari began to sing, her voice rising with the wind, the notes pure, the pitch perfect. The song was one of joy and laughter, adding to Branislava's perfect moment.

Branislava looked around her at the people she loved. Her nephew Razvan, who had been so horribly tortured by his own grandfather, Xavier. Ivory, who had been betrayed by Xavier and chopped to pieces by vampires in league with him. Fen and Tatijana, her beloved sister, trapped with her in the wall of ice there in Xavier's laboratory. Dimitri and Skyler, a young woman made by Xavier through Razvan's body and then sold into sex slavery by her great-grandfather.

There was joy here and true happiness. Xavier and his brothers were pure evil and yet somehow, good had triumphed here, and her perfect moment proved it.

Look at them all, Zev. These people, most of them, are our family. Xavier tried to destroy them all, everyone here, really, and yet we can come together like this, in fun and laughter, an impromptu party with no real reason except you love me enough to dance with me because you know I enjoy it.

Zev kissed the junction between her neck and shoulder. *I would dance with you anywhere, Branka, and enjoy every single moment of holding you.*

Happiness welled up. That was the wonderful thing about Zev. She knew he was telling her the truth. He would dance with her anywhere simply because she loved to dance. She glanced at her sister, held so close by

Fen. Fen was a good man and she already thought of him as a brother. The way he looked at Tatijana was beautiful. Tatijana's gaze met hers and they smiled.

"I love her so much, Zev," she whispered against his chest. "I wanted so much for her to escape and to be able to live life, to dance like this whenever possible and to find a man who loved her above all else. I believe my wish came true." Satisfaction edged her words.

"I see you are having a party practically on my front step, but I don't believe I was invited, so I'm crashing." Mikhail announced his presence.

He swung Raven around and the two of them came together, moving with a flowing grace to the music. Alexandru ran over to Jennifer and Andor. Jennifer took both boys' hands and they began to dance together in a circle.

Zev laughed. "Look what you started, Branka."

"And I got us in trouble with the prince. Who knew he liked to dance?"

"Doesn't everyone?" Zev nudged her and indicated the couple coming into the clearing.

Gregori and Savannah joined them, which wasn't a surprise since Gregori tended to be wherever the prince was. Their two little girls, Anya and Anastasia, ran to join the other children while their parents danced.

The small area seemed to be transformed, growing larger even, with the brush and shrubbery cleared away, giving the couples a dance floor. The moon looked down on them, adding light while the band played. Stars scattered across the night sky, sparkling like diamonds, giving them a ceiling of beauty.

Branislava turned her face up to Zev's. "This is all you, Wolfie; you're such a miracle." She kissed her way up his neck, her fingers laced around his nape, beneath the long, thick pelt of hair. "I don't know how you make everything so wonderful."

Fen and Tatijana just happened to be dancing close. Fen gave a little snort of derision. "*Wolfie?* Did I just hear you call that man *Wolfie?*"

"No, you didn't," Zev denied, giving him a fierce scowl. "Go away, Fen."

"Dimitri." Fen continued to hold Tatijana close to her sister and Zev while they danced. He waited until Dimitri was very close to him and leaned over. "She calls him *Wolfie.*"

Dimitri glanced over at Zev with a wide grin on his face. He opened his mouth to tease him, but caught a glimpse of Branislava's mortified expression. Tiny little flames were beginning to flicker in her eyes.

He closed his mouth and raised his eyebrow at his brother. "Really, Fen, you shouldn't be eavesdropping on private conversations." It was all he could do not to laugh, but he kept a straight face as he fanned Branislava's rising wrath.

"But *Wolfie*? Come on, bro, that just suits our little brother to a tee. He's kind of like a big teddy bear, don't you think?"

As Fen whirled Tatijana out away from him, he stepped back, his left foot sinking just a little into the forest floor. Myrmica rubra, the fire ant of Romania, swarmed up his leg, biting and stinging.

Fen waved his hand and the ants calmed instantly, rushing back to the ground and disappearing. He glared at Branislava, who was looking far too innocent. "*O jelä peje teräd, emni*—sun scorch you, woman!" Tatijana didn't help his cause, covering her mouth and clearly laughing at her sister's antics.

"Having trouble there, Fen?" Mikhail asked. His features appeared relaxed, much younger. Laughter welled up and spilled into his usually somber eyes.

"Blasted Dragonseeker women have this penchant for revenge, Mikhail," Fen said. "You need to talk to them about it."

"Not me," Mikhail hastily denied. "I'm not getting on their bad side." He danced away laughing.

Fen laughed, too, bringing Tatijana close to him. "Your sister is a fiery little thing. Imagine taking offense just because I overheard her calling Zev that ridiculous nickname."

"Imagine," Tatijana echoed, snuggling closer. "At least she didn't set your hair on fire." She smoothed her hand over his long, very thick and distinctly silver hair with black strands woven into the waves falling down his back. It was secured at his nape with a leather cord, but hung nearly to his waist. "I'd hate to have you bald and scorched."

Fen caught her closer as if for protection. "She wouldn't dare."

I would dare, Branislava assured him.

Fen couldn't help the laughter welling up. He and Branislava burst out laughing at the same time. Zev and Tatijana, then Dimitri and Skyler joined in.

Branislava felt as if she were at a family celebration. It felt right. Normal. Beautiful. *Perfect*. She had never once imagined she could have such fun and happiness, not when she was freezing and frightened, there behind that wall of ice.

More dancers showed up. To her surprise Zacarias De La Cruz led Marguarita onto the forest floor with the others dancing. She should have known he would be a graceful dancer. He held his lifemate close, very lovingly, not at all appearing to be the dangerous, dark predator she knew him to be.

Nicolas, Zacarias's brother, came behind him, leading Lara, his lifemate. Branislava's heart leapt with joy. Lara, her great-niece, looked beautiful and happy, glowing even, obviously happy with her lifemate. Lara had been the one to return to the ice caves, searching for her aunts, but she'd been a little girl, a child when they'd helped her to escape, and she hadn't even been certain her childhood had been real. Still, she had come to free them from their horrible prison. It was good to see her so happy.

Rafael and Colby, another De La Cruz brother and his lifemate, came into the clearing with Juliette and Riordan, the youngest brother. Laughing, the men whirled the women into the flow of dancers. Last came Manolito De La Cruz, with MaryAnn. They were of mixed blood like Dimitri, Fen and Zev, carrying both Lycan and Carpathian blood. They were considered *Sange rau* by the Lycans and under a death sentence, while Carpathians believed them to be *Hän ku pesäk kaikak*—guardian of all. MaryAnn laughed softly as Manolito spun her around and drew her in close to him again.

"This is so wonderful," Branislava said. "Look at the children. Listen to them laughing."

In her world, deep beneath the ice, neither she nor Tatijana had ever had the chance to be a laughing child. Little Lara had also been used by Xavier for food. Even Razvan, taken control of by Xavier, had fed on her. No doubt that, like Branislava's and Tatijana's, Lara's arms and wrists were covered in scars.

Branislava wanted to replace every ugly moment of her own childhood with special moments such as this one. Shea and Jacques's son Stefan had joined the circle of laughing children. She looked around for Falcon and Sara's children. Usually, where one child was, the others always followed.

"Sara is about to give birth and the children wanted to stay close to her," Zev said. "Gregori just gave me the news that she's in labor. She was human before Carpathian and she's much more comfortable using a human delivery. Shea's a doctor and she's with her, that's why Jacques is here alone with his son."

"Are there complications?" Branislava was suddenly anxious. In between the attacks by the Sacred Circle army there was little time for fun or rejoicing. A baby born would add to the beauty of the night.

"If there were complications, Gregori and Skyler would be called immediately. Probably you and Tatijana as well," Zev assured. "Close your eyes."

She did, her head pillowed on his chest, directly over his heart. Immediately she had the sensation of floating through the clouds, her body light and airy. His scent, that masculine, keeper of the forest scent combined with his feral, predatory smell filled her lungs and sent heat rushing through her veins. She would always want him, whether they were alone, or in the middle of a crowd. The feeling filled her with happiness.

She had seen ballroom dancing in Tatijana's mind. The two of them had replayed the dances over and over, committing the steps to memory, but the actual sensation of dancing with Zev, floating over the forest floor and up into the clouds was far more amazing than the dances she'd envied so much.

Eventually, Zev and Branislava found a place off to the side where they could sink into the soft grass and watch the other couples. She snuggled close to him. One of Ivory's wolves poked his head over her shoulder while another lay beside her, watching Ivory and Razvan's every move. Branislava sank her fingers into the thick, soft fur. She loved every tactile feel she could find; when locked in the form of a dragon behind a wall of ice, she'd never had the opportunity to know much other than cold and pain.

She had learned patience and acceptance—they all had. They had no other recourse, but now that she was free, she couldn't stop touching things, wanting to experience everything for herself. Tatijana was the same. Sitting so close to Zev, the grass under her, the stars over her and his arm holding her close, a wolf in her lap, she experienced true happiness.

Branislava put her head on Zev's shoulder, forcing the wolf standing behind them to use Zev's other shoulder. "I love watching the children. Look at little Anya dancing. She's got the moves, doesn't she?"

Zev followed Branislava's gaze to the little girl wiggling enthusiastically. Her sister was just as wild, both clearly feeling the beat of the earth and Syndil's drums more than the guitar. "They're beautiful. We'll have to have twins. Little girls. I can just imagine the trouble they'll get into with you as a mother and Tatijana as their aunt." His heart swelled at the thought of his child, or children, growing in her.

Branislava laughed softly. "Or you for a father. I refuse to accept all the blame. I can imagine what kind of a bossy boy you were."

He had been bossy. He'd often taken over leadership of any activity and other children always followed. Later, when he was barely seven and allowed to hunt with his father and the pack members, he was usually given a key position. "It was a relief to my father and the others in the pack hierarchy when I was sent to the elite school," he admitted. "They sent me when I was just a boy, but I could come home on visits. Eventually, the visits were further and further apart." There was regret in his voice. "My personality was too alpha, and it was difficult to have more than one alpha in the same pack, even if I was a boy."

She rubbed her cheek along his arm, like the kitten he often referred to her as being. He thought he actually heard her purr, but when he looked at her, she had her eyes closed.

"I love you the way you are, Zev. Fen and Dimitri are both alpha males and they get along with you very well," she murmured, her voice loving.

He wanted to smile at her. She was his fierce kitten, coming to his defense even when there was no need. He was who he was and he'd accepted it long ago. Perhaps the ferocity of his Dark Blood had driven him to be the fierce wolf that he was. Intelligence played a large part, he knew that, but one also had to be willing to walk fearlessly and alone into extreme danger with utter confidence.

"I had no idea when I crossed that rogue pack path a few short weeks ago," he said, nuzzling the top of her head with his chin, "that I would ever have such a gift handed to me. I won't lie, which would be impossible anyway, I had certain urges to be with a woman, but I never once thought about having a partner in life. Not one time. I didn't think it would be possible to find a woman who could accept me the way I am. Or one who would be willing to be by my side fighting rogue packs, hunting vampires or protecting council members."

Zev threaded his fingers through hers and brought her hand to his mouth, teeth scraping gently back and forth over her knuckles. He felt her answering heat, her body nearly glowing with the rush spreading through her veins. How could he not enjoy the instant acceptance of his attention to her? If he touched her, he knew she would be damp and ready for him. It didn't take much for him to ignite the fire that always smoldered in her.

"I love that you belong to me," he whispered against her ear, his teeth teasing her lobe.

Fen whirled by with Tatijana. *Don't set the grass on fire, you two,* he cautioned.

Both Zev and Branislava looked down hastily to make certain there were no flames or sparks to catch the vegetation on fire. The ground was cool to the touch and the foliage remained unscorched. They looked at one another and laughed like children.

"He's so mean," Branislava said. "For a minute there I actually fell for it and believed him. Can you imagine if we set the forest on fire with everyone dancing? Especially the prince? Gregori would have a few things to say to us."

"It would be worth it," Zev said firmly.

"True, but behave yourself anyway. Maybe we need a couple of the wolves to sit between us," she suggested, but she didn't move.

Gregori and Savannah sank down beside them. Gregori's lifemate looked happy. The moment she was sitting, her two little girls rushed her, flinging their little bodies on top of her. She toppled over backward, dragging them both with her, laughing as they hugged her tightly. Both popped up quickly and hurried over to pet the wolves. Neither touched them until they looked to Gregori for permission, although clearly they were already communicating with them.

Gregori indicated Ivory and Razvan. "Those two are their pack leaders. If you want to play with them, you need to ask politely. And if they say no, don't pout. If they say yes, thank them immediately."

Alexandru ran up and flung himself in Gregori's lap. Instantly Gregori's arms wrapped around the boy, holding him close. He dropped a kiss on top of Alexandru's head. "Are you having fun?"

Alexandru nodded and circled Gregori's neck with one small arm, leaning in to whisper something in his ear. He pointed to the wolves and Gregori's daughters.

"They're asking permission of Ivory and Razvan right now," Gregori assured, keeping an eye on his daughters as they raced through the crowd to the two wolf keepers.

Branislava hid her smile behind her hand. Stern Gregori was certainly far more than the prince's protector and right-hand man. His normal dangerous mask was completely replaced around the children and lifemate. She imagined Zev just like that with his children—and with her. To others he might appear very frightening, but his family would always know the real man, just as Savannah and her children did. Apparently the prince's son did as well.

She watched Anya and Anastasia run up and tug on Razvan's pant leg. He immediately stopped dancing and crouched down to eye level with both girls. Ivory leaned down to hear what was said. Branislava noted that although Gregori appeared to have his attention on Alexandru, his gaze flickered often to his daughters.

Razvan looked up at Ivory. Alexandru held his breath. Razvan said something and Ivory nodded. Both girls clapped their hands, smiling, but sobered as the couple continued to talk to them. They nodded over and over, and then turned. Branislava caught Gregori's instant frown, but he smiled when they turned back, clearly thanking the couple. She noted that both Razvan and Ivory communicated with their wolves. As Razvan turned back to take Ivory into his arms, two more wolves peeled off his back and loped over to the two sitting patiently on the sidelines with Branislava and Zev.

Alexandru jumped down from Gregori's lap and hurried over with the girls to pet and love on the wolves.

Branislava noted that Mikhail and Raven danced close to Ivory and Razvan, clearly thanking them for giving the children the opportunity to be with adult wolves. She knew that wolf pups were often brought in for the children to learn how to treat them, but Razvan and Ivory's wolves were part of a hunting pack and usually stayed apart from the other Carpathians.

Branislava watched the girls approach the wolves. They did so slowly, hands extended toward the animals to allow them to smell. Alexandru wiggled his way between the two girls so that Anastasia moved over. She leaned close and whispered in his ear.

Branislava felt her heart turn over at the sight of the two little heads pressed so close together. Clearly Anastasia was instructing Alexandru on how Ivory and Razvan had told the twins to approach the wolves. The prince's son was very solemn as he extended his hand to the alpha wolf first. He bowed his head as if showing his respect.

"They're beautiful," she told Savannah. "Truly beautiful. When Alexandru walked over and stood between the twins, there was a moment when I thought the ground rippled. Did you feel it, too?"

Savannah exchanged a look with Gregori. She nodded slowly. "Yes. The three are powerful together, even at their age. It's a little disconcerting."

Gregori reached out and took his lifemate's hand. "They're intelligent and have good spirits, all three of them. It will be an adventure raising them, but they'll be fine." He kissed her hand. "We'll be the ones with gray hair."

Zev laughed. "I was just telling Branislava that we needed to have twin girls."

Fen and Tatijana sank down beside them. Fen gave a snort of derision. "You'll be the only Carpathian with gray hair."

Since Fen's hair was streaked with a very impressive silver, Zev couldn't help but laugh at his statement. "Wait, you'll be the one with quads. Has it ever happened? Four little Dragonseeker girls all with a penchant for revenge."

Dimitri thumped his older brother's head. "That would be suitable punishment for you."

Skyler winked at Branislava. "I'll bet we could make it happen, too."

"I'd help," Gregori volunteered.

"Hey," Tatijana protested. "I'd be the one carrying them. I'd be a balloon."

"But cute," Fen said, pulling her close. "Very cute."

Mikhail held up his hand, and the dancers immediately stopped dancing as the music faded. He stepped into the middle of the clearing, a smile on his face. "We have a newborn. Sara and Falcon have a beautiful—and healthy—baby girl."

A cheer went up and Branislava found herself yelling with the others. She hugged Zev close. "I couldn't have asked for a better ending to this night's fun," she whispered.

"They have chosen the name Isabella for their daughter. Isabella Sara," Mikhail announced.

16

Branislava stared into Arno's room, her heart sinking. She should have known Xaviero wouldn't wait long to strike at them. The Lycans were under lockdown and watched at all times, so who had committed such a terrible crime?

"At least we had last night together," she whispered to Zev, and reached behind her to make contact with him. She needed to feel her rock, her anchor when the world around her spun into madness.

The night before had been perfect, and even later when they sat around Mikhail's home, they had discussed the three mages only very lightly, as if all of them knew they needed to take a brief respite from touching too close to evil.

Zev started to move her out from in front of him, his arm pressuring her to step behind him, but she shook her head.

"Not yet, Zev. Something isn't right, and I need to figure out what's wrong before anyone enters. Skyler was bringing a meal to him and discovered the body. She didn't go in or touch anything. She said when she started to step through the entrance to check, her skin crawled and inside she felt jittery."

"Arno's obviously dead," Zev pointed out. "There's a silver stake sticking out of his chest. Skyler's young. Of course she felt jittery."

"She may be young, Zev, but she's sensitive to any magic and there's magic here. Black magic. Evil. I can feel it."

"The moment the other council members find out Arno is dead, they'll want answers," Zev insisted. "They'll expect me to have them."

"I'm just asking for a minute to assess the situation," she insisted, biting back a snappish tone. She was already nervous, fearing she already knew who had been there and why.

Zev immediately brought his hand to the nape of her neck, fingers easing the tension out of her. "I'm sorry, Branka. I had no right to take my emotions out on you. Arno has been my friend for many years. I liked him very much. He was a very wise man and he never jumped to conclusions. Even when his own beliefs said one thing, he tried to keep an open mind and really listen and give credence to the other side of issues. He leaves behind a loving family who counted on me to keep him alive."

She leaned her head against his chest in an effort to comfort him, even as her restless gaze searched the room. Floor to ceiling. All four walls. The room looked untouched, and if it hadn't been for Arno's body in the exact center, his body in a pool of blood, laid out with his arms and legs spread wide and a silver stake protruding from his chest, she might not have been so cautious.

She raised her arms outward and drew symbols in the air.

I call upon Thurisaz, that which reacts,
I call upon Kenaz, that which gives vision and insight,
I call upon Algiz, that which gives protection and safe harbor,
I call upon Ansuz, that which reveals what is unseen.

Immediately runes appeared all over the walls, climbing high, up to the ceiling and spreading across it. Her breath caught in her throat. "Zev, he used blood. This is a very dangerous spell. Until I can undo what he's wrought, we don't dare enter."

"Who is he?" Zev asked, his fingers tightening around her nape.

"Only a High Mage could do this. He's here. Close. This is Xaviero's work. He preferred to use the old alphabet to cast, unlike Xavier or Xayvion. I would recognize this anywhere."

"He couldn't have sent an apprentice to do his dirty work?"

She shook her head, fighting to keep her heaving stomach in place. There had never been a doubt in her mind that Xaviero had produced the mage-shadows in the Lycans. She had heard his voice, but he'd been far away—so she thought. He had to have been present in the room to place such a spell.

"No. He was here." Her mouth was so dry she could barely get the words out. She touched her sister's mind to make certain she was safe. *He's here, Tatijana. In the Carpathian Mountains. He's killed Arno. Go to ground where he can't enter. The sacred warrior cave perhaps, but get to safety.*

She knew Zev heard her, he was merged very deeply with her. She felt him in her mind, pouring strength into her.

"Why would he risk everything and come here himself?" Zev gestured toward Arno's body. "Why kill him and not come after me?"

"He needed to know his enemy. If you've been inadvertently a thorn in his side, pouring water on the fires he's created among the council members and among the packs, destroying rogues and killing his assassins, he will want you dead. He knows now that I'm with you, that by killing one of us, he'll kill us both," she explained.

"How?"

"Arno told him, of course. Arno, no matter how he tried, would never have been able to hold out against the High Mage, any more than Lyall was able to do with me questioning him."

"I can find out exactly what Arno told him, and perhaps even his plans," Zev said. "I can access Arno's memories."

"Don't you think Xaviero knows that? He left the head intact. He wanted someone to come into the room and try to save Arno. The room is a huge, dangerous trap. Arno's brain will be as well. Once we get in there, it will be far better to sever the head and burn the body as quickly as possible," Branislava objected.

"Can you remove the danger?" Zev asked.

She realized he hadn't agreed with her. She turned to look at him over her shoulder, her heart sinking. Zev was a man of integrity. Of loyalty. Of duty. He would find his answers one way or another, and danger wouldn't play a part in whether or not he did his job.

"I can get us into the room," she said slowly, her gaze clinging to his.

She didn't want him to do this, but he would, and if he was going down that path, she was going with him.

Gregori came in behind them. "Skyler and Dimitri just told me. Mikhail's on his way."

"No!" both said simultaneously.

Zev sighed. "The mage was here. Xaviero. Branka's certain he killed Arno and has set traps in the room and probably on the body as well."

Gregori looked past them to the walls, ceiling and floor covered in bloody runes. He frowned. "Can you unravel that? Or find a way to counter it? Is there even a spell for that? Maybe we should just burn it all down, Branislava."

Zev shook his head. "You know we need the information Arno can give us. If Branka really can't find a way in, we'll burn it all, but we need information. Anything at all to give us clues to where Xaviero is and what his plans are."

"He wouldn't tell those plans to Arno, knowing you're going to try to access his memories," Gregori protested.

"That's true," Zev said. He slipped his arm around Branislava and held her for a long moment. "But the clues will be in the traps. He won't be able to set them without giving something of himself away. Isn't that how it works, Branka?"

She didn't want to admit he was right. In order to get the information, they needed to face each trap, dismantle it and move to the next one. The more traps, the more information Xaviero would be forced to leave behind, whether he wanted to or not. First, she would have to be certain she had made the room safe and that the information wasn't a red herring planted by Xaviero. No one else, other than Tatijana, knew him that well. She had to be the one facing the mage's work, because she wasn't about to let her sister do it.

"Yes," she answered reluctantly. "That's how it works."

"Is it possible for you to instruct us telepathically?" Zev asked. "You look at his work and then tell us how to unravel it? I'm merged with you, won't I be able to see what needs to be done when you are figuring it out?"

Branislava shook her head. "To pit yourself against a High Mage spell is too dangerous without knowing what you're doing. It's very complicated and detailed, layers upon layers. Anything this dangerous can't be managed that way, Zev, but thank you. I know you're just trying to spare me his presence. Arno will have told him about me. He saw me question Lyall, and no doubt, Xaviero already knows who I am. There isn't any point in trying to hide from him."

Zev stiffened, his arm tightening around her. "If he knows you, his trap will be very specific to you, won't it?"

She shrugged. "That would make sense, but I think more likely, it will be specific to you. Perhaps not the first one, the first snare is set to use Arno's body to lure another victim into the room. If Skyler hadn't been the one to find the body, Xaviero may have done just that. *You* almost entered the room. He would have triumphed right then."

Mikhail appeared in the hallway behind Gregori. "Arno is dead." It was more a statement than a question. The question was for Gregori, asking what happened.

I thought you were going to keep him away from here, Zev said.

Gregori shook his head and gestured to the runes written in blood covering the walls and ceiling of the room. "He had a visitor. A mage can slip past guards during the day."

There is no controlling Mikhail. He is responsible for the Lycan council and carries that weight heavily on his shoulders. I can only protect him, not control him, Gregori replied to Zev.

I do not envy you your job, Zev said to Gregori.

Gregori looked into the room and the bloody symbols covering the walls. *At this moment, I do not envy yours.*

"Who specifically was assigned to protect him?" Mikhail asked.

Branislava's gaze jumped to the prince with sudden apprehension. She could feel the change in Zev. His face remained expressionless, but deep inside, there was a small ripple of unease. She hadn't considered who might have been guarding Arno and what happened to him—or that the Lycan would be someone close to Zev.

"One of my best," Zev answered slowly. "Arnau. And he's Arno's son. He's an elite hunter and a member of my pack. His room is right there." He indicated the door just to the left of Arno's sleeping quarters.

Gregori stepped to one side of the door and waved his hand to the prince, as if shooing him aside. Branislava would have laughed at the gesture if the tension wasn't so high. The prince didn't move a step. Gregori thrust his hand toward the door and it sprang wide open.

Arnau leapt through the open space, already half man, half wolf, his muzzle dripping with saliva, madness in his red-rimmed eyes. He had one target and he landed squarely on her, driving Branislava to the floor, his claws tearing at her stomach and his teeth clamping down around her left shoulder, up high, toward her neck.

Zev reacted first, hurling through the air at a blurring speed, both boots hitting Arnau squarely in the ribs, driving the Lycan off of Branislava. The Lycan rolled and came back to his feet, his gaze targeting Bronnie. Clearly for him, there was no one else in the narrow hallway. He made no sound, just attacked a second time, propelling himself forward, closing the distance between them fast.

Mikhail stepped in front of Branislava, a silver stake in his fist. The Lycan used his claws to go up and over the prince, raking flesh from his chest and shoulders as he whipped past him. Gregori swore and yanked Mikhail back and away from the mage-maddened Lycan.

Arnau hit Zev squarely in the chest as Zev materialized right where Branislava had been. They stared into each another's eyes. The stake in his fist penetrated right through the chest wall, through muscle and tissue, straight to the heart. Zev put his arm around Arnau and gently lowered him to the ground. He went with him, crouching low.

Arnau tried to speak. Zev nodded several times. His sorrow was palpable, so intense Branislava felt tears burning behind her eyes.

"I know," Zev said softly to Arnau. "Good journey my friend." One hand around Arnau's, he held the Lycan's gaze with his own as the life faded from the elite hunter's eyes.

He stayed beside the body for a long minute, his hand smoothing back the hunter's hair and then slipping his fingers over the mask of death to close Arnau's eyes. He stood slowly, as if the weight of his friend was heavy on his shoulders. Taking a breath, he drew his sword and severed the head from the shoulders in one smooth movement.

There was silence in the hall. Gregori was the first to move. "Mikhail, this will be a long job for Bronnie and Zev. Perhaps it is best if we take care of other matters and allow them to get to it. I've sent for Fen and Dimitri. They work well with Zev, and if their lifemates are present, both are powerful in their own right. The combination of these six could very well defeat Xaviero's plans."

"In other words," Mikhail said. "You'd like to put me in a bubble and keep me safe."

Zev cleaned his sword and put it slowly and reverently back in its scabbard. "We all want you safe, Mikhail. Whatever Xaviero has done here cannot touch you, or he will win." He turned his head, his eyes meeting the prince's. "I'm not willing to let him win. He's taken too many good men with his evil. We have to stop him."

Mikhail nodded. "I agree. Just be careful."

Branislava moved under Zev's shoulder, slipping her arm around him as they turned back to the open door and the body of Arnau's father.

I'm so sorry, Zev. There were no right words. She felt his pain, that intense sorrow he refused to allow others to see. The death of his friend had only increased his determination to destroy Xaviero before he could hurt anyone else.

Zev's only indication that he heard her was a soft brush of his mind against hers. His face didn't change expression and his gaze didn't stray from the room.

"Where do we start?" he asked.

Branislava straightened her shoulders and stepped to the doorway, carefully studying the symbols. "First I have to cleanse the room and drive away the demons he set here. He brought them through the gates of hell. I've seen them do it more than once, and whatever comes through can get trapped on this side."

Zev frowned. "I can't fight what I can't see."

"This won't be that kind of fight," she replied. "You can't physically enter that room without being killed. The demons stand guard as they've been commanded to do and wait for their reward, the flesh and blood of a living creature."

"I've heard of shadow warriors, the dead brought back to serve the mage."

She shook her head. "Shadow warriors were men who fought with honor, and a mage captured their spirit and forced them into service. These are demons, evil beings the mage can't force into service. He makes an exchange with them. In this case, he's trading their service for the chance to taste flesh and blood. Yours or mine, specifically."

Zev ran his hand down his knife as if eager for battle. "Let's get to this. Tell me what to do."

"We're one, our souls tied together, so he believes if he kills one of us, he kills the other," she explained.

"And he's right," Zev confirmed.

"He doesn't know our spirits are tied together. If either of us gets pulled into the other world, which from what I see here, could be their plan, the demons devour our body and our spirit will enter the other world where his brother waits to collect it in the hopes that he can be resurrected."

Zev swore under his breath. "I'm a man who fights what's in front of me, not ghosts," he said, his voice turning gravelly, the growl not far off. "How the hell do you prevent your spirit from entering another realm, or your body from being devoured by demons?"

She reached out and gently rubbed his wrist. "I don't know if that is the plan, Zev," she admitted. "I'm trying to guess and prepare myself for any likelihood. I know they spoke of such things, and the spirit has to be one known to them."

Zev was a man of action, and this fight required finesse, the knowledge of spells and both white and black magic. His breath hissed out, a harsh blast of protest. "He wants your spirit."

"He didn't know I was here until he questioned Arno," she reminded. "But he is an opportunist. I'm just being careful."

She glanced behind her and Arnau's body was already gone, the hall clean as if no violent death had ever taken place. She touched her belly where the claws had raked her. "There can be no trace of blood on me," she added, lifting her fingers to examine the evidence of the Lycan's attack.

Instantly Zev spun her around and really looked at her. "Branka, I'm sorry. I was selfishly thinking of the loss of my friend." He placed his palm over the bite marks on her neck.

Rather than soothe the wound, pain flashed through her body. She jerked away from him, her eyes going wide. "I need Skyler and Tatijana right away," she said and let herself sink down on the floor right in front of the door. "Tell them to hurry," she added.

Fen and Tatijana emerged first, Tatijana going to her knees beside her sister. Her gaze went into the room and she gasped at the sight of the bloody symbols.

Branislava grasped her hand tightly. "I was bitten by Xaviero's servant."

"Arnau was not Xaviero's servant," Zev protested. "He was a good man." He crouched beside his lifemate. "When I tried to heal her with my palm, my touch burned through her. I felt it, Tatijana."

Tatijana and Branislava stared at one another in a kind of horror. Tatijana gripped her sister's hand. "He injected you with demon's bait, didn't he? They'll rush right to you."

Zev wrapped his arms around his lifemate. "Speak a language I can understand."

"We have to get it out of her," Tatijana said. "They'll find her. In this realm or the next, they'll come for her. I know this spell. I saw them all working on perfecting it. We both did. Bronnie, we can get it out of you."

Branislava nodded several times, took a deep breath and settled back against Zev. "Now, Tatijana, you and Skyler. Get her here. Where is she?"

"Dimitri and Skyler were out running the wolves this evening with Ivory and Razvan," Fen explained, his voice so gentle Branislava had to fight tears. "All of them are on their way and should be here soon."

She knew she was emotional. Most of it had to do with Zev's emotion— or lack thereof. He pushed his feelings aside in order to survive the things he had to do, but she felt it, that burning sorrow at the loss of a man he considered family. He blamed himself for not tending to her wounds immediately and for not finding a way to prevent what had transpired. Losing a council member was a huge blow to him. Losing Arnau, a member of his pack, was even more of a personal blow. And now knowing he had waited to heal her and she was infected . . .

"We're here," Skyler said, breathing hard, as if she'd been running. "Ivory, too. What do you need?"

"She's been bitten. Demon bait was transferred into her body," Tatijana explained.

Both Ivory and Skyler looked past the Dragonseeker sisters into the room. Thousands of bloody runes covered the walls and ceiling, while a dark pool of blood covered the floor.

"I can use the bait to draw the demons into the open," Branislava explained. "It's the only way to send them back to where he pulled them from. He's brought them through from hell."

Ivory's fingers sought the cross she always wore hanging around her neck. Her fist closed over it. "I saw Xavier, at least at the time I thought it was Xavier, it may have been one of the others, but I swore the gates of hell opened and he emerged."

Branislava went pale, but she didn't reply. Instead she looked to Tatijana. Tatijana stepped back at once and lifted her arms. Her eyes grew larger, the emeralds darkening to a much deeper hue.

Thurisaz, I call upon thee,
That which can bring chaos, instinctive will,
Help me to draw forth that which will draw forth the darkness
     of demons,
Born of blood, by the blood I command thee to come forth.

Dark bubbles appeared around the wounds in Branislava's neck and stomach. The bubbles beaded together to form long strands. The strands wiggled and danced, until finally a head appeared on each one. The small creature writhed and squirmed, feasting on the droplets of blood before being suddenly lifted up by a blast of icy wind and driven into the room where Arno's body lay.

Branislava spun around and came to her feet all at once, a blur of motion, her hands up like two weapons. Her breath caught in her throat. Tatijana stood as close as possible. Power leapt between the two women. Branislava could feel the flow of energy pouring from her sister to her. Skyler and Ivory joined with Tatijana and the power was so strong, it was almost too difficult to wield. She felt Zev close, steadying her.

Inside the room, the long, wormlike creatures rushed to feed off the pool of blood beneath the dead body. There was a moment of absolute stillness, and then the chamber came alive. Dark shadows appeared from every direction of the room and one dropping from the ceiling, bodies stretching obscenely, mouths yawning wide as bony, clawed fingers reached greedily to snatch at the demon bait. There were five of them. The shadowed shapes circled the dark worms and the body on the floor.

Branislava waved her hands gracefully, drawing symbols in the air, all the while chanting in a soft, but commanding voice.

That which comes from the dark,
I see you, I know you,
I take back from you the spirit and energy that was stolen,
I call upon Hagalaz, that which can be destructive uncontrolled,
I call forth your energy now, Hagalaz, to use your forces of control.

Branislava's voice swelled with power. She felt the additional boost as Skyler joined Tatijana, feeding her energy to counter the dark spell the High Mage had left behind.

I call upon the spirit of air,
Winds that blow freely,
Bring forth your gales,
Cleanse and seal this place,
So that which would do harm may not leave this place.

In unison, the demons whirled around to face her, mouths gaping at her, eyes glowing red with hatred. They clawed at the wormlike creatures, snatching them up as the cleansing wind began to whirl around the room. Shrieking in fury, the demons thrust the worms into their mouths, gobbling fast in an effort to get something in return for their daylong vigil. Even as they devoured the worms, they rushed toward the opening where she stood unflinching, her hands as graceful as ever, determination in her every move as well as in her voice.

The demons hit an invisible barrier and were pulled back toward the center of the room. The wind whipped around the walls of the room in a circle, traveling faster and faster, howling, seeking prey. It caught at the shadowy figures and tugged, dragging at their reluctant forms, pulling them apart until they looked more like dust particles scattered in the air.

Still the shrieking could be heard. The walls of the room swelled outward. The ceiling raised higher, the bloodied runes writhing, looking as if they were alive and making an effort to counteract Branislava's commands. She kept the wind building speed, calling once more for aid from above.

That which is bound by darkness,
I call forth light.
Fire that burns and cleanses bright.
I call forth your energy, separate and dispel,
That which would be bound, sending it back to hell.

The particles in the room slowly began to be drawn into the very vortex of the wind, spinning faster and faster, a funnel of black sand and shadow. Hands emerged, great long bony fingers tipped with claws, and just as suddenly were pulled back into the maelstrom. Faces pressed through the twister, mouths screaming, eyes distorted and then those too disappeared.

Branislava kept the pressure on, building on the power fed to her by Tatijana, Skyler and Ivory. She refused to relent, again weaving symbols in the air, the pattern intricate, a replica of the runes written in blood on the walls and ceiling, but in reverse order.

As fire burns and ashes fall,
I call forth the abyss, hear my call.
Open your maw so that I may return,
That which was born of blood and must be returned.

Heat burst through the room. Orange-red flames danced up the walls and licked across the ceiling, devouring the runes. As the fire spread and leapt higher, the demons shrieked and moaned in protest. The cleansing wind continued rushing around the room, howling in fury, fanning the flames until every last rune was consumed. The demons tried to flee the firestorm, but the winds were too strong for their insubstantial bodies. They were drawn in by the ferocious gale and consumed by the flames.

Branislava drew a deep breath and allowed the wind and flames to slowly subside. She felt her legs tremble. Turning, she went into Zev's arms, uncaring who was watching and might see her weakness—her vulnerability. She needed the comfort of his strength, of the rock that he was for her.

"I know now what the three of them were doing when Xavier seemed to kill Xaviero and then Xayvion," she murmured into Zev's shirt. She lifted her head and looked at her sister with stricken eyes. "They were practicing bringing each other back from the other side. That's what Ivory saw. They were practicing for a time just like this one."

"Do you mean he intends to bring Xavier back?" Razvan asked. His voice was steady, his face expressionless.

"He needs a soul, or a spirit," Tatijana said. "To send down the tree of life."

"Arno, a council member?" Zev asked. "Or his son, Arnau, an elite hunter?"

Branislava sighed and pulled herself out of his arms. "No, Zev. He means to trap you or me. Once he extracted the information from Arno, and he knew I was his enemy, he knew he had the ideal person for his plan. He wants the two of us dead. I have mage blood. Xavier is my father. He would recognize my soul or my spirit immediately. Xaviero is probably rubbing his hands with glee right at this very moment."

Zev shook his head. "Well, he doesn't get you or me. Too bad for him. If he wants to see his brother so badly, we'll just have to arrange a little trip for him."

"What's next, Branislava?" Fen asked.

"We go in, just Zev and me. There's no point in risking anyone else. If we fail, Tatijana and Fen should just burn the body right from the doorway. There has to be another trap set inside, around the body itself. He knows someone will attend the body."

"Can you build a circle of protection around the body before you touch it?" Skyler asked. "At least then, while you're doing whatever needs to be done, you can't be attacked from outside the circle."

Branislava inclined her head with a small smile. "I think that's a good idea, little sister-kin. Wish us luck." She turned and hugged her sister fiercely.

"I'll be waiting for you," Tatijana whispered. "Right here. I'll be waiting."

Zev stepped through the doorway first. She knew he would. Of course he would. He wasn't about to allow Branislava to go into danger without checking it out himself. She followed him, one hand fisted in his shirt as she stepped into that demonic room. Her breath left her lungs in a rush of fear. It was a gut reaction she couldn't stop, and Zev instantly flooded her mind with warmth and assurance.

"I can feel him, Zev, that's all. I'm all right," she declared. "His presence is strong in this room. It just threw me for a minute, that's all."

Zev crouched beside the body, hands reluctantly keeping away from Arno, even though she felt his need to touch the man in a kind of salute. He looked at her over his shoulder. "I've got this one, Branka. I'm your detail man, remember?"

She nodded. Zev knew Arno far better than she did. If there was something out of place he would spot it. "Take your time," she cautioned. They couldn't afford a mistake.

"The stake isn't right," he said. "The cord holding his medallion of the Sacred Circle isn't the one he normally wears." Without touching the fallen council member, Zev peered closer, studying the small intricate tattoo on Arno's wrist. "This isn't right, either, Branislava. Can you look at this for me? I'll show you what it should look like and you tell me what's different and why."

In his mind, Zev produced an exact replica of the Sacred Circle tattoo worn on the wrist by every member. He felt Branislava look it over carefully before she studied the one on Arno. He heard her suck in her breath sharply.

"He's woven in a death spell. See the black runes between the double rows of the scrolls? Don't touch the body. Don't move it. Not yet. And don't let his blood get on you."

Zev sank back on his heels, avoiding any contact with Arno.

She passed her hand over the stake, careful not to get too close. "Yes, he's added some kind of spell to the stake. The cord is definitely rigged as well and looks as if I'll have the most trouble with it."

She took a deep breath and stood up, glancing over her shoulder at the three women watching. They nodded to her, prepared to help her.

"What happens if I sever the head and we just walk away from this?" Zev asked. "That's what you wanted in the first place. I can see your reasoning."

"I have no doubt that he made that impossible as well. He's driving us toward Arno's brain and his memories."

"We already know his intent now, Branka. Why continue? We can burn the body."

A small sound escaped from Branislava's sister. Clearly burning the body wasn't a good idea. There were few things that made him lose his temper, but feeling helpless was one of them. He couldn't stand in front of his lifemate and protect her when he didn't know how. This kind of mage magic was out of his realm of experience.

"Just do what you have to do, Branka, and let's get this over with."

Branislava cast her protection circle and then stood for a long moment gathering her courage. Facing Xaviero was becoming easier. She had been so terrified of him, but each time she was successful in destroying his work, she realized how much she really did know. Her education had been complete.

The three brothers had all worked in the laboratory, learning and perfecting skills over and over. There hadn't been a spell, from the smallest to the most dangerous, that she hadn't seen and committed to memory. She had nothing else to keep her mind occupied in those long years of captivity. *The three High Mages didn't know more than she knew.*

She concentrated on the tattoo first. The dark death spell was woven carefully within the tattoo itself. She knew Xaviero well enough to know he would find it amusing to weave such a deviant spell into what was considered a sacred symbol. Had Zev not recognized that there was that tiny difference, the High Mage would have had his entertainment for the evening.

That which is marked, drawn in black,
I call forth your energy to send you back,
Twist and turn, swirl that burn,
I draw forth your power, which now I return.

Branislava watched the runes slowly disappear from the tattoo. She took a deep, cleansing breath and let it out. "Really study the tattoo, Zev, make certain there isn't anything else hidden."

Zev took his time, looking at the tattoo he'd seen a thousand times on various people. The pool of blood prevented him from getting too close, but eventually he nodded. "It looks like it's supposed to, Branka."

"The stake is filled with power. I can feel it, much like an explosive. It's a simple enough spell designed to kill as many people as possible." The memory of Xavier placing the spell in objects and then sending in his apprentice to retrieve the article for him rose like a nightmare. Both Tatijana and she had tried to warn the various unsuspecting young mages. They had never succeeded and had watched the apprentices die when the spell was triggered.

That which is silver, born of fire,
I call back your essence, drawing back your power.
As fire burns, so water cools,
I call to water, release evil's hold.

She passed her hand over the part of the stake protruding from Arno's chest. The sensation of dark power was no longer there. She nodded slowly. Her mouth had gone dry. The cord was an altogether different proposition. She was certain there was a spell on the woven strands, but she wasn't yet certain how to counteract it. She needed to reveal it first.

That which is woven,
Reveal to me,
That which is evil,
So I may see.

At once she could see that the cord held life. One wrong movement and the cord would attack. She swallowed hard and once again traced symbols in the air while she murmured her counterspell.

That which would do harm,
I dispel your power.

I take what was woven, so these threads have no power,
As you were woven, so now I unweave,
Each particle I harvest so no death may there be.

Branislava dropped her arms to her sides and forced air through her lungs. She spent the next few minutes making certain there were no more traps hidden around or under Arno's body. She cleansed the blood and then sank down to the floor beside Zev.

"I believe we actually did it," she said, relief in her voice. She brushed her cheek against his shoulder. "I think we can look at his last memories."

"I'll do it," Zev said. There was distaste in his voice. The idea of desecrating the council member by invading his private thoughts didn't sit well. Still, it had to be done.

"You can see his memories that way," Branislava agreed, "but it's dangerous. We can go into his mind and see them the Carpathian way and perhaps, if we're lucky, we'll see more of Xaviero than Arno remembers. People pick up details without knowing it. We can find them when he wasn't aware. The circle will protect our bodies, and the others can watch over us. It's safe for them to enter now."

Zev wasn't as used to the Carpathian ways, but he was willing to follow Branislava's lead when it came to mage magic. He nodded.

Branislava didn't wait, afraid she might lose her newfound courage and confidence. She shed her body and became pure spirit, entering the council member's mind. The moment she did, she knew she had made a terrible mistake. Xaviero's splinter shadow waited, crouched like a dark demon in the night. He attacked triumphantly, catching at her spirit with claws and teeth, and dragging her through the portal to the other realm.

17

Zev! Branislava reached for her lifemate as she was drawn into that icy cold realm of the half-life.

Zev recognized the tree. He'd been there before with Branislava when he'd nearly died. She had held him to her. Now it was an altogether different fight. This was his kind of fight.

They need me alive. They won't kill me. They're counting on the fact that no one will find me.

My spirit is woven to yours. We travel together. He used his calmest voice, steadying her. More than anything, Branislava hated the cold. She felt alone and isolated, that child forced into a dragon's form and placed behind a wall of ice.

Focus on the thing holding you prisoner. He's obviously taking you to Xavier. We have to stop him. What is it? He suspected it was nothing more than a small sliver of Xaviero, a shadow that he'd left behind to capture Branislava or him.

He felt her shiver, and then the woman he knew so well came forth, a warrior of old. She stopped shivering and he felt the steel running through her

Xaviero left a tiny piece of himself behind.

He could see that the shadow was delighting in ripping at her spirit, tin holes, to wear her out and make her more vulnerable to Xavier's possession. There was no doubt in either of their minds that Xaviero's shadow was taking her spirit to his brother.

Xaviero had no idea that Branislava wasn't alone. He hadn't yet detected the weave binding Zev's spirit to Branislava's.

If he can gleefully tear holes into your spirit, this shadow thing can be destroyed, right?

The sliver of Xaviero is far too small to do more than what it was programmed to do—give Xavier the spirit he needs to return to the land of the living. Xaviero wasn't about to give away too much of himself even to get Xavier back, she replied.

Zev could hear and feel pain creeping into her. The capacity for cruelty in Xaviero amazed him. Even the little sliver of Xaviero *had* to torment.

Zev studied the shadow from every direction. The claws dug into Branislava and the demon fought with her, attempting to drag her down the tree trunk to the icy cold below. He could feel greedy eyes on them. He heard teeth gnashing. Moans. Wailing. Branislava refused to go easily, pitting her strength against the demon—and her spirit was strong.

Fen, Dimitri, I need a massive storm. Lightning that is supercharged. Build it for me fast and let me know when the lightning is forming its peak.

Neither man questioned him, nor did they respond verbally, but he felt their immediate acquiescence.

Catch the next branch, Branka. Hang yourself up on it.

She did as he said, reaching with her light to wrap firmly around the branch. Below, he heard an ominous rustle as something began to drag itself up the tree trunk out of the icy dark. Xavier was coming to claim his prize.

Zev was both Carpathian and Lycan—mixed blood—impossible to detect, even for a mage. His energy was completely muted. Neither Xavier or the splinter of Xaviero knew Branislava wasn't alone, and that was their advantage. Before Xavier reached them, something had to be done fast.

Zev felt the storm even deep as he was in the other realm. The air above and below him suddenly charged with a current of pure electricity. Xavier seemed to know something wasn't right, redoubling his efforts to get to the spirit trapped in the other realm.

The storm is massive and lightning is directly overhead, Fen informed Zev.

Zev held tighter to Branislava as she fought to stay on the branch. *Say the words we need. Words of war. My kind of war. Physical. Now, Branka.* Xavier was close, too close. He could feel him now, the slime of evil that reached them before Xavier's malevolent spirit.

Branislava gasped in his mind. She hadn't considered that they might reveal a physical particle, but once Zev gave her the idea, she caught on quickly.

That which was shadow,
Now must take on form.
From gray existence,
A body be born.

Branislava delivered the words in her most powerful voice, projecting through the light to the dark slice of the mage. The splinter demon stiffened, clearly suspicious of her audacity. His dark shadow wavered and suddenly shifted from wraithlike to substance.

Zev struck hard, calling down the lightning so that it ran down the tree fast, seeking a target. He wrapped himself around Branislava to protect her. It was his first time calling down the lightning, but he was a warrior through and through and his aim was absolutely accurate. The bolt hit the sliver of Xaviero squarely through the center of the particle. The particle turned black, curled and then turned to ash. It floated away, while the odor of rotten eggs lingered in the air behind it.

Zev redirected the lightning down the trunk of the tree in the hopes of destroying Xavier once and for all. He heard a scream of pain, of anger, of absolute hatred. The sound vibrated through their spirits, jarring them both. Zev kept his spirit wrapped tightly around Branislava's, fairly certain Xavier would retaliate if at all possible.

The bolt must have scored a hit, although he'd directed it blindly, by sound alone. The voice continued to screech. It took a moment to realize Xavier was incoherent, but trying to hit back with a spell.

Zev drew Branislava up the tree to the thicker branches closer to the top, moving fast, whipping around to the other side of the trunk. The blast shook the tree, but hit branches a good distance from them. The branches exploded, splintering, and then coming back together. The tree trembled and then began to shake.

It's angry. It wants us to leave now, Branislava whispered into his mind. *The only reason it isn't punishing us is because Mother Earth has claimed us as her own. But it will discipline Xavier harshly. The mage is used to being the one giving orders and it's humiliating for him to subjugate himself to the tree. He thinks to destroy it somehow, but he cannot.*

The tree shook violently, leaves churning in the air. Below them, they heard pitiful cries and pleas. Zev wasn't waiting around for the tree to change its mind. He'd been the one to zap its trunk with lightning and he couldn't blame it for being angry.

They sped through the branches, dodging the worst of the flailing limbs, and quickly entered their own bodies. Zev, as he collapsed, reached for Branislava, holding her body in his arms to prevent her from hitting the floor hard.

The fight had cost them strength, but that was all, both were intact. He could feel Branislava's sense of triumph. Together they had faced both Xavier and Xaviero and they had triumphed.

Branislava turned over, looking up to his face. "I can't believe you thought of forcing him into a physical form. That was brilliant."

"Don't give him a big head," Fen cautioned. "Both of you need blood. You're in the middle of a protection circle. You might want to let us in."

Zev drew in his breath. "I still need to attend to Arno's body and then inform the council members," he told Branislava. "I suppose we have no choice but to let them give us blood. You're looking a little pale. Did Xaviero's demon shadow hurt you?"

"I feel a little ragged around the edges," she admitted, "but I'm alive and you're alive, and that small piece of him was destroyed. Xavier was sent back down into the depths of hell and he can just stay there."

Ivory crossed herself and gave them a small smile. "You two work very well together, a true alpha pair."

"Don't even think it," Razvan cautioned, his arm sliding around Ivory's waist. "No more wolf pups. Mikhail will not turn a blind eye forever."

"I know." She rested her head against his shoulder briefly. "But they would be perfect, just like Dimitri and Skyler are."

"So would we," Fen said, daring to tease her when no one else but her lifemate did. "Don't listen to Razvan, Ivory."

Branislava waved her hand and the protection circle opened. Zev made an effort and got to his feet. He didn't want to sever Arno's head, but it had to be done. The man needed to be given peace. He drew his sword and waited for Branislava to step back. Fen and Dimitri drew her to them, Dimitri steadying her while Fen offered her his wrist.

"Good journey, old friend," Zev whispered as he swung his sword.

The wrench in his gut was expected. The burning behind his eyes not so much. He looked away from the others, unable for a moment to catch his breath. At once, she was there. Soft. Warm. Pouring into his mind, filling him with her special brand of love. How had he ever done without her?

"Zev," Razvan said softly. "Take what is offered freely." He held out his wrist.

Zev didn't look at him, although he was fairly certain courtesy dictated that he do so. Razvan's voice was too gentle, too understanding. He didn't want sympathy, or even understanding. He let himself consume the hot nutrients, without actually tasting or even thinking about what he was doing. He had to get through the next few hours and do what had to be done. He'd grieve for his friends later.

"We'll need to prepare a pyre for the bodies," Zev said when he had drunk his fill. "The other members of the council will want to be there to send them on their journey. A private place, but big enough for the Lycans to gather."

"Zev," Fen said softly. "It isn't a good time to have a large gathering, not now that we know Xaviero is close by. He'll know the Lycan traditions and he'll be expecting a funeral pyre."

"He'll be angry," Tatijana added. "No one ever defied them, or outsmarted them. He'll be so maddened, he might try to bring the mountain down on top of all us."

"No one move," Branislava said suddenly.

Zev froze in place. Her voice had gone still. A warning. He wasn't the only one who believed her low, incredibly soft voice. He looked down at Arno's body and the severed head. For a moment he could see nothing out of place. He was a man of small details and the only thing different was that the necklace had dropped onto the floor. What had she seen that he hadn't?

"What is it?" Fen asked.

The room had flooded with tension. All of them were well aware of what a High Mage was capable of.

He saw it then. One strand of the cord had dropped into the pool of Arno's blood and was now thoroughly soaked in it. The blood had begun to travel down the cord on one side and up the other so that the red stain spread slowly through the rest of the cords.

"The necklace," Branislava whispered, her voice almost hoarse. "Arno's necklace. Tatijana, it's inside the circle with us."

The cord had remained still under Zev's watchful gaze. As far as he could tell, it was simply a weave of twine now soaked in blood. He believed Branislava's fear, but he couldn't see the why of it. Of course the necklace would get blood on it if it fell into the pool beneath Arno. Still, he waited, touching her mind. She was frightened.

Tatijana moved first. She stepped into the circle of protection that Branislava had made earlier. Ivory and Skyler joined her. The three began to walk together, following the circle, chanting softly. Zev didn't allow himself to get distracted. He kept his gaze on the necklace, now pumped up from the blood. The strands of twine appeared to have swelled, nearly doubling in size. When the three women began to move, one piece near the medallion seemed to break off enough to turn toward the movement.

Fen's breath hissed out. "It's alive. That thing's alive."

Branislava reached out very slowly and touched Fen's arm to quiet him. He was standing closest to the blood-filled creature and at the sound of his voice, it swung its head toward Fen. The movement was fast, as if sound and motion triggered aggression. The organism appeared to be listening again.

Zev could see the head now. It was round like a swollen bulb, but the strands at the top were frayed as if some of the twine was embedded within the head and stuck out like spiked hair. The blood continued to fill the strands so that it doubled, then tripled in size. The three women stepped away from the circle, and again the creature swung its head toward them. They froze halfway to the door.

How do we get rid of it? Zev asked. He used the common Carpathian path of communication, rather than his private one with Branislava.

I'm trying to think. I've seen this before, but only once. The tension in her voice indicated the creature was extremely dangerous. *No one talk or make a move. It's lightning fast. You won't be able to outrun it. Tatijana, do you remember?*

No. No, I don't. There was terror in Tatijana's voice, so much so that Zev feared Fen wouldn't be able to stop himself from going to her. He must have said something privately to her because some of the fear on her face eased.

It's okay, Branislava said to her sister. *I'll figure it out. I just need a minute.*

Zev detested the fear in Branislava's voice. He wanted to wrap his arms around her and hold her safe, to keep her from having to deal with mage magic and blood and death. She'd had enough of such things in her childhood and the years that followed, trapped as she was in dragon form watching an endless parade of tortures.

Branka, you can remember. Your fear is a childlike fear. Go back to those days. That is where you will find the memory.

He realized the moment he gave her the information that she already knew it. She didn't want to remember. Whatever memory was associated with the wormlike blood-filled creature, had been traumatizing and she didn't want to recall it.

I'm sorry, mon chaton féroce. I should have known better. I'm with you this time. You won't face it alone.

He might not be able to fight the thing physically, but he could stand in front of her.

Branislava shut herself off from the rest of them, but not Zev. She sank into his mind, merged deeply with him, drawing on his strength. He was a rock, a steady anchor, and she knew she could count on him to keep her just as steady.

Tatijana and Branislava had turned ten. Xavier had let them out of their dragon forms as an unexpected birthday present. Xaviero and Xayvion had arrived with packages wrapped in brown paper and twine.

We both were so happy to be in our natural forms that we ran around, holding hands, just grateful for the opportunity.

They wanted their father to see them as something other than objects to feed on. He understood how they must have latched on to any kindness from him, needing to hope.

Every time he seemed to make an effort, we put blinders on and fell for it. There was a birthday cake. And presents. Xavier had us sit in the center of the room on the floor. He said he wanted to watch us open our presents.

He felt her give a mental shudder. Her body was tense, the memories affecting her physically. She was nauseated and fighting it. Still, she had the control to remain still.

First, he had a special surprise. He brought in our only friend. He was thirteen, a mage and apprentice. He was always kind to us. He sneaked food to us and would talk about the world outside.

Zev's stomach lurched. He feared what would come next. Branislava was pale. She looked lost. *Look at me, Branka. Only at me. No one is moving. That thing has no target. Just keep looking into my eyes.*

Her gaze jumped to his. He felt the impact of her green eyes. Two jewels pressed into a stark white face. Her red-gold lashes stood out against her pale skin.

His name was Jules and he sat between us, right where Xavier told him to. He brought us a present as well.

There was a hitch in her voice and tears burned in her eyes. He surrounded her with warmth and love, the only thing he could do when he couldn't physically hold her.

We opened his gift first. He gave us bracelets he'd made himself.

Don't! He said it sharply, knowing she was about to rub her wrist where she'd first put the bracelet. He felt her involuntary movement start in her mind.

Branislava drew herself up sharply mentally. She had to keep it together. If Zev hadn't stopped her she would have drawn the attention of the blood worm and it would have attacked. Already it had grown more, feasting on the blood of the dead man.

Tell me, Branka, but you don't have to remember anything but the way to kill this thing.

She wanted that to be the truth. She stayed drowning in his eyes. He had beautiful eyes. Calm. Steady. There was never panic in him. She wondered how such a man had come to be. Still, she had no choice but to remember the sequence of events, because she had to see Xaviero in the background as he cast the spell upon the twine and then later, destroyed his blood worm.

Xavier gave us both a conjuring ball made of fine crystal. We tore through the other wrappings, scattering them on the floor. I remember we were laughing. We'd never had presents or cake. Xavier gave us the cake as we opened Xaviero's present. It was a very ornate dagger. The hilt was covered in jewels and the blade actually had three diamonds going down the center of it. I thought it was fake, just because it was so beautiful.

The tension in her was explosive. Zev tried to hold her to him, using steady calm in his eyes. *This memory is from long ago, Branka. You were a child then. He cannot touch you now. I'm standing between you.*

His voice would always steady her. And those eyes. She took a breath and let herself fall deeper into his eyes. She could be safe there.

Tatijana lifted the dagger from the wrapping. Xaviero told her to cut her palm and to let the blood drip over the wrapping and twine. I heard the laughter in his voice—that cruel laughter that I'll never forget—and I knew something bad would happen. Tatijana refused. She tried to drop the weapon, but Xayvion was behind her and he forced her to carve an X into her palm. She still has the scar.

Zev didn't glance over toward Tatijana as she assumed he would. He didn't so much as blink. He kept his gaze squarely on hers, holding her to this time and place when she could so easily have slipped back.

Branislava swallowed. *They made her drip her blood all over the wrapper. Xaviero took the knife and handed it to me. I didn't want Xayvion to touch me, so I did it myself. I didn't cut nearly as deep as Tatijana because I did it myself. I didn't wait for them to tell me what to do. I just allowed my blood to mingle with Tatijana's on the wrapping paper.*

You both must have been so frightened.

We knew something horrible was going to happen. The birthday, presents and cake were long forgotten at that point. At first we stared at the wrapping paper expecting something there, but then the twine began to absorb the blood and we knew it was alive. The three of them, Xavier, Xaviero and Xayvion, were so gleeful. They rubbed their hands together in anticipation. I remember thinking they did it exactly at the same moment and that their expressions were the same

Zev sent her another wave of reassurance and she realized deep inside panic was beginning to set in. She didn't want to remember what happened next. She took another calming breath and tried to distance herself.

Tatijana moved when she saw the body doubling in size and the thing swung its head toward her. We could see the teeth, serrated and sharp. Xavier hissed at her to be still or it would eat her alive, starting with her feet. We froze. So did Jules. For a few minutes everyone just sat there on the floor, afraid to breathe, with that horrible creature growing in size. It consumed the blood fast.

Zev frowned at her, but he didn't move a muscle. *Could the three mages talk without drawing its attention?*

And move. Somehow it seemed the creature was a part of them and wouldn't attack them. They each moved behind one of us. Xaviero chose me. I could feel him there and knew something terrible was about to happen. He whispered to me that we were playing a game, that games were always played at birthday parties. I couldn't move or speak. The one who did lost the game and was eaten by the blood worm.

She knew what it cost Zev not to close his eyes or look away from her. He was a man who always protected those he loved. He'd lost two, one lay on the floor in front of him. Now, he couldn't stop this memory from consuming her once again. But he stayed with her, lived it with her. That moment she felt pain slicing through her.

"Don't you move, Tatijana. If you do, I'll start jumping around. I mean it. Don't you move." I kept calling to her, over and over while they tortured us. All three of us. She knew I would, too. I tried to keep them from ever focusing on her. I didn't think about trying to help Jules.

Branka. Zev's voice held pure love. *You were a child fighting to survive. Trying to keep your sister alive. You did nothing wrong and your friend Jules would have been the first to say so.*

He screamed and the worm was on him, attaching itself to his leg and eating fast right through his flesh. It wrapped around his leg like a snake would, and each segment and strand seemed to have teeth, biting into him. His screams were horrible. Tatijana and I froze at first, watching as the thing ate him alive, just as they said it would. We couldn't stand it. I grabbed the dagger and began stabbing it over and over. Tatijana hit it with the crystal ball, trying to smash it, but it wouldn't stop and it wouldn't die.

Did it turn on you?

It was so caught up in a feeding frenzy, it didn't even look at us. I could hear the three brothers laughing as they watched us and watched poor Jules. He kicked and fought and nothing stopped that eating machine. Their laughter was maniacal, diabolical and so evil. She choked back a sob. *Zev.* She whispered his name, needing him.

We're past this. We know Jules dies. But the creature is still alive. How did they get rid of it?

They called it to them. I remember the words. And then they commanded it to die. I think because they made it, they were able to stop it.

You know how. You don't need them. You can use any tone, speak any words of any language. You know Xaviero's tone, his exact pitch. Even if Xayvion is alive, he wouldn't have come with Xaviero. He would stay safe waiting to see if this trap worked to free Xavier. This creature was made by Xaviero, and you can use his spell and his tone to stop the thing.

The blood on the floor was nearly gone and the creature had wrapped its bloated body around Arno's leg. Branislava glanced at her sister, using just her eyes. Tatijana stared at the blood worm, horrified. Fen was the closest to the worm and she had to be terrified that he would be attacked.

Branislava is going to try to kill this thing, Zev informed the others. *No one move or speak. Give her the chance to do this.*

Branislava didn't dare wait. She closed her eyes and found the voice and intonation of Xaviero. Zev was there with her, perfecting the pitch in her mind before she opened her mouth to speak.

That born of blood and earth,
I call your name.
To me you must crawl,
Hearing no others' claim.

Her voice was commanding, reverberating through the room. Tatijana flinched mentally, but stayed absolutely still, her eyes as round as saucers. Her hand, however, was on the knife strapped to her waist.

The worm stiffened. Shook its head. Let out a high-pitched shriek that hurt her ears. She repeated the command, making certain that every inflection was exactly as it had been when the three mages had called the creature back to them.

That born of blood and earth,
I call your name.
To me you must crawl,
Hearing no others' claim.

Still the creature protested, thrashing, but still sucking at the flesh of the fallen man. Branislava pressed her lips together. *Something's wrong. He isn't attacking me so I've got the correct tone and inflection, but he isn't responding.*

That's not true. He is listening, but he's confused. Now that I think about it, Xaviero would have prepared that twine somewhere else. He just had to switch it with the cord Arno wore after Arno was dead. Xayvion could very well have been with him. I am able to listen to any tone or accent and speak languages nearly flawlessly. It is a gift I was born with. Share Xayvion's tone and I'll do my best to reproduce it.

Branislava didn't want to take the chance that he might accidentally draw the blood worm's attack, but she had no choice. The confusion wouldn't last long and the worm would be looking to kill. She repeated Xayvion's voice and intonation, nearly a replica of Xaviero's only a tiny bit deeper.

She gave an almost imperceptible nod and together, their voices rang out through the room.

That born of blood and earth,
I call your name.
To me you must crawl,
Hearing no others' claim.

This time the worm reacted immediately, swinging around and slithering toward them like a trained dog might to his master. It stopped directly between them, almost touching Zev's boots. She had no idea if blood called it and if it would detect the difference. She didn't dare take the chance. She pushed the next spell into Zev's mind, repeating it several times.

I'm ready. Let's kill this thing.

He made her feel confident. That was the thing about Zev she loved th
most—his belief in her abilities—in their ability when they were together

She took a deep breath and nodded to him. Once again their voices fille
the room—not their voices—but the voices of the two mages combined.

Of blood you were born,
I call to your spoor.
I see that which is hidden,
May your path be no more.

As you were made,
So shall you die.
That which was created,
Shall now be untied.

The blood worm lifted its head and shrieked even as it began to brea
apart. Blood spilled out of it in streams, the twine binding it together shred
ding to reveal an empty shell that was nothing but teeth and blood. Th
creature continued to make long, hideous noises until its head unraveled a
well and it fell to the floor in the middle of the pool of blood, no more tha
regular twine.

There was a long silence. Branislava let her breath out slowly and backe
away from the innocent-looking string and the widening pool of blood. Sh
pressed a hand to her heaving stomach. It was all too much for her, th
memories, the sight of Arno's body and the worm breaking apart.

Zev was there immediately, enfolding her into his arms, turning her s
that his body shielded her from the others. "Let's get you outside, *cheri*," h
said softly. "You need to be in the fresh air."

"But you have things to do here," she protested, although everything i
her yearned to get out of that room and away from the smell of blood an
death.

"Arno can wait. It will take a little time to prepare the bodies for th
funeral pyre. All Lycans present as well as the council members will war
to pay their respects. A member from the Sacred Circle will want to say
few prayers over the bodies before they're burned." Zev brushed a kiss acros

the top of her head. "Right at this moment, Branislava, there is nothing more important than taking you out into the night where we can both breathe. We have a little bit of time before the ceremony must take place."

She was grateful that he included himself. She nodded and he wrapped his arm around her waist, tucking her under his shoulder and took her right out of the room, down the hall and out into the fading night. The moment she was outside, she drew in a deep lungful of air to try to counteract her protesting stomach.

"That was so awful . . . that blood worm."

He nodded, holding her closer. "It was. It always amazes me what the mind of someone evil can conceive."

"Jules died, you know. He died hard." She looked at him with stricken eyes. "We couldn't save him, and they laughed. They *enjoyed* his pain and terror. He'd served them, admired and respected them. He had no idea what they were like until he realized they kept us prisoners inside the bodies of dragons and behind the wall of ice."

He ran his fingers through her silky hair. "I know, *mon bébé*, we'll find him and destroy him. We won't let him keep hurting people."

"Xavier was a monster. He really was, but while he enjoyed other's pain, it was his experiments he was obsessed with. Don't get me wrong, he loved hurting others, but not like Xaviero. Xaviero *had* to torture. It was the only thing that ever made him happy. Xavier despised Carpathians and he was determined to ruin them, to wipe them from the face of the earth. But he was somewhat dispassionate about his tortures as a rule."

"He sounds despicable."

She nodded, threading her fingers through his and walking a little faster as if she might outrun the conversation. "He was despicable. But Xaviero was worse. He *needed* to torture others, especially women and children. He thrived on it. Nothing made him happier. I could tell when it had been too long for him. He was moody and irritable even with his brothers, and Tatijana and I would stay as still and as quiet as possible. Eventually Xavier or Xayvion would tell him to go have fun and we knew what that meant. There is no possible way that he could have been in the Lycan world and not tortured others. He wouldn't have been able to help himself."

"I believe you." Zev ran his hand through his hair. "Bodies turned up in other packs and other countries. I know, I investigated. Most were women, some children. We put it down to vampires stalking the packs. Or rogues. It's happened before. I even considered a serial killer, a human. We never found enough evidence. Sight, scent, it just wasn't there, but I did suspect many of the killings were connected."

"Xaviero thought snatching children out from under their parent's noses was such a thrilling feat. He got the pleasure of tormenting the child, torturing him or her and then allowing the parents to discover the body. He wanted to see their sorrow. He often spared them so they would have to live with guilt and turn their grief into anger at one another."

Zev was silent a moment. "Rannalufr counseled those who lost children. The suicide rate definitely rose sharply, but no one ever suspected soft-spoken, kind Rannalufr of pushing grieving parents to kill themselves."

"He would have enjoyed that power immensely."

"And Xayvion?" Zev asked, knowing she needed to talk.

He kept her walking, away from the village, doubling back toward the forest where he knew she felt safer. Trees closed around them, branches reaching up to the night sky. A few stars had emerged from the strange, violent storm that had come out of nowhere earlier. The last of the dark clouds dissipated to allow the half-moon to reappear.

Zev knew Fen had called in Daciana and Makoce, the two Lycans he trusted the most, to attend Arno and Arnau's bodies. The Carpathians would have to go to ground soon. Branislava was worn out, and in truth, he was as well. Traveling outside one's body took a toll, especially when fighting demons in another realm. Had someone told him he'd be doing such a thing a year earlier he would have laughed at them.

"Xayvion was always quiet. He rarely said much, and Xavier always seemed in charge, but if Xaviero got out of hand, it was Xayvion who stopped him, usually with a look. It was eerie when it happened. Unbelievable almost. And it was rare. Xayvion conducted all the experiments with his brothers, but it was as if he was disconnected completely from everyone. He didn't see us, or their victims as anything alive. When he laughed, it never seemed real to me. He sounded hollow. Dead. I don't really know how to explain it, you'd have to see him in action."

Zev guided her toward their home. If they had time, he would have taken her back to their crater in the snowcapped mountains, but she needed to go to ground and he needed to be up as early as possible to help the Lycans prepare for the service. He wanted it done and over before the mage had a chance to know where or what they would be doing.

"Zev, why did you insist on Arno and Arnau being burned at a service when you know what a risk it is to have everyone together in one place like that?"

He winced. He should have known she was shrewd enough to figure out it was the last thing he would do if he wanted to keep the other council members safe. He had hoped she wouldn't ask him that question.

"They're already in danger from Xaviero. If he can kill Arnau, one of my best men, and then kill Arno, who was already leery of everyone, he can get to anyone. Better to draw him out where all the Lycans and all the Carpathians will be waiting for him."

"They won't get him," she said.

"No, they won't," he agreed. "But if he comes to the funeral pyre—and after you described him, I know he will for certain—he won't be able to resist seeing everyone's pain and guilt, and then I can track him. I'm mixed blood and elite. I know what to look for. I can track him back to his lair."

Branislava looked at him with wide, green eyes. "That's what I thought," she said softly.

18

Beneath the ground, Zev's eyes snapped open and he was instantly alert. What had disturbed his sleep? Waving his hand, he opened the dirt above him so that he could see the basement floor like a ceiling over his head. It was intact. He lay quietly, listening to the sound of his own heartbeat. Nothing seemed out of place. No sound. No movement. He just had this odd feeling in his gut.

Beside him, Branislava lay quietly, her head on his chest, one arm thrown around his waist while her leg was sprawled carelessly over his. She was like the fierce kitten he often called her, cuddly one moment and capable of lethal claws the next. He ran his palm over her strikingly beautiful face.

Seeing her, he relaxed, the tension draining from his body. She looked like an angel to him, a being from a heavenly realm rather than one from earth, one caught up in blood and death. He rubbed his hand over her face again, and then he touched her reverently with the pads of his fingers, marveling at the contrast of her soft skin and his much rougher hands.

Branislava moved slightly, her eyes suddenly opening, showing that gift of green emeralds. She smiled at him, a soft, loving smile that stole his breath and pushed need and hunger into his body.

What is it? Do you have need of me?

The Carpathian paralysis was at its heaviest and yet she managed to return to him. Again, he was a little in awe of his luck. *I'm just wondering how a man of war like me could be so lucky as to get a woman of grace like you.*

Her long lashes swept down, but not before he saw the pleased amusement in her eyes.

I am the lucky one, Wolfie, and I am well aware of it. Sleep. You need to rest.

She called him *Wolfie* when she loved him so fiercely she felt a little overwhelmed by it and had to lighten the moment. He found himself smiling. Happy. Content. Except for the fact that he was awake when he should have been fast asleep. There was just a nagging feeling of unease. He knew he had no choice but to check it out.

Branka, I'm going to walk around a bit and make certain everyone is safe. Continue to rest. I'll return as soon as I've made the rounds.

A small frown came over her face. He couldn't help but rub his finger over her full, pouting lips. Her lashes fluttered, but she didn't lift them. Answering wings fluttered in his stomach, teasing his groin into growing in length and girth.

You're Carpathian, you can't go out this time of day.

I've always been able to go out this time of day. Why should anything be any different just because the ancients acknowledged me?

Her little frown deepened. His heart did a slow somersault in his chest and this time he smoothed the line between her eyes.

I forgot about the Dark Blood lineage. They are the only ones to be able to do such a thing. Combine that with your Lycan blood and there you go. Not a good thing when your lifemate can't do the same.

Her petulant tone made him smile. *And why is that?* he asked her, bending down to brush his mouth gently across hers.

Who knows what trouble you'll get into without me.

He laughed softly, once again finding himself happier than he'd ever been in his life. It mattered little the circumstances surrounding them, the danger or the battles, only this fiery woman lying curled so close to him.

He cupped her breast, his thumb sliding over her nipple. She shivered and her nipple peaked. He had known that even during the time when Carpathians couldn't move, she would respond to his touch. He was fascinated by her body, the shape of her, those soft curves, all that silky satin skin.

Mmm, she whispered. *Your touch always makes my body sing.*

She was more than half asleep to say something like that to him. His smile broadened. *I like the way your body sings for me. Have you ever dreamt of making love during the time you cannot move? Your body seems so alive to me.*

To tease her, he ran his hand down her flat stomach to the junction between her legs. There was smoldering heat when the rest of her body felt cool to his touch. *I do believe you're dreaming of me.* He cupped her mound and felt the small rush of liquid response.

She gave a little sniff of disdain, her lips curving into a smile. *Not really. A wolf man? Why ever would I do that?*

Because, my darling woman—he bent his head again to draw her breast into the heat of his mouth—*if you dreamt of another man and responded like this, wet and ready with your fire growing, I would have to hunt him down and kill him.* He flattened his tongue, stroking and teasing, using the edge of his teeth while he suckled, showing her the wolf lying in wait.

She laughed softly, the sound vibrating through him, teasing his body like the touch of her fingers. *You're such a big bad wolf sometimes.*

You have no idea just how bad a wolf can be. Here you are lying so helpless, and I have no problem taking advantage of you.

His teeth nipped his way down to her belly button, his tongue easing the sharp sting. His sank one finger deep into her waiting body, feeling her readiness, that eager reception he always anticipated.

Should I be afraid? I believe my body belongs to you. It is saying so right this minute.

Her laughter teased at his groin, as if her mouth was so close to him, breathing warm air over the burgeoning shaft and sensitive head. He could have sworn he felt the brush of her tongue over him. His cock jerked and he circled his girth with his hand, already on fire for her.

You're playing with fire again, she said softly, intimately, into his mind. Her tone was pure seduction. A temptress with her body calling to his and her mind touching him with her fingers and tongue and mouth.

Hunger was savage. Tearing at him unexpectedly the way it often did when he was close to her. The scent of her called to the wolf in him, and his body reacted with urgent, brutally hard need. He plunged two fingers into her tightness, trying to prepare her when he knew he would join them fast and hard.

I am always ready for you, my love, always. I look at you and my body drips with welcome. My breasts cannot wait for your mouth and hands. I am more than ready.

Zev didn't waste any more time. He parted her thighs and moved her body so he could slide into her fiery sheath in one, fast forceful surge, burying himself to the hilt. He went so deep he felt her womb, that warm, snug place she would carry their child. Despite the hour of the day, her sheath was hot vibrant silk, moist and ready for him, opening reluctantly and then clamping around him like a tight fist of pure fire.

His breath hissed out as he began to move, locking her hips in place while he pounded his body into hers, burying himself over and over in that scorching blaze. She couldn't move, couldn't stop him from doing anything to her body, and the wonderful thing was, she didn't want to. He could touch her anywhere, kiss her, taste her and just explore, and his woman gave herself into his keeping.

He gave himself up to sheer feeling, letting the sensations pour over him and into him. There was a kind of wonder in being able to always be what he was—a wolf, an alpha, a predatory animal claiming his mate. Branislava never objected to the wild pounding or rough handling, matching him flame for flame.

This time, because she couldn't move, there was a sense of power mixed with lust and love, an intoxicating combination. The knowledge that she trusted him implicitly, that she would allow him to use the sanctuary of her body during this hour, was the most sensual of all.

His hands moved over her, stroking and kneading her body, feeling the answering response as her muscles clamped down around him tight. The heat built and built until even the ground seemed to glow with a red-orange hue. He lifted her buttocks and surged forward again and again, driving into her so that each stroke sent her breasts swaying.

Her mouth formed a small round *O* and her eyes glazed. He could see the marks of his possession on her skin, all those nips and bites, the press of his fingers, marking her, claiming her as his own. Satisfaction rose along with a primitive need to possess her. A wolf chose his mate wisely, and Branislava would always be his choice. His destiny.

You are becoming more wolf by the moment, she hissed, her mind chaotic with the building pleasure. His hands seemed to be everywhere, bringing her body to life when the sun had drained her of all strength. He had magic in him, a beast bringing mind-numbing pleasure bent on her destruction. And she was more than willing to give herself up to him, to allow them both to burn in her fire.

His thrusts were strong and the rhythm a fierce pace, a machine driving through her soft folds, feeling like a steel piston covered in velvet. She knew the meaning of velvet over steel now. The friction turned her body into a firestorm, hot and needy and seeking the wind to fan the flames. She felt him swelling more, an amazing feat. It seemed impossible to accommodate him and yet, there was always more pleasure, a never-ending coiling of tension building in her until fear skittered down her spine and she feared he might tip them both over the edge to insanity.

A good way to go, he observed, leaning down to bite at her breast and then suckle strongly. *I could just eat you up. I've thought about it enough times. I could spend hours devouring you and all that cinnamon-honey that really belongs to me.*

She squirmed at that thought, her sheath flooding him with scorching hot liquid. *I'm not arguing with you. You get anything you want, you know I'm crazy mad about you.*

He laughed softly. *You're crazy mad about what my body can do to yours.*

Okay, that was the truth as well. And right now, she desperately needed him to give her release, but she couldn't move, couldn't bring her hips to his. He was using his arms now, bracing himself as he pounded into her. She could almost hear the flames crackling around them. The glow in the soil deepened.

Zev. Just his name. Her miracle. The man who could remove every ugly bit of her past and replace it with such blissful experiences and memories. *I need . . .*

I know what you need, amoureux, I'll always know. He moved in her, against her, filled her, the friction building over her most sensitive spot until her body seemed to go up in flames, the orgasm tearing through her like a crown fire, leaping from her groin to her belly, up to her breasts and bursting down her thighs.

Zev threw back his head and howled like the wolf he was as her body took his with it on that fiery ride of sheer bliss. He stayed locked with her a long time, sharing one body, one skin, complete in each other.

Kiss me and let me go back to sleep.

All over again, she sounded drowsy and sensual, enough that his cock jerked and thought about coming to life. She opened one eye and managed a small laugh. *You're insatiable. You're lucky I love you that way.*

He thought about all the things he could do with her. She was sleepy and needed to rest and rejuvenate in the soil. And there was that strange nagging feeling he couldn't quite put to rest, but still, the temptation of her body . . .

"Does it ever bother you that you're not Carpathian and everyone else is?" Travis Amiras asked Paul Chevez as they tossed a ball back and forth in the front yard of the house where the Carpathian children were housed together to better protect them while the adults slept.

Paul was twenty, a man already filled out with wide shoulders and defined muscles. He was already battle-scarred at his young age. He'd fought vampires, helped to run a massive cattle ranch, had been shot and recently helped to save Dimitri from death by silver. Travis hero-worshipped him.

"I'm not quite ready for that yet," Paul said. "Carpathians age at a much slower rate than we do. My friend Josef is in his twenties, but is considered a kid. I work hard on the ranch and take care of my little sister. It would annoy me to be treated that way. Besides, I take looking after Ginny seriously. I wouldn't want to be in the ground while she was above it."

Travis nodded. "I can understand that. You've only got one sister to look out for. I've got seven brothers and sisters, now that Sara has had the new baby, little Isabella." His voice went soft when he mentioned the baby. "It's hard for Sara and Falcon to go to ground and leave us all. They rely on me."

Paul nodded. "Falcon talks about you all the time. He was upset that Gary was no longer able to be with you during the day."

Travis shrugged. "I have to admit, I don't like it, either. Gary is cool.

He teaches us the most interesting things. Marie, the nanny for the kids, can be a little boring. She looks after the little ones and sometimes tries to boss me around. It drives me crazy."

"But Slavica and Mirko, the innkeepers, have that beautiful daughter, Angelina. I've noticed you like spending time with her," Paul observed with a faint grin.

Travis tried to look innocent and then broke out laughing. "She's really cool, too. She doesn't treat me like I'm a kid."

"I noticed her coolness," Paul said. He caught the ball and looked uneasily toward the west. "Travis, let's go inside."

The smile faded from the younger boy's face. His eyes turned old and he took a long look around him. "You feel something, don't you? Something is wrong."

It was still a good couple of hours before any of the adult Carpathians would be rising, and he was a little uneasy as well. He had no idea why. He was eleven, closer to twelve and already he had taken on the ways of his Carpathian adopted father, Falcon. He walked like him and wore his hair long like him. "Do you feel uneasy?"

Paul walked up the steps to the small house. There were only two other adults with them to protect the children and he felt the responsibility heavily. He had fought vampires and Lycans, but this felt different. He wasn't certain if it was his imagination or not until he glimpsed Travis's eyes. The boy was psychic and very sensitive.

"I have no idea if we're both a little tense and our imaginations are getting away from us because of all that's happened," Paul admitted, "but it's better to be safe. Let's get the children in the sealed room Mikhail and Gregori provided. We can come back up here and scout around a little. I'll call in Jubal."

"It's weird not to have Gary with us anymore," Travis admitted. "During the day, he always stayed close to protect us and I felt as if he could stop anything."

"It's probably nothing at all," Paul said again, although his gut was beginning to churn and he was certain there was cause for alarm. He just didn't want the kid to panic. "Let's get the others down below."

"Falcon's trained me to fight. Peter and Lucas are way better than anyone gives them credit for," Travis told him. "They like to pull pranks, but they'll fight if they need to."

"Let them know we're counting on them to stand in front of the others," Paul said. "Make certain they take you seriously."

Travis nodded. He went into the first playroom. Marie was there with the baby and his two younger sisters, Chrissy and Blythe. Chrissy was eight and Blythe six months younger. Chrissy was reading aloud. She stopped when he entered and immediately her face fell. She went to Blythe and put her arm around her.

"Paul thinks it's a good idea to move everyone down below, to the safe room," Travis said, trying to use his most matter-of-fact voice. "Just as a precaution. It's probably nothing, but just in case."

Marie came to her feet immediately. "Chrissy, we'll need those two bags right there. Hurry and do as your brother says."

Travis waited until Chrissy and Blythe had the bags Marie had indicated before turning to leave the room.

"Trav, wait," Blythe said. Her voice shook. "Are you coming, too?"

"In a few minutes. I need to get the boys. Peter and Lucas will be with you until I get there. Jubal is coming. Paul and I are just going to look around outside." Travis tried to reassure her, but her eyes had grown big and she looked about to cry.

He walked back into the room and gave her a clumsy hug, not looking at Marie. He was always a little embarrassed showing his affection, but he loved his brothers and sisters, and Falcon had told him repeatedly that men showed those they loved their feelings and it wasn't at all girlie. Blythe clung to him and then Chrissy joined in the hug.

After a moment, Chrissy took Blythe by the hand. "Help me carry the bags for Marie. We don't want the baby to wake up."

Travis left them to it and went to find his brothers. Peter and Lucas had tied Jase, their six-year-old brother, to a chair and were running around him yelling like banshees. It took a few minutes to get their attention. The only way he managed it was to stand in their path and let them run into him.

"We've got real trouble," he announced soberly.

Peter immediately loosened the bonds so Jase could get up. Lucas put his arm around Jase, pulling him close.

"What do you want us to do?" Peter asked.

"I'll be bringing Anya, Anastasia, Stefan and Alexandru down soon. Jennifer is with them and so is Angelina and Ginny. They'll know something is wrong, but you still have to act like everything is going to be all right. Whatever Marie and Angelina say to do, just do it, keep the peace, no matter how long this takes. If something happens, Peter, you and Lucas have to stand between whatever the danger is and the younger ones."

Peter nodded. Travis gripped his brothers' forearms in the traditional warrior's greeting, making the ritual solemn, so they understood the danger coming. When he was certain they would get Jase to safety and take their mission seriously, he went to the last room to tell Angelina.

Angelina, Ginny and Jennifer were playing games with the younger children. Laughter ceased the moment he entered. Stefan stood up, placing his body in front of Alexandru. The twins, Anya and Anastasia, moved up on either side of the prince's son. They all faced Travis with somber faces.

He forced a smile, but the dread in his stomach had grown and he knew something was definitely wrong. "Just as a precaution, everyone needs to move down to the safe room. Don't give Marie or Angelina any trouble, even if it takes a long time. Remember the new baby. We don't want her to be alarmed. Jubal is coming, and we'll be all right, but we have to make certain everyone is in the safe room just in case."

Ginny picked up Alexandru and Angelina took the twins. Jennifer took Stefan's hand. They immediately complied without asking questions.

Travis went room by room, making certain all the children were safely down in the room Mikhail and Gregori had provided. He made his way back to the sitting room. Paul was outside on the verandah, pacing back and forth. He had gathered up weapons, slinging them over his shoulder and looping them through his belt. Travis's mouth went dry but he did the same, slowly donning all the weapons one needed to fight off a vampire or his puppets. Rogue packs of werewolves required silver stakes and silver knives. He added those as well before joining Paul on the front porch.

The feeling of impending doom grew in him, a dark dread that seemed to swallow him whole. He risked a quick glance at Paul, hoping he would see something there to help him shake off his anxiety, but Paul looked every bit as grim as he felt.

"They're all in the safe room," he reported, managing to keep his voice steady.

"Jubal is around the back. He feels it, too."

"A vampire?" Travis asked almost hopefully.

"No vampire can be out at this time of day. Not even the *Sange rau*. Our own mixed bloods have managed every now and then, but it still takes a toll. To battle in the sun, I don't know what that would do to one of them." Paul shook his head. "We just have to hold out until the sun goes down."

"What are we facing? A rogue pack?" Lycans could be out during the day, and certainly a pack of werewolves could as well.

The wind rushed toward them, carrying the scent of burning brimstone, a sulfuric stench much like burnt rotting eggs. Paul caught Travis by the arm. "Get inside now. Hurry. Don't argue with me, just do it."

Travis wanted to protest. He needed to help protect the younger children, but the urgency in Paul's voice alarmed him. He retreated indoors, going to the window, notching an arrow tipped in silver into his crossbow.

"Jubal," Paul called. "Do you smell that? What is that?"

"Hellhounds," Zev answered, striding into the yard, his long dark coat swirling around his boots. "Hounds of hell. Mage magic."

Jubal skidded to a halt when he caught sight of Zev, his eyes going wide in shock at the sight of a Carpathian walking boldly in the sun. Travis came out of the house as well, standing uncertainly on the porch.

"It just made sense, after all the things Branislava told me about the High Mage, that he would come after the children," Zev said. "I caught their scent in the wind and pushed it toward you, hoping you'd be prepared."

"How do we prepare?" Jubal asked.

"This is not the first time I have encounterd them. We need oil. Hyssop oil." Zev looked around, found an old cooking pot and quickly summoned the oil. "Dip your arrows in that. Coat every weapon you have. If necessary, pour it over yourself. The oil will continue to flow as needed."

"They'll be faster than you can possibly imagine. When you fire at them, aim well ahead of them. Some will have more than one head. They'll be huge and frightening. Their eyes will glow, some red and some a hideous yellow. Try not to look directly at them."

"Hounds of hell," Paul muttered. "Heralders of death. Anyone who looks . . ."

Zev shot him a look and Paul fell silent. "They are that only because the mage puts a spell on them and uses them to bring his plague to those he wants dead. Don't let their saliva get on you, or their blood. They'll carry the plague in teeth and claws. Shoot them through their eyes, and if you can't hit that target, aim for the throat. It won't kill them, but it will slow them down."

The ground vibrated. The pot of hyssop oil shook, the oil forming large rings.

"Take cover," Zev commanded. "Take your time with each shot. Place it ahead of the hound. Remember, if there's more than one head, all three have to be hit in the eye." He turned his attention to Travis. "Go for the throat, it will buy you the time you need to take a steady, true aim. Don't panic, that will get you in trouble every time. I'll be right here." Zev used his calmest, most steady voice, low yet carrying the weight of his authority and knowledge.

Travis nodded and dropped to one knee, sheltering behind a heavy column there on the porch. The scent of burning brimstone grew stronger and with it, the smell of fire, or rather burned grass and foliage, as if the traveling hounds were leaving behind a barren wasteland.

Zev turned toward the west, his long coat swirling around him. He watched as the first of the hounds broke out of cover and into the open. He was massive—a huge black hound with burning coals for eyes and gigantic teeth and claws, running full out toward them. Behind him, several more burst into the open, looking like a galloping herd of wild beasts, monsters so foul they could only be conceived in hell—or by a fiendishly evil mind.

With one hand, he picked up the cooking pot and poured the hyssop oil over his head so that it ran down his hair and over his face and shoulders. In one motion, he put it down, lifted his crossbow and fired the first arrow.

The arrow went true, straight into the left eye of the lead hellhound. It leapt into the air, bellowing, snarling, snapping the air with its teeth. Black blood ran down its face as it landed hard, shook its head and kept coming.

Zev heard Travis's soft hiss of fear, but the boy didn't run. "Steady. Don't fire yet. I'll take out their leader," he cautioned softly, hoping his calm voice and matter-of-fact demeanor would give the boy courage.

He lifted his crossbow again and fired off a second arrow dipped in the hyssop oil, scoring a direct hit to the right eye. The massive black-furred hound was nearly to the porch. He snarled, pulling back his lips to reveal his razor-sharp teeth and the long, almost saber-toothed tiger canines. His body shuddered and he slowed, took two more steps and seemed to skid, his back claws still digging in for purchase as his legs propelled him forward. His muzzle hit the ground hard almost at Zev's feet. The hound thrashed around, howling and biting the air.

"Pick one of them," Zev instructed the others. "Hit the eyes. Make certain you're covered in oil and if those teeth or claws get to you, yell out immediately. I'll take care of the wound. Travis, if you're uncertain . . ." He fired at the hound nearest to the house, once again scoring a hit directly in the left eye. The beast was running full out, its body nearly the size of a large pony. Its head was massive, the muzzle filled with giant teeth. "Aim for the throat. Take your time. You can do this."

Paul shot the hound to the right of the one Zev had hit. His arrow hit the hound squarely between the eyes and bounced off. Paul swore softly, took a breath and sent a second arrow, this one much truer, straight into the beast's right eye. Both hounds were running flat out, deadly venom hanging in great long strings from their muzzles. His hound veered sideways and rammed the one Zev had struck. The two hellhounds tangled for a moment, tumbling over one another, snarling and snapping.

Jubal and Travis both fired at a two-headed monster almost simultaneously. Travis's arrow hit the hound in the throat, burying deep. Jubal's arrow found one of the eyes. The two-headed hellhound leapt over the snarling, fighting beasts and hit the railing of the verandah, smashing the wood, landing almost on Travis.

Travis stood up, crossbow in hand, staring into the malevolent yellow eyes of the two-headed hound. It stood glaring back at him, black blood running from one eye on its left head and its throat. The animal pulled back its lips in a deadly snarl, the strings of venom increasing tenfold. The boy let out his breath and as the animal took a slow, stalking step toward him, fired his crossbow straight into the other eye of the left head.

Zev reached back with one hand, even as he let another arrow fly toward the hound, which had managed to get to its feet. Picking up the pot of oil, he threw the contents at the two-headed beast leaping at Travis. The boy backpedaled fast as he fit another arrow into his bow, firing as he stumbled away from the hellhound.

Zev felt the blast of black breath from the beast, hot and wild and tainted with evil, as he stepped between the hound and the boy. He fired calmly into the eye of the right head. Travis's arrow had hit the throat a second time. Oil dripped from both heads of the animal, running off the fur in streams. The fur came with the oil, leaving long raw patches of blistering skin.

Maddened with pain, the hellhound thrashed around, and then hit its head against one of the columns, shaking the roof and cracking the column. One side of the roof partially collapsed over the porch as the animal hit the railing and then the side of the house. The two-headed beast spun in circles, teeth snapping at everything in its path.

Zev yanked Travis off the porch, thrusting the boy behind him as the hound Jubal fired at rose from the ground and galloped toward them with blurring speed. Zev fired rapidly, three arrows in quick succession, aiming just ahead of the hellhound. The beast leapt the last few feet, his glowing eyes not on Zev, but on the boy. One eye had two arrows sticking out of it, but the second eye was clear. The third arrow had hit him through the nose.

Zev dropped the crossbow, and caught the beast with his bare hands, snapping the massive head away from Travis.

"My knife," he hissed, over his shoulder at the boy. He was grateful for his mixed blood, blood that gave him enormous strength, although the beast burned him right through the thin gloves he wore. Using leverage he flipped the hellhound off his feet, but his arm was dangerously close to the snapping teeth.

He felt Travis step up beside him, pull the knife from his belt and without being told, without hesitation, thrust the oil-covered blade into the eye of the beast. Jubal had his hands full with the beast Zev had shot earlier, trying to prevent it from reaching the verandah.

Zev and Travis leapt back and away from the thrashing, dying animal, turning back to the porch. It was empty. Where the window had been, there was now an enormous hole. His heart sinking, Zev caught up his crossbow, dove through the window, somersaulted to his feet, and ran toward the hallway.

The trail of black blood led through the house to the kitchen where there was another enormous hole where the door to the basement should have been. The hellhound had been programmed to find and kill the children, and it was following their scent trail.

He took the stairs two at a time, jumped one-handed over the railing when he was halfway down and landed in a crouch just a few feet from the two-headed hound. One head lolled to one side, two streams of black blood pouring from the sightless eyes. Black fur was gone from the head, neck and shoulders, leaving blistering skin that seemed to bubble up loosely as if underneath, the oil was dissolving everything it touched.

The beast used its deadly claws to rip at the wall, tearing great long strips from the structure, but as fast as he dug, the wall repaired itself. Each time the claws sank into the wall, the hellhound lifted its head and bellowed with pain, the wall creating a current of electricity that clearly went right through the animal. Smoke rose around him, the stench of rotting, burned eggs intensifying, but even the pain didn't slow the monster down.

"Travis, are you with me?" Zev asked.

"Yes." The answer was very faint, but steady.

"I'm going to ask you to do something that will be very scary and equally as dangerous. Are you up for it?"

"If it keeps that thing away from my family," Travis replied.

Zev drew his sword. "I'm going to sever both heads. You have to keep track of the one with the eye still intact. It won't be easy. The hound is going to rage at us. It will likely attack me, headless. The two heads will roll around and black blood will be everywhere. You can't look at anything but that one spot, the eye that needs to be closed. Fire your arrow and hit what you're aiming at."

"What if I miss?" Travis's voice trembled.

"You can't miss. Do you understand me? You can't miss. You know how to shoot. Falcon taught you. You'll hit what you're aiming at."

"Yes, sir," Travis said.

Zev took a breath, let it out and stepped close to the massive hellhound. He brought his sword down hard, using the combined strength of Lycan and Carpathian, using his centuries of experience in battle. The sword cut cleanly through the gruesome creature, severing the two heads so that they fell to the floor.

A blast of heat rose from the severed neck, smoke rising and black blood pouring from the hole. Zev jumped back to avoid the splatter, placing his feet carefully as the headless body whipped around, claws ripping at the air around it.

The two heads rolled, leaving a trail of poisonous blood on the floor. One eye glowed a ghastly yellow, shining like a beacon each time it came around to the surface. Travis didn't look to see what the headless body of the gigantic hound was doing to Zev. He did every single thing Falcon had taught him. He took a breath. Let it out. Counted to himself to get the rhythm of his target. Visualized the arrow going straight and true. He waited and as the head rolled, he let his arrow fly, and just as quickly fit another in the crossbow, just as Falcon had instructed.

His arrow hit the yellow eye dead center. It stared at him malevolently, wide open, the arrow protruding. The head rolled closer to him. He didn't take his gaze from his target. When the eye rolled back up to the surface, he let lose the second arrow and just as quickly reloaded.

The head stilled, the eye open and staring, but now it appeared a faded yellow, hollow, with no real life or intelligence behind the glare. Still, Travis couldn't tear his gaze away, fearing that the creature would come to life again. He was afraid to look behind him, fearing Zev wouldn't be there and the headless body would be about to rip him to pieces with those terrible claws.

"Travis." Zev's soft voice reached him through the roaring in his ears. "Thank you. You killed it. We need to go back and help Jubal. If you need a minute, you can join the others in the safe room and let them know we're almost done here. Jubal and I will clean up."

Zev's voice was that same calm, steady miracle of complete confidence. But he was moving up the stairs fast, a graceful, fluid exit, but an exit all the same. Travis was well aware the elite hunter was making certain Jubal was still alive and had killed the last of the hellhounds. He didn't want to be left alone in the same room with the macabre two-headed beast, even though it appeared dead. He wasn't about to open the safe room door until he was absolutely certain it was safe to do so. He ran after Zev.

Zev hated to leave the boy after he'd shown so much bravery, and was happy to hear his footsteps as Travis raced after him, but his mind was already on the fiends from hell trying to get to the children. There had been five of them. He'd killed the leader. The two-headed monster was dead. The two hounds that collided together had been slain as well. That left one. They'd been lucky. Jubal had good aim, and so had Paul and Travis. The oil had come in handy. Without it, the beasts would come at them again and again, in spite of the arrows. There was no other real way to kill the hellhound without the oil. It acted like poison to them.

Zev burst out onto the porch, ready for anything—other than the scene in front of him. Paul and Jubal sat on the ground a few inches from a dead hellhound, both laughing almost hysterically. They looked up as he approached. The hound and both men were covered in oil and puddles of it lay on the ground.

"Were either of you hurt? Bitten? Clawed? Did you get any blood on you?"

"No," Jubal said. He looked at Paul and they broke into laughter again. "We're just covered, ready for the fryer. How about you?"

Zev let the tension drain out of him, although he was fairly certain the two men were bordering on hysteria. "I'm covered in oil as well." He sank down onto the ground beside them and surveyed the four massive bodies. "So are they. What did you do?"

Paul grinned and wiped his face with the back of his hand, smearing more oil. "I kept throwing buckets of the stuff at it while Jubal kept shooting. Eventually, the darn thing went down, but it took about ten arrows and five full buckets of the stuff. I can't believe you managed to conjure up a replenishing container of oil."

Travis came and sat down between Paul and Zev. He looked at the three men. "I'd much rather fight a vampire," he declared with a small shudder.

"You're not alone in that," Paul agreed.

"We've got a mess to clean up," Zev said. "Although I think I'm feeling little sleepy."

Jubal threw a handful of dirt at him. "Don't even think about running out on us."

Zev yawned. "Really. The sun is getting to me."

"We'll get to you," Paul declared, making a move as though he might tackle Zev.

Zev was too fast, leaping to his feet, nearly skidding in the oil. "Fine. I'll help. But you two made a mess."

"We saved the day," Jubal announced solemnly. "We were discussing medals of valor."

Zev's eyebrow shot up. "Medals?" he repeated, as if he wasn't certain what that was.

"Of valor," Paul said. "Trav can get in on it, too. We even designed one." He looked at Jubal and the two of them roared with laughter.

Zev shook his head. "Young Travis, this is clearly a side effect of getting too close to one of the hellhounds. Their brains are addled."

Travis nodded. "I can see that. We'd better leave them to it and clean up downstairs so the kids can get out of the safe room. They'll be frightened."

They turned away and Paul yelped in panic. "Wait! You can't leave. You have to burn all this."

Turning back, Zev laughed at the stricken faces of Jubal and Paul. Even Travis laughed with him. "I notice I get the work and you get the medals." He called down the lightning and directed it over the bodies, incinerating them and the black, shiny blood that had spread throughout the yard.

"As it should be," Paul muttered under his breath, just loud enough for Zev to hear.

A whip of lightning struck a few feet from Paul's feet, getting the last of the blood from the ground. Paul practically leapt over the top of Jubal to get away from the sizzling tip.

"I'm telling Branislava on you," he called out, using the last resort he had to even the odds.

19

An unholy mist crept through the forest, weaving through the trees close to the ground. Tendrils rose from the foot-high bank of fog, long tentacles inching through brush and leaves to wind like snakes and climb higher into the tree trunks. A strange odor of burning sulfur accompanied the dense vapor. The smell was faint, yet wildlife shied away from the creeping mist, whirling around when it approached and running as if their very lives were in danger.

A wolf sank down onto its haunches and lifted its muzzle skyward, emitting a long warning note. Another joined it.

To me now! Dimitri ordered the two alphas sharply. *Hurry. Skyler, move it. We have no time. Zev! Fen! We're surrounded. The wolves are calling, can you hear the warning?*

Dimitri held out his arms for his wolves to leap aboard. They came running out of the deeper forest to leap at him. He felt the jolt as they shifted at the last moment. The little alpha female was getting it, but she still hit him harder than necessary. He reprimanded her automatically, reminding her to shift a little faster.

Skyler's wolf Moonglow rushed toward them and she turned, arms wide, to make it easier for her to leap aboard. Dimitri kept his eyes on the fog as it inched its way toward the clearing where the ceremony to send Arno and his son Arnau off with honors was taking place.

He couldn't describe it as mist any longer—the matter was far too dense and gave off an eerie, flickering, yellowish-gray glow. He signaled Skyler to start moving, back in the direction of the clearing. The fog was taking over the forest and he didn't want her or the wolves in it.

Wolves began howling from various positions in the forest. Skyler gasped and reached for his hand. "The wild ones are warning us to get out," she interpreted.

Dimitri lifted his head and howled back, emitting a series of notes and cries, perfectly pitched like a wolf, responding to the warnings of the wild wolves.

Ivory and Razvan came from the direction of the west, their wolves already riding on both of them. "Are you two all right?" Razvan asked, looking Skyler over carefully.

Skyler nodded. "One of my wolves, Frost, hasn't returned yet. Dimitri called them in."

"I've told the wild ones to get out of this part of the forest and avoid the fog," Dimitri said. "They knew, they were warning us, but I wanted to make certain they understood how dangerous it is."

Razvan indicated the yellowish vapor. "It appears to be climbing the trees. Look how it wraps around the trunk and goes up. It goes up the trees it touches before it creeps forward again along the forest floor."

Ivory and Skyler stepped toward the fog, both determined to find the missing wolf. Dimitri caught Skyler's arm to halt her.

"He'll come back or he won't, *csitri*, but you can't get near that stuff. If every animal in the forest is running away from it, you have to heed the warnings."

Ivory had halted as well, looking back at Razvan as if he'd communicated with her privately. Her long lashes hid her expression but she dropped her chin and shook her head. Razvan put his arm around her briefly as if comforting her.

"We can't just leave him," Skyler protested.

"You knew from the beginning we could lose the wolves," Dimitri said, his tone gentle, but brooking no argument. "You can't sacrifice your life hunting a stray. This fog is dangerous. We've got to go."

"He'll come back. He always strays too far, but he comes back," Skyler said, leaning into Dimitri for a moment. "I've reprimanded him over and over but he just seems to get lost when he runs free, meaning he loses track of time and what he's supposed to be doing."

Insects poured out of the ground, running ahead of the fog as it continued to move toward the clearing. Ants, termites, beetles, every insect that sought refuge in the ground or fallen trees, turned the vegetation into a living carpet,

Dimitri tugged at Skyler's hand. "We're leaving *now*."

Skyler hesitated. "Dimitri, the air feels heavier, almost as if there is a dark spell hidden with the fog." She looked at her birth father. "Do you feel it?"

Razvan nodded. "Nature has been twisted and bent to another's desire."

"But more," Skyler speculated. "It's more than that. It's darker. Evil. As if there are things wrought within the fog that come from another realm."

Dimitri held up his hand for silence. He kept catching small murmurs, sounds, yet the others clearly couldn't hear. He shook his head and took two steps back as the fog inched closer.

Frost came running from the direction Ivory and Razvan had come at a frantic pace, eyes a little wild. Dimitri held his arms out and the errant wolf leapt for the safety of his alpha's back.

"There's something in the fog, moving, talking. I can hear it," Dimitri told the others. "It's not only climbing the trees, but as it gets closer to the edge of the forest it's building height on the ground as well. Let's get back to the clearing and help get everyone out of there."

Gregori, get the prince to safety. There is something out here beyond my knowledge, but there is no doubt it is dangerous. Whatever it is, it's heading your way. It's moving slow, but hidden within there is something evil. Dimitri sent the warning ahead of them, tasking Gregori with getting their prince to safety.

Gregori Daratrazanoff sighed heavily. Mikhail had attended the honor ceremony for Arno and his son as any good diplomat would. The Lycans insisted, in spite of all the warnings, that the fallen council member had to have a full ceremony, and be sent off with honor. Instead of holding the funeral the following rising, Rolf had insisted on preparing the ground and waiting three days and nights. No amount of arguing had changed his mind.

"You heard Dimitri. I have to get you out of here, Mikhail. Dimitri is warning Zev and he'll do his best to persuade the Lycans to leave, but you can't take the chance."

"Do you know how many times you say that to me?" Mikhail asked with a small sigh.

"You've given your speech and paid your respects," Gregori said. "Already the children were attacked. Had Zev not been Dark Blood, we could have lost them. Our last defense is you. You know that. Better to protect our children than to stay and protect the Lycans when they're insisting on staying. If things get bad here, we can send reinforcements."

"What is he up to, this Xaviero? Why would he suddenly reveal himself to all of us? The brothers hid among our different species and did their damage in secret. What is so important that they keep coming at us? Clearly Lycans and Carpathians are not going to go to war with one another. He can't wipe us out, not here. We're spread out over the world. We need the answer to this, Gregori. Whatever Xaviero wants is too important for us not to know about it."

Mikhail rose with obvious reluctance. He signaled Zev over to them. "Dimitri has warned you?"

Zev took a deep breath and let it out, nodding his head. There were very few times when he had clashed with Rolf, head of the Lycan council, but Rolf had insisted on sending off Arno and his son with honor. He insisted on waiting the prescribed three days so those far away could make the journey. That just gave Xaviero all the more time to prepare. After the attack on the children, Zev was absolutely certain Xaviero would strike at the service. He'd been right. He hated being right.

"Yes. I've talked to Rolf numerous times and he refuses to listen. I tried to tell Rolf it wasn't safe for anyone to be here, but he pointed out the large number of Lycans and Carpathians who have come to pay their respects He thinks there is an army here and no need to leave."

"Perhaps if I spoke to him again," Mikhail offered. He had already don so once, after their children had been attacked. Clearly Xaviero was not going to stop until he reached his goal—whatever that was.

Zev shook his head. "This ceremony is ingrained deep in our culture. It's important to all Lycans and especially Rolf. He is head of the council. Arno is a fallen council member, murdered by an enemy. He will stay here alone if necessary."

From the moment he'd entered the clearing, Zev had known something was terribly wrong. The feeling in the very soil bothered him. The air. He felt uneasy and trapped. He'd gone to Rolf immediately and tried to get him to at least change the location of the ceremony, but the ground had been purified and the pyre already built.

Zev had argued that the feeling in his gut was never wrong and had kept him alive all these long years—more, that he had expected Xaviero to strike at them. Rolf had actually turned his back on Zev and stormed away, refusing to listen to reason.

"Still, I have to try," Mikhail said, ignoring Gregori's slashing silver eyes.

He made his way through the crowd of Lycans to reach the head of the council. A man, one of many who had come that Mikhail had never seen before, was speaking from the podium. He wore a long brown robe with a hood and spoke in a soft, carrying tone. He looked grief-stricken as he spoke of Arno and the fallen elite hunter. Not only did he look devastated, but he projected such sorrow that even Mikhail felt desolate.

He nearly turned back, aware that the Lycans were all grieving for the much-beloved council member and his son, but Gregori was waiting, arms folded across his chest, his silver gaze impossible to ignore. Rolf rose reluctantly when Mikhail gestured to him and they found a small space off to one side.

"Rolf." Mikhail pitched his voice low. "We're getting reports of trouble heading this way. The consensus from our most experienced warriors is that we should leave immediately. I agree with their assessment. We need to start getting everyone to safety."

Swift annoyance crossed Rolf's face and he glanced over at Zev, as if the elite hunter had been the one to irritate him. His features settled into his usual calm mask when he looked back at the prince of the Carpathian people.

"Zev had no right to ask you to come and talk to me," he said, his teeth snapping together, revealing the wolf lurking close to the surface.

"He didn't ask me," Mikhail countered. "My security people did. Zev explained that this ceremony was important to the Lycans and I respect that. I respected Arno. But you and I are responsible for our people, and I thought you would want to know that time is of the essence. We have to get everyone to safety."

Rolf's mouth tightened. "Perhaps you've never gone into war zones, but I have many times during my career as a council member for my people. We accept the risks."

"For yourself," Mikhail agreed. "But for so many others? Look at the number of Lycans who have come from so many places to pay their respects. They're in jeopardy as well."

"Arno served these people for well over a hundred years. He deserves their respect and the honor of their presence. He was a highly decorated and revered member of the Sacred Circle. He believed in the old ways and codes of honor. This was his way. This is his belief. I will not dishonor him because I am afraid for my life," Rolf said firmly. "Nor will any Lycan. I do appreciate you coming, but this is a Lycan matter and you and your people must do as you see fit. We will stay." He whirled around and stormed back to his place in the front of the Lycan packs, his shoulders square and his jaw set stubbornly.

Mikhail glanced at Gregori. There was no getting around the Lycan council leader. He had made up his mind and there would be no changing it. Rolf was not only grief-stricken; he was weighed down with guilt.

"Put the word out to our people. There is trouble coming and we're leaving."

"Zev isn't going to leave the Lycans," Gregori said. "He's been their protection for years and it won't matter that Rolf is being stubborn about this. Zev was born into their culture and, although from a protection standpoint he'd like to get them all out of here, he understands. His brothers will stand with him. Ivory and Razvan as well."

Mikhail nodded. "I would expect nothing less. If it wasn't for my responsibilities to our people, I'd stand with them as well. Xavier nearly pushed our species into extinction. Xayvion has nearly done so with the Jaguar race. Xaviero is determined to ruin the Lycans. They have to be stopped."

Gregori inched Mikhail away from the Lycans. Two more council members had come to honor Arno and with them, their guards. Leaders or representatives of many other packs had arrived as well. Gregori used the common Carpathian path to warn their warriors of the coming danger Dimitri and Skyler had observed in the forest.

Mikhail and Gregori made their way to Zev. Mikhail shook his head sadly when Zev raised an eyebrow. He stepped forward and gripped Zev's forearms in the traditional way of Carpathian warriors. He was pleased when Zev instinctively gripped his. "You are prepared?"

Zev nodded slowly. "We've tried to think of everything that might be thrown at us. I think we're as prepared as we can be." Who could ever be fully prepared for mage magic? Not just any mage, but a High Mage?

The sense of urgency in him was growing. He wanted Mikhail gone, far away from the clearing and the fog Dimitri had warned him of. If nearly all Carpathians were wiped out, there would be hope as long as Mikhail lived. Mikhail might chafe the bonds that held him prisoner of his people occasionally, but he knew his duties and Zev could see that he wouldn't argue with either him or Gregori. He was leaving.

Can you hear them? That's not just our wolves, Zev, that's the wild ones. I've sent them away.

I hear. The ceremony has started. What is happening out there? Zev stayed calm. Panic caused one to lose the ability to think. He was responsible for the council members, their Lycan guards and all the alphas and representatives that had come from many of the packs.

He motioned to his elite hunters. Daciana's eyes were swollen and red, something he'd never witnessed in the long years they'd been together. He couldn't blame her. Losing Arnau was wrenching and adding his father Arno's death to the mix only added to the sorrow—and guilt.

The fog here is unnatural and not made by any Carpathian, Dimitri reported, using the common Carpathian path. *It has a foul feel to it. Skyler says she detects darker spell within the mist. All wildlife, including birds are retreating from it. Insects are pouring out of the ground.*

Smoke rose in the air, the purifying leaves burning white and giving off the sweet odor of jasmine in preparation for the burning of the bodies. Arno and Arnau lay within the flowers and branches of the funeral pyre, high up where their spirits would have an easy ascension.

Daciana, Makoce and Lykaon joined him.

"We're going to be attacked. Rolf and the others won't listen to anything I say. They're insisting on completing the ceremony. Be ready. Stay close to the council members. Any other guards you really trust, warn, and get them to surround the council."

They didn't ask questions. He'd known they wouldn't. He was alpha of their pack and his word was law. They nodded and moved into the crowd surrounding the ceremonial pyre.

Branislava reached out to him, settling her fingers around his wrist as he came up to her. "He's here, Zev," she whispered, leaning into him. "I feel his presence."

Just her light touch made him feel as if he had a home. A haven. She had a way of looking at him that made the world right, even when everything around them seemed to be falling apart.

"We knew he would come, Branka, if for no other purpose than to see the grief his handiwork caused. We knew he wouldn't be able to help himself."

Branislava looked around at the precautions and intricate safeguards the Carpathians had used to protect the Lycans as they gathered for the service. "He's here for a purpose. Not just to thumb his nose and prove his superiority. I know you feel it, too. And now Dimitri has found the mist. It will come creeping out of the forest surrounding us, and there are foul things he could conjure up that can kill."

"You know him better than anyone else, Branislava. You've done a study of these three mages for centuries when no one else knew of their existence. You're our authority. Tell me what you think he's going to do."

He had faith in her ability to defeat Xaviero. She was every bit as skilled and she had the advantage. She'd seen him cast, knew his every spell, when he had never considered her a threat and hadn't known the three mages were educating a very bright pupil. *She* just had to believe in herself. He knew she had to overcome the terror instilled in her from her birth.

Branislava chewed nervously on her lower lip. "He'll want to get as close to the funeral pyre as possible. He would most likely want to give the talk . . ." She trailed off, her eyes meeting Zev's. She shook her head hastily. "But he wouldn't dare."

"It's *exactly* what he'd do," Zev countered. "Can you imagine how smug he would be if he got away with it? Standing in front of Carpathian and Lycan alike and giving what essentially would be a eulogy for the two men he murdered? He wouldn't need to exact revenge—that alone would reaffirm his superiority."

Dimitri, how fast is the fog moving toward us? It was imperative to know Xaviero's timetable. Zev needed to clear out the civilians and prepare the available warriors for battle.

It's building very slowly. And thick. And very, very foul.

Branislava glanced nervously toward the surrounding forest. *That's not good. I don't like that insects are pouring out of the ground, either. He's up to something, something much deadlier than we first thought.*

The fog started about a foot off the ground and is now winding up to the top of the trees like thick snakes, Skyler added.

Stay away from it, Branislava advised. *Don't let it touch your skin. And whatever you do, don't get inside of it.*

I see glowing eyes. Red. Yellow. And we're beginning to hear voices—or I am, Dimitri said. *Skyler feels things moving, but she hasn't heard anything yet.*

Zev's heart seemed to skip a beat. *His army. The Sange rau. We knew he was building an army. Dimitri can feel them because he's mixed blood as well. Xaviero has an army of Sange rau and hellhounds waiting to annihilate us.*

But if that were the case, why aren't they here already? Branislava asked. *Why send the fog. We're in the middle of a clearing.*

Zev frowned. *He's holding them back. To what purpose?* he mused aloud, inviting the others to speculate. *Why is he taking the chance that we might discover them before he unleashes them on us?*

"Who from the Sacred Circle was scheduled to give a talk?" Branislava asked, whipping around to look toward the funeral pyre.

"Roberto Hans," Zev answered slowly, avoiding looking too hard at the Lycan considered one of the greatest leaders of the Sacred Circle. "He's speaking now."

Zev recognized him as one of the more prominent members of the Sacred Circle. Roberto Hans had been speaking with Rolf just moments earlier. The face and body appeared to be Roberto's, along with the deep voice, yet to Zev's trained ear, there was a lack of depth to the sound. Something missing. As if the voice was a recording and not the real thing.

There was no way to prove he was right, but still, he was certain. Zev recalled that Roberto and the Lycan known as Rannalufr had been good friends. Had Xaviero, disguised as Rannalufr, approached Roberto just to talk about the death of their old friend Arno, Roberto would have allowed him in without hesitation.

Branislava watched Zev move away, back toward the Lycans crowded so closely around the funeral pyre. She didn't like that they were so close to Xaviero—if that was the High Mage—and she was fairly certain it was. She didn't want to keep staring at him, afraid he would realize they were on to him. She moved to get into a better position to aid Zev when a peculiar odor drifted from the crowd, just the faintest of smells, but she caught it and stiffened, stopping instantly.

Zev. Branislava's voice quivered, but she couldn't help it. *That thought of both mages so close in such a large crowd was utterly terrifying. I think both of them are here. Xayvion as well as Xaviero. I caught a whiff of incense, a powerful combination of herbs that are used to send a spirit along on his journey. Just a small passing scent, but Xayvion favored spells where he used incense to aid him. Whatever they're doing, I think they plan to do it right here.*

Perhaps someone else used this incense in the hopes of sending Arno and Arnau on a safe journey.

It wasn't just that, Zev. It was a combination of scents. Xavier was using it in the laboratory when he stabbed Xaviero. Her heart began to pound as she pulled up the memory. *There was a thick fog in the lab that night. I couldn't see Xaviero's body once it fell to the floor. I saw Xavier grab his feet and pull him out of the lab, but I couldn't see his actual body because the mist was too thick, lying about a foot above the floor.*

Branka, listen to me. You can do this. Figure this out. No matter what happens, you have to stay focused on what you believe is Xaviero's ultimate goal.

She could see Zev working his way toward the front and Fen on the other side of the crowd doing the same thing. Zev's calm voice always steadied her. He had a way of looking and speaking with such a composed, sure manner, that everything in her settled. Not this time. This time she was fairly certain she knew what Xaviero and Xayvion were up to.

They are going to trade the spirit of the living for the spirit of the dead. That's why I smelled the combination of incenses on Xayvion as he moved through the crowd. They have a live body here, one they want to put Xavier's spirit into. They need deaths, souls and spirits wailing. The more the better. They intend to open the gates of hell.

There was a small silence. She could feel Zev around her. In her mind. As always, he was as steady as a rock. He wasn't in a panic as she was. Perhaps because he didn't know how bad it was going to get.

Dimitri, Skyler, Ivory and Razvan burst from the forest, running toward them, drawing her attention. Directly behind them, a mottled snake slithered up a particularly large tree. When it was halfway up the trunk, it reared back and struck the tree, sinking its teeth deep. Color ran up the bark, changing it from the normal darkish gray to a sickly white. The color spread to the branches and then to the leaves.

Branislava gasped and turned to look behind her. Another tree directly across from the first one, on the other side of the clearing, was lit up in the same ghostly way. She knew without looking that there would be one tree directly across from the ceremonial pyre and two more lit above it, forming an inverted pentagram.

Several Lycans began to turn their heads away from the funeral pyre, uneasy, feeling the evil dread spreading throughout the clearing. The elite hunters moved in closer to better protect the council members. *They've started, Zev. You have to get to their sacrificial victim. He'll be somewhere close to the pyre. They'll want his body, so they'll have to drive his spirit out at the precise moment the gates open so they can make the exchange. They'll slay as many as possible to accomplish their goal.*

Fog leaked through the trees into the opening surrounding the clearing, a thick yellowish-gray vapor. Tentacles swirled up the trees, climbing toward the sky. The ground fogbank was high, a good six feet or more, like a great wall moving toward them, although still slow. Branislava couldn't help herself. She looked toward the speaker standing on the raised podium. His eyes met hers. She would recognize that malevolent, evil stare anywhere.

Xaviero. He threw back his hood, extending his arms wide as if in supplication, just as Zev fired a shot at him.

The bullet flew true, speeding directly at Xaviero's forehead, right between his eyes. Xaviero smiled, a malicious, vile, spiteful promise of pure glee.

In her shared mind with Zev, Branislava screamed in alarm. *Zev, duck, hit the ground.* She tore her gaze from Xaviero's and frantically chanted a protection spell.

That made of lead,
Fired to kill,
I remove your force,
Now shall you be stilled.

The bullet hit some kind of barrier, stopping just between Xaviero's eyes, hovering there for a moment and then reversing, to streak through the air straight at the shooter. Zev hit the ground and rolled, the bullet obeying Branislava's order at the last moment, falling harmlessly to earth.

Xaviero saluted her with a small bow, his smile widening until he looked almost grotesque, an unholy monster from another realm. She realized he'd spent time in the very place Xavier was trapped. The three brothers had prepared for the inevitable moment when one of them was killed.

Zev, find his sacrifice. Do it fast, all hell's about to break loose. She needed help fast. *No matter what happens, keep them off of us. Tatijana, Skyler, Ivory. I need you now. We're in the battle of our lives. Xaviero and Xayvion will strike at us. We're the only ones able to stop them. You have to protect us. We'll need time to counter their spells.*

The spell of the inverted pentagram had closed the clearing off from all help. She was certain no one could get in and no one could get out. The fog winding up the trees and into the sky, coming together in a dense bank above their heads, was all about preventing Carpathians from using storms, or taking to the skies.

The three brothers had a long time to perfect their ambush and they knew how each species fought. No doubt they had prepared for every eventuality. Zev had been correct in saying three days was too long to give the mages—not when they'd been preparing for centuries.

The fogbank crept out of the forest, surrounding the clearing like a great army. She could see eyes glowing, both red and yellow.

Hellhounds, Zev. He's got hellhounds coming at us.

They emerged out of the fog. Snarling. Slobbering. Dripping great strings of venom from their muzzles. Lips were drawn back, revealing large razor-sharp teeth. Their heads were massive and many of them had two heads. One had three. Their bodies were the size of ponies, thick and roped with muscle. Black fur appeared spiked and bristling, as if one could get seriously wounded touching them. As they approached slowly, the ground beneath them blackened, the grass withering and curling under each step. Behind each of the hounds was a man, or rather a creature, half man, half wolf.

Sange rau. Branislava breathed the name into his mind.

This was the Lycans' worst nightmare—an army of *Sange rau*—mixed bloods, faster, stronger and more intelligent than everyone else.

Take down the barriers he's built, Zev said. *Don't think about anything else. We're prepared for hellhounds. We knew he had an army of Sange rau.*

His voice calmed her as it always did. He was matter-of-fact. There was no panic in him, no terror. She realized it was the trait that others relied on as well. Zev could truly face danger and not flinch. His mind was always working, always finding a way.

Someone screamed, a high-pitched voice of terror. Branislava swiveled around. The ground erupted, first with insects and right behind them, mutated red-striped toads with serrated teeth. Venom dripped down their chins. They snapped at the insects and as people shifted, the movement attracted their attention.

Toads began hopping onto the nearest warm body and injecting a par-alyzing venom into their victim as quickly as possible. Each time a toad sank its teeth into its prey, it emitted a loud croak, calling to the others. More leapt at the hapless targets, attaching themselves on calves and thighs, rip-ping away clothing to reach the flesh beneath. The accumulated poison brought their quarry crashing to the ground fairly quickly.

The moment their prey went down, dozens leapt on them, swarming over the top of them like in some macabre horror movie. Blood ran into the ground beneath them, but most of the victims were so weighed down by the toads, she couldn't see them, just the moving mounds of toads. To her shock, the toads appeared to be growing, or they were bloated from the repulsive feast.

Other Lycans tried to help their fallen friends, kicking at the slavering creatures and trying to yank up the paralyzed victims. Those injected with the toad venom could only stare up at their comrades, unable to move or talk or even scream as the toads began to devour them.

Tatijana, you have to take care of those toads, Zev commanded. *Branka, get that barrier down and then get rid of the fog.*

She wanted to hiss at him in anger. Did he think she was a miracle worker? All around her was complete chaos, Carpathians pouring hyssop oil over them, turning, taking careful aim and firing oil-dipped arrows at the hellhounds.

"Pack leaders, take your points and defend your positions," Zev ordered as he ran.

Branislava saw him disappear behind the smoking pyre. The smoke was no longer white and clean-scented. More smoke rose toward the overhead bank of fog, rushing up to the sky to gather in one spot, staining the yellow-gray vapor a dark, malevolent shade of black. Flames licked at the wood and flowers, burning the first layer of the pyre and igniting the logs and branches holding the bodies of Arno and Arnau.

Her heart pounded at the thought of Zev so close to Xaviero. The mage was locked in a circle of protection and she didn't yet know where his brother was. But if they were unlocking the gates of hell, he would be forming a triangle with his brother and the ceremonial pyre where their sacrifice would be—and Zev was running straight into their powerful web.

She forced herself to block out the screams and the fighting as well as the terrible baying and howls of the hounds. She couldn't even look at the toads and their victims. Her job was to remove the five-pointed inverted pentagram. The massive zone the mages had created was the key to their power. Without it, they would be unable to open the gates and they couldn't exchange spirits and bodies.

Can you get rid of them, Tatijana? The toads? Can you destroy them?

I can figure out the toads, Bronnie, Tatijana assured her. *You just keep working on that.*

Tatijana moved back-to-back with her sister. She closed her eyes for a moment. Around her the noise was hideous with the cries of the injured and the gasps of the dying. She could hear the breath rattling in their bodies, as she had when she was a child watching her father and uncles performing their experiments on living species. She had to force her mind back to the present, focusing on countering the deadly mutated toads.

She knew the toads were a distraction from Xaviero's real plan. They needed dead bodies and chaos reigning. The more souls and spirits trapped within their web, the more power generated for the two High Mages to use. Still, the toads did their job, springing on legs and eventually pulling their prey down. They grew fatter and bloated, but still, they didn't stop, although their size began to slow them down.

She stood in the middle of the clearing and, lifting her hands, she began to weave a pattern in the air. As she began, she felt tearing at her leg and then a slow burn that began to make its way up her leg, running from nerve to nerve.

Dimitri kicked at the frog, tearing it from her body. The hateful creature took a large chunk of skin with it as it went flying across the clearing.

Tatijana didn't follow its path. The toads hopped close, ringing her. Targeting her. Dimitri, Skyler, Ivory and Razvan took up positions to protect her while she continued. Dimitri removed the poison from her body even as she worked.

Her voice was steady, pitched low, yet carrying through the clearing, the singsong notes adding to her power.

> *Creatures of earth,*
> *Warped in design,*
> *As your voices are raised,*
> *Let earth take your bite.*

The toads opened their mouths in protest. The serrated teeth fell to the ground with every note coming out of them. Each time they tried to call to the others to join them, more teeth spilled out. Venom ran freely into the soil.

That which is cold-blooded,
Dwelling beneath the soil,
I call to you, snake,
Come forth and clear this peril.

Snakes slithered from the holes in the ground where the toads had emerged and began hunting the vile, bloated creatures. The snakes were long, olive green, with yellow half-moons on either side of the neck. Dark bars ran along either side. The grass snake was considered by some to be a protector, not an aggressor. They struck fast. The toads were too bloated to move quickly, allowing the snakes to find them easily.

Tatijana heaved a sigh of relief and dropped her arms, grateful she had, at least, managed to cut down one threat. She heard Razvan grunt and looked up as a huge hound leapt on him, nearly crushing his chest, driving him over backward, taking him to the ground. Instantly wolves leapt from Ivory directly onto the massive beast, all soaked in hyssop oil, tearing at the hellhound's underbelly, biting its legs and throat. They were fast, but the beast was faster, dropping Razvan and turning to clamp its giant maw around the male wolf.

Razvan rolled, coming up under the hellhound, his knife slitting the beast's belly with the blade also soaked in the oil. The hound opened its teeth, allowing the wolf to drop to the ground. As Razvan rolled, more wolves leapt from his back to join the others tearing at the huge hound. The hyssop oil, more than the knife, the wolves or Razvan, began to take its toll on the hellish creature. It staggered as it tried to whip around, snapping in the air at the wolves.

Ivory took the blade of her knife, fiery hot, and pressed it into the teeth marks on Razvan, cauterizing the wound. He shot her an agonized glance and turned back to the hound lurching toward the wounded wolf, putting his body squarely between the hellhound and his wolf. Ivory fit an arrow into her crossbow, shooting the beast in the eye. She stepped closer as the slavering beast whirled around, snapping at the air, knocking into Razvan and sending his body tumbling into the fallen wolf. Ivory threw her knife, the one with the glowing red blade, and Razvan, from his position on the ground, slapped it against the bite on the wolf's body.

Farkas, one of Ivory's wolves, howled, adding his voice to the chaos of the terrible battle. Screams erupted near the ceremonial pyre. Tatijana swung her head to look. Xaviero held his arms wide and issued a command. Two Lycans walked in blind obedience into the leaping flames while a line formed behind them, its members waiting their turn.

Horror filled her. She felt Branislava reaching behind her and slowly closed her fingers around Tatijana's hand. She glanced over her shoulder to see that they were ringed, not only by hellhounds, but behind them *Sange rau*. Four of them.

Behind the wall of hellhounds and *Sange rau*, a robed figure stepped out. He threw back his hood and smiled grotesquely. She found herself staring at Xayvion.

20

Branislava whipped around, gripping Tatijana's hand. She barely allowed herself to see the hellhounds with their glowing eyes fixed on their small group, or the four *Sange rau* directly behind them. Her gaze was drawn straight to the flames shooting up to the sky.

Xaviero was collecting his souls, anguished beings unable to prevent themselves from obeying his command. He sent them to their slaughter, death by fire, a putrefying blend of incense he had mixed with poisonous tree branches hidden among the flowers and branches after the pyre had been built.

She was only partway through figuring out exactly what Xaviero had done to build his inverted pentagram. She couldn't do that and save people, and right now, feeding people into his fire to claim their souls was far too much for her to bear.

Branka, I can't stop them.

Zev came into view, rushing to shove the next two Lycans out of line. They went flying to the ground, landing a distance away, but both picked themselves up and simply went to the end of the line, falling into place in spite of Zev's interference.

Help me, tell me what to do.

These were his friends, some he'd known from birth. There was no countering any of the intricate spells as easily as Tatijana had done away with the toads. Each spell was wrapped in a layer and had to be peeled back like an onion. How did one stop a master?

Dimitri, Fen, I have to get to the fire right now. They were her biggest hope. Fen was fighting his way back to Tatijana, Skyler, Ivory and her, knowing they had to be protected while they tried to deal with Xaviero's hellish spells. She had to break free of the ring of hellhounds and *Sange rau* in order to aid those walking haplessly into the fire. *I'll try to clear a path, but it won't last more than a few seconds.*

Tatijana, Skyler and Ivory would have no choice but to counter Xayvion. He was obviously there to keep them busy and not allow them to interfere in any way with Xaviero and the ceremony he was conducting.

Branislava tried to drown out the sounds of the battle going on all around, the cries of the dying and horror-stricken as well as the sight of the hellhounds with their glowing eyes and slavering jaws. She couldn't think about the *Sange rau* directly behind the massive beasts. They were tall, broad-shouldered and savage, nearly impossible to kill; she needed Dimitri and Fen to run interference if she was to have a chance of getting past them.

Mask my energy so they have no idea I'm shifting. It would be tricky. The *Sange rau* as well as the Lycans could feel energy coming toward them. They had to time it just right. The hellhounds were already closing in, forcing the ring smaller.

Now, Dimitri responded.

Branislava leapt into the air, over the hellhounds, almost directly in the path of one of the *Sange rau*, shifting into her dragon form. Branislava recognized Sandulf from Lyall's memories. The *Sange rau* was far faster than she anticipated, leaping after her, shifting into half-wolf, half-man form and hooking the dragon's belly with terrible claws, ripping to try to eviscerate the dragon.

Great drops of blood rained down on the hellhounds so that for a moment they paused in their attack on those gathered in the tight circle. They abandoned their stalking to leap into the air, trying to get to the dragon and help bring it down. The fresh blood maddened them so even the commands of Sandulf did no good.

Dimitri shifted into half-man, half-wolf, slamming into Sandulf claw-ing at the dragon, attempting to drag it to earth. They came together with bone-shaking force, so hard Dimitri knocked the mixed blood from the dragon, allowing her to rise just enough to escape the hellhounds' attack. He landed on the back of one beast while Sandulf fell on the neck between the two giant heads of a two-headed hound.

Dimitri, covered in hyssop oil, burned the back and fur so that the pain-maddened hound shrieked in fury, snapping at everything in sight, includ-ing other hellhounds. Rolling, Dimitri straddled the monster and jammed an arrow into one wicked yellow eye, using the combination of his mixed blood to penetrate to the brain.

Assaulted by the neighboring hound biting repeatedly at it and having a large, heavy man hit between its heads, the two-headed beast lowered its heads, looking malevolently left and right and sank teeth into the two hell-hounds beside it. Dimitri managed to jam a second arrow into the eye of the monster he rode. The hound shuddered, took two steps and dropped.

Sandulf got up slowly and faced Dimitri, wiping his hand across his mouth, looking down at the blood smeared on his fingers. He spit contemp-tuously. He was a brute of a man, much like his uncle, Randall, but where Randall was gentle and kind, Sandulf enjoyed the power of his build. His eyes glittered with rage as he rushed Dimitri.

Dimitri didn't move, waiting, a matador meeting the rush of bull. At the last possible moment he sidestepped, plunging the silver stake deep, using the momentum of both their attacks to push through the chest wall to penetrate the heart. He whirled around as he drew his sword and severed the head from the shoulders.

Branislava's dragon rose just enough to get out of the way of the hounds, spun and aimed her tail at the hounds and *Sange rau* surrounding the others. With a vicious slap, she sent them all tumbling away from Skyler, Tatijana and Ivory. She couldn't stay and protect them, not with Zev and the Lycans in such trouble. She left them, sending up a prayer that Dimitri, Fen and Razvan could protect them.

Zev continued to shove Lycans out of line, forcing them to go to the back and wait for their turn to walk into the fire. He was hot and sweaty and furious. He couldn't wake any of them, no matter how hard he tried. It was a difficult and tiring business. Just a few feet from him was Xaviero, his hands moving in an intricate pattern as he faced the fire, feeding it with live fuel in order to perform the task he desired. He was close, yet Zev couldn't touch him, not with the protective circle around him.

The fire dragon plopped herself down at the edge of the large fire now shooting halfway to the thick fog overhead. Billowing black smoke ran along the ceiling, turning the fog charcoal in color. The dragon lifted her wedge-shaped head and poured a steady stream of fire around the protection circle, lighting the ground so that flames shot up around Xaviero, ringing him. The blaze couldn't touch him, but it would make him uncomfortable and unable to see what was happening around him. More, it would force him to stop what he was doing, just as she had done while trying to bring down the inverted pentagram, to counter her moves.

She wouldn't be able to stay long in the fire, preventing the Lycans from throwing themselves into the inferno, so she had to neutralize Xaviero's spell. She knew Xaviero very well, she had studied him carefully. Even if he'd made a thousand more spells in the intervening years, his style was still the same—arrogant and self-serving.

Zev did his best to turn each of the Lycans away from the fire. They seemed empty bodies, their spirits gone, although he could see the horror in their eyes as they walked into the flames. He'd lost four only, but he'd had to be aggressive, even using his fists to knock them to the ground. Shoving hadn't been enough with the more determined—or those deep under Xaviero's command.

Hurry, Branka. They're moving around to the other side.

He knew she was hurrying, doing her best. She had to be uncomfortable there in the fire, even in her dragon form, but these were real men and women just walking calmly under the High Mage's command into the conflagration. *On some level, they know what they're doing. Xaviero has removed their free will, but they can see what's coming and have no way to stop it.*

Branislava heard the anguish in his voice. It was like Xaviero to do such a thing. It wasn't enough for him to sacrifice all the Lycans to his nefarious plan; he had to make certain they suffered emotionally and mentally. She would bet her last dollar they suffered physically as well, they just couldn't cry out.

Choices have been taken,
No will is left to see,
I call to that which is hidden deep inside of thee.
I call to the fire of passion,
I call to the spirit within,
Break these bonds that bend,
Allowing free will to reign again.

The Lycans returned to themselves with a terrible war cry, spinning around, away from the fire and looking with hatred and anger toward Xaviero. Eight of the warriors peeled off to surround the circle of protection.

No! Zev, you must stop them. They can't attack him.

Terrified of what the High Mage could do with the angry wolves, twisting their hatred and anger to his purpose, she shifted from her dragon form, leaping away from the flames and running to intercept, her hands already sketching a pattern in the air as she tried to place a holding spell on the Lycan warriors.

Time that is movement,
Root them,
Hold each within their place,
Let all now be frozen so no further harm may take place.

Already it was far too late for the fastest and strongest of the Lycans. Four leapt through the flames surrounding the hated mage and struck the protection barrier. One tried for the back of Xaviero's neck, hoping to use his wolf to sever the spinal cord. Two others closed in from both sides, and the last chose a frontal attack, going for the throat.

The flames surrounding the protection circle disappeared in a blue puff. Xaviero caught the Lycan coming at him, snapped his neck and threw him casually into the flames several feet away. He smiled at Branislava as he did so, that evil, contemptuous smirk she remembered from long ago. She would never forget the macabre showing of his teeth and his cold, dead eyes that glowed with a kind of glee when he hurt others.

The Lycan leaping at his neck was caught in the air, held prisoner by burning runes and then, casually, with his unholy sneer, the mage reached up, caught the Lycan by the neck and tossed him after the first one into the blaze.

Both Lycans screamed as they caught fire, whirling around trying to put out the flames running over their bodies. As if they'd been coated in an accelerant, the fire burned right through them, as they screamed and wailed, the sound never to be forgotten.

The last two warriors hit the protective circle, and runes leapt over their bodies, running up their legs and hips, to their torsos and around to their backs, climbing higher and higher until they reached their necks. Both men in their Lycan form put clawed hands up to their throats, their eyes going wide, seeming almost to pop out of their heads as they fought for air. It was a slow, cruel strangulation and all who watched were helpless to do anything at all. The two men, as if they were doing a ghoulish ballet fell to the ground in slow motion and lay at the mage's feet.

Around them, the battle blazed between Carpathians and the Lycans led by Daciana, Makoce and Lykaon and the hellhounds and *Sange rau* army the mages had created. Still, in that moment, it seemed as if there was only Xaviero and Branislava staring at each another.

Branislava moistened her lips and waved her hand to restore the Lycans' abilities to move. "He's baiting all of you. You can't defeat him," she said aloud. "You can't. Join the others in fighting off his army and leave him to me." She forced absolute confidence into her voice, the confidence Zev instilled in her. His belief in her overcame her childhood terror of this man.

Eyes darkened with anger, the mage stared at Branislava, a clear warning that he would retaliate if she tried anything at all.

Zev took a step toward the mage, drawing his attention. Branislava shook her head, but said nothing. Zev wasn't a man who fought battles with anger or made impetuous moves. He'd deliberately caught the eye of the mage to give her time to get back to taking down the barrier and removing Xaviero's inverted pentagram and the unholy fog.

Staring at Zev, the mage slipped his hands into the pockets of his robe and took out two very benign-looking pebbles. They were about the size of a man's eye and smooth as if they'd been polished over and over. With slow deliberation, Xaviero opened his hands, allowing the pebbles to slip out of his palms and drop onto the furred chest of the two dead Lycans at his feet. He never once looked down to see if his aim was true. He only stared at Zev with his sneer of absolute contempt.

Zev could see that the pebbles landed directly over the hearts of both Lycans. There was no bouncing or sliding off the thick mats of fur. The pebble blazed into a curious blue-purple flame and sank into the chests of the Lycans. His breath caught in his throat as the two dead warriors spasmed. Convulsed. Began to grow. Where there had been fur, great spikes burst through skin, covering back, chest, arms and even legs. The muzzles expanded to accommodate a second row of serrated teeth. The two creatures stood up on their legs, claws growing until they were twice the size of a grizzly bear's.

Zev sighed and looked around at the Lycans staring in disbelief. There was little of the two men they knew recognizable under the monstrous builds. "I'll need Fen and Dimitri here to help me deal with porcupine boys," he said in a carrying voice, going for humor when it appeared they were all doomed.

A few of the pack leaders smiled. He signaled to Branislava to move back away from the fire and into the circle of Lycans.

"You must protect the women. More than anything else that matters. You know how to kill the hellhounds, and you must deal in packs with the *Sange rau*. There're more of us than them. Mob them if you have to, but take them down. And protect the women. They have to deal with the mages."

Branka, you have to break his circle of power. I haven't been able to find his sacrifice as of yet. I'm drawn to the other side of the fire. I'm certain that's where he's kept, but Xaviero keeps throwing things at me I can't ignore.

He'll go back to work once he's satisfied that you're occupied with the giant porcupines. I'll see what I can do.

No, it's more important that you figure out how to bring down the inverted pentagram and the fog barrier. I can sense Mikhail and Gregori with reinforcements on the other side, but they can't get in.

The large monsters Xaviero had created shook themselves, and then turned black vacant eyes on not Zev, but Branislava. Clearly the mage knew which of them his greatest enemy was.

Get out of here, Branka. Right now. Stay inside that circle and get back where the Carpathians can help protect you.

Somehow, Zev, you have to retrieve the pebbles from their chests. Nothing else will actually kill them. The pebbles give them life.

Got it. Now go. And be safe.

Zev needed to keep his attention on the porcupines. Each took a shuddering step as if testing their new body to see how it worked. The first one stepped out of the circle of protection with one leg, and Zev, using his mixed blood speed, whirled forward and severed the limb with blurring speed, gliding out of reach in one continuous movement.

The porcupine howled and tipped forward, a slow ponderous fall as black blood poured into the ground around him. To Zev's disgust the creature licked at the blood and then tried to get to his one remaining knee.

Zev whirled in close a second time, coming in from above at the last moment. His sword flashed, severing the head as he continued his trajectory, landing a few feet away in a crouch. The head bounced and rolled, spilling more of the black blood across the field. Relief swept through him. It was a delaying tactic, but as tactics went, the porcupine wasn't the worse thing on the battlefield. Branislava hadn't considered that Xaviero wanted to delay them as well.

"Zev, what the hell?" Fen was beside him.

Dimitri took up position on the other side. All three stared in a kind of appalled fascination at the severed parts of the fallen creature. The leg shook and shuddered. The body did the same. The head elongated grotesquely.

"I don't think cutting them up is a really good idea," Fen said. There was the faintest humor in his voice. "We need a different plan."

Zev, maybe I can help, Branislava said, terror in her voice again.

He's targeting you. Get out of his sight. I want you safe, Branka, you're our hope to get out of this mess.

She winced at the lash of pure authority in his voice. He was impossible to ignore when he spoke like that. She knew he commanded armies, and right now, both Carpathian and Lycan alike were under his orders. He commanded the battlefield like a general and clearly knew what he was doing. It was just that he didn't know about mages—*these* mages—as she did. She couldn't help but be afraid for him.

Still, she wasn't going to argue in the middle of a battle and distract him from the three new porcupines coming at him. Or the second original porcupine lumbering out of the circle of protection. Already, Xaviero was back to ignoring them, his arms wide, facing the fire, his features settling into lines of concentration.

Zev muttered under his breath, wishing he knew a few incantations. "We have to know which one of the new ones was the torso. Branka says we need to retrieve the pebbles, that, by the way, turned into blue flames before they entered their bodies. So you know, this is going to be easy."

Dimitri sent him a little smirk. "It always is, isn't it?"

"They don't move as fast as his hellhounds, or the *Sange rau*," Fen pointed out with a small frown. "So what is it that is lethal about them, other than teeth and claws?"

"If they look like a porcupine," Zev said, with a small grin. "You might consider that their quills could be dangerous. All those sharp spikes? Just a guess."

Fen shot him a look. The four porcupines lumbered closer, attempting to surround the three hunters. "They look exactly alike. Which one has the pebble we're looking for?"

"The one directly facing you, Fen, is the one who split into threes, but that particular one with the strange-looking ridges was the torso," Zev said. "Be careful about severing parts. We don't want any more to pop up. I'm assuming, and that could get us all killed, that if we get the two pebbles the other two new ones will fall."

"Let's hope," Fen said, and leapt straight into the air, above the porcupine in front of him.

As if the movement had triggered them into violence, all four of the large Lycans turned puppets, shot out deadly quills. They were much like arrows although streamlined and tipped with venom. The three hunters could see the venom glistening on the tops, which meant the bodies of the porcupines produced the venom and it ran through the hollow quill to the tip.

The only thing that saved Zev and Dimitri from being covered in poisonous quills was their mixed blood speed. Both leapt into the air, although Zev felt the burn as one of the quills passed through his ankle. Hot and ugly pain ripped through him like a freight train, stealing his breath.

"Push the poison out through your pores," Dimitri instructed, his eyes on his brother.

As Fen dropped from his leap in the air, he came down on the porcupine Zev had pointed out as the one Xaviero had released his pebble into. His legs wrapped around the neck of the beast, the only spot that wasn't covered with quills. He drove the huge Lycan puppet nearly into the ground with the velocity of his attack, so that the porcupine couldn't move, his legs trapped in the dirt.

Fen plunged his knife into the chest of the beast, following the path with his fist, swearing in his native language as venom burned through his flesh, but his fingers managed to find the small pebble. He snatched at it, dragging it into his palm, even as the beast attacked him, ripping at his arms and shoulders with great, tearing claws. He held on to his prize with tenacity, ignoring what was happening to his body while he extracted the pebble.

Two of the porcupines rushed to help, but their footwork was clumsy, and Dimitri managed to slow them down by taking their legs out from under them. Fen pushed off the porcupine's head, the pebble in his hand. It was surprisingly clean and smooth, cool when it should have been covered in blood and warm.

Branka, what do we do with the pebble once we have it? They're still alive and coming at us, Zev said.

He didn't like Fen's apparent fascination with the small round stone, either. Rather than hurling the thing away, as instinct might demand and running from the creatures bearing down on him, Fen stood staring at the pebble as if mesmerized.

Use a cloth to touch it. Don't use skin.

Now she told him. Zev ripped his shirt and took the pebble right out of Fen's hand, shoving him out of the path of one of the marauding porcupines. Fen blinked rapidly, frowned and looked at his torn arms with a kind of shock.

I've got it. What do I do with it? Already the other puppets were coming after him, ignoring both Fen and Dimitri. He was grateful he'd pushed the poison out of his system as Dimitri had instructed, something he'd never done before and would have come in handy in a few of the battles he'd been in.

Hurl it straight at Xaviero. Just like the time you shot at him. Aim between his eyes and don't miss.

He's inside a protective circle.

Exactly. His own magic will destroy the pebble.

"Get the other one and try not to touch it. If you do, you risk zombie land, although Fen looked pretty dreamy," Zev pointed out.

Dimitri used the same tactic as Fen had, leaping into the air, his legs scissoring around the puppet's neck, driving him down into the dirt to trap his legs while he slammed his knife inside the chest. He'd wrapped the inside of his fist with a piece of his shirt, and when he felt the small pebble, he used two fingers to scoop it into the middle of his palm.

The porcupine tore at him. Dimitri felt sorry for the creature, despite the pain it caused as it ripped at his arms and tried to embed quills into his skin. He'd once been a Lycan warrior, fierce and fast and loyal to his people. To do this to such a man was wrong.

"I'll give you the peace you deserve," he whispered softly as he ripped the pebble out of the Lycan's chest.

He leapt away from the creature, and sprinted to Zev's side. "What now?"

"We throw them at Xaviero's forehead. Aim right between his eyes and Branislava says not to miss. So don't miss," Zev cautioned. "Right after me. A one-two punch, so he has no time to counter."

Dimitri nodded. Zev hurtled the first pebble so hard it sang as it moved through the air. Dimitri followed suit, giving the small stone a voice as they whistled low all the way to the protective circle. Both stones hit the protective shell hard, aimed exactly for the middle of Xaviero's forehead. Blue flame burst from the protective shell, sputtered and then was gone. For a moment the ring around the mage lit up and he stumbled back as if hit with a great force.

Anger flared in his eyes as he glared at the three of them. His puppets collapsed on the battlefield. Zev sent him a little salute.

It's done, Branka. We're coming to you.

And all of you are all right?

A little beat up, but we're fine, he assured. *The Lycans he made into puppets are at rest.*

It was impossible for any soul dying there on the battlefield to escape. Xaviero had seen to that with his foul fog and the blackened, greedy smoke from his fire, but she didn't want to point that out to Zev. Branislava deliberately began to inch her way away from the roaring blaze, knowing the closer she was to Xaviero's center of power, the more it would interfere with hers. She had to be just as powerful in her own right—for good. Where there was evil, there was always good. Where there was darkness, one could find light. One didn't exist fully without the other.

Tatijana, are you all right?

Before she blocked out everything else, she needed to know the other three women could handle Xayvion.

Tatijana heard her sister as if she was far away, not merged in her mind. Her concentration was wholly on Xayvion. Already he had countered her spell, turning her wholesome and helpful garden snakes into venomous vipers, slithering around the field just waiting for a hapless Lycan or Carpathian to make a misstep.

> *To those that are filled with venom,*
> *A healing charm I apply,*
> *I call you forth with music, hear my healing rhyme.*
> *Each serpent I now call, return to what you were,*
> *Releasing that which would harm,*
> *Banishing that which is fear,*
> *Dissolve that which is poison,*
> *Let all that is venomous disappear.*

Xayvion's simply using delaying tactics, Ivory warned. *He's worked his way around until he's in the position needed to form a triangle with his brother and the fire.*

The three of us can drive him out of there, slow down his petty little spells, Skyler said. *He's playing with you, Tatijana. He doesn't care about the battle or actually doing anything but adding souls to the fire for Xaviero to open the gates.*

If we throw him off his game, Ivory added, *it will slow Xaviero down and give Branislava more of a chance to unravel the source of power.*

All three felt much safer with Dimitri, Fen and Zev close to fight off the lightning-fast *Sange rau,* but the packs taking their places had all trained in the event they ever came across such a creature in their lifetimes. Like the Carpathians, they used hyssop oil to cover themselves and coated their silver arrows and knives with it as well.

Tatijana tried to block out the fierce battle and the sometimes hot breath of a hellhound that managed to get too close.

"Let's try it," she murmured, and held out her hands to Skyler and Ivory.

They bent their heads as Ivory said a small prayer before they merged into one unit of power. Tatijana lifted her head and looked directly at Xayvion.

I call to the power of earth,
Mother who created us,
I call to the power of air,
Lend me your force.
I call to the power of water,
Protect me from that which can burn,
I call to the power of fire,
Bring forth through me, your explosive blast.

Xayvion hadn't been expecting them to attack him directly. The force hit him mid-center, folding him in half like a paper doll, lifting him up and flinging him across the field straight into the inferno Xaviero had fed the Lycans to. He screamed, spinning like a top, trying to gather enough wits to counter their spell. Even as he emerged, his robes singed and his white hair burned, Tatijana was ready for him.

Twist and turn, spin and churn,
Into this fog you must now turn,
Let what is within not be seen,
So that you wander sightless deep within.

Whatever was in the fog, the thickness of the black enveloping smoke, was no better for the mage than for the Carpathians or Lycans. They had released foul things into the dense barrier to aid them when the time came to sacrifice the souls Xaviero had ripped from the dead. He gathered them, keeping them in the smoke, pressed against the fog.

Xayvion felt angry spirits reaching for him, locking clawed, greedy fingers into his spirit in an attempt to drag him into the realm where they waited helplessly for Xaviero to send them into the realm of dark hopelessness.

Instantly he fought back, shocked at the strength of the women. Tatijana was no more than fodder—food to keep the three brothers alive. There was nothing there, no brain, no gifts, no skills. A stupid child to devour when hungry. How could she counter his moves and then become aggressive? He recognized Ivory. He had helped Xavier kidnap her for Draven's dark desire, that stupid boy, first in line to be prince before Mikhail, who had no idea of the power he could have wielded had he not had such an obsession with one woman. Xaviero had been the one aiding the vampire, chopping her maliciously into pieces and scattering her body across the meadow for the wolves to devour her. He had deliberately not killed her, knowing she would suffer horribly. If the wolves didn't eat her the sun would take her, and yet, there she was, adding her power to Tatijana's. The third woman was a stranger to him, but he could feel her touch, and he recognized it with a shock.

Xaviero, her child lives. You know who I mean. We killed her, didn't we? Xavier said she was dead, yet her child lives. This one is hers and Razvan's child as well. There was panic in him. He pushed it down to fight his way out of the smoke.

Kill them. Kill them all now! Xaviero ordered, fear shimmering in his voice in spite of himself.

Join your strength with mine, Xayvion insisted.

He waited until Xaviero turned from his appointed task and sent power flowing to him in a steady stream. Lifting his arms, he retaliated against the three women, but for the first time, he was afraid.

Giant worm underground,
I call you forth from your mound,
Encompass all, leave none behind,
So from your core our magic may be entwined.

The ground beneath Tatijana, Ivory and Skyler shifted ominously and then burst apart, as if it had been ripped in two and a giant sinkhole had formed. From the hole a giant worm burst into the open, serrated teeth catching all three women, driving them thirty feet into the air and then disappearing just as fast down the hole.

This worm is one of their pets, Ivory warned. *Don't fight. There are venom sacs everywhere, the poison preventing all of us from shifting. I mix this venom with a few other chemicals and coat my weapons with it to prevent vampires from shifting. Try to relax. Razvan will come,* she added with complete confidence. *We've fought them before.*

Branislava felt the instant Xaviero's power shifted and she struck at the first of the trees where he had attached his weave of black magic. He had used multiple layers, all foul and powerful, a testament to the fact that he'd worked on the inverted pentagram and barrier for years to create such a strong force. No, that was wrong. She felt the touch of each of the brothers. She recognized them separately now. As long as she could block out everything happening around her, she could concentrate on what the three brothers had done. And she was growing in confidence.

She had successfully, without drawing Xaviero's attention, taken off several of the layers. One by one. Peeling them back carefully. She felt as if he'd created a giant spider's web and she had to delicately remove the silken threads without warning the spider sitting there waiting for a feast.

Without his sustained power feeding the grid he'd created, she could work a little faster, although just as carefully. She was confident she could find a way to stop him.

I call to alder,
Battle witch,
Isa's calming treacherous ice,
Focus my will,
Hear my call,
Fox of the wood, it is our day to battle,
Move silently following this unknown path.
I call to that which is unseen,
Guide me through this web of darkness,
Crystalline essence light my way,
So that I may unbind that which has been bound.

The tree shivered. The sickening grayish white of the trunk and branches dulled. Branislava took a deep breath and pushed more power at the first of the five points. Tiny sparks leapt around the tree like dancing fireflies. She was wrapped in fire. In passion. There was no way to contain what or who she was. She'd been lucky that Zev was as passionate as she was, was able to take her fierce heat and wild cravings. She poured that same fire into her spells, using her love, not allowing hatred or fear into her craft.

Alder protect me as I pass from one form to another,
Fire, I call your spirit,
Be mindful of my call,
She who bleeds feeds forth your fires of life.
As a spider spins her web,
I now unweave this charm.
That which was woven in darkness,
I bring forth light's fire to encompass and disarm.

The tree's bark went from a sickly white to a darker, more natural hue. Branches and leaves took on a normal tone and the fog receded from the tree, driven back away from it by the glowing fireflies. The sparks danced read and orange, leaping about joyously through the limbs of the tree, and flickering through the leaves, bringing back life.

Xaviero threw back his head and roared with rage. Roared. The ground shook. Nearly everyone fell hard. The mage's arms shot out, encompassing the field. The air vibrated with his anger. Electricity crackled and snapped, sizzling like whips overhead. The fire leapt, flames roaring.

"Feast, my pets. Kill them. Kill them all. Tear apart the woman. Devour her and leave nothing behind. Feast. Kill. Devour."

The hellhounds sprang on the Lycans between them and Branislava. The hellhounds leapt through the air to land on the Lycans and Carpathians nearest them, holding them down with great claws while razor-sharp teeth tore chunks out of flesh. Vipers sank teeth into ankles, regardless of having no venom. The *Sange rau* launched themselves at Branislava, determined to get past her guards and kill her as their master desired.

Zev actually used three hellhounds as a springboard, hitting the *Sange rau* closest to Branislava squarely in the chest with both feet. He used his mixed blood strength and speed as well as his momentum of flying forward and the *Sange rau*'s momentum of blurring speed. The two crashed so hard together Zev felt every bone in his opponent's chest smash under his assault. The shock ran up his legs, but he dropped harmlessly to the ground in a crouch.

A hellhound knocked him flat, but he sliced open the beast's belly as he went down. When it lifted its muzzle to scream, he slit its throat. Rolling, he came up and slammed one arrow into its right eye and left it for Fen to finish off as he raced to protect Branislava.

Fen used a hellhound to leapfrog, rolling over its back to slam a silver stake deep into the chest of the *Sange rau* Zev had taken to the ground. As he rushed past the thrashing hellhound with one arrow in its eye and burned coat, he thrust a second arrow deep into the left eye and kept running.

Dimitri came after him, using the silver sword, slashing downward in a long arc to sever the head of the *Sange rau* both Fen and Zev had wounded. The hellhound was down, but the one Fen had rolled over, burning its back with the hyssop oil, was snarling and ready for him, its great jaws wide open, displaying the wicked set of teeth. A chunk of flesh hung from the side of one jaw, along with strings of venom mixed with blood.

Dimitri didn't bother to slow down—he shoved the long blade of his sword coated with hyssop oil right down the gruesome throat and out the back of the massive head. They stood together, Fen, Dimitri and Zev, Razvan fighting his way to them, so the four stood back-to-back, prepared to keep everything and anything off of Branislava.

Dimitri's eyes narrowed. *Where is Skyler?* he demanded, trying to see everything on the fierce battlefield.

Tatijana is missing as well, Fen added, his heart in his throat.

Razvan indicated the huge hole in the center of the field where the three women had disappeared.

Xaviero sent a worm for them. He backed away from the hole, although it was the hardest thing he'd ever done. *We have to guard Branislava. Without her, we're lost, and now both mages can work to kill her. Trust Ivory. She's dealt with these worms and will bring them back safely.*

He closed his eyes briefly. *Ivory, be safe. Come back to me.*

21

Ivory bit back an exclamation of pain as the worm's teeth closed around her. *It's going to take us down into the hole. Don't fight it. The more you fight, the more venom it will inject into your body. No matter how much it hurts, or how frightened you are, stay very still,* she warned the others.

It's taking us up, not down, straight to that foul fog, Skyler hissed, trying to keep still when she felt as if the thing was sawing her in half.

It's rising fast, but it will go straight down again. Just hold on. Ivory injected calm into her voice. She'd seen the worms before, fought them, taken back Razvan from one.

Tatijana shuddered. *It's taking me back to the mage's lair. I'd rather die than go back.*

Don't fight, Ivory reiterated. *I know what to do. Just stay calm. Once we enter the hole, the worm can move fast underground. The tunnel is already dug and it just has to slide through. The ride will be much smoother. I've got some weapons we can use, but when it hits back to ground, it's going to hurt like hell. I can't risk losing them.*

The worm shot up about thirty feet, just enough for them to feel the foulness of the fog overhead and hear the screams and wails of the spirits trapped in the black smoke. It paused there for a moment and then backtracked with tremendous speed, down into the earth where it was most comfortable.

I tried shifting, Tatijana said. *It's impossible.*

The worm has a venom that prevents that from happening. I've milked these worms and used the venom along with my own chemicals to improve the solution. I dip my weapons into the compound before I go hunting to prevent vampires from shifting. Ivory did her best to sound matter-of-fact.

Now that they were sliding through the air at a dizzying rate of speed, the hold on them eased. For all its ferocity, the worm had a delicate touch when bringing prisoners to the mage. She knew what it cost both Skyler and Tatijana to stay so still within the grasp of the worm. When the teeth of the creature met flesh, it injected its venom to hold that form. Not only was it painful, it was terrifying to be dragged through a tunnel beneath the earth knowing the destination was far worse than the worm.

Skyler was very young and new to their world. Her lifemate had only just claimed her. She'd been human, living with Carpathian adopted parents who protected her from such things. Tatijana had been a prisoner nearly her entire existence in the mage laboratories. Of course she wouldn't want to return. Still, neither struggled, using tremendous discipline to do as she told them.

Fighting a worm is very dangerous. Everything about them is venomous. The spikes he uses to propel himself forward and dig are especially perilous. He has a barb on the end of his tail. When you do get loose, stay far away from that.

Education was always the key to success. The more information one had, the more power to defeat. She eased a crystal-centered circular weapon from her belt. Very gingerly she pushed one into Tatijana's hands and a second into Skyler's, before pulling a third out for herself.

His mouth contains double rows of serrated teeth, and inside are sacs of venom. We're going to have to go inside. If you find yourself outside of him, remember his tail can also break every bone in your body with one swipe and his hide is so tough it will slice your skin if you come into contact with it.

I've seen them, Tatijana admitted. *Xavier fed them humans.*

Skyler shuddered and then had to suppress a cry of pain.

I'm going to disorient the worm with sound. Try to close your ears. The vibration alone will hurt your insides, but the sound itself is most troublesome. I know of no other way to distract it. It will thrash a bit and then open its mouth. That's what we want and we'll have only a couple of seconds. I can't stress that enough. He'll recover fast. Push the poison from your body and shift to molecules. Skyler, have you ever done that? Pushed the poison or shifted into something that small?

She had to know if her young stepdaughter could do such a thing on her own.

Absolutely, Ivory. I can do this. I will do this.

The young voice quavered, but Ivory heard the absolute steel. *Are you both ready? The moment the mouth opens and you can, follow me inside. Keep your weapon ready and don't touch anything inside.*

She sent up a prayer that they would make it out, and then, using a pitch that caused vertigo and notes that disoriented and vibrated the very insides of the worm, she began to chant in a singsong voice.

I call to the element of air, used for sound,
Drum to the heartbeat of evil that digs through the ground.
Pitch, harmonics, combine and align,
Fight by attacking the warp evil's mind.

She had fought the worms several times, but it was always with her heart in her throat, a terrible, frightening fear that was nearly overwhelming. She had a deep faith and she prayed urgently not to be abandoned, not when she had two other lives depending on her.

She continued to sing, but the rhythm of her song changed as Mother Earth responded to her discordant notes, changing the very vibrations within the soil, drawing it inward. The ground shivered with the sound, trembled as the wave of sound went crashing through it. The worm tube began to collapse in on itself. Soil, rock and debris fell around them, tumbling into the tube.

A roar of thunder boomed down the hole just behind the worm and it hesitated, slowing almost to a stop. The entire body shuddered and shivered. Ivory sang again, the pitch reverberating through the dirt, the sound hurting all three of them right along with the worm. The notes crashed through their bodies, shook their minds and turned their insides into a quivering mass of congealed gelatin.

Disoriented, the worm halted all progress, its mouth yawning wide in a terrible shriek that resounded through the ground, releasing all three at the same time.

Ivory pushed the poison from her body and shifted to vapor, still holding the weapon so that it seemed to float through the air. *Hurry. Hurry. Keep that weapon close and follow me inside.* She didn't have time to look to see if they followed, but she sensed them behind her as she streamed inside the open mouth of the worm.

Both Skyler and Tatijana could feel the vibration of the disc in their hands as they followed Ivory deep into the creature's mouth. They went past the double rows of what looked like shark teeth, continued past dripping fangs and thick pockets of amber-colored venom, down into the very throat of the worm.

Ivory had constructed the disc of natural elements, everything gifted from Mother Earth herself, minerals and gems to form the weapon. She had used it many times against the worm, and like always before, it felt a natural part of her. She could tell Skyler and Tatijana were both daughters of the Earth in the way they held the weapon as well.

You're looking for scar tissue somewhere inside the throat. The worms have only two vulnerable spots and the second is deep inside the body where we definitely don't want to go. Whatever you do, don't scrape up against the walls of this worm. Don't touch anything because everything inside is thick with its venom. The scar tissue is where the master can attach himself and give instructions.

It was dark and dank, very humid inside the throat of the worm. Great streams of amber hung like icicles from the roof of the mouth and dripped continuously. Membranes were covered by strange high ridges, deep valleys of scarring and large misshapen bumps, above and all around them.

The worm shrieked again, the sound echoing up the throat, nearly throwing them against the walls. The creature grew frantic as the tunnel continued to collapse, fighting to make it through to the other side by wiggling, bucking and even whirling like a drill.

The three women searched for the telltale spot inside the desperate worm. As the creature spun madly in an attempt to get out of the collapsing tunnel, venom sprayed around its throat. Only the fact that the three women were in the form of vapor saved them from being doused.

Is this it? Skyler asked.

Tatijana had stayed close to her, hoping to protect her if everything went bad fast, not that she could imagine much worse. She peered at the strange markings on the inside of the worm's throat. Small raised wounds and blemishes were scattered in a pattern of seven whorls and deep circular indentations, marks she was certain the mage had made.

Skyler's right. This has to be his mark, Ivory. There's a fresh wound here.

Ivory inspected the small ring. *Perfect. Good eyes, Skyler. This disc is iolite,* she identified. Already there was a thin thread of blue-violet light emanating from the disc.

It's a violet stone that enhances vision on the astral realm, Tatijana explained to Skyler just in case she didn't know.

Very volatile under the right circumstances, Ivory added. *Do exactly as I do and then get out of here fast.*

Ivory didn't wait, shimmering into her natural form, careful to avoid the strings of amber venom seeping in long strings from the roof of the mouth as she hovered in the center of the worm's throat.

Skyler gasped as fibers reached for Ivory, like tentacles following the source of heat. Ivory was fast, dodging them and using the light like one of her arrows, striking deep, penetrating into the worm's tough wall. When she let go of the disc, the weapon followed the light, crashing hard into the pattern of scars.

Both Skyler and Tatijana followed suit without hesitation, releasing first the light like a spear and then the disc, nearly simultaneously. All three weapons pulsed with light and then burst into a violet wash that bathed the walls of the worm's throat in vivid color. A shrill, penetrating sound followed, the piercing notes threatening to destroy all sense, so that all three hastily muted the volume.

Hurry, hurry, Ivory urged, rushing toward the mouth of the worm.

The giant cavernous body of the creature rolled again. Bucked harder. Began to thrash violently. Tatijana and Skyler kept up with Ivory, dodging the venom and avoiding touching the walls of the spiraling worm. Condensation formed, an eerie haze when the violet light spread like a smoky red tide staining everything in its path a bluish purple.

The three women hovered just behind the double rows of serrated teeth.

The sense of urgency was strong in all of them, as if they shared one mind—and one goal.

The worm rocked violently again, thrashing as more smoky violet light poured from the three discs and curled as vapor in every direction. Ivory appeared to be concentrating hard.

Three, two, one, she counted down and then burst forward.

The worm's throat contracted. Squeezed. The walls narrowed behind them. The mouth of the worm gaped open to cough, every muscle constricting violently.

Ivory didn't need to tell them to hurry. They followed her frantic attempt at reaching the surface. The ground trembled and shook with intensity as the worm thrashed, maddened by the burning in its throat. Shock waves like seismic anomalies reverberated through the ground. Dirt fell in on itself all around them.

I can get us out faster, Tatijana volunteered. *Let me.*

Tatijana squeezed past Ivory, shifting into her dragon form so that she could dig their way out far faster than they could. Her wedge-shaped head burst through the surface, continuing upward so that she could use her long neck and front claws to protect the others from the fierce battle taking place aboveground.

Branislava saw Tatijana's dragon head emerge from beneath the surface and something deep inside her settled. Behind Tatijana's dragon came first Ivory and then Skyler. She wasn't alone fighting a war against two, possibly three mages. Her lifemate and the others were holding off the mage's army to give her the chance to bring down Xaviero's seat of power, and she was close. She could feel it now, the taste of victory. It was all about not making a mistake.

All three women had gone through a fight, but they'd emerged alive and victorious. They hurried to make their way through the battlefield to get to her side. With the exception of Ivory, three had been born of Dragonseeker blood. Ivory was lifemate to a Dragonseeker and over the years his blood had become hers, so technically, the mages would be dealing with four powerful Dragonseeker women.

Tatijana, I need you and Ivory to take the two trees there. Branislava indicated the tree directly opposite from the one she had released. *Ivory, if you could take the one at the bottom of the pentagram, that would be helpful. Skyle you and I are going to work on the ones on either side of Xaviero. He's setting up a triangle with the fire and his brother. You can see his position.*

She dug a small diagram in the dirt with the toe of her boot. *I've figured out what he's doing and how he set up his power grid. We'll have to open our minds to one another for this to work properly.*

Ivory was a loner. Other than Razvan she didn't share her life—or her mind—with anyone else. If this was to work, they'd have to do it together.

Ivory knew her meaning immediately and simply nodded. *I am a warrior first. Whatever needs to be done, I will do.*

Branislava breathed a sigh of relief. She'd put her sister closest to Ivory in order to give Ivory aid if needed. She would be positioned with Skyler. Both women were powerhouses in their own right, and all four of them connected had every chance of bringing down the two mages. She did her best to convey that confidence while she instructed them on how to peel back the layers of magic Xaviero had wrought.

Skyler's eyes widened in shock, Branislava's only warning. A massive hellhound hit her squarely in the chest driving her over backward, the gaping mouth with rows of terrible teeth driving straight for her throat. She tried to fend it off with outstretched hands, a pitiful attempt, but the hot breath blasted her in the face and what looked like a thousand teeth rushed at her. At the last moment she squirmed enough that the beast clamped his jaw down tight around her shoulder, not her throat.

She heard her own scream, a frightened, pain-filled cry, torn from her in spite of all resolution not to show Xaviero weakness. Of course he'd targeted the women. She'd been so wrapped up in her work, she hadn't thought to keep one eye out for an attack.

The hellhound ripped a great chunk of flesh from her shoulder, and clamped down a second time on the bone. His teeth seemed to meet in the middle and he shook her like a rag doll. There was no way to shift, no way to reach into her belt and retrieve the knife there.

Skyler rolled on the ground beneath the hellhound, a knife in her fist, blade up. She cut the legs of the beast, slicing tendons and ligaments as she rolled to the other side. As she came up in a crouch, she slammed the blade into the eye of the hellhound and leapt away from the creature before it could release Branislava and attack her.

Razvan came out of nowhere, covered in blood, his face a mask of intent, eyes blazing fire as he leapt over one hellhound, slamming his arrow deep into its eye, knocked down a *Sange rau* and launched himself in the air at the last moment, to land squarely on the back of the hellhound attacking Branislava.

He wrapped one arm around the beast's head, jerking it back hard as he plunged his knife into the animal's remaining good eye. The hellhound shuddered. Took a step and collapsed over the top of Branislava. Razvan pulled her out from under the heavy creature, his fingers moving over her shoulder to determine how much damage had been done.

"Thanks. Both of you." She included Skyler. "Thank you."

Razvan nodded. "It's not broken, but right now, drive out every bit of bacteria. You'll need to cauterize it as fast as possible."

It hurt, even when she did her best to push the pain away. Even pushing out the strands of bacteria was painful. Burning it clean hurt even more. She set her teeth and nodded to Razvan that she was good and could go back to work. A part of her was very grateful that he stood guard over the four of them. The thought of another hellhound getting ahold of her was terrifying. With a little shudder she turned back to begin peeling the layers back on the heavy strands of magic protecting the mage's power grid.

The fire let out a roar, as if alive, and maybe it was with the aid of the mages. The flames turned blue in the middle of the conflagration, a storm of defiant color in the midst of the raging blaze. The flames leapt higher and higher, nearly climbing to the fog ceiling, the black smoke spreading like a cancer overhead. The tremendous heat drove everyone away from the site, not because the Carpathians couldn't control their temperatures, but because the fire melted everything in its range.

The ground shifted, a jarring warning that stopped nearly everyone in their tracks. Even the few remaining hellhounds paused uneasily. Xaviero walked out of the protective circle, unbending, unafraid, a blue light glowing around him. His brother came from the other side, just as impressive, wrapped in that same mystique that set them apart from the rest of the world.

They kept to the shadows, making no sound at all, yet commanding the attention of every combatant. The hellhounds rushed to them, slinking low, like pets who had been beaten but were at the command of their masters.

Both mages waved their hands and a candle on either side of the triangle they formed with the fire leapt to life, the flames flickering blue to match the center of the larger blaze.

The ground trembled a second time, a great crack zigzagging through the center of the triangle Xaviero, Xayvion and the fire formed, in the exact center of power between the trees the two had prepared in advance. Soil erupted into a geyser and then collapsed in on itself, forming a sinkhole several feet in diameter.

The candles on either side of the triangle leapt in glee, the flames turning blue to answer the blue crystals both mages scattered on the ground surrounding the sinkhole. A blast of heat rose from below, as if a great volcano lurked just beneath the surface. The fog above their heads reflected an orange-red hue cast from the melted rock deep in the sinkhole.

A hush fell over the battlefield. Both mages stepped out of the shadows, ringed by the hellhounds to guard them as they performed their ritual. Dressed in purple robes, they lifted their arms and opened them wide. In complete synchronization, the two chanted the foulest of dark magic, demanding the gates of hell be opened.

> *I call to the devil of black rock's depth,*
> *Let these souls travel the devil's spine.*
> *Let them be the offering to all that is dark,*
> *So that none may undo this time.*

> *Let these souls serve as fodder,*
> *As hunger feeds.*
> *Let their blood seal the bond,*
> *Let their blood seal this need.*

Branislava winced at the demonic, vile incantation, the deal they were making. They ordered and cajoled. They commanded and yet supplicated. The arrogance of the two mages shocked her. What they would bring back from the dead would be far worse than what Xavier had been. She shuddered thinking of the reign of terror he would provide. The mage voices rose in volume as they continued with their bid to free their brother.

Each soul I send,
I exchange for life.
I sign with you now with blood and life,
From this day forward I am bound to serve.

Be ever to be immortal,
For what has been served.
From spirit and blood, flesh and bone,
I sign this pact now with immortality won.

Xaviero gestured toward the fire, crooking his little finger, summoning their offering. The prisoner was wrapped from head to toe in silver chain. A tall, broad-shouldered *Sange rau* dragged him from behind the fire and shoved him into the triangle so hard he fell facedown in the dirt. The *Sange rau* moved back quickly, clearly not wanting to get too close to the mage. With no hands to stop him, the prisoner's face buried itself in the grime. He lay unmoving for a moment, no sound escaping. Very slowly he turned over and in spite of the chains, managed to get into a sitting position.

Zev's heart stuttered. Went still. *Branka. That is my grandfather. That's Hemming. I would know him anywhere, even though the silver has burned into his skin and he's been tortured beyond endurance. That's Hemming.*

Don't move. Don't speak or draw attention to yourself in any way, Branislava cautioned. *You are alpha. Above all matters. He cannot feel your emotion or he can draw more power from it. Your grandfather carries your grandmother's blood. He is now mixed blood as you are, and he is a strong Dark Blood.*

Zev hadn't really considered that. He'd been told by the Carpathians that he was of the Dark Blood lineage many times, but he never really understood what it meant. He thought of himself as Lycan. If he considered himself Carpathian at all, it was as a brother to Fen and Dimitri. Now, with his grandfather chained and about to be slain so Xavier could have his body and his spirit could go to hell in exchange, he realized that all along, it was this the mages had been looking to do.

They wanted the body and blood of a Dark Blood, and his grandfather had probably walked right into their trap. He had gone looking for those who had murdered his mate. One by one he had hunted them down. Of course Xaviero would have heard the rumors. It would have taken little effort to lure Hemming to him.

They can't have him, Zev said, absolute determination in his mind and voice.

Of course they can't. We're close to tearing down his powerhouse, but it takes time to unravel what he's wrought. Inch your way to the weakest side, the side of the fire. He won't be expecting an attack from that side, Branislava advised.

Because it's impossible. The fire is so hot it's melting anything within several feet of it. He's burning blue flames inside of it. My body can't withstand such a temperature, Branka. I've tried regulating it, but he has magic in that fire.

My love—her voice overwhelmed him with tenderness—*trust me. Wrap yourself in me. My spirit is woven to yours. My body belongs to you. My soul is the other half of yours. I am fire. Cloak yourself with my dragon scales and in darkness make your way to your grandfather. It can be done.*

You should have been a general, mon chaton féroce. He had much to learn about being Carpathian. His woman was brilliant.

Fen. Dimitri, he said. *Step slowly in front of me. Slowly, so you don't draw the attention of either of the demon brothers.*

Fen moved first, gliding without seeming to, his body coming in at an angle to allow Zev to slip behind him. Dimitri immediately shifted his weight from one leg to the other, effectively blocking Zev from sight. Instantly Zev shifted, going completely invisible. He moved through the crowd with stealth, careful to keep from alerting a hound or making one of the remaining *Sange rau* nervous.

He realized the packs had done a tremendous job in bringing down the mage's army. There were very few of the *Sange rau* left alive. The mages had given the illusion that there were many more, but he counted no more than a dozen left, including the one who had shoved his grandfather into the dirt.

Zev conveyed the information to Fen and Dimitri. They would spread the word and the Carpathians would make certain they were in a good position to take down the remaining *Sange rau* if need be. He hoped if they managed to kill the mages and destroy their plan, the mixed bloods would understand what and who they had worked for. Perhaps they were under some kind of spell. They certainly weren't members of the Sacred Circle, although one or two of those he'd killed, he recognized from meeting them in their packs. They'd definitely started out as Lycan.

He inched his way through the crowd, staying as low to the ground as possible, winding his way without form toward the fire. Even without his body he felt the terrible melting power of the blue flame. He knew as he approached it that that flame was part of the power grid Branislava and the others were trying to take down.

Zev wrapped his body in his lifemate, feeling her dragon scales close over his skin, those fiery protective scales that warded off even the heat of a magical blue flame. He sent her the overwhelming love he felt for her, his faith in her, and most of all his gratitude for her. Even in the middle of her working at destroying Xaviero's web of power, she enfolded him in love. He was not going alone through that fire.

He wore the red-gold scales like a long hooded coat of armor. He moved slowly even though he felt the fierce heat. The scales reflected the hot blue flames back away from him and he found he could actually breathe as he inched his way toward his grandfather.

For the first time he was truly grateful for his mixed blood. With those silver chains, Hemming would never be able to run. He would have to sling him over his shoulder and carry him away from that triangle and the fearsome opening in the ground. He couldn't look into that hellhole.

As he neared his goal, Xaviero stood over Hemming, his ceremonial knife held high in his hand. The knife was much larger than he had ever seen in a ceremony, looking more as if it could kill a huge animal, much less a man. Runes danced across the silver blade, continually moving as if thirsty for the blood of the Dark Blood the mage intended to murder, yet not sever his head, preserving the body for Xavier.

Hemming didn't try to move away, nor did he look away from Xaviero. The silver chains had to be agony, burned so deeply into his skin Zev could barely make out that there was actually skin left on his grandfather. The prisoner was fully aware of his surroundings and the intentions of the mage, but he didn't blink, staring defiantly at Xaviero as he chanted, his voice rising with Xayvion's.

The four women had cast their circle of protection right under the noses of the mages' watchdogs. Each time a *Sange rau* or a hellhound got near them, Daciana's pack, along with Tomas, Andre, Lojos, Mataias and Razvan, kept them back. Fen, Dimitri or Zev had come in to finish the job of taking down any threat to the women.

Branislava lifted her arms, uncaring that either of the mages or their sentinels might spot her. It was now or never. Tatijana, Skyler and Ivory followed her actions.

Alder, battle witch, heed to my call,
It is time for battle, evil must fall.
Cedar known as the tree of life,
I call to you now as the gates of hell come to life.

The four women joined their power, merged minds and became one single entity, one heart and goal—to stop the mage from his dark deeds.

Blackthorn straif, Dark Crone of the woods,
I have need of your power, stand and slay that which must be undone,
Ancient oak Dagda,
Dominion of power I call to you now, feast on this blackest of powers.

Now, Branislava whispered into his mind. *Hurry.*

Zev didn't hesitate, trusting her. The flames of the two candles flickered, leapt and then died. The four remaining trees that helped formed the inverted pentagram each began to change, starting in their root systems. A healthy mottled bark replaced the sickly white color from the ground up the tree to the reaching branches, and finally the leaves turned silvery green.

Zev burst into the triangle as the source of power faded, careful not to touch the mage, but literally snatching the chained body out from under the knife plunging downward toward the heart. He rolled with his grandfather, away from the mage and out of the triangle, coming to his feet and shifting Hemming's body over one shoulder in a fireman's carry.

The hellhounds reacted, snarling and charging him, their speed utterly incredible. Zev ran at them, closing the distance between them every bit as fast. When he was just feet from the massive beasts, he hurdled them, using the strength from his mixed blood, the Lycan's ability to spring and the distance and speed of the combination of species.

Fen and Dimitri closed ranks, facing the hellhounds chasing Zev. Covered in battle wounds, slashes and fierce bites, Andre, Tomas and Lojos joined them while Mataias dropped back to protect Zev as he carried his grandfather's body back to the circle of protection the four women had cast around them.

The blue flame in the fire sputtered and faded, was consumed by the rich red gold of the natural flames. At once the color of the smoke changed, and the fire itself died down so that the flames weren't reaching for that unhealthy bank of fog overhead. As the white smoke mingled with the black and eventually devoured it, the dense wall of fog began to break up into smaller, ragged patches.

The wall of foul fog surrounding the clearing, making it impenetrable, thinned as a cooling wind began to blow through it. The spirits trapped in the unnatural smoke drifted into the purified smoke, rising upward toward the clouds where the wind took them.

Xaviero roared with rage as molten lava burst from the hole in the ground. The smell of sulfur claimed every other scent, drowning out even the smell of blood. For one moment voices could be heard. Wailing. Shrieking. Demonic. The lava rained down inside the triangle, forcing Xaviero and Xayvion to flee the safety of their refuge.

The four women turned as one unit to face the fleeing mages. Xaviero threw his hands in the air, tracing a pattern of destruction, twisting the raining lava into fireballs of magma and hurling them toward his enemies. As one, Branislava, Skyler, Tatijana and Ivory flung up their hands, tracing symbols and chanting softly under their breath to turn the firebombs into harmless rain.

The earth shook violently, throwing everyone to the ground. Once. Twice. A third time. One lone spirit shot close to the surface, hovered there in the fading smoke, mouth gaping wide in a silent scream of protest. His hollow eyes stared accusingly. It wasn't difficult to recognize Xavier as he tried desperately to escape.

Ivory stepped forward, pushing air at the smoke, clean, crisp, fresh air right into the middle of the apparition. There was no malice on her face. No hatred. Just acceptance of what had to be done.

I call to wind chaos and destruction,
Phlegmatic energy of air,
Blow through that which is shadow,
Dispersing all with marked protective care.

The face distorted grotesquely. Small holes appeared, the wind drifting through the mask almost sedately. Xavier hovered there, reaching through the smoke toward his brothers. Both took a step toward him as if they could yank him out of the abyss. Something reached up from below and hooked wicked claws into the smoke, yanking the spirit below. Xavier's desperate wail hurt their ears, and then the earth slammed shut with a decisive crash.

Xaviero slowly lifted his gaze to the women. Hatred was in every line of his face. His mouth pulled back in a snarl. He lifted his arms to the sky and then made a throwing gesture. A large, spinning rock with crystal spikes burst from the earth and hurtled toward them.

Skyler pushed air at the rock, stopping it before it could strike. *You are too old to be throwing a childish tantrum,* she chided. *We are daughters of the Earth. Do you think our mother would allow you to harm us? Choose another weapon, this one will not work.*

The rock dropped harmlessly to the ground. She didn't fling it back at him, or send it smashing into the hellhounds ringing him. She just let it drop, showing no animosity toward him whatsoever.

His anger grew to a festering rage. *You,* Xaviero hissed at Skyler. *You are the child that should never have been born. The child of every species. Mage, Jaguar, Carpathian, Lycan and human. Your mother deceived us. She was too powerful and had to be killed. We couldn't risk her coming against us as she eventually would have. And yet our brother stupidly used Razvan's body to impregnate her. His mistake. His ultimate mistake.*

Skyler stared into his eyes, unblinking. Unafraid. Her mother had warned her to stay away from the mages, to hide who she was and her abilities, but she was no longer that helpless child and she never would be again. *You did not frighten my mother nor do you frighten me. I pity you with your grandiose schemes and desperate need for control. You have nothing, and you are nothing.*

Your mother was nothing. She crawled before us, a child we created. Mage, Jaguar and human for our purposes. Ours. She danced to our tune. She was no more than a puppet, he screamed.

Skyler recognized that he was trying to anger her. That he was using her mother's past to fuel her temper so he could use that against her, twist her emotions into something ugly. She shook her head. *You feared her power and her goodness or you wouldn't have wanted her dead. Again, I'm sorry for you.* She lifted her hands into the air and began sketching a pattern.

For those who lost will,
Let it now be returned,
Taking back their power,
So freedom may be earned.
Your evil will not prevail.
These men no longer belong to you,
Just as my mother never belonged to you.

Most of the mixed bloods who had served Xaviero stopped fighting abruptly, looking confused and disoriented. A few sat down and buried their faces in their hands.

Xayvion slipped into the shadows. *Brother. Leave with me now. We cannot defeat them.*

They are women. Nothing. Xaviero spit on the ground. *These warriors cannot touch me, the hellhounds obey. I will kill all four of them.*

Brother. I entreat you. Leave now. Xayvion's voice faded.

Sputtering, his face red, Xaviero stomped hard on the ground, and then threw two crystal spheres he produced from the pockets of his robe into the hollows he'd made in the dirt. Furious that his brother would think the women, even combined, could wield more power than the two of them left him wanting to tear the four hated women apart limb by limb.

Water bubbled up from the indentations his heels had made, shot into the sky and then rained down over the four women, an acid rain that threatened to consume them.

Tatijana shifted partially into the blue dragon, her wedge-shaped head lifted to the sky, mouth open while her hands followed a complicated pattern.

Waters chemical, acid rain,
I drink your strength having no pain.
You quench my thirst, revive my will,
I transmute this water making it evil's swill.

When the last drop was gone and Xaviero stood gaping at her, she shifted back and smiled almost gently at him. *You taught me that trick when I was ten years old. Have you forgotten? My dragon is a water dragon and you used me, forced me to consume acid rain. My dragon seems to have developed a taste for it.* She smiled serenely and gave the mage a small salute.

Xaviero whirled around, ignoring the scattering hellhounds who howled like lost souls, uncertain what he wanted them to do. They began snapping at one another. Two went down in a fierce fight while the others rushed to bite and claw the combatants.

So intent on destroying the four women he blamed for thwarting his plan, Xaviero appeared not to notice. He continued spinning, his robes flaring out in a wide circle, scattering sparks over the ground. Blue flames burst from his fingertips, so that he looked as if he was circled by one long, continuous blue flame. He produced a wild wind that fanned the dying flames of the pyre into a fearsome conflagration.

His hands flowed, his voice rising as he sent the blue fire streaking overhead straight at Branislava. She ignored the screams and shouts to get down, standing her ground, holding Xaviero's gaze as he smirked at her, certain the flame would devour all four of the women.

As the heated missile bore down on them, Branislava stepped forward, just a little ahead of the others, lifting her arms straight over her head as if putting on a long gown. Her hands moved gracefully in the air, like a dancer telling a story.

Born in fire, honed in ice,
I call to the four corners.
Make your energies mine,

I call to fire, sister kin,
I absorb your abilities,
Taking all within.

She turned to embrace the battlefield.

I call to Pisionics swinging blades,
Spontaneous combustion,
Magick is made.
Take that which is evil,
Return it to realm,
Encasing all in your fire,
So none may return.

Her body shimmered red gold and then the blue flame hit her. Her entire body glowed blue and flames erupted all around her, seemingly engulfing her.

Xaviero laughed gleefully, the sound shrill over the silent battlefield. He didn't seem to notice the great beasts standing for a moment, uncertain there on the battlefield and then tucking their tails and wandering off. As they stepped into the forest, out of sight and mind of the mage, they dissolved into nothing.

The blue flame danced for a moment, whirling around Branislava almost playfully. Through the blue of the fire gleamed first gold and then red, followed by orange. The colors swirled around her from head to toe and then slowly faded into her body, as if she'd absorbed the flames.

Seriously, Xaviero, is your mind going? she taunted. *You actually used elements to try to harm us? You must do better than that or the four of us will have to send you straight through the gates of hell to join your brother. You signed a deal with the devil in blood. I believe that paper is in your pocket, and he will hold you to it.*

Xaviero cursed her in several languages. *All of you are dead. Every person you care about is dead. They just don't know it yet,* he promised.

Smiling at Xaviero, seemingly unaffected by his rage or his promise, she lifted her hands and sketched symbols in the air between them. The symbols hung there, runes of flames. Xaviero tensed, trying to read her attack on him. His hands came up in answer for another round in their battle.

Zev struck him from behind. Xaviero's eyes went wide in absolute shock. He hadn't noticed that his hellhounds had disappeared and that he was no longer within a protective circle. It never occurred to him that Branislava was merely keeping his attention on her—that all four women were using delaying tactics, simply playing a game with him while the real attack came from elsewhere.

In Lycan form, Zev's wolf bit through the scrawny neck and clawed down the mage's back, ripping open flesh to pull the spinal cord free. He flung it on the fire, whipped the body around and plunged his fist deep into the mage's chest, clawing for the heart. He tossed that on the fire as well. Shifting to his natural form, he drew his sword and severed the head, throwing that on the fire. The body followed.

That's one way to do it, Branislava whispered into Zev's mind.

"Feel better?" Fen asked.

"A little bit of overkill?" Dimitri suggested drolly.

"That was me keeping my cool," Zev answered. He looked around. "There's mop-up to be done, but I need to attend to my grandfather. He's in bad shape."

"We've got this," Fen said.

22

Z ev hurried to the spot where he'd left his grandfather, Dimitri pacing along beside him. Daciana, Makoce and Lykaon guarded him. All three looked grim as they stepped back to allow Zev to kneel beside Hemming.

Silver chains, wrapped close together, were embedded deeply into the skin. Clearly some skin had grown over the chains, making them a part of his body. Dimitri had suffered a few weeks wrapped in silver chain and he remembered every second of the merciless agony. He couldn't imagine how long Zev's grandfather had endured such torture.

"Get them off," Hemming gasped in greeting. "Zev, get these chains off of me now."

Zev took a deep breath, nearly shook his head but Dimitri's fingers settled around his arm, preventing him from speaking. *Skyler can do it. Let me call to her. She removed mine.*

Call her then. Hurry.

Zev smoothed his hand through his grandfather's hair in a rare gesture of affection. "The woman who can remove the chains is on her way. I had no idea you were still alive. I thought you long dead after one of your hunts."

Branislava appeared at his side, Skyler, Tatijana and Ivory close behind. *I brought them in case we could help with healing,* she confided.

Zev was grateful she was there, grateful he had her. The moment she was close to him, he felt as if he could endure anything—even losing his grandfather for the second time.

Skyler knelt down on the other side of Hemming, running her hands over his body and the tight silver chains embedded so deep. She looked up at Dimitri with stricken eyes. He laid his hand gently on her shoulder.

Zev, if I remove the chains, he will die. He's lived too long in them. They're embedded in his very bones, and have become part of his system. He lives in agony, but . . . Skyler trailed off, tears in her eyes. She looked up at Dimitri again, as if somehow her lifemate could change what was. *Perhaps I'm wrong. Bronnie? Tatijana? Ivory?*

Branislava positioned her palms just above Hemming's body and ran her hand from head to toe. Zev felt her instant reaction and knew without her saying so that Skyler's evaluation had been correct.

Zev bowed his head for a moment before looking his grandfather straight in the eye. "If we remove the chains, Grandfather, you will die."

Hemming smiled at him. For the first time his face seemed to relax beneath the terrible bands of silver. "I long for peace, Zev. For the chance to be with Catalina once again. I miss her every moment of my existence. Get the chains off of me."

Skyler shook her head. "I don't want to be the one. I don't, Zev. What if you look at me as the person who killed your grandfather? I can't do it."

Hemming turned his head slowly to look at her. "You're so young. I can't remember ever being that young. The chains are . . ." He seemed to have to search for the word. "Painful."

Zev felt his heart contract. If Hemming couldn't remember the actual word to describe pain, he'd been in the chains too long suffering the torture of death by silver. The mage hadn't put the hooks into his body, so that the liquid silver could eventually find his heart and kill him. Xaviero had been far too clever for that. He'd merely wrapped him in the chains, rending him helpless and in total agony.

Zev felt Branislava steel herself and knew what she was going to do. His heart nearly burst with gratitude and love for her.

"I'll remove them," Branislava said firmly. "Skyler can show me how."

Skyler nodded several times. "Of course. If that's what he really wants."

Hemming smiled at her. "More than anything else, I desire to be free of these chains. To experience true freedom one last time. Of course, I would like to remember what it is to live without pain."

Branislava slipped her hand into Hemming's hand. "I'm Zev's lifemate, Branislava. He calls me Branka."

Hemming studied her with intelligent, all-seeing eyes. "Of course he does. He is a lucky man to have you. I expect that you will take good care of him."

"Always," Branislava whispered. She glanced at Skyler.

Zev could feel his lifemate choking up. He couldn't blame her. Up close to Hemming, one could feel his power. He had resisted the mage's demand and been tortured for far too many years. He'd held out when others would have succumbed.

"I'm going to try to loosen the chains first," Branislava said. "The other healers will join with me so the power will be extensive, but the chains are deep in your body and this may be even more painful to you. We'll try to keep that at a minimum as well."

A shadow fell across them. She looked up to see Gregori and Mikhail joining Fen and Dimitri, standing like guardians. For some reason the sight of the prince coming to pay tribute to Zev's grandfather choked her up all over again. Tears burned behind her eyes and in her throat.

Hemming stroked his rough fingers over her palm. "You are saving me. Saving my heart and soul. I will go with honor."

She nodded at him, afraid to speak.

"If I may," Gregori said, crouching down beside Hemming's head. "I cannot save your life, but I can help ease the pain."

Hemming kept his eyes on Zev's. Zev's nod was almost imperceptible. Gregori placed both hands on either side of Hemming's head and looked to Branislava.

She took a deep breath.

Chains of silver bedded within,
Chains of silver under tissue and skin,
Chains of silver connected to bone,
Chains of silver now may you be undone.

Her gaze jumped to Hemming's face. His hand closed around hers, his grip like a vise. Tiny beads of blood seeped all around the chains. There was agony on his face. She started to sit back on her heels, sickened by what she'd done. Skyler had been right to refuse his request.

"No," Hemming said, his voice hoarse. "Don't stop."

"The five of us can join to ease his pain," Gregori said. "Push your power to me."

The four women did so without hesitation and Gregori, his hands still on either side of Hemming's head, bowed his own head.

I call to valerian to relax and release,
White willow I send you to embrace and ease,
That which is silver, toxic to bone,
I bid you to cease as goldenseal roams,
That which is natural and of earth's healing core,
I bid you to ease that which is tattered and torn.

The agony in Hemming's eyes receded. He smiled at his grandson. "They are handy friends to have—and keep."

"It is so," Zev agreed. *Take them off of him, mon chaton féroce. I can't stand to see him like this another moment.*

Branislava took another deep breath and let it out. She knew if she succeeded in removing the chains, Hemming would only have a short period of time until he died. There was no way to repair the damage to bone and flesh and organs when the silver had eaten through him and become an operating part of his body.

I am with you, Branka, Zev assured her. *Soul and spirit bound together. This is our decision to free him and send him to the woman who waits for him.*

Grateful for Zev's reassurance, she squeezed Hemming's hand to warn him before she started.

Chain of silver buried deep within,
Chain of silver wrapped like a serpent's skin.
Chain of silver that cuts to the bone,
I seek out your making so that you will now be known.

Hemming's hand squeezed hers so tightly she nearly gasped aloud. When she looked closely at his face, he appeared serene, still staring into his grandson's eyes, as if he found strength there. She knew what that was like, relying on Zev. He was a rock, always steady, no matter what was happening. There was something in Zev, something so strong, so deep, that she knew she could always count on. He was unswerving in his duties, his loyalty and his calm demeanor. He had the ability to lead under any circumstances—even when his heart was breaking.

I trace your pattern and follow your path,
Removing your roots as I seal and cast.
In each valley and burn I insert a balm,
So that your poison is ceased and can do no more harm.

The chains slackened. On the silver rings she could see blood and bits of flesh and bone. Branislava closed her eyes briefly and bit back a sob. She had known, of course, but seeing the evidence made his imminent death all too real.

Zev, Fen and Dimitri carefully pulled the chains up so they could be cut from Hemming's body, and removed completely. Zev tossed them a distance away. Branislava found it difficult to look at the man who had once been like Zev—strong and muscular and reliable. His body was ravaged by pain, lack of food and exercise. His muscles were atrophied. Every inch of his body welled up with blood. His flesh had been eaten away by the silver in the chains, leaving a raw, bloody mess.

Gregori continued to hold his head, helping to ease the man's suffering. Branislava held his hand, but it was Zev that Hemming looked to.

"I was born Lycan and I fell in love and mated with what I believed was another Lycan—your grandmother. She believed she was Lycan as well. Her parents found her on a battlefield, after the *Sange rau* had destroyed most of the pack." Hemming coughed and blood trickled out of the corner of his mouth.

Mikhail, Fen and Dimitri moved closer, almost protectively, although there was little any of them could do for the man.

"She was everything to me." Hemming's eyes lit up. "She was a thing of beauty on the battlefield and we were always together. Never apart. We had a beautiful daughter—Aubrey." He looked as if he was seeing back into the past and the memories were pleasant. "Both of us we quite enamored with our little girl."

He coughed again and more blood trickled down his chin. Zev wiped it away with his thumb. Branislava switched places with Gregori to cushion Hemming's head in her lap so that his head was at a higher angle. She smoothed back his hair with trembling fingers.

"Your mate was from a very revered Carpathian lineage," Mikhail said, his voice pitched low and soothing. Almost singsong. A voice that could easily usher a man gently into another realm. "She was the last remaining Dark Blood. Her parents must have been killed by the *Sange rau* when they tried to help defend the pack. They were traveling in that area and most likely stumbled across the battle."

Hemming nodded. "She didn't remember them. She was little more than an infant when her Lycan parents found her. None of us, least of all her, thought she was anything but Lycan. She began to have troubling dreams. Visions came to her of the future. Of a split between Lycan and Carpathian. She sent a message to the Carpathians of her visions, but she was murdered shortly after that and we didn't know if it had gotten through or not. It was then that we realized she was more than Lycan—that she could have been Carpathian, and now, because of me, she was both. She had become the hated *Sange rau.*"

"Not the *Sange rau,*" Mikhail corrected in his gentle way. "She was *Hän ku pesäk kaikak,* which in our language, is 'guardian of all.' She was not rogue or vampire, Hemming, she was a great warrior."

Hemming nodded, grateful for the explanation of the difference. "She often gave me blood during hunts or battles when I was wounded. I realized that I was becoming as she was."

Branislava squeezed his hand. "Zev is *Hän ku pesäk kaikak*. Fen and Dimitri are as well. They fought this day with honor. You would have been proud of your grandson."

"I've always been proud of my grandson. He has been a thorn in Xaviero's side almost from the first day the mage became aware of an elite hunter who advised the council. Xaviero couldn't break Zev's hold on them, not even the members of the Sacred Circle."

Another coughing fit seized Hemming hard. His body was slippery from all the blood leaking from so many places the chains had opened up. Branislava looked to Gregori, her sorrow so heavy she could barely breathe.

The pain is gone now. His body is numb, Gregori assured her. *Can you not feel his joy? He is going to be with his lifemate. They are bound, whether or not tied soul to soul. He cannot wait to be with her.*

Branislava knew Gregori spoke the truth. Hemming's head fell back into her lap and once more his gaze jumped to his grandson's.

"He never knew you were my grandson. He didn't even suspect—not until recently. It was amusing to see him rail and rant, throwing temper tantrums like a child because he couldn't kill the six of you he wanted dead. He used my blood to build servants, but he didn't understand that the making of a true *Sange rau*—or rather a *Hän ku pesäk kaikak*—took time. He expected the Lycans he forced into his service to be faster and smarter and better than all they encountered."

His hand went out to Zev. Trembling. Weak. The loss of blood was telling on him and he choked several times, fighting for breath. Branislava didn't care if Hemming was numb or not. She couldn't stand that fact that he was drowning in his own blood and knew it.

> *I call to water's life source pay heed to my call,*
> *I bid you to bend and reform to my will,*
> *I take that which is lifeblood and turn it aside,*
> *So that air may now flow giving peace to this life.*

Hemming looked up at her and smiled. "I'm not afraid, little granddaughter. The pain of the chains is gone and I'm free. I feel as if I'm soaring across the sky. I have this time to be with my grandson and to meet you and his friends. No man could ask for more as he passes. I thank you for your care."

Clearly her small spell had worked, and he was able to find an alternative method of breathing enough to talk as his time ran out. Branislava shoved her free hand in her mouth to keep from sobbing aloud. Hemming clearly wanted to be free of the life he had led. She didn't want to ruin his passing with her tears.

"These men. Lycans. The ones Xaviero forced into his service," Hemming said. "They were good men, Zev. Kind men. Some did their best to ease my suffering. They had no choice once Xaviero took away their free will. They will feel tremendous guilt. And they will be forever shunned by Lycan society, and yet they need to belong to a pack."

"I hear you, grandfather," Zev said softly. "I understand."

"You can't risk them going rogue. They need a strong alpha they can look up to."

"You tried to be that alpha for them, didn't you?" Zev asked, with sudden comprehension. "Even wrapped in chains of silver you tried to help the others."

"They can't continue without a pack, you know that. They're good boys. Some of them must have survived."

Not the one who had thrown his grandfather facedown in the dirt in front of Xaviero. That *Sange rau* had not survived. Dimitri had dispatched him quietly and quickly while the rest of those in the field had watched in horror as Xaviero and Xayvion had opened the gates of hell.

"Maybe a dozen," Zev said.

"So few. Xaviero took so many lives so casually. He was cruel, Zev. So cruel. If the Lycan he wanted in his service didn't join with him, the mage tortured and killed his family. Then, just to rub salt in the wounds, he took on his Lycan image and became the kindly Rannalufr, to counsel the rest of the grieving family members. More than likely he made them feel such guilt they quickly killed themselves. He would dance with glee around the laboratory whenever he managed to ruin an entire family."

The coughing was continuous now. The bleeding was steady, no matter how many times Zev wiped the blood from his grandfather's mouth.

It won't be long now, love, Branislava said. *He's close. I don't know why he's still holding on when he could embrace death.*

Zev feared he knew. "Rannalufr means 'plundering wolf.' I suppose if any of us had just thought about how that name didn't fit the imagery we might have looked closer at him."

Hemming made a movement as though he might shake his head, but the effort was too much and sent him into another violent coughing fit. Zev took his free hand.

"You want *me* to be responsible for these displaced Lycans. To form a pack with them and become their alpha. Not someone else. You want me to be their leader."

Hemming nodded, too exhausted to speak.

"I give you my word, Grandfather. I'll take care of them." Inwardly Zev sighed. He knew what his grandfather wanted all along. But that many *Sange rau*, all relatively newly made, shunned by the Lycans and their council, would be a handful. "They will make tremendous elite hunters once trained properly. If they wish to join my pack, I'll take them on."

Now he was a schoolteacher. Zev couldn't contain the little sigh. A flash of amusement lit up Hemming's eyes. He squeezed Zev's hand and then allowed his lashes to drift down.

There was a moment where he took a breath and exhaled. Peace settled over his ravaged features. A kind of joy. His lips curved into a soft smile, and he was gone.

Branislava held Hemming's hand for a few more moments and then gently extricated herself, allowing his head to lie on the ground once again. She reached out to Zev, who immediately wrapped his arm around her.

"He wanted to go," Gregori said, his voice a little rougher than normal. "I'm sorry, Zev. He was a good man. It would have been a pleasure to have had more time with him, if for any other reason than to learn from him."

Zev nodded. He looked past Mikhail to see the four silent sentinels, Andre, Tomas, Lojos, and Mataias standing guard between Mikhail and the *Sange rau* lined up behind them, watching in silence. He noted each of the faces of the mixed bloods. They looked grief-stricken. Confused. Ashamed. All of them had bowed their heads at Hemming's passing. Two wore the Sacred Circle tattoo, and one crossed himself. Another looked as if he murmured a prayer.

The moment Zev looked up, all eyes jumped to his face. Waiting for him to judge them. To pass sentence on them. He was weary of blood and death. Of fighting. He had lost friends this day—they all had. But these men had lost everything. They were no longer Lycan and most Lycans wouldn't welcome them home. Even if the council ruled to lift the death sentence on the *Sange rau*, there would be prejudice until education finally won the old ones over.

Their free will was taken from them. They tried to fight against Xaviero's orders. Some embraced his rule, while these did not. You can see marks on them. Some of them were disciplined by the mage. His disciplines are brutal. Cruel, Branislava informed him.

I will not force them to join my pack. They've had enough of others making choices for them. They can make up their minds.

Most likely they'd heard the conversation with his grandfather, but he was held to that promise—not any of them.

Slowly he stood up and made his way to them. The row of *Sange rau*—no, not that—they were *Hän ku pesäk kaikak*. "In spite of what others have told you, in spite of every ancient belief, a mixed blood is not an abomination. Just as a Lycan can make the choice to become a rogue werewolf, and the Carpathian can make the choice to become a vampire, you also have a choice in how you want to live. At this moment, you are considered *Hän ku pesäk kaikak*, which means 'guardian of all.' I am *Hän ku pesäk kaikak*. I make no apologies for this. I take my role very seriously. I guard all species. Lycan. Carpathian. Jaguar. Human, and yes, even mage."

One man stepped forward. "I'm Caleb," he introduced himself. "We fought for the mage and have committed terrible crimes."

Zev nodded his head gravely. It would do no good to dismiss things done in battle. "War brings out the worst in all of us," he agreed. "Especially when we have no choice. Xaviero took your will from you. In some ways, he took all of our wills, forcing us to fight against one another. He was a powerful mage and he had centuries of planning the downfall of our people. He made you pawns and turned you into the thing you were taught to hate the most. That doesn't mean he should continue to rule you. You all have choices to make."

"Where can we go?" Caleb asked. "My pack will never accept me back. I have no family to go back to."

The others nodded.

"It is entirely up to you. I can teach you the ways of the elite hunter. With me, you can learn the ways of the Carpathian so that your skills will improve even more. You will be expected to understand the full meaning of what it is to be a guardian of all and to live your life with honor. You are free to leave now and choose your own way. If you choose the way of the *Sange rau* and you decide to go rogue or vampire, we will hunt you down and kill you. That is a fact I cannot deny."

"Are you saying you would have us?" Caleb asked. "All of us? After what was done here?"

"Xaviero and Xayvion did this. You were victims of his cruel magic. We all were." Zev shrugged. "Look around you. Do you see condemnation? That is not the way of the Carpathian people. You are both Lycan and Carpathian. Your loyalty must be first to your pack and then to both species if you remain with me."

Gregori stirred, but said nothing when Mikhail flicked him one telling glance.

The twelve men looked around the battlefield. Carpathians had called down the lightning to burn their dead, and Lycans had chosen to fuel the ceremonial pyre to incinerate their dead. Rolf, the other council members and the pack leaders huddled together. Some shot the twelve suspicious glances, but no one challenged them as they talked with Zev.

"They will not accept us," Caleb pointed out.

Zev shrugged. "That's their problem not ours. They had no trouble allowing us to fight for them—and they'll call on us again."

The guardians looked at one another as though uncertain what to do. Zev shook his head. "Any time you join a pack and swear allegiance to the alpha pair, it is solely an individual choice. It has to be. Each of you make up your own mind."

He glanced at Gregori and then back to the others. "Know this about the pack leader you will serve under. I am fair and loyal, but I absolute demand your best at all times. I don't tolerate insubordination. I have women in my pack who are as good or better warriors than any of you, and I expect them to be treated with respect at all times. If you can't handle those things, you don't belong in my pack."

He noted each of their expressions, especially the ones with the tattoos of the Sacred Circle. Many of those who believed in the sacred code didn't believe women should fight with men.

"You also need to know my allegiance is given to Mikhail, prince of the Carpathian people. I am Carpathian, just as I am Lycan. I am a guardian of all and I will defend him with my life. I will expect my pack to do the same."

Again he watched them closely. Two frowned, but they appeared more puzzled than dismayed.

"We're both Lycan and Carpathian," Caleb said, with a little bit of wonder in his voice.

Zev nodded his head in agreement. "Think about it and let me know. You're free to go wherever you like. And you're free to contact me when you make up your mind."

Caleb shook his head and stepped forward, gripping Zev's shoulders hard. "I cannot be without a strong pack leader. Hemming was my acknowledged leader, though most of the time I couldn't do the things he would have wished. I would be more than honored if you would accept me into your pack."

It looks like we're going to have a very big family, Branislava said.

I know, Branka. I'm sorry. I don't want to complicate our lives, but I can't leave them without a leader.

She laughed softly, wrapping him up in her love. *We asked for wolves, remember? I think the old adage "be careful what you wish for" might apply here.*

He laughed softly in his mind with her, sharing that moment of humor while each of the twelve guardians swore their fidelity to him and to their new pack. He had to learn their names quickly before he performed the introductions to his lifemate, their alpha, and Daciana, Makoce and Lykaon, before bringing them before the prince.

The four silent guards watching over Mikhail moved a little closer, as did Gregori, but no one objected to the formal introductions.

"I have much left to do here," Zev pointed out. "Daciana, Lykaon and Makoce can find you a place to stay until we can make homes within the forest where you'll be more comfortable."

He watched his pack move off the battlefield. *Life just became a lot more complicated.*

I have no doubt that you can handle it.

"We couldn't get here any faster," Gregori apologized. "We brought reinforcements, but the barrier kept us out."

"Xayvion slipped away, but Xaviero is dead. Let's hope he stays that way," Zev said.

Mikhail shook his head. "We lost a couple of our warriors, but the Lycans were hit particularly hard it seems."

"Those closest to the mage were lost," Zev explained. "He needed souls for his exchange. His toads were more of a delaying tactic but his hellhounds and his *Sange rau* killed quite a few. He also sent some into the fire before we managed to stop him." He looked down at the body of his grandfather. "All this time Xaviero had him, torturing him, and I didn't know."

"I'm sorry for your loss," Mikhail said sincerely. "And I'm sorry we couldn't get here faster with more men. Perhaps the losses would have been less."

"Rolf had the choice to send everyone away," Zev said, a little surprised at the bitter feeling welling up. "He chose to force his people to stay without even properly warning them or giving them the choice." He turned his head, his gaze finding the council leader. "Excuse me, please, Mikhail. I need to talk to Rolf."

"We'll take your grandfather's body to the cave of the warriors," Gregori offered. "We'd like to do something to help."

Zev inclined his head. He dropped to one knee beside Hemming and rested his palm on his grandfather's forehead in a silent tribute. It was covered in blood and deep scars where the chains had been. "They would have sentenced him to death. The council. Do you realize that?" He looked up at Branislava. "They killed my grandmother. Not the mage, but her own pack. They would have done the same to Hemming had he not fled in the night with my mother."

"They only knew the *Sange rau*," Branislava reminded gently. "Not the *Hän ku pesäk kaikak*. They didn't know there was a difference."

Zev shook his head and stood, shoving both hands through his hair, looking more a wild wolf than ever. "They would have killed me, Branka. Knowing me, they would still have killed me. All those men." He waved his hand toward his new pack members who followed Daciana out of the clearing. "There's no compassion on the faces or in the hearts of the council members for them. Mikhail feels more and he's a stranger to them. Caleb was right. So was Hemming. They will never be wholly welcomed by our people. I won't, either. In time, you won't. They saw what was done to Dimitri, but rather than condemn themselves for being so medieval, they wanted to talk and make excuses. They never really looked at him as a person."

Branislava laid her hand gently on his arm. "Seeing your grandfather wrapped in chains, seeing what silver can do to a Lycan's body has really upset you, Zev, as it should, but perhaps it would be much better to wait to speak with Rolf."

"He didn't even warn the other Lycans, Branka. He knew the danger and yet he said nothing to them. Had we held the ceremonial service immediately after Arno and Arnau were killed, Xaviero wouldn't have had time to set up his trap. He would have been forced to hold his ritual somewhere else. I could have tracked him, but Rolf refused even that."

She rubbed his arm. "I know." What else could she say? He had argued with Rolf for hours, trying to get him to agree to send the slain council member and his son off the next rising without telling anyone where they would build the funeral pyre. There had been a stubborn set to Rolf's jaw she'd never noticed in the few times she'd seen him. He had been dismissive, and almost rude to Zev.

Zev leaned into her unexpectedly, his arms pulling her close, just holding her while he breathed away his anger. She wrapped her arms tightly around him, giving him as much strength as she could. All of them were battle-scarred, but she knew this night had taken its toll on her wolf.

Zev brushed a kiss along Branislava's mouth. "I love you," he whispered. He didn't say it often enough to her, he was certain, but he felt it with every breath he took.

"I know. I'll be right here."

He appreciated that she didn't argue with him. He needed to do this tonight. He was a man who could stay in control—and he would—but he didn't want to. He wanted the satisfaction of curling his fingers into a fist and punching Rolf in his pompous face.

He strode over to the small group of Lycans, the pack leaders with Rolf and Randall. Randall broke into a smile the moment he caught sight of Zev.

"As always, you pulled us through. I've never seen anything like that in my life." He held out his hand.

Zev took it almost reluctantly. He couldn't blame Randall for Rolf's decision. "I'll miss working with you, Randall," he said quietly.

Instantly all conversation ceased and the pack leaders turned to face him, shock on their faces. Rolf scowled at him.

"I don't understand," Randall said. "Of course you'll be working with us. You're our enforcer. Our elite hunter. You're invaluable. This wasn't your fault. No one could have predicted such a thing. Hellhounds. An army of *Sange rau*. Poisonous frogs." He shuddered. "And to think all this time Rannalufr was really this evil mage."

"His plan was to bring about the downfall of the Lycans. His brother Xavier tried with the Carpathians, and Xayvion has nearly destroyed the Jaguar species. I think they came close to their goal. We nearly allowed a war between Lycan and Carpathian."

"Have those remaining traitors, Xaviero's *Sange rau* army, been taken into custody? I saw them leaving with Daciana and the others," Rolf demanded.

Zev shook his head. "Xaviero took their free will from them. They fought against him, but he gave them the blood to become mixed bloods. He murdered their families and tortured them when they went against him. In the end, he took their will because it was the only way he could get them to cooperate. They are innocent."

"That's not your place to judge," Rolf pointed out.

Zev smiled at him. "I'm resigning. I will no longer aid a council who do not serve all their people or have their best interests at heart. As for the twelve men who need support and won't get it from their own people, they'l have it here with me. If you wish to pass judgment on them, you'll have to talk to their pack leader as is the way of all Lycans."

"You can't resign. We don't accept your resignation," Randall said.

"I'm sorry, Randall. You're a good man. But I gave my counsel to Rolf and he refused to listen to me. He didn't go to you and discuss it. He made an arbitrary decision to put his pack leaders and you in unnecessary jeopardy."

Randall's eyebrow shot up. "Is that true, Rolf? Why? That goes against everything the council stands for."

"You would have sided with Zev and my vote is the tiebreaker. There were only two of us," Rolf defended.

The other two council members who had come for Arno's ceremony looked at one another with raised eyebrows.

Rolf waved his hands dismissively. "Why waste time arguing? Zev, think what you're doing. If a mistake was made here, and I concede I may have been wrong, that doesn't mean a resignation is in order."

Zev spread his hands out in front of him. "The prejudice against mixed blood is so strong in Lycans, Rolf, that even you wouldn't listen when I told you what would happen here."

Rolf shook his head. "That's not true, Zev."

"It is true. In all the long years I've been the council's leading elite hunter, every time I've given you advice based on my knowledge and my instincts, you've followed it. You didn't this time. Arno was very conflicted about those of us who are mixed blood because of his belief in the sacred code, but at least he admitted it and struggled with what was the right thing to do. You didn't listen this time because you found out I'm a mixed blood and you no longer trusted my judgment."

Rolf shook his head but he didn't deny it aloud.

"The thing is, I've always been a mixed blood. My mother was of Carpathian descent. All those centuries I served this council, you had a mixed blood giving you advice and fighting your battles for you. I protected all of you. Even knowing that, you would have sentenced me to death. Rolf, this could have been a slaughterhouse. We were fortunate that the four Carpathian women here with us today could defeat the mages. You should have listened to me. I hope you listen to whoever is chosen to take my place."

Once again he touched Randall's hand, lifted a hand in salute to the pack leaders and turned on his heel to walk away from them. He didn't belong with them anymore. Not until they figured it out and changed their policies. He was mixed blood—both Lycan and Carpathian and he would never turn rogue or vampire. They had seen Dimitri, Fen and him fight for them and still, not one of them had given their condolences on his grandfather, or made a comment on how appalling it was that Xaviero had used silver to torture a man for years. It hadn't occurred to them that he was a man. Or a Lycan. Or a Carpathian. Or all three. Hemming was simply *Sange rau* to them and that was all they saw.

He wrapped his arm around Branislava, not missing a step as he continued away from the battlefield toward the forest where they could shift in privacy and join Gregori and Mikhail in the cave of warriors. Fen and Tatijana, Dimitri and Skyler as well as Razvan and Ivory were already waiting for them.

He had no doubt they would give his grandfather the honors due him before laying him to rest. These were the people he chose to be with. He was Lycan in his heart and he always would be, but he was also *Hän ku pesäk kaikak*—guardian of all. Right now, the only thing in his mind was paying proper tribute to Hemming in a private and loving way.

23

Zev woke to the moon directly above him, the beams shining like a spotlight over him. The sky was clear with thousands of brilliant stars glittering like diamonds. He turned his head and Branislava smiled at him. His heart did that slow, melting somersault it often did when she gave him that particular smile.

"You opened the earth."

"I wanted you to wake to the night. It's so beautiful, Zev."

The heat of her body warmed him, her skin, hot silk, gliding against his, making him feel alive. Her head rested on his arm, and she lay snuggled tight against him, his body curved protectively around hers. He knew she was trying to ease not only the pain of losing his grandfather, but the bitter reality that the two men he'd considered close friends for more years than most could count had turned on him. Certainly not openly and maybe they didn't even realize it yet, but in their hearts, they thought differently of him because he was mixed blood.

"Zev," she said softly, reading his thoughts. "They will come around. Rolf was ashamed and guilty. Randall didn't realize the man in chains was your grandfather. Mikhail spoke with both of them and they're devastated that you resigned. They'll be the ones to persuade the Lycans to accept mixed bloods."

He sighed and nuzzled the top of her head. Her hair, usually more red gold, was very red and all over the place, just the way he liked it. "Maybe you're right." He wanted her to be. He couldn't help the affection he had for the two men he'd protected for a good portion of his life. The fact that they didn't reciprocate was difficult to accept.

She brushed a kiss along his bicep. "They reciprocate. They don't know how to backtrack, but they will. Give them time, Zev."

"You were right to insist we come to our little crater," he murmured against her wild hair, willing to let her make him feel differently. He was happy with her. He would always be happy with her, no matter what else was going on in his life. "I should always listen to you."

He felt her smile against his bicep. Her small teeth nipped, sending a thrill vibrating through his body. "Of course you should. When it comes to you, Wolfie, I'm the woman who plans to see to every detail of your happiness and health."

He heard that little bite in her voice. "I'm sorry I was such a fool last night. I should have allowed you to heal my wounds before we laid my grandfather properly to rest. I know you weren't the least bit happy with me."

Her mouth curved against his arm. He felt the warmth of her breath and then the brush of her lips. "So coming up to our special mountain was a little compensation."

Of course she'd known. He knew she wasn't happy with waiting, so when she suggested going to the mountain where they'd spend the day nestled in the crater high up in the dome, beneath the rich soil, surrounded by cooling mist and snowcaps, he'd agreed just to appease her.

"I like taking care of you, Zev. It matters to me."

He heard the honesty in her voice and winced. Not only did it matter, but as his lifemate she was driven to care for not only his happiness, but his health.

"I know, Branka," he admitted, and nuzzled the top of her head with his chin again, enjoying the way her hair caught in the shadow on his jaw. Silken strands, weaving them together in intimacy. He liked the image although it was far too corny to ever admit to her.

"You insisted on healing me," she pointed out.

His smile came instantly at that little sulky note in her voice. He felt jo sweeping through him. He had gone to ground with the weight of the world on his shoulders, still upset—and hurt—over Randall's and Rolf's reactions to the death of his grandfather. He had woken to Branislava and his shaken world had righted itself.

"I did, didn't I?" He couldn't help the lazy satisfaction creeping into his tone. He tracked a shooting star before he turned his head to brush kisses along her temple. "I'm sorry."

She frowned. "For what?"

"I promised you I wouldn't make arbitrary decisions that affected both of us, but without consulting you or even thinking about consulting you, I committed us to taking on those twelve very lost men—the mixed bloods. They're traumatized and it won't always be easy. I should have asked you what you wanted to do."

Branislava rolled to her side, propping herself up on one elbow to look into his eyes. "Silly wolf. Of course you had to take those men into your pack. If you hadn't, I would have been disappointed in you. That's the man I love, the man I know and respect. Aside from that, your grandfather practically gave you an order. He wanted those men taken care of." She leaned in, drawing his attention to her swaying breasts. "My mouth is talking and it's just a little higher up than where you're looking."

"I know," he murmured, "but you're intentionally distracting me."

He leaned over and helped himself, licking at her nipple and then tugging with his teeth until her breath came in ragged gasps. He drew her breast into the heat of his mouth, discovered she was even hotter, all that wonderful natural fire coming to the surface just for him.

Branislava ran trembling fingers through Zev's hair in a long caress, enjoying the sensation of the soft strands against her skin while his mouth devoured her breast. "I love watching you," she confided. "It's a very erotic sight to see your hunger for my body."

She could feel his hunger as well. His desire was always intense, almost tangible. The pull of his mouth was strong, the suction, the moist heat, his teeth scraping seductively and the small nips that sent electrical charges straight to her dampening center.

He lifted his head and his eyes stared straight into hers. Her breath caught in her throat at the absolute possession stamped in his face and the fierce desire in the depths of his eyes. In that moment, he was wolf all the way, a sexual creature of insatiable appetites. And he was hers.

She pushed herself up on her hands and knees, straddling his hips to trail kisses down his scarred chest. "I fed this morning. Enough for both of us," she confided, her voice dropping to a low siren's whisper.

His body tightened wickedly, every muscle contracting as she licked at his pulse, the stroke of her tongue creating an answering throb in his veins. The sensation was pure pleasure, moving through him, consuming him. There was no way to prepare for the erotic burst of pure decadence, of indulgence, as her teeth sank into him. The bite of pain simply added to the intensity of his desire. She was an addiction, his greatest asset, his greatest love. He fisted both hands tightly in her luxurious hair. The feel of all that fiery silk in his rough palms maddened him with need.

Still, there was a part of him that simply enjoyed that slow, leisurely awakening of desire in his mind, when his body was already hot and hard. He could already taste her in his mouth, the wonderful combination of cinnamon spice and honey that was in her blood, in the hot liquid seeping from the very core of her body—for him. Only for him.

He was alpha enough, wolf enough, to enjoy the fact that he was the only man who would ever have her, ever know her passionate fire, her devotion to pleasing him, the minute details she employed to give him absolute pleasure. Branislava always focused so completely on *him* when they made love, never herself. She gave and gave to him. He was in her mind, in her heart, in her very soul. She wanted him to be sated, completely satisfied and utterly spent with each joining.

He didn't want to tell her that would never happen. The more she gave, the more he craved his beautiful addiction, the more his love felt all encompassing, overwhelming even. She licked across the small pinpricks on his chest, closing them, adding one more shudder of pleasure before she moved up and over him.

His hand slid up her silken inner thigh and he felt her muscles tighten in anticipation. Her heat was growing, that wonderful secret haven he always lost himself in. He slipped a finger inside her and felt her gasp, felt hot liquid surround him and tight muscles clamp down like a vise. Very slowly he withdrew his finger and brought it to his mouth.

"Nothing tastes as good as you," he whispered, meaning it. He could spend a lifetime indulging his cravings with her body.

Her tongue slid across the pinpricks on his chest, as her body heated more. She pushed back, coming over the top of him, her breasts sliding over the muscles of his body, causing them to react, drawing every bit of blood to his groin until he was bursting with urgent need. He caught her arms, providing a soft carpet of thick grass to surround her. He wanted the hard earth beneath it to hold her in place while he took her, but he didn't want her uncomfortable.

In one smooth motion, he rolled her under him and bent his head to the swell of her breast where her pulse beat so strongly, beckoning him, calling to him with a frantic urgency. Her spicy fragrance rose, his mate making her own demands, there in the secret cradle of new life they'd discovered. He thought of that small crater inside the mountain as their own private paradise.

He teased her nipple into a tight peak with a flat, broad stroke of his tongue, enjoying the way her body flushed, all that hot passion rising like a tide, a volcano, so close to the surface, so close to a fiery explosion. He indulged himself, his mind needing the slow, leisurely enjoyment of her body while his body continued to demand a wild instantaneous satisfaction.

He kissed his way up the slope of her breast to that throbbing beat and without preamble sank his teeth deep. She arched into him, her soft cry music to his ears. He loved every sound she made, every whimper, every plea, the way she chanted his name. His rough hands moved over her soft body, a claiming, an exploration. Every part of her was his. This amazing, beautiful woman gave herself to him, gave her body to him to play and worship there.

Her blood grew hotter and her skin flushed a beautiful rose as she writhed under him. He lifted his head and watched the two small trickles of ruby-red blood make their way down her breast. With a smile he chased them, lapping at them before closing the two small holes he'd made. At once he closed his mouth again over her left breast, the fingers of his hand tugging and rolling at her other nipple. She cried out, this time a little louder, pushing her breast into the heat of his mouth while he bit down softly.

He lifted his head to look down at her with satisfaction. Her breasts were covered with small strawberries, marks of his possession, tiny little nips, and most of all her nipples were hard peaks. "I saw a woman once wearing only a small fancy, decorative golden chain connecting one breast to the other, from nipple to nipple, and I couldn't understand why until this moment. You have the most beautiful breasts, Branka, so beautiful. I could see you wearing little but a decorative chain. She had one that was five strands wrapped around her hips and nothing more."

"Where in the world did you see such a sight?"

His hand stroked between her legs and he felt the flood of liquid at the idea. "I chased a Lycan who had murdered his neighbor into a club where there was dancing."

She laughed softly. "There was obviously a lot more going on than dancing."

"Probably, but I didn't have the time to stay and watch. Although, if you want to dance for me, I would be more than willing to sit back and enjoy the show."

"You think I wouldn't?" She caught his head in her hands, framing his face. "I would do anything for you. Anything you asked or wished of me."

"Then dance for me, *mon chaton féroce*. I would love to sit here and watch you dance."

He rolled off of her, reclined back on their thick mat of grass and watched as she gracefully got to her feet. She turned her back to him and the sound of music began to drift into the cradle, through the leaves of the few trees, an exotic, sexy sound that matched the beat of his heart.

She swept her hair up in an intricate do, long tendrils looking as though they'd escaped to drift down her back to her bottom. When she turned, his heart skipped a beat and then began pounding. She wore a decorative chain, several strands of finest gold woven in an intricate pattern strung from one breast to the other. The clamps on her nipples were jeweled and tiny bells hung from the loops of the chains.

His cock, already full, nearly burst. His hand moved down to casually circle his burgeoning erection while he inspected the series of chains wrapped around her hips. Little strands of bells hung like fringe, dipping low, nearly covering her fiery mound and the damp heat between her legs, but each movement gave him teasing, enticing glimpses.

She swayed, a sultry movement, undulating her body, a ripple of pure sexual intent. She kept her eyes on his, moving around him, her small bare feet making no sound in the grass so that she appeared to be dancing almost in the air.

The small bells tinkled and added their notes to the music. He realized that each bell sent a small vibration through his cock. His fist tightened, slowly sliding in time with that beat up and down his shaft. He had never seen anything more sensual in his life. She danced gracefully, but every movement was about sex, was an invitation to claim her body—was a claiming of his body.

The wind drifted through the small crater and caught at her hair, tugged at the bells and brought him her enticing fragrance. He crooked his finger at her and she swayed closer. He reached up and caught the chain, tugging gently. She gasped and came down to her knees, her breath hissing out of her, her green eyes going wide as fire raced from her nipples to her groin. He kept tugging, bringing her lower until her mouth was over his cock.

She laughed softly, a sound of pure joy, the warmth of her breath teasing the broad head, and then he inhaled sharply as her tongue lapped at the small pearls waiting for her. She enveloped him, her mouth gloriously hot, eager to taste him, to please him, happy that her dance had given him such happiness. He caught her hair in one hand and played with the chain with the other as she suckled him, her mouth tight, her tongue dancing. He let his head fall back and he watched the stars above him. "No other man could ever be this happy, Branka," he whispered.

Her fingers danced over his tight sac, her mouth perfection; at times she took him so deep the constriction shocked him while the sensation bordered on ecstasy. When he knew she was going to drain him, he tugged the chain again, forcing her forward, forcing her to lift her head.

Her jeweled gaze met his. She pouted at him. "I was hungry."

"So am I," he said, his voice close to a growl. He pushed her gently to the ground. "Very hungry. A wolf's hunger."

She shivered, and made a move as if she might remove the chains. He shook his head. "Leave them. I'll remove them later. I like the bells and the way they look on you." He tugged again at the chain between her breasts, lifting the two soft mounds slightly. "I never thought an adornment would look so beautiful against your skin. Your skin is flawless, amazing, and such a perfect color." Her skin felt—and looked—like soft rose petals flushed with heat.

"I have scars," she said softly and went to touch the raised ridge between her breasts.

He caught her hand and pushed it back to the ground. "This body belongs to *me*," he snapped, and leaned down as he pulled up on the chain, lifting her breasts so that he could nip at the underside of her left breast. "*Mine.* And it's perfection. You don't get to ever say anything disparaging about this body." He ran his tongue along the ridged scar from one breast to the other, teasing and tugging at the chain.

He'd made the declaration half in humor and half serious. He loved her body and he never wanted her to feel less than beautiful. He kissed his way down from the jeweled tips of her breasts to her intriguing belly button. He spent some time there, teasing and nipping before moving lower to inspect those mysterious little bells. If she moved, bucked her hips, would that same vibration run through his cock? A small experiment was in order. The music continued to play, drifting on the wind, the branches of the trees swaying gently, as if keeping time. He lifted her hips, wedging his shoulders between her thighs to hold her open to him. She was a beautiful flower full of nectar and he wanted it all.

He bent his head and lapped at the honey spilling from her. She bucked hard. The tiny bells jingled along the chain running from one nipple to the other as her breasts swayed. The bells around her hips chimed, soft little musical notes that vibrated through his cock, sending electrical shocks singing through his entire body.

He held her firmly, a hungry wolf, doing what he did best—devouring her. He used his tongue to draw out the nectar he craved. He used the edge of his teeth to tug on her sensitive bud to keep the bells playing. He suckled strongly, listening to the beauty of her voice crying out as he drove her up fast and hard, over and over, sending her body into a series of wild orgasms that rocked her.

Each movement sent the bells frantically singing and his cock nearly exploding with the intensity of the vibrations. He shifted position again, kneeling between her legs, needing to be inside of her. Her lashes were a half-mast, the green eyes glazed and sensual. Her full lips were parted, her breathing ragged as he moved over her, entering her in one brutal thrust.

She sobbed his name as he paused, holding himself deep in her while he bit down on the chain between her breasts, sucking it into his mouth and holding it between his teeth. He surged into her again and again and each time he did, the chain tugged on her breasts. All the while he stayed merged mind to mind, better to feel the hot pleasure streaking through her nipples, down her belly and into her tight sheath as he thrust in and out of her. Her fiery core had never been quite so scorching, fisting around him, clamping down like a vise so that the friction as he pounded into her nearly sent them both up in flames.

Fire arced from one nipple to the other as he tugged the chain with his teeth. The bells chimed and the flames jumped to his cock, scorching him like white lightning. He could feel exactly what she felt, that fire burning through her breasts, a delicious, sweet burn that flashed through her body like a storm to center around his shaft.

He didn't want the sensations to ever stop for either of them, but he could feel her body growing hotter, tightening around his cock mercilessly, almost to the point of strangulation. The ground turned a subtle shade of red, her body was a magnet, drawing the magma that was at the very earth's core just as it sought to draw the seed from him.

She whispered his name, a soft plea, and he took her over the edge, soaring with her, freefalling through space, while her muscles clamped down around him, milking him, surrounding him with her particular fire. He didn't wait for the aftershocks to cease. He leaned down and carefully removed one jewel from her nipple, and drew her breast into the soothing heat of his mouth.

Her breath hissed out and her lashes drifted down, a look of intense pleasure on her face. He stroked her nipple over and over with his tongue, ending with kisses before attending to the other breast. Her sheath tightened around him, clamping down hard as he released the jewel and took her breast into his mouth. The soft moan added to his conviction that the fire in her only seemed to be growing, and no matter how passionate they were, how often he took possession of her body—or even how he took possession—the fire between them would only get hotter.

"Do you have any idea how much I love you, Branka?" he asked, his voice low, a strange lump choking him. He had to clear his throat several times.

"Yes," she said quietly, reaching up with her slender arms to circle his neck. "You love me as fiercely as I love you. And it grows with every moment we're together."

"Did the chain hurt you at all?"

She laughed. "I'm Carpathian, wolf. I would never play with something that hurt in the way you mean. I felt fire, but you know I love that burn. If it got to be too intense, I simply turned down the heat a notch. You were in my mind, feeling what I was feeling, watching to make certain you weren't hurting me in any way. I felt you there, caring for me. Protecting me. That's why I trust you so much, Zev. You put me first."

"You're my mate. The love of my life. My everything. Of course I'm going to make certain you feel nothing but pleasure, any way I can give it to you."

"Naturally," she agreed, "although, Zev, your nature dictates who and what you are. You would put my health, happiness and pleasure above your own regardless of whether we were lifemates or not. That's what I love most about you. *Who* you are."

She raised her face to his, kissing him slowly, taking her time, the fire in her mouth sending a fiery arrow straight to his heart. He kissed her back with the same passion, the same fire, but his mouth was infinitely tender, showing her without words how much he felt for her. When he lifted his head she was smiling at him. He found himself smiling back and once again began moving in her body, this time slow and leisurely. They had all the time in the world.

APPENDIX I
Carpathian Healing Chants

To rightly understand Carpathian healing chants, background is required in several areas:

1. The Carpathian view on healing
2. The Lesser Healing Chant of the Carpathians
3. The Great Healing Chant of the Carpathians
4. Carpathian musical aesthetics
5. Lullaby
6. Song to Heal the Earth
7. Carpathian chanting technique

1. THE CARPATHIAN VIEW ON HEALING

The Carpathians are a nomadic people whose geographic origins can be traced back to at least as far as the Southern Ural Mountains (near the steppes of modern-day Kazakhstan), on the border between Europe and Asia. (For this reason, modern-day linguists call their language "proto-Uralic," without knowing that this is the language of the Carpathians.) Unlike most nomadic peoples, the wandering of the Carpathians was not due to the need to find

new grazing lands as the seasons and climate shifted, or the search for better trade. Instead, the Carpathians' movements were driven by a great purpose: to find a land that would have the right earth, a soil with the kind of
richness that would greatly enhance their rejuvenative powers.

Over the centuries, they migrated westward (some six thousand years
ago), until they at last found their perfect homeland—their *susu*—in the
Carpathian Mountains, whose long arc cradled the lush plains of the king-
dom of Hungary. (The kingdom of Hungary flourished for over a
millennium—making Hungarian the dominant language of the Carpathian
Basin—until the kingdom's lands were split among several countries after
World War I: Austria, Czechoslovakia, Romania, Yugoslavia and modern
Hungary.)

Other peoples from the Southern Urals (who shared the Carpathian language, but were not Carpathians) migrated in different directions.
Some ended up in Finland, which accounts for why the modern Hungarian and Finnish languages are among the contemporary descendents of
the ancient Carpathian language. Even though they are tied forever
to their chosen Carpathian homeland, the wandering of the Carpathians

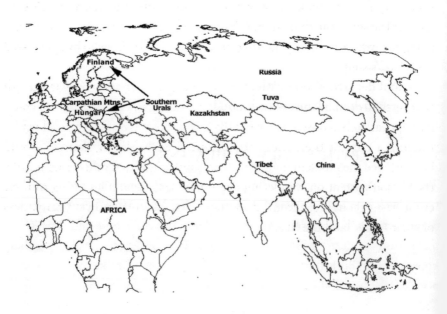

continues as they search the world for the answers that will enable them to bear and raise their offspring without difficulty.

Because of their geographic origins, the Carpathian views on healing share much with the larger Eurasian shamanistic tradition. Probably the closest modern representative of that tradition is based in Tuva (and is referred to as "Tuvinian Shamanism")—see the map on the previous page.

The Eurasian shamanistic tradition—from the Carpathians to the Siberian shamans—held that illness originated in the human soul, and only later manifested as various physical conditions. Therefore, shamanistic healing, while not neglecting the body, focused on the soul and its healing. The most profound illnesses were understood to be caused by "soul departure," where all or some part of the sick person's soul has wandered away from the body (into the nether realms), or has been captured or possessed by an evil spirit, or both.

The Carpathians belong to this greater Eurasian shamanistic tradition and share its viewpoints. While the Carpathians themselves did not succumb to illness, Carpathian healers understood that the most profound wounds were also accompanied by a similar "soul departure."

Upon reaching the diagnosis of "soul departure," the healer-shaman is then required to make a spiritual journey into the netherworlds to recover the soul. The shaman may have to overcome tremendous challenges along the way, particularly fighting the demon or vampire who has possessed his friend's soul.

"Soul departure" doesn't require a person to be unconscious (although that certainly can be the case as well). It was understood that a person could still appear to be conscious, even talk and interact with others, and yet be missing a part of their soul. The experienced healer or shaman would instantly see the problem nonetheless, in subtle signs that others might miss: the person's attention wandering every now and then, a lessening in their enthusiasm about life, chronic depression, a diminishment in the brightness of their "aura," and the like.

2. THE LESSER HEALING CHANT OF THE CARPATHIANS

Kepä Sarna Pus (**The Lesser Healing Chant**) is used for wounds that are merely physical in nature. The Carpathian healer leaves his body and enters the wounded Carpathian's body to heal great mortal wounds from the inside out using pure energy. He proclaims, "I offer freely my life for your life," as he gives his blood to the injured Carpathian. Because the Carpathians are of the earth and bound to the soil, they are healed by the soil of their homeland. Their saliva is also often used for its rejuvenative powers.

It is also very common for the Carpathian chants (both the Lesser and the Great) to be accompanied by the use of healing herbs, aromas from Carpathian candles and crystals. The crystals (when combined with the Carpathians' empathic, psychic connection to the entire universe) are used to gather positive energy from their surroundings, which then is used to accelerate the healing. Caves are sometimes used as the setting for the healing.

The Lesser Healing Chant was used by Vikirnoff Von Shrieder and Colby Jansen to heal Rafael De La Cruz, whose heart had been ripped out by a vampire as described in *Dark Secret*.

Kepä Sarna Pus (**The Lesser Healing Chant**)
The same chant is used for all physical wounds. "Sívadaba" ["into your heart"] would be changed to refer to whatever part of the body is wounded.

Kuńasz, nélkül sívdobbanás, nélkül fesztelen löyly.
You lie as if asleep, without beat of heart, without airy breath.

Ot élidamet andam szabadon élidadért.
I offer freely my life for your life.

O jelä sielam jőrem ot ainamet és soŋe ot élidadet.
My spirit of light forgets my body and enters your body.

O jelä sielam pukta kinn minden szelemeket belső.
My spirit of light sends all the dark spirits within fleeing without.

Pajńak o susu hanyet és o nyelv nyálamet sívadaba.
I press the earth of our homeland and the spit of my tongue into your
    heart.

Vii, o verim soŋe o verid andam.
At last, I give you my blood for your blood.

To hear this chant, visit: http://www.christinefeehan.com/members/.

3. THE GREAT HEALING CHANT OF THE CARPATHIANS

The most well-known—and most dramatic—of the Carpathian healing chants was *En Sarna Pus* **(The Great Healing Chant)**. This
chant was reserved for recovering the wounded or unconscious Carpathian's
soul.

Typically a group of men would form a circle around the sick Carpathian
(to "encircle him with our care and compassion") and begin the chant.
The shaman or healer or leader is the prime actor in this healing ceremony.
It is he who will actually make the spiritual journey into the netherworld,
aided by his clanspeople. Their purpose is to ecstatically dance, sing, drum
and chant, all the while visualizing (through the words of the chant) the
journey itself—every step of it, over and over again—to the point where the
shaman, in trance, leaves his body, and makes that very journey. (Indeed,
the word "ecstasy" is from the Latin *ex statis*, which literally means "out of
the body.")

One advantage that the Carpathian healer has over many other shamans
is his telepathic link to his lost brother. Most shamans must wander in the
dark of the nether realms in search of their lost brother. But the Carpathian
healer directly "hears" in his mind the voice of his lost brother calling to
him, and can thus "zero in" on his soul like a homing beacon. For this reason, Carpathian healing tends to have a higher success rate than most other
traditions of this sort.

Something of the geography of the "other world" is useful for us to
examine, in order to fully understand the words of the Great Carpathian
Healing Chant. A reference is made to the "Great Tree" (in Carpathian: *En*

Puwe). Many ancient traditions, including the Carpathian tradition, understood the worlds—the heaven worlds, our world and the nether realms—to be "hung" upon a great pole, or axis, or tree. Here on earth, we are positioned halfway up this tree, on one of its branches. Hence many ancient texts often referred to the material world as "middle earth": midway between heaven and hell. Climbing the tree would lead one to the heaven worlds. Descending the tree to its roots would lead to the nether realms. The shaman was necessarily a master of movement up and down the Great Tree, sometimes moving unaided, and sometimes assisted by (or even mounted upon the back of) an animal spirit guide. In various traditions, this Great Tree was known variously as the *axis mundi* (the "axis of the worlds"), Ygddrasil (in Norse mythology), Mount Meru (the sacred world mountain of Tibetan tradition), etc. The Christian cosmos, with its heaven, purgatory/earth and hell, is also worth comparing. It is even given a similar topography in Dante's *Divine Comedy*: Dante is led on a journey first to hell, at the center of the earth; then upward to Mount Purgatory, which sits on the earth's surface directly opposite Jerusalem; then farther upward first to Eden, the earthly paradise, at the summit of Mount Purgatory; and then upward at last to heaven.

In the shamanistic tradition, it was understood that the small always reflects the large; the personal always reflects the cosmic. A movement in the greater dimensions of the cosmos also coincides with an internal movement. For example, the *axis mundi* of the cosmos also corresponds to the spinal column of the individual. Journeys up and down the *axis mundi* often coincided with the movement of natural and spiritual energies (sometimes called *kundalini* or *shakti*) in the spinal column of the shaman or mystic.

En Sarna Pus (The Great Healing Chant)
In this chant, ekä ("brother") would be replaced by "sister," "father," "mother," depending on the person to be healed.

Ot ekäm ainajanak hany, jama.
My brother's body is a lump of earth, close to death.

Me, ot ekäm kuntajanak, pirädak ekäm, gond és irgalom türe.
We, the clan of my brother, encircle him with our care and compassion.

*O pus wäkenkek, ot oma śarnank, és ot pus fünk, álnak ekäm ainajanak,
pitänak ekäm ainajanak elävä.*
Our healing energies, ancient words of magic and healing herbs bless my
brother's body, keep it alive.

*Ot ekäm sielanak pälä. Ot omboće päläja juta alatt o jüti, kinta, és szelemek
lamtijaknak.*
But my brother's soul is only half. His other half wanders in the netherworld.

Ot en mekem ŋamaŋ: kulkedak otti ot ekäm omboće päläjanak.
My great deed is this: I travel to find my brother's other half.

*Rekatüre, saradak, tappadak, odam, kaŋa o numa waram, és avaa owe o
lewl mahoz.*
We dance, we chant, we dream ecstatically, to call my spirit bird, and to
open the door to the other world.

Ntak o numa waram, és mozdulak, jomadak.
I mount my spirit bird and we begin to move, we are under way.

*Piwtädak ot En Puwe tyvinak, ećidak alatt o jüti, kinta, és szelemek
lamtijaknak.*
Following the trunk of the Great Tree, we fall into the netherworld.

Fázak, fázak nó o śaro.
It is cold, very cold.

Juttadak ot ekäm o akarataban, o sívaban és o sielaban.
My brother and I are linked in mind, heart and soul.

Ot ekäm sielanak kaŋa engem.
My brother's soul calls to me.

Kuledak és piwtädak ot ekäm.
I hear and follow his track.

Saɣedak és tuledak ot ekäm kulyanak.
Encounter I the demon who is devouring my brother's soul.

Nenäm ćoro, o kuly torodak.
In anger, I fight the demon.

O kuly pél engem.
He is afraid of me.

Lejkkadak o kaŋka salamaval.
I strike his throat with a lightning bolt.

Molodak ot ainaja komakamal.
I break his body with my bare hands.

Toja és molanâ.
He is bent over, and falls apart.

Hän ćaδa.
He runs away.

Manedak ot ekäm sielanak.
I rescue my brother's soul.

Alᴈdak ot ekam sielanak o komamban.
I lift my brother's soul in the hollow of my hand.

Alᴈdam ot ekam numa waramra.
I lift him onto my spirit bird.

Piwtädak ot En Puwe tyvijanak és sayedak jälleen ot elävä ainak majaknak.
Following up the Great Tree, we return to the land of the living.

Ot ekäm elä jälleen.
My brother lives again.

Ot ekäm weńća jälleen.
He is complete again.

To hear this chant, visit: http://www.christinefeehan.com/members/.

4. CARPATHIAN MUSICAL AESTHETICS

In the sung Carpathian pieces (such as the "Lullaby" and the "Song to Heal the Earth"), you'll hear elements that are shared by many of the musical traditions in the Uralic geographical region, some of which still exist—from Eastern European (Bulgarian, Romanian, Hungarian, Croatian, etc.) to Romany ("gypsy"). Some of these elements include:

- the rapid alternation between major and minor modalities, including a sudden switch (called a "Picardy third") from minor to major to end a piece or section (as at the end of the "Lullaby")
- the use of close (tight) harmonies
- the use of *ritardi* (slowing down the piece) and *crescendi* (swelling in volume) for brief periods
- the use of *glissandi* (slides) in the singing tradition
- the use of trills in the singing tradition (as in the final invocation of the "Song to Heal the Earth")—similar to Celtic, a singing tradition more familiar to many of us
- the use of parallel fifths (as in the final invocation of the "Song to Heal the Earth")
- controlled use of dissonance
- "call and response" chanting (typical of many of the world's chanting traditions)

- extending the length of a musical line (by adding a couple of bars) to heighten dramatic effect
- and many more

"Lullaby" and "Song to Heal the Earth" illustrate two rather different forms of Carpathian music (a quiet, intimate piece and an energetic ensemble piece)—but whatever the form, Carpathian music is full of feeling.

5. LULLABY

This song is sung by women while the child is still in the womb or when the threat of a miscarriage is apparent. The baby can hear the song while inside the mother, and the mother can connect with the child telepathically as well. The lullaby is meant to reassure the child, to encourage the baby to hold on, to stay—to reassure the child that he or she will be protected by love even from inside until birth. The last line literally means that the mother's love will protect her child until the child is born ("rise").

Musically, the Carpathian "Lullaby" is in three-quarter time ("waltz time"), as are a significant portion of the world's various traditional lullabies (perhaps the most famous of which is "Brahms' Lullaby"). The arrangement for solo voice is the original context: a mother singing to her child, unaccompanied. The arrangement for chorus and violin ensemble illustrates how musical even the simplest Carpathian pieces often are, and how easily they lend themselves to contemporary instrumental or orchestral arrangements. (A wide range of contemporary composers, including Dvořák and Smetana, have taken advantage of a similar discovery, working other traditional Eastern European music into their symphonic poems.)

Odam-Sarna Kondak (Lullaby)

Tumtesz o wäke ku pitasz belső.
Feel the strength you hold inside.

Hiszasz sívadet. Én olenam gæidnod.
Trust your heart. I'll be your guide.

Sas csecsemõm, kuñasz.
Hush my baby, close your eyes.

Rauho joɲe ted.
Peace will come to you.

Tumtesz o sívdobbanás ku olen lamt3ad belső.
Feel the rhythm deep inside.

Gond-kumpadek ku kim te.
Waves of love that cover you.

Pesänak te, asti o jüti, kidüsz.
Protect, until the night you rise.

To hear this song, visit: http://www.christinefeehan.com/members/.

6. SONG TO HEAL THE EARTH

This is the earth-healing song that is used by the Carpathian women to heal soil filled with various toxins. The women take a position on four sides and call to the universe to draw on the healing energy with love and respect. The soil of the earth is their resting place, the place where they rejuvenate, and they must make it safe not only for themselves but for their unborn children as well as their men and living children. This is a beautiful ritual performed by the women together, raising their voices in harmony and calling on the earth's minerals and healing properties to come forth and help them save their children. They literally dance and sing to heal the earth in a ceremony as old as their species. The dance and notes of the song are adjusted according to the toxins felt through the healer's bare feet. The feet are placed in a certain pattern and the hands gracefully weave a healing spell while the dance is performed. They must be especially careful when the soil is prepared for babies. This is a ceremony of love and healing.

Musically, the ritual is divided into several sections:

- **First verse**: A "call and response" section, where the chant leader sings the "call" solo, and then some or all of the women sing the "response" in the close harmony style typical of the Carpathian musical tradition. The repeated response—*Ai Emä Maye*—is an invocation of the source of power for the healing ritual: "Oh, Mother Nature."
- **First chorus**: This section is filled with clapping, dancing, ancient horns and other means used to invoke and heighten the energies upon which the ritual is drawing.
- **Second verse**
- **Second chorus**
- **Closing invocation:** In this closing part, two song leaders, in close harmony, take all the energy gathered by the earlier portions of the song/ritual and focus it entirely on the healing purpose.

What you will be listening to are brief tastes of what would typically be a significantly longer ritual, in which the verse and chorus parts are developed and repeated many times, to be closed by a single rendition of the final invocation.

Sarna Pusm O Mayet (Song to Heal the Earth)

First verse
Ai Emä Maye,
Oh, Mother Nature,

Me sívadbin lañaak.
We are your beloved daughters.

Me tappadak, me pusmak o maγet.
We dance to heal the earth.

Me sarnadak, me pusmak o hanyet.
We sing to heal the earth.

Sielanket jutta tedet it,
We join with you now,

Sívank és akaratank és sielank juttanak.
Our hearts and minds and spirits become one.

Second verse
Ai Emä maγe,
Oh, Mother Nature,

Me sívadbin lańaak.
We are your beloved daughters.

Me andak arwadet emänked és me kaŋank o
We pay homage to our mother and call upon the

Pōhi és Lōuna, Ida és Lääs.
North and South, East and West.

Pide és aldyn és myös belső.
Above and below and within as well.

Ŧondank o maγenak pusm hän ku olen jama.
Our love of the land heals that which is in need.

ṫtanak teval it,
Ṽe join with you now,

Maγe maγeval.
Earth to earth.

O pirä elidak weńća.
The circle of life is complete.

To hear this chant, visit: http://www.christinefeehan.com/members/.

7. CARPATHIAN CHANTING TECHNIQUE

As with their healing techniques, the actual "chanting technique" of the Carpathians has much in common with the other shamanistic traditions of the Central Asian steppes. The primary mode of chanting was throat chanting using overtones. Modern examples of this manner of singing can still be found in the Mongolian, Tuvan and Tibetan traditions. You can find an audio example of the Gyuto Tibetan Buddhist monks engaged in throat chanting at: http://www.christinefeehan.com/carpathian_chanting/.

As with Tuva, note on the map the geographical proximity of Tibet to Kazakhstan and the Southern Urals.

The beginning part of the Tibetan chant emphasizes synchronizing all the voices around a single tone, aimed at healing a particular "chakra" of the body. This is fairly typical of the Gyuto throat-chanting tradition, but it is not a significant part of the Carpathian tradition. Nonetheless, it serves as an interesting contrast.

The part of the Gyuto chanting example that is most similar to the Carpathian style of chanting is the midsection, where the men are chanting the words together with great force. The purpose here is not to generate a "healing tone" that will affect a particular "chakra," but rather to generate as much power as possible for initiating the "out of body" travel and for fighting the demonic forces that the healer/traveler must face and overcome.

The songs of the Carpathian women (illustrated by their "Lullaby" and their "Song to Heal the Earth") are part of the same ancient music and healing tradition as the Lesser and Great Healing Chants of the warrior males. You can hear some of the same instruments in both the male warrior healing chants and the women's "Song to Heal the Earth." Also, they share the common purpose of generating and directing power. However, the women's songs are distinctively feminine in character. One immediately noticeable difference is that, while the men speak their words in the manner of a chant, the women sing songs with melodies and harmonies, softening the overall performance. A feminine, nurturing quality is especially evident in the "Lullaby."

APPENDIX 2

The Carpathian Language

Like all human languages, the language of the Carpathians contains the richness and nuance that can only come from a long history of use. At best we can only touch on some of the main features of the language in this brief appendix:

1. The history of the Carpathian language
2. Carpathian grammar and other characteristics of the language
3. Examples of the Carpathian language (including The Ritual Words and The Warrior's Chant)
4. A much-abridged Carpathian dictionary

1. THE HISTORY OF THE CARPATHIAN LANGUAGE

The Carpathian language of today is essentially identical to the Carpathian language of thousands of years ago. A "dead" language like the Latin of two thousand years ago has evolved into a significantly different modern language (Italian) because of countless generations of speakers and great historical fluctuations. In contrast, many of the speakers of Carpathian from thousands of years ago are still alive. Their presence—

coupled with the deliberate isolation of the Carpathians from the other major forces of change in the world—has acted (and continues to act) as a stabilizing force that has preserved the integrity of the language over the centuries. Carpathian culture has also acted as a stabilizing force. For instance, the Ritual Words, the various healing chants (see Appendix 1), and other cultural artifacts have been passed down through the centuries with great fidelity.

One small exception should be noted: the splintering of the Carpathians into separate geographic regions has led to some minor dialectization. However the telepathic link among all Carpathians (as well as each Carpathian's regular return to his or her homeland) has ensured that the differences among dialects are relatively superficial (e.g., small numbers of new words, minor differences in pronunciation, etc.), since the deeper, internal language of mind-forms has remained the same because of continuous use across space and time.

The Carpathian language was (and still is) the proto-language for the Uralic (or Finno-Ugrian) family of languages. Today, the Uralic languages are spoken in northern, eastern and central Europe and in Siberia. More than twenty-three million people in the world speak languages that can trace their ancestry to Carpathian. Magyar or Hungarian (about fourteen million speakers), Finnish (about five million speakers) and Estonian (about one million speakers) are the three major contemporary descendents of this proto-language. The only factor that unites the more than twenty languages in the Uralic family is that their ancestry can be traced back to a common proto-language—Carpathian—that split (starting some six thousand years ago) into the various languages in the Uralic family. In the same way, European languages such as English and French belong to the better-known Indo-European family and also evolved from a common proto-language ancestor (a different one from Carpathian).

The following table provides a sense for some of the similarities in the language family.

Note: The Finnic/Carpathian "k" shows up often as Hungarian "h." Similarly, the Finnic/Carpathian "p" often corresponds to the Hungarian "f."

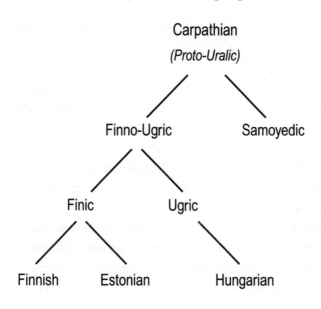

Carpathian
(Proto-Uralic)

Finno-Ugric   Samoyedic

Finic   Ugric

Finnish   Estonian   Hungarian

Carpathian (proto-Uralic)	**Finnish** (Suomi)	**Hungarian** (Magyar)
elä—live	*elä*—live	*él*—live
elid—life	*elinikä*—life	*élet*—life
pesä—nest	*pesä*—nest	*fészek*—nest
kola—die	*kuole*—die	*hal*—die
pälä—half, side	*pieltä*—tilt, tip to the side	*fél, fele*—fellow human, friend (half; one side of two) *feleség*—wife
and—give	*anta, antaa*—give	*ad*—give
koje—husband, man	*koira*—dog, the male (of animals)	*here*—drone, testicle
väke—power	*väki*—folks, people, men; force	*val/-vel*—with (instrumental suffix)
	väkevä—powerful, strong	*vele*—with him/her/it
vete—water	*vesi*—water	*víz*—water

2. CARPATHIAN GRAMMAR AND OTHER CHARACTERISTICS OF THE LANGUAGE

Idioms. As both an ancient language and a language of an earth people, Carpathian is more inclined toward use of idioms constructed from concrete, "earthy" terms, rather than abstractions. For instance, our modern abstraction "to cherish" is expressed more concretely in Carpathian as "to hold in one's heart"; the "netherworld" is, in Carpathian, "the land of night, fog and ghosts"; etc.

Word order. The order of words in a sentence is determined not by syntactic roles (like subject, verb and object) but rather by pragmatic, discourse-driven factors. Examples: *"Tied vagyok."* ("Yours am I."); *"Sívamet andam."* ("My heart I give you.")

Agglutination. The Carpathian language is agglutinative; that is, longer words are constructed from smaller components. An agglutinating language uses suffixes or prefixes whose meaning is generally unique, and which are concatenated one after another without overlap. In Carpathian, words typically consist of a stem that is followed by one or more suffixes. For example, *"sívambam"* derives from the stem *"sív"* ("heart") followed by *"am"* ("my," making it "my heart"), followed by *"bam"* ("in," making it "in my heart"). As you might imagine, agglutination in Carpathian can sometimes produce very long words, or words that are very difficult to pronounce. Vowels often get inserted between suffixes to prevent too many consonants from appearing in a row (which can make the word unpronounceable).

Noun cases. Like all languages, Carpathian has many noun cases the same noun will be "spelled" differently depending on its role in the sentence. Some of the noun cases include: nominative (when the noun is the subject of the sentence), accusative (when the noun is a direct object of the verb), dative (indirect object), genitive (or possessive), instrumenta final, supressive, inessive, elative, terminative and delative.

We will use the possessive (or genitive) case as an example, to illustrate how all noun cases in Carpathian involve adding standard suffixes to the noun stems. Thus expressing possession in Carpathian—"my lifemate," "your lifemate," "his lifemate," "her lifemate," etc.—involves adding a particular suffix (such as "-*am*") to the noun stem (*"päläfertiil"*), to produce the possessive (*"päläfertiilam"*—"my lifemate"). Which suffix to use depends upon which person ("my," "your," "his," etc.) and whether the noun ends in a consonant or a vowel. The table below shows the suffixes for singular nouns only (not plural), and also shows the similarity to the suffixes used in contemporary Hungarian. (Hungarian is actually a little more complex, in that it also requires "vowel rhyming": which suffix to use also depends on the last vowel in the noun; hence the multiple choices in the cells below, where Carpathian only has a single choice.)

	Carpathian (proto-Uralic)		Contemporary Hungarian	
person	**noun ends in vowel**	**noun ends in consonant**	**noun ends in vowel**	**noun ends in consonant**
1st singular (my)	-m	-am	-m	-om, -em, -öm
2nd singular (your)	-d	-ad	-d	-od, -ed, -öd
3rd singular (his, her, its)	-ja	-a	-ja/-je	-a, -e
1st plural (our)	-nk	-ank	-nk	-unk, -ünk
2nd plural (your)	-tak	-atak	-tok, -tek, -tök	-otok, -etek, -ötök
3rd plural (their)	-jak	-ak	-juk, -jük	-uk, -ük

Note: As mentioned earlier, vowels often get inserted between the word and its suffix so as to prevent too many consonants from appearing in a row (which would produce unpronounceable words). For example, in the table on the previous page, all nouns that end in a consonant are followed by suffixes beginning with "a."

Verb conjugation. Like its modern descendents (such as Finnish and Hungarian), Carpathian has many verb tenses, far too many to describe here. We will just focus on the conjugation of the present tense. Again, we will place contemporary Hungarian side by side with the Carpathian, because of the marked similarity of the two.

As with the possessive case for nouns, the conjugation of verbs is done by adding a suffix onto the verb stem:

Person	Carpathian (proto-Uralic)	Contemporary Hungarian
1st (I give)	-am (andam), -ak	-ok, -ek, -ök
2nd singular (you give)	-sz (andsz)	-sz
3rd singular (he/she/it gives)	— (and)	—
1st plural (we give)	-ak (andak)	-unk, -ünk
2nd plural (you give)	-tak (andtak)	-tok, -tek, -tök
3rd plural (they give)	-nak (andnak)	-nak, -nek

As with all languages, there are many "irregular verbs" in Carpathian that don't exactly fit this pattern. But the above table is still a useful guideline for most verbs.

3. EXAMPLES OF THE CARPATHIAN LANGUAGE

Here are some brief examples of conversational Carpathian, used in the Dark books. We include the literal translation in square brackets. It is interestingly different from the most appropriate English translation.

Susu.
I am home.
["home/birthplace." "I am" is understood, as is often the case in Carpathian.]

Möért?
What for?

csitri
little one
["little slip of a thing," "little slip of a girl"]

ainaak enyém
forever mine

ainaak sívamet jutta
forever mine (another form)
["forever to-my-heart connected/fixed"]

sívamet
my love
["of-my-heart," "to-my-heart"]

Tet vigyázam.
I love you.
["you-love-I"]

Sarna Rituaali (**The Ritual Words**) is a longer example, and an example of chanted rather than conversational Carpathian. Note the recurring use of *"andam"* ("I give"), to give the chant musicality and force through repetition.

Sarna Rituaali (**The Ritual Words**)

Te avio päläfertiilam.
You are my lifemate.

Éntölam kuulua, avio päläfertiilam.
I claim you as my lifemate.

Ted kuuluak, kacad, kojed.
I belong to you.

Élidamet andam.
I offer my life for you.

Pesämet andam.
I give you my protection.

Uskolfertiilamet andam.
I give you my allegiance.

Sívamet andam.
I give you my heart.

Sielamet andam.
I give you my soul.

Ainamet andam.
I give you my body.

Sívamet kuuluak kaik että a ted.
I take into my keeping the same that is yours.

Ainaak olenszal sívambin.
Your life will be cherished by me for all my time.

Te élidet ainaak pide minan.
Your life will be placed above my own for all time.

Te avio päläfertiilam.
You are my lifemate.

Ainaak sívamet jutta oleny.
You are bound to me for all eternity.

Ainaak terád vigyázak.
You are always in my care.

To hear these words pronounced (and for more about Carpathian pronunciation altogether), please visit: http://www.christinefeehan.com/ members/.

Sarna Kontakawk (**The Warriors' Chant**) is another longer example of the Carpathian language. The warriors' council takes place deep beneath the earth in a chamber of crystals with magma far below that, so the steam is natural and the wisdom of their ancestors is clear and focused. This is a sacred place where they bloodswear to their prince and people and affirm their code of honor as warriors and brothers. It is also where battle strategies are born and all dissension is discussed as well as any concerns the warriors have that they wish to bring to the Council and open for discussion.

Sarna Kontakawk (The Warriors' Chant)

Veri isäakank—veri ekäakank.
Blood of our fathers—blood of our brothers.

Veri olen elid.
Blood is life.

Andak veri-elidet Karpatiiakank, és wäke-sarna ku meke arwa-arvo, irgalom, hän ku agba, és wäke kutni, ku manaak verival.
We offer that life to our people with a bloodsworn vow of honor, mercy, integrity and endurance.

Verink sokta; verink kaɳa terád.
Our blood mingles and calls to you.

Akasz énak ku kaŋa és juttasz kuntatak it.
Heed our summons and join with us now.

To hear these words pronounced (and for more about Carpathian pronunciation altogether), please visit: http://www.christinefeehan.com/
members/.

See **Appendix 1** for Carpathian healing chants, including the *Kepä Sarna
Pus* (The Lesser Healing Chant), the *En Sarna Pus* (The Great Healing
Chant), the *Odam-Sarna Kondak* (Lullaby) and the *Sarna Pusm O Maγ et*
(Song to Heal the Earth).

4. A MUCH-ABRIDGED CARPATHIAN DICTIONARY

This very much abridged Carpathian dictionary contains most of the Carpathian words used in these Dark books. Of course, a full Carpathian dictionary would be as large as the usual dictionary for an entire language
(typically more than a hundred thousand words).

Note: The Carpathian nouns and verbs below are word stems. They generally do not appear in their isolated, "stem" form, as below. Instead, they usually
appear with suffixes (e.g., "*andam*"—"*I give*," rather than just the root, "*and*").

a—verb negation (*prefix*); not (*adverb*).
agba—to be seemly or proper.
ai—oh.
aina—body.
ainaak—forever.
O ainaak jelä peje emnimet ŋamaŋ—Sun scorch that woman forever
   (*Carpathian swear words*).
ainaakfél—old friend.
ak—suffix added after a noun ending in a consonant to make it plural.
aka—to give heed; to hearken; to listen.
akarat—mind; will.
ál—to bless; to attach to.

alatt—through.

aldyn—under; underneath.

alə—to lift; to raise.

alte—to bless; to curse.

and—to give.

and sielet, arwa-arvomet, és jelämet, kuulua huvémet ku feaj és ködet ainaak—to trade soul, honor and salvation, for momentary pleasure and endless damnation.

andasz éntölem irgalomet!—have mercy!

arvo—value; price (*noun*).

arwa—praise (*noun*).

arwa-arvo—honor (*noun*).

arwa-arvo olen gæidnod, ekäm—honor guide you, my brother (*greeting*).

arwa-arvo olen isäntä, ekäm—honor keep you, my brother (*greeting*).

arwa-arvo pile sívadet—may honor light your heart (*greeting*).

arwa-arvod mäne me ködak—may your honor hold back the dark (*greeting*).

ašša—no (*before a noun*); not (*with a verb that is not in the imperative*); not (*with an adjective*).

aššatotello—disobedient.

asti—until.

avaa—to open.

avio—wedded.

avio päläfertiil—lifemate.

avoi—uncover; show; reveal.

belső—within; inside.

bur—good; well.

bur tule ekämet kuntamak—well met brother-kin (*greeting*).

ćaða—to flee; to run; to escape.

ćoro—to flow; to run like rain.

csecsemõ—baby (*noun*).

csitri—little one (*female*).

diutal—triumph; victory.

ći—to fall.

k—suffix added after a noun ending in a consonant to make it plural.

ekä—brother.

ekäm—my brother.

elä—to live.

eläsz arwa-arvoval—may you live with honor (*greeting*).

eläsz jeläbam ainaak—long may you live in the light (*greeting*).

elävä—alive.

elävä ainak majaknak—land of the living.

elid—life.

emä—mother (*noun*).

Emä Maɣe—Mother Nature.

emäen—grandmother.

embε—if, when.

embε karmasz—please.

emni—wife; woman.

emnim—my wife; my woman.

emni hän ku köd alte—cursed woman.

emni kuŋenak ku aššatotello—disobedient lunatic.

én—I.

en—great, many, big.

én jutta félet és ekämet—I greet a friend and brother (*greeting*).

én maɣenak—I am of the earth.

én oma maɣeka—I am as old as time *(literally: as old as the earth)*.

En Puwe—The Great Tree. Related to the legends of Ygddrasil, the axis mundi, Mount Meru, heaven and hell, etc.

engem—of me.

és—and.

ete—before; in front.

että—that.

fáz—to feel cold or chilly.

fél—fellow, friend.

fél ku kuuluaak sívam belső—beloved.

fél ku vigyázak—dear one.

feldolgaz—prepare.

fertiil—fertile one.

fesztelen—airy.

fü—herbs; grass.

gæidno—road, way.

gond—care; worry; love (*noun*).

hän—he; she; it.

hän agba—it is so.

hän ku—prefix: one who; that which.

hän ku agba—truth.

hän ku kaśwa o numamet—sky-owner.

hän ku kuulua sívamet—keeper of my heart.

hän ku lejkka wäke-sarnat—traitor.

hän ku meke pirämet—defender.

hän ku pesä—protector.

hän ku piwtä—predator; hunter; tracker.

hän ku vie elidet—vampire (*literally: thief of life*).

hän ku vigyáz sielamet—keeper of my soul.

hän ku vigyáz sívamet és sielamet—keeper of my heart and soul.

hän ku saa kuć3aket—star-reacher.

hän ku tappa—killer; violent person (*noun*). deadly; violent (*adj.*).

hän ku tuulmahl elidet—vampire (*literally: life-stealer*).

Hän sívamak—Beloved.

hany—clod; lump of earth.

hisz—to believe; to trust.

ho—how.

ida—east.

igazág—justice.

irgalom—compassion; pity; mercy.

isä—father (*noun*).

isäntä—master of the house.

it—now.

jälleen—again.

jama—to be sick, infected, wounded, or dying; to be near death.

jelä—sunlight; day, sun; light.

jelä keje terád—light sear you (*Carpathian swear words*).

o jelä peje terád—sun scorch you (*Carpathian swear words*).

o jelä peje emnimet—sun scorch the woman (*Carpathian swear words*).

o jelä peje terád, emni—sun scorch you, woman (*Carpathian swear words*).

o jelä peje kaik hänkanak—sun scorch them all (*Carpathian swear words*).

o jelä sielamak—light of my soul.

joma—to be under way; to go.

joŋe—to come; to return.

joŋesz arwa-arvoval—return with honor (*greeting*).

jŏrem—to forget; to lose one's way; to make a mistake.

juo—to drink.

juosz és eläsz—drink and live (*greeting*).

juosz és olen ainaak sielamet jutta—drink and become one with me (*greeting*).

juta—to go; to wander.

jüti—night; evening.

jutta—connected; fixed (*adj.*). to connect; to fix; to bind (*verb*).

k—suffix added after a noun ending in a vowel to make it plural.

kaca—male lover.

kadi—judge.

kaik—all.

kaŋa—to call; to invite; to request; to beg.

kaŋk—windpipe; Adam's apple; throat.

kać3—gift.

kaδa—to abandon; to leave; to remain.

kaδa wäkeva óv o köd—stand fast against the dark (*greeting*).

kalma—corpse; death; grave.

karma—want.

Karpatii—Carpathian.

Karpatii ku köd—liar.

käsi—hand (*noun*).

kaśwa—to own.

keje—to cook; to burn; to sear.

kepä—lesser, small, easy, few.

kessa—cat.

kessa ku toro—wildcat.

kessake—little cat.

kidü—to wake up; to arise (*intransitive verb*).

kim—to cover an entire object with some sort of covering.

kinn—out; outdoors; outside; without.

kinta—fog, mist, smoke.

kislány—little girl.

kislány kuŋenak—little lunatic.

kislány kuŋenak minan—my little lunatic.

köd—fog; mist; darkness; evil (*noun*); foggy, dark; evil (*adj.*).

köd elävä és köd nime kutni nimet—evil lives and has a name.

köd alte hän—darkness curse it (*Carpathian swear words*).

o köd belső—darkness take it (*Carpathian swear words*).

köd jutasz belső—shadow take you (*Carpathian swear words*).

koje—man; husband; drone.

kola—to die.

kolasz arwa-arvoval—may you die with honor (*greeting*).

koma—empty hand; bare hand; palm of the hand; hollow of the hand.

kond—all of a family's or clan's children.

kont—warrior.

kont o sívanak—strong heart (*literally: heart of the warrior*).

ku—who; which; that.

kuć3—star.

kuć3ak!—stars! (*exclamation*).

kuja—day, sun.

kuŋe—moon; month.

kule—to hear.

kulke—to go or to travel (on land or water).

kulkesz arwa-arvoval, ekäm—walk with honor, my brother (*greeting*).

kulkesz arwaval—joŋesz arwa arvoval—go with glory—return with honor (*greeting*).

kuly—intestinal worm; tapeworm; demon who possesses and devours souls.

kumpa—wave (*noun*).

kuńa—to lie as if asleep; to close or cover the eyes in a game of hide-and-seek; to die.

kunta—band, clan, tribe, family.

kutenken—however.

kuras—sword; large knife.

kure—bind; tie.

kutni—to be able to bear, carry, endure, stand, or take.

kutnisz ainaak—long may you endure (*greeting*).

kuulua—to belong; to hold.

lääs—west.

lamti (*or* **lamt3**)—lowland; meadow; deep; depth.

lamti ból jüti, kinta, ja szelem—the netherworld (*literally: the meadow of night, mists, and ghosts*).

laña—daughter.

lejkka—crack, fissure, split (*noun*). To cut; to hit; to strike forcefully (*verb*).

lewl—spirit (*noun*).

lewl ma—the other world (*literally: spirit land*). *Lewl ma* includes *lamti ból jüti, kinta, ja szelem*: the netherworld, but also includes the worlds higher up *En Puwe*, the Great Tree.

liha—flesh.

lõuna—south.

löyly—breath; steam (*related to lewl: spirit*).

ma—land; forest.

magköszun—thank.

mana—to abuse; to curse; to ruin.

mäne—to rescue; to save.

maγe—land; earth; territory; place; nature.

me—we.

meke—deed; work (*noun*). To do; to make; to work (*verb*).

mića—beautiful.

mića emni kuŋenak minan—my beautiful lunatic.

minan—mine; my own (*endearment*).

minden—every, all (*adj.*).

möért?—what for? (*exclamation*).

molanâ—to crumble; to fall apart.

molo—to crush; to break into bits.

mozdul—to begin to move, to enter into movement.

muonì—appoint; order; prescribe; command.

muonìak te avoisz te—I command you to reveal yourself.

musta—memory.

myös—also.

nä—for.

nâbbŏ—so, then.

ŋamaŋ—this; this one here; that; that one there.

nautish—to enjoy.

nélkül—without.

nenä—anger.

ńiŋ3—worm; maggot.

nó—like; in the same way as; as.

numa—god; sky; top; upper part; highest (*related to the English word: numinous*).

numatorkuld—thunder (literally: sky struggle).

nyál—saliva; spit (*related to nyelv: tongue*).

nyelv—tongue.

odam—to dream; to sleep.

odam-sarna kondak—lullaby (*literally: sleep-song of children*).

olen—to be.

oma—old; ancient; last; previous.

omas—stand.

omboće—other; second (*adj.*).

o—the (*used before a noun beginning with a consonant*).

ot—the (*used before a noun beginning with a vowel*).

otti—to look; to see; to find.

óv—to protect against.

owe—door.

päämoro—aim; target.

pajna—to press.

pälä—half; side.

päläfertiil—mate or wife.

palj3—more.

peje—to burn.

peje terád—get burned (*Carpathian swear words*).

pél—to be afraid; to be scared of.

pesä (n.)—nest (*literal*); protection (*figurative*).

pesä (v.)—nest (*literal*); protect (*figurative*).

pesäd te engemal—you are safe with me.

pesäsz jeläbam ainaak—long may you stay in the light (*greeting*).

pide—above.

pile—to ignite; to light up.

pirä—circle; ring (*noun*). to surround; to enclose (*verb*).

piros—red.

pitä—to keep; to hold; to have; to possess.

pitäam mustaakad sielpesäambam—I hold your memories safe in my soul.

pitäsz baszú, piwtäsz igazáget—no vengeance, only justice.

piwtä—to follow; to follow the track of game; to hunt; to prey upon.

poår—bit; piece.

põhi—north.

pukta—to drive away; to persecute; to put to flight.

pus—healthy; healing.

pusm—to be restored to health.

puwe—tree; wood.

rambsolg—slave.

rauho—peace.

reka—ecstasy; trance.

rituaali—ritual.

sa—sinew; tendon; cord.

sa4—to call; to name.

saa—arrive, come; become; get, receive.

saasz hän ku andam szabadon—take what I freely offer.

salama—lightning; lightning bolt.

sarna—words; speech; magic incantation (*noun*). To chant; to sing; to celebrate (*verb*).

sarna kontakawk—warriors' chant.

śaro—frozen snow.

sas—shoosh (*to a child or baby*).

saγe—to arrive; to come; to reach.

siel—soul.

sieljelä isäntä—purity of soul triumphs.

sisar—sister.

sív—heart.

sív pide köd—love transcends evil.

sívad olen wäkeva, hän ku piwtä—may your heart stay strong, hunter (*greeting*).

sívamet—my heart.

sívam és sielam—my heart and soul.

sívdobbanás—heartbeat (*literal*); rhythm (*figurative*).

sokta—to mix; to stir around.

soŋe—to enter; to penetrate; to compensate; to replace.

susu—home; birthplace (*noun*). At home (*adv.*).

szabadon—freely.

szelem—ghost.

taka—behind; beyond.

tappa—to dance; to stamp with the feet; to kill.

te—you.

Te kalma, te jama ńiŋ3kval, te apitäsz arwa-arvo—You are nothing but a walking maggot-infected corpse, without honor.

Te magköszunam nä ŋamaŋ kać3 taka arvo—Thank you for this gift beyond price.

ted—yours.

terád keje—get scorched (*Carpathian swear words*).

tõd—to know.

Tõdak pitäsz wäke bekimet mekesz kaiket—I know you have the courage to face anything.

tõdhän—knowledge.

tõdhän lõ kuraset agbapäämoroam—knowledge flies the sword true to its aim.

toja—to bend; to bow; to break.

toro—to fight; to quarrel.

torosz wäkeval—fight fiercely (*greeting*).

totello—obey.

tsak—only.

tuhanos—thousand.

tuhanos löylyak türelamak saɣe diutalet—a thousand patient breaths bring victory.

tule—to meet; to come.

tumte—to feel; to touch; to touch upon.

türe—full, satiated, accomplished.

türelam—patience.

türelam agba kontsalamaval—patience is the warrior's true weapon.

tyvi—stem; base; trunk.

uskol—faithful.

uskolfertiil—allegiance; loyalty.

varolind—dangerous.

veri—blood.

veri-elidet—blood-life.

veri ekäakank—blood of our brothers.

veri isäakank—blood of our fathers.

veri olen piros, ekäm—literally: blood be red, my brother; figuratively: find your lifemate (*greeting*).

veriak ot en Karpatiiak—by the blood of the Prince (*literally: by the blood of the great Carpathian; Carpathian swear words*).

veridet peje—may your blood burn (*Carpathian swear words*).

vigyáz—to love; to care for; to take care of.

vii—last; at last; finally.

wäke—power; strength.

wäke beki—strength; courage.

wäke kaða—steadfastness.

wäke kutni—endurance.

wäke-sarna—vow; curse; blessing (*literally: power words*).

wäkeva—powerful.

wara—bird; crow.

weńća—complete; whole.

wete—water (*noun*).

Do you love fiction with a supernatural twist?

Want the chance to hear news about your favourite
authors (and the chance to win free books)?

Keri Arthur
Kristen Callihan
P.C. Cast
Christine Feehan
Jacquelyn Frank
Larissa Ione
Darynda Jones
Sherrilyn Kenyon
Jayne Ann Krentz and Jayne Castle
Lucy March
Martin Millar
Tim O'Rourke
Lindsey Piper
Christopher Rice
J.R. Ward
Laura Wright

Then visit the Piatkus website and blog
www.piatkus.co.uk | www.piatkusbooks.net

And follow us on Facebook and Twitter
www.facebook.com/piatkusfiction | www.twitter.com/piatkusbooks

piatkus